The Dying Place

Charly Cox was born in the South, raised in the Midwest, and now resides in the Southwest United States. She enjoys jigsaw and crossword puzzles, hanging out with her husband and her spoiled Siberian husky, visiting her son in Arizona, and traveling.

Also by Charly Cox

Detective Alyssa Wyatt

All His Pretty Girls
The Toybox
Alone in the Woods
The Devil's Playground

THE DYING PLACE

CHARLY COX

San Diego, California

 **Canelo US**
An imprint of Printers Row Publishing Group
9717 Pacific Heights Blvd, San Diego, CA 92121
www.canelobooksus.com

Printers Row Publishing Group is a division of Readerlink Distribution
Services, LLC. Canelo US is a registered trademark of Readerlink
Distribution Services, LLC.

First published in the United Kingdom in 2023 by Hera Books.

Published in partnership with Canelo.

Correspondence regarding the content of this book should be sent to Canelo
US, Editorial Department, at the above address. Author inquiries should be
sent to Canelo, Unit 9, 5th Floor, Cargo Works, 1–2 Hatfields, London SE1
9PG, United Kingdom, www.canelo.co.

Publisher: Peter Norton • Associate Publisher: Ana Parker
Art Director: Charles McStravick
Senior Developmental Editor: April Graham
Editor: Julie Chapa
Production Team: Beno Chan, Julie Greene

Library of Congress Control Number: 2023948766

ISBN: 978-1-6672-0644-8

Printed in India

27 26 25 24 23   1 2 3 4 5

To anyone who's ever had a dream they might be afraid to follow — and to all the fans out there who continue to help me follow mine.

Chapter One

Saturday, May 28

Heart pounding, lungs gasping for every precious intake of oxygen, Kennedy Farmer propelled herself forward, knowing the end of her five-mile run through Coyote Canyon waited just around the corner. With her calves burning and begging for mercy, she pushed back against the pain, and with a renewed surge of energy, gathered steam until she burst onto the last leg of the trail. When she finished, a quick peek at her phone strapped on her arm showed she'd beaten her personal best time by seventy-two seconds.

Hands on her knees and bent over at the waist, her breaths sawing in and out of her chest, she smiled. She loved this time of the evening with the golden hues casting a pink glow over the Sandia Mountains, giving them the watermelon color for which they'd been aptly named, when everything around her sparkled in the sun or hid in the shifting shadows of the coming nightfall. Off in the distance, a pack of coyotes yipped and howled, startling a rabbit to dart in front of her and dash the other way.

With the buzzing background noise of traffic, she marveled, as she often did, at the contradictory nature of her favorite running trail, where human sightings were even rarer than wild animals. Still, despite the quiet beauty and illusion of a peaceful, hidden country solitude, she really remained just a hop and a hill away from the interstate that ran through the canyon.

Overhead, a murder of crows scattered from the treetops, and Kennedy imagined they must be on their way to pick at whatever remained of the coyotes' feast. Inhaling a deep breath of fresh mountain air, she stood still and simply appreciated the serenity of her surroundings.

As she did, she heard a faint whisper of movement behind her. Excited that it might be the fox she'd spotted a few days ago trying to sneak through undetected, she started to turn around – only to find a man less than a foot away, his hard, calculated stare unblinking as he lunged toward her.

Kennedy's heart jerked once inside her chest as one word raced through her mind – *run*. Spinning toward the parking lot, she thought only of reaching the safety of her car. But before she could take more than a step, the man latched onto her ponytail and yanked her backwards. When his hand reached around her to clap across her mouth, Kennedy's survival instincts took over. Struggling to escape, she scrabbled for purchase, one shoe falling off as the man dragged her along the dirt and off the trail.

Suddenly lifted off her feet and thrown to the hard-packed ground, she gasped for breath as her attacker followed her down, crushing her with the heavy weight of his body. And then his thick, sweaty hands wrapped around her neck and squeezed, his thumbs pressing into her windpipe and cutting off her air. With black dots dancing in her vision, her wide eyes locked onto a pair of cold, dark ones. Staring up at his face, a flicker of recognition rippled through her.

Desperate to force out the scream her throat held hostage, she bucked and twisted, her hands grasping at his immoveable grip as he leaned forward and pressed harder, his gaze never leaving hers.

With the pressure in her chest expanding, anger at allowing herself to become complacent to her surroundings warred with her rising terror. Her tenuous hold on consciousness remained a hopeless breath away as her mind turned into a blurred mess of lines and hazy colors popping behind her eyes.

As the fight for life began to slip helplessly from her grasp, her attacker shifted positions to straddle her body, his thighs pressing like a vise grip against her ribcage and trapping her arms against her sides as one muscled forearm replaced his hands. With his free hand, he grappled for something at his side. And then suddenly, the unmistakable touch of a cold, sharp blade pressed into the corner of her mouth.

'If you scream or try to fight me, I will slice out your tongue before I peel your skin away and leave you out here for the scavengers to pick your bones apart. Do you understand?' The evil promise that he meant every word blazed from his murderous eyes.

Desperately trying to cling to any hope for escape, Kennedy did the only thing she could: she nodded.

Seconds later, when something pricked her neck, she was filled with the sickening clarity that she'd been drugged. Fighting to hold onto consciousness, she forgot she'd agreed not to scream, and so she sucked in a mouthful of air, only to have it cut off when her attacker ground his palm against her lips.

Eyes bulging, heart hammering, Kennedy stared up at his dispassionate glare. With his face swimming in and out of focus, a fleeting image of this man sitting somewhere in a car flashed in her memory, but as she tried to hold onto the picture, her eyelids felt a magnetic pull to close. The siren ringing inside her head warned her that if she succumbed to the drug, she would die, and so she fought a losing battle to stay awake.

When the man lifted her into his arms, she could do nothing but allow herself to be carried away, her limbs flopping in the air like a rag doll's. Her eyes slit open just enough for her to spot her car sitting in the parking lot, waiting for her. Weakly, she lifted one hand as if she could somehow summon it to come to her rescue.

Metal scraped a deep gouge into the back of her head when her attacker tossed her into the trunk of his own vehicle. The distinct ripping sound of tape breached the fog in her brain and the blood thundering through her ears as she lay there, helpless to move. Within seconds, her wrists and ankles were bound together with zip ties before a strip of silver buried her cries inside her mouth.

The trunk slammed closed, sealing her fate. With her final sliver of consciousness slipping away, a deep cold stole into the center of Kennedy's bones, knowing her lapse in attention, despite how careful she'd always been in the past, had just gotten her killed.

The last thought she had before her slide into black oblivion was that maybe the crows had been circling for her.

Chapter Two

Saturday, May 28

Huddled into a corner with her arms wrapped around her knees, Kennedy rocked back and forth, her eyes glued to the blood-streaked floor as her head repeatedly ran the reel of horror playing out in front of her. Powerless to help either of them, she listened as her abductor pummeled the limp body of a young girl handcuffed to and suspended from a metal bar spanning the narrow width of the room.

Across the small space, the girl's dying gaze landed on her face. A muted scream butted up against the duct tape sealing Kennedy's terror inside as, unable to watch, she turned away from the sight. Even after it became clear the girl had stopped breathing, the monster's murderous beating neither slowed nor ceased, not until the girl's head lolled forward, no longer responsive to the kicks and punches or the inarticulate grunts and threats that had been part of what had finally dragged Kennedy's drugged mind back from unconsciousness.

A sonorous roar bellowed from deep inside her abductor as he rained down a final series of blows before his rage sputtered to a standstill. Frightened at the man's sudden silence, Kennedy opened her eyes just as he reached into his pocket and removed a key. And then, as if he hadn't just slain another human, he slipped it into the lock that would unchain the girl from her tethered position. Stepping back, he watched with dispassion as the girl's body flopped down in a heap, her head striking the cold cement floor with a sickening crack. And then he wrenched a knife out of the sheath strapped to his belt and dropped to his knees beside her, raising his arm high above his head before bringing it down again and again.

Whimpers gurgled and simmered inside Kennedy when her abductor finally turned his leering, blood-spattered face toward her and demanded she look.

'I want you to watch what's in store for you so that every time you close your eyes, you feel my fists on your body, draining your life from you.' With his wet knife pointed in her direction, he advanced until the tip pierced her cheek, and he dragged it down her skin, whispering in a voice as cold as an Alaskan winter, 'Except I'll be sure to take more time with you.'

With nowhere to go, Kennedy crowded herself deeper into the corner, her head whipping back and forth, as if by denying her situation, it would no longer be happening.

The man leaned in closer. 'What did you think would happen, running out there all alone, tempting fate? It's like you wanted me to find you. Maybe if you'd been a little smarter' – he tapped the hilt of his knife against her temple – 'then you wouldn't be here now. If you think about it, this is *your* fault.' He tossed a look over his shoulder to the dead girl's body. 'Just like that was *her* fault. If she had made any other choice than the one she did, she wouldn't have left me without one.'

Against her will, Kennedy's eyes fell on the extremely beaten and battered face of the girl and wondered what misstep had landed her in the crosshairs of this psychopath.

Her abductor laughed – a low, cruel sound that turned Kennedy's blood to ice – as he rose to his feet before calmly stepping over the dead girl as if she were nothing more significant than a pile of dirty laundry. Then he strolled out of the room and closed the door behind him, leaving Kennedy alone with the body and a pool of dark red trickling her way.

Too terrified to do anything else, she drew her bound legs closer to her chest and watched through the glass walls as the man moved over to a sink, where he splashed water on his face. As he scrubbed away the incriminating evidence, Kennedy's eyes were drawn to a wall where a multitude of hammers and other everyday tools hung – all of them now taking on a far more sinister meaning. Her body quaked as she tore her gaze away, only to find the man's burning stare aimed at her as he removed his shirt and used it as a washcloth to scrub his neck and arms before dropping the sodden mess into the basin.

When he finally finished cleaning up, he paused at a set of stairs, casting her a grin that turned her stomach into a gurgling earthquake of nausea. As he disappeared, his chilling words raked at her sanity, leaving her with two questions hammering inside her head.

How in the world had she ended up here, waiting to be murdered? And who was the dead girl lying on the floor in front of her?

Chapter Three

Perched on the edge of a dark gray leather sofa, Detective Alyssa Wyatt and her partner of the past eight years, Detective Cord Roberts, sat across from Ben and Barbara Pembroke in their luxurious house nestled in the foothills of Albuquerque. Ellary, their oldest daughter, stood behind them with one hand gripping tightly to the back of a chair.

Earlier, Alyssa and the rest of her team had been minutes from leaving the precinct, excited at the prospect of enjoying that too rare occurrence of being home in time for dinner, when the captain had stopped them with the announcement of a possible missing woman. So, instead of sinking her teeth into her husband's fresh-out-of-the-oven lasagna, she found herself trying to wrap her mind around the Pembroke family's delay in contacting the police. Her eyes strayed to the grandfather clock in the corner of the room as it chimed seven o'clock.

'You said you believed your daughter, Rheagan, went missing yesterday. Is that correct?'

Barbara wrung her hands together as if washing them with air. 'Yes, that's right.'

'But you waited until this evening to make a missing person's report?'

8

The lines around Ben's mouth tightened as he drilled his intense stare in Alyssa's direction. 'Detectives, please try to understand that we didn't actually believe our daughter was missing. We fully expected she'd return home by this afternoon. Clearly, that never happened, and so we contacted the police immediately.'

Clearly, not *immediately*. Though the thought popped into Alyssa's head, she managed to keep it hidden from her expression.

Barbara lowered her head. 'We just assumed she'd gone out with friends.'

'Would Rheagan not tell you if she was going out?' Alyssa asked.

In a move that Alyssa had already witnessed at least half a dozen times since she and Cord had arrived, Mrs. Pembroke nibbled on her bottom lip as she peered up at her husband before answering. 'Rheagan frequently overlooked mentioning such things. And so, if she had plans, we weren't aware of them.'

The eyeroll Ellary executed while she sucked air in through her clenched teeth spoke louder than her mumbled comment. 'Maybe someone should've asked – or demanded – to know once in a while.'

Alyssa mentally shook her head. Perhaps because of the line of work she was in, she couldn't imagine not insisting on knowing where her children were going and with whom. Of course, her daughter, at twenty-one, no longer lived at home, but the rules still applied to her nearly eighteen-year-old son. 'Have you tried calling her?' she asked now.

Barbara's head bobbed up and down emphatically. 'Yes, several times. But she never answers.'

Cord rested his pen on his notebook and studied the Pembrokes. 'What about her friends? Have you contacted any of them to see if they've heard from her?'

Ellary Pembroke sighed heavily and spoke before either of her parents could. 'Listen, I love my little sister madly, but to be completely honest, we're still not entirely convinced she's *actually* missing.'

This time Alyssa really shook her head. 'I'm sorry, but I'm not certain I understand why Detective Roberts and I are here then.'

Ellary's eyes flickered in her parents' direction before she squared her shoulders and spat out something she'd clearly been hesitant to admit. 'Look, what my parents are afraid to tell you is that this wouldn't be the first time Rheagan has simply decided to head out on some kind of adventure without bothering to tell anyone. Around this time last year, she decided to attend some festival in Colorado. The entire time she was gone, my parents assumed she was hanging out with me since I'd just moved into my new apartment. It wasn't until she returned home three days later that we discovered the truth.'

'And none of you were in contact with her at any point during those three days?' Cord asked.

'No. I was busy getting my apartment in order, and my parents didn't want to interrupt our "sisterly bonding time."'

Alyssa directed her question to Mr. and Mrs. Pembroke. 'Did Rheagan say something to you before she left for Colorado that made you think she was simply going to her sister's?'

Two pink circles blossomed on Barbara's cheeks. 'At breakfast, she asked if I thought Ellary needed help settling in.'

'You said this wouldn't be the first time Rheagan disappeared without telling someone where she was going. Were there other incidents aside from that one?' In Alyssa's mind, she found just that one occurrence even more of a reason for the Pembrokes to insist on knowing their daughter's plans, eighteen years old or not.

When neither of her parents seemed inclined to answer, Ellary did it for them. 'There were times Rheagan would say she was going somewhere and then change plans without telling anyone. But the Colorado thing was the biggest.' She darted a quick peek down at her parents. 'Aside from a lecture not to do it again, and despite me warning Mom and Dad that it would keep happening if they didn't impose some kind of punishment, there were no real consequences, so in my opinion, Rheagan really didn't learn anything from it.'

Ellary continued. 'What I'm about to say might sound harsh, but the truth is: Rheagan has a knack for acting without thinking things through. To her, everything is just one big adventure, so she never takes time to consider how her actions impact anyone else. As the baby of the family, you'd think she wouldn't crave that kind of attention since attention is pretty much all she's ever gotten from the moment she squealed her way into this world.'

Alyssa wondered if the resentment she detected in Ellary's voice stemmed more from jealousy or because she felt her parents hadn't done enough to try to rein her sister in, and now she might be missing. Based on everything she'd heard so far, it didn't take a big leap of logic to see that Ben and Barbara allowed Rheagan to get away with just about anything. In her opinion, both as a member of law enforcement and as a mother herself, she couldn't help but feel they were perhaps a bit too indulgent.

'Look, I hate to say this,' – Ellary met Alyssa's eyes with a steady gaze – 'but the truth is that my sister gets a thrill out of people's reactions to her antics. And I think that's probably why I'm not quite convinced she isn't just waiting for the exact right moment to reappear so she can revel in how she had all of us fawning over her safety.'

The memory of the day Alyssa's own little brother had been kidnapped thirty-nine years ago pushed itself to the forefront of her mind. Like Ellary now, she'd believed Timmy had been trying to play a trick on her. The truth had destroyed her parents and led her into law enforcement. Cord, sensing exactly where her head had gone, gave her an imperceptible nudge, enabling her to shove that recollection back into its rightful compartment.

'Then let me ask you this,' Alyssa said. 'When was the last time you actually saw or spoke to Rheagan?'

Barbara didn't hesitate. 'Nine thirty Saturday night, just before I went off to bed.'

Alyssa and Cord exchanged startled expressions. She'd expected them to say Sunday sometime. 'And how did she seem then?'

Barbara's forehead scrunched with her confusion. 'She seemed fine. She told me good night, and that was that.'

Cord had already tried asking, but Alyssa tried again. 'Have you reached out to any of her friends?'

Ellary nodded. 'I sent Bridgette Palmer and Laila Solomon, her two best friends, a text to see if she was with them, but they said they hadn't seen her. If Rheagan had made plans, that's who it would've been with.'

'Would you mind getting us their contact information?' Cord asked. 'Detective Wyatt and I can drop in and see if they can shed some light on things.'

Barbara's head snapped in Cord's direction. 'But… you're still going to file the missing person's report, right? I mean, Rheagan has never been gone this long without her car.'

Alyssa rushed to reassure her. 'Yes, ma'am. We're just trying to get as much information as possible so we can run down the last few days and determine where your daughter is.' On that note, she turned back to Ellary. 'You said your sister does things oftentimes for the attention it brings her. Can you give us some examples of what you mean?' What she was really asking was if Rheagan's attention-seeking behavior included meeting up with strangers. Because the bottom line remained: whether Rheagan Pembroke disappeared of her own free will or not, she was still, technically, missing.

'Do you think that will help you figure out where she is?'

'To be honest, I don't know. But it helps to have as much information as possible, to try to understand who your sister is as an individual. At this point, the more you can tell us, the better chance we'll have of finding out where she's gotten off to.'

Ben answered Alyssa's question before Ellary had a chance. 'I really don't see how this could help you locate her, but an example of one of her more serious stunts would be when Rheagan went on an end-of-school-year class trip to Cliff's Amusement Park.' He turned to his wife and daughter. 'She was what, thirteen, fourteen at the time?'

As she answered, Barbara began weaving her hands together once more. 'Fourteen, dear. That was the summer before her freshman year of high school.'

Ben nodded. 'That's right. Anyway, on one of the rides, she somehow managed to unbuckle her safety belt after the ride took off – or maybe she did it beforehand. I don't know. Either way, thank God, nothing actually happened.'

Ellary snorted. 'Nothing happened except she damned near gave everyone a heart attack. Including you and Mom when you found out. I'd say that's something.'

Unable to hide her stunned reaction, Alyssa's mouth dropped open. She didn't know exactly what she'd been anticipating, but she knew it wasn't hearing that Rheagan had done something so utterly, completely life-threatening. In her opinion, that sort of stunt sailed well beyond an adrenaline-fueled drive for adventure and dipped more into foolish, reckless, and outright stupid territory.

A vision of the beautiful girl pictured in a family photograph lying dead somewhere because of her irresponsible behavior stuck in Alyssa's mind.

Ellary picked up the story where her father had left off. 'Her friend freaked out and began screaming for help, and so the park attendant finally stopped the ride. As soon as he realized what had happened, security kicked Rheagan out and banned her from returning for an entire year.'

The hard glint of anger that momentarily stamped itself on Ellary's face harbored years of bitterness, and Alyssa couldn't help but wonder if it was directed more at her younger sister or her parents. Or both.

'Anyway, Mom was fighting a nasty flu, so she called me at work to ask if I would pick Rheagan up. When I got there, I expected to see shame or maybe even some guilt, but instead, Rheagan practically floated to the car, she was so giddy. She just kept going on about what a thrill it had been. Her biggest regret about the entire thing? She hadn't been able to grab a snapshot of the expressions on everyone's faces.'

Ellary's eyes dropped to the top of her mother's bent head. 'My mom tends to try to hide some of Rheagan's transgressions, so I decided to tell Dad myself. I told him they absolutely couldn't ignore Rheagan's behavior this time because she'd put her own life, and possibly others, in danger.'

'And were there consequences then?' Alyssa asked.

Mrs. Pembroke's voice crackled as she answered. 'I grounded her for two weeks, cancelled her traditional beginning-of-summer party, and took her phone and tablets. Rheagan pouted but took her punishment in stride.'

Alyssa's first thought was that it clearly hadn't been enough if their daughter continued to act out in such dangerous ways. She approached her next question with caution. 'Rheagan's behavior, as you've described it, seems… risky, at best, and might point to other dormant issues. Have you ever considered taking her to see someone about why she does such things?'

Mr. Pembroke's voice carried the weight of insult when he responded. 'Of course, we worried and insisted she speak to someone. But as Ellary has already mentioned, Rheagan does these things all in fun, and the therapist she saw a few years ago claimed he found nothing to the contrary.'

'How long did Rheagan see this therapist?' Cord asked.

'Once a week for three months.'

Mrs. Pembroke broke in. 'Detectives, I don't want you to go away with the wrong impression about my daughter. It's true that she certainly doesn't think through what her actions might mean for others, but honestly, she has a heart of gold and really cares about people. My moth-erly instincts are telling me that she's not merely being thoughtless here. Despite what Ellary may or may not believe' – she turned her head to her oldest child and whispered, 'Sorry, dear' – 'I don't think Rheagan's off on some grand escapade. I think' – her fear-filled eyes bored into Alyssa's – 'I can *feel* that something has happened to my daughter, and I need you to find her and bring her back home to me. Please.'

'If she's missing, we'll do everything we can to bring her home,' Alyssa promised. 'You said you inquired with her friends, but what about asking any of your neighbors if they'd seen her?'

Before Alyssa had even finished the question, Ellary was shaking her head. 'The Hoyts' – she pointed to the right – 'left early yesterday morning and won't be back until later this week.' She swept her arm in the other direc-tion. 'Mayor Kelson lives next door, and when Dad spoke to him earlier today, he and his wife said they hadn't seen her either. And I'm sure you noticed when you arrived that there's no one across from us.'

'You said Rheagan's never been gone "this long" without her car. Could she have gone for a walk, or is it possible someone just picked her up?'

'No,' Ben said. 'I'm a light sleeper, and I would've heard if a car pulled into the drive. And as for her just going for a walk, I suppose she could've, but I highly doubt it. Rheagan is not what one would call a nature lover.' He looked down at his hands.

'What about her leaving the house to meet someone?' Alyssa asked.

Ben rubbed his knuckles across his forehead. 'It's possible, of course, which is one of the reasons we believe she might be missing and not just out having a fun time. But if our daughter met someone new, I'm sure she would've at least told us about him. Or her. She always has in the past, and I can't imagine why she'd keep it a secret this time.'

Cord asked the question sitting on the tip of Alyssa's tongue. 'Rheagan had *no* other friends she hung out with besides the two you mentioned?'

All three of the Pembrokes stared uncomfortably at each other before Ellary finally answered. 'Not really, no. Bridgette and Laila are the only two who've managed to stick with her through all her crazy stunts. So, they're the ones Rheagan trusts the most, I guess. If I'm being honest, I've always hoped they would somehow coax her to calm down, at least a little. But so far, that hasn't happened.'

For the first time since they'd arrived, Alyssa spotted the beginning signs of fear that something truly might've happened to her sister on Ellary's face. She turned to Barbara. 'What was Rheagan wearing when you told her goodnight on Saturday?'

'White shorts and a red tank top with a black stripe around the middle.'

Despite knowing her next question could cause the concerned family to panic, Alyssa knew of no other way to pose it than to just ask. 'Does Rheagan have any distinguishing marks you can tell us about? Birthmarks, piercings, tattoos?'

Immediately, a moan slipped between Barbara's pursed lips as she squeezed her arms around her stomach and rocked slowly back and forth.

Ben glanced at his wife before turning his attention back to Alyssa. He pointed to a spot behind his right ear. 'She has a rose tattoo here.' He touched his arm. 'And another one here. It's a bouquet of red and yellow roses interlaced with barbed wire and a slithering snake moving between them.'

Half an hour later, after they'd asked permission to go through Rheagan's room, Alyssa and Cord, armed with a current photo, as well as addresses and phone numbers for Rheagan's friends, headed back out to her government-issued Chevy Tahoe.

As Alyssa pulled away from the curb, Cord asked, 'Well, what's your gut feeling on this one? Is Rheagan Pembroke missing or just off on an adventure?'

'I honestly have no idea. But I have to admit hearing about her propensity for dangerous activities has me a little concerned. I'm hoping a conversation with her friends will give us a little more insight into that, or at least give us a direction to look.'

Cord nodded his head in agreement and buckled himself in. 'That's kind of where I was leaning, as well.'

Chapter Four

Informed Monday night by Bridgette Palmer's parents that their daughter wouldn't be home until late, and with Laila Solomon neither answering her phone nor her door, Alyssa and Cord had finally conceded they'd have to wait until the next day to speak with Rheagan's best friends. And even though the time on her dash showed only seven forty-five when she pulled to a stop in front of the Palmer residence on Tuesday morning, Alyssa already felt the day slipping away. When it came to possible missing persons cases, she and her team were well aware how one second could make the difference between saving a life or... not. Not to mention they might've already lost more than those first crucial twenty-four hours.

Unlike the Pembrokes' neighborhood, where all the homes were custom-built, Bridgette Palmer and her family lived in a well-maintained but classical, middle-class tract home with many of the surrounding houses bearing similar facades and much smaller yards. A stunning redhead, who appeared to have just stepped from the pages of a glossy magazine, passed in front of a large window that passersby could easily peer into.

Alyssa locked her Tahoe and followed Cord up the sidewalk lined with an innumerable variety of colorful, fragrant flowers she couldn't identify.

The redheaded girl opened the front door wearing a short dress that exposed trembling legs. Alyssa didn't put much weight behind the girl's obvious nerves because, as her son had often pointed out, nobody liked talking to the cops, even if they knew they'd done nothing wrong.

'Ms. Palmer?' Alyssa asked.

The young girl flashed a beautiful white smile that showed off her perfect teeth. 'Bridgette. Ms. Palmer sounds like my grandma.'

The sound of a strained engine caught everyone's attention, and Alyssa and Cord turned in time to see an old, yellow Ford pickup sputter to a stop in front of Bridgette's house. The loud, grating music blasting through the open windows went blessedly quiet when the young girl behind the wheel turned off the ignition.

'That's Laila Solomon. The two of us had already made plans for breakfast and mani-pedis today, so she was already on her way here when you called. I figured if you're here to talk about Rheagan, you could talk to us both at the same time.' As soon as Bridgette finished explaining, her eyes widened, and her smile fell away. 'Oh my God. I hope that was okay.'

'Actually, that works out great,' Alyssa said. 'It'll save us an extra trip.'

Laila slipped past Alyssa and Cord on the porch and stuck out her hand to introduce herself. 'I'm Laila Solomon, one of Rheagan's best friends.'

Bridgette giggled. 'I already told them.'

Laila dropped her hand and shrugged. 'Oh.' Unlike her friend, Laila's face was makeup free, and her hair spilled out of the rubber band that barely contained the messy ponytail atop her head. If Bridgette had just stepped away from a photo shoot, Laila had just rolled out of bed.

Alyssa introduced herself and Cord. 'I'm Detective Wyatt, and this is Detective Roberts. Thanks for meeting with us. I understand the two of you have plans, so we'll try to be as quick as we can.'

Bridgette invited them in and turned to a couple walking down the hall. 'The detectives who wanted to talk to us about Rheagan are here.'

The thick-jowled man they'd met last night nodded a greeting before turning back to his daughter. 'Why don't you take them to the living room? Mom and I will head to the kitchen.'

Bridgette waved Alyssa and Cord to a well-worn but comfortable leather sofa while she and Laila sat across from them in a matching loveseat.

If either girl thought their friend was missing, neither exhibited signs of it. Alyssa wondered if it had been one of these girls who'd been with Rheagan at the amusement park the day she'd unbuckled herself on the ride. She made a mental note to ask before they left.

In a show of nerves, Bridgette picked at the old polish on her fingernails. 'So, you said on the phone that you needed to talk about Rheagan. Is she in trouble or something?'

If not for the Pembrokes painting the picture that they had of Rheagan's personality, Alyssa might've found the question odd. However, in light of what they'd just learned, she found it to be an acceptable and even expected one. She smiled in an effort to put the girls at ease.

'Not that we know of. Actually, her parents and sister have reported her missing.'

Mouths dropping open in identical fashion, both Bridgette and Laila jerked their heads in each other's direction before snapping them back toward Alyssa. 'Wait, missing? I mean, Ellary sent us both a text yesterday to see if Rheagan was with us, but she didn't mention anything about thinking she was missing.'

Laila's head bobbed in agreement. 'Like at all.'

'Can you tell us when the two of you last saw or spoke to Rheagan?' Cord asked.

Both girls answered at the same time. 'Saturday night.'

The same day Barbara Pembroke last saw her daughter. 'And what time was that?'

Bridgette's phone magically appeared in her hand, making Alyssa wonder where in the world she'd had it stashed. She did a one-handed swipe over her screen, tapped one of the icons and then swung it around for Alyssa and Cord to see. 'Nine thirty-eight.' One long fingernail tapped the screen. 'The three of us had plans, but she cancelled.'

Alyssa read the string of messages that included all three girls.

> Hey, R, what time are you planning on getting here?

> Sorry. Gotta bail. Stomach hurting. Have fun w/o me. Talk tomorrow.

> K. Sry bout your stomach. Feel better. TTYT.

Laila followed up with a crying emoji.

For two individuals who were supposed to be Rheagan's best friends, Alyssa found the girls' replies, void of questions, a bit strange.

As Alyssa handed Bridgette's phone back to her, the young girl responded to Alyssa's thought as if she'd read her mind. 'I was kind of annoyed that she blew us off. But it wasn't like it was totally unexpected or surprising because she has a habit of doing that.' In the way of typical teenagers around the globe, she rolled her eyes. 'She likes to keep her options open in case something better or more exciting comes along. She never says that out loud, of course. But Laila and I know it anyway.'

'Do you mind if we ask where you girls were planning on going?' In Alyssa's mind, it was a place to look, if nothing else.

'Sure, but we hadn't actually decided yet. We usually figure it out once we all meet up, and we almost always meet up here.'

Laila's chin dipped toward her chest so that she gave a softly spoken confession to her clasped hands. 'If I'm being honest, I was kind of relieved that Rheagan bailed. I mean, I know that sounds awful. She's always a ton of fun, but…' Embarrassed at the admission, Laila's words trailed off.

'She's always a ton of fun, but what?' The kindness in Cord's voice brought Laila's head back up with her deer-in-the-headlights eyes on full display.

Bridgette reached over and gave her friend's hand a quick, reassuring squeeze before answering Cord's question herself. 'Please don't think we're bad friends. We love Rheagan; we really do. But she can sometimes be a bit extra, especially if we're around her for a long period of time. And with this being our last summer break before we head off to college, we've been hanging out a lot lately.'

'We don't think you're bad friends at all,' Alyssa promised. 'But can you tell us what you mean by Rheagan can sometimes be a bit extra?' She was curious if their stories would be similar to what the Pembrokes had already told them.

'Um, well' – Bridgette shifted in her seat – 'she absolutely loves being the center of attention, and so she kind of has this super edgy side that makes her do things without thinking them through. Like one time, our junior year, someone dared her to climb on top of the school and spray-paint *Hollister Sucks.* That was our principal's last name. And she totally did it.'

Laila's eyes widened as she stared at Bridgette, her head tipped toward Alyssa and Cord.

Accurately reading the teen's concern, Alyssa rushed to reassure them both. 'We're not here to ask questions that will get your friend in trouble. We're here to find out if she's really missing and where she might have gotten off to.'

Laila sucked in a deep breath of relief. 'That wasn't even one of her crazier things, either. One time, she unbuckled herself on a ride at Cliff's Amusement Park.'

Well, that answered Alyssa's as-yet unasked question as to whether one of them had been the friend with Rheagan at the time.

'I mean, she apologized, but couldn't really understand why we were so upset since no one actually got hurt.'

Curiosity bubbled up inside Alyssa, both as a detective and as someone who simply wanted to understand this missing teenager. 'It sounds like you've all been friends for a long time. Did Rheagan ever confide in you *why* she does these things?'

Bridgette and Laila both shook their heads.

24

'But I know her mom and dad forced her to go to counseling for it,' Bridgette said.

Laila tapped her friend's leg. 'That's right! I forgot about that.' She turned back to Alyssa and Cord. 'Like her mom was mad pissed at her after the amusement park deal. I don't think I've ever heard her mom so upset. Both her parents are always so chill about *everything* she does. Right, Bridge?'

Bridgette nodded.

Rheagan's best friends were corroborating what Alyssa and Cord had already learned, but nothing they'd told them so far hinted at where she might be. Alyssa took a few seconds to think about how to pose her next question. 'You mentioned Rheagan liked to keep her options open in case something "better" came along. Would that include meeting up with strangers?'

Bridgette's answer was immediate. 'No way. She might do some pretty dumb things sometimes, but she doesn't have a death wish, not really.'

Was it possible Rheagan had just run away for a few days like Ellary first believed? 'Can you think of somewhere she might've gone?'

Bridgette and Laila looked at each other before Laila said, 'No. If she was planning on slipping away for a few days, she never mentioned anything to us about it. And I'm pretty sure she would've because she usually does.'

'What was her situation like at home?' Cord asked.

Laila shrugged. 'Well, she pretty much gets whatever she wants because her parents almost never tell her no. Like, Bridge and I joke that we're going to get it tattooed on her forehead whenever she gets pissed at them so she can be reminded how lucky she really is.'

Bridgette's smile could best be described as awkward. 'It's not just that, though. She doesn't usually even get in trouble when she pulls one of her crazier stunts. Her parents just sweep things under a rug like nothing happened. Instead of boys being boys, it's just Rheagan being Rheagan. Like when she did that to the roof, they talked the principal into suspending her for a week instead of having her arrested for vandalism. Then they paid to have it painted.'

Alyssa watched as Bridgette paused to look at Laila. They must've agreed on whatever silent communication passed between them because she turned back and continued.

'There are only two things Rheagan struggles with. One is that she's always felt inferior to her sister because Ellary is the kind of student who always got straight As, had the cutest, most popular boyfriends, got accepted into some of the top schools, and is really just an all-around golden child. I mean, not that that's bad. Just telling you what Rheagan says.'

Laila nodded. 'Rheagan even admitted that's why she does some of the dumb things she does.'

'What do you mean she admitted it?' Cord asked.

'A few years ago, Ellary got an award from the mayor for something, and Rheagan made the comment that there was no way she'd ever be as perfect as Ellary so she might as well keep on "earning her reputation" her own way. So, I guess we were wrong a minute ago when we said she'd never told us why she does any of it.'

It made sense. After all, the term *sibling rivalry* existed for a reason. 'You said there were a couple of things Rheagan really struggled with,' Alyssa said. 'What was the other?'

Another brief round of silent communication passed between the teens before Bridgette answered. 'She and her dad fought about her neighbor, Raider, after he caught them making out one day and straight up freaked out. I guess he didn't like that Raider's a year older than her' – Bridgette rolled her eyes in an expressive show of disagreement – 'even though, seriously, it's closer to like eight months, so what's the big deal, really? Plus, I guess Mr. Pembroke told Rheagan she didn't need to be hanging out with someone who has kind of a reputation for being a troublemaker.'

Laila snorted. 'Not that we said this to Rheagan, of course, but Bridge and I thought it was just a tad bit hypocritical that her dad had this major beef about Raider's "troublemaking" reputation, but not his own daughter's. I mean, seriously.'

'Can you give us an example of the kind of trouble Raider got into it?' Cord asked.

'More than anything else, he has an attitude problem. Like he doesn't like to be told what to do, and so he mouthed off a lot, at least in school. But he never got into fights or anything that I can remember. Anyway, Mr. Pembroke demanded Rheagan steer clear of Raider altogether. And if I'm being honest, I really think that's why Rheagan keeps hooking up with him, just to get a rise out of her dad. Especially because she knows Raider's way more into her than she's into him.'

Alyssa glimpsed at the top of Cord's notebook where he'd written *Raider* and circled it. 'What's Raider's last name?'

'Hoyt. They live right next door to the Pembrokes.'

Ten minutes later, after asking the girls to notify them if they heard from their friend, Alyssa and Cord left. In the

Tahoe, she turned to Cord. 'Well, we know the Hoyts aren't home until later this week, but we have a name, so let's go see if we can find a way to contact Raider. Maybe he'll have some answers for us.'

Driving away, Alyssa was hit by the feeling that Rheagan's vanishing act wouldn't be something as simple as her and her neighbor deciding to hook up without letting her family know. As much as she hoped to be wrong, the itch at the back of her neck warned her not to count on it.

Chapter Five

Dragging the dead girl's body behind him, Kennedy's abductor disappeared into the gaping hole of darkness hidden behind a secret door. Trapped wails scaled the walls of her throat as the blood-soaked cement mocked her with the reality that her once carefree world had dissolved into this glacial glass chamber of torture and torment, where not only was she faced with her imminent death, but her own murder. Unable to stop it, her mind replayed the past few days on a never-ending reel of disbelief.

After killing the girl on Saturday, her abductor had left the body locked in the room with Kennedy. Then he'd disappeared up the wooden steps, and the next time she'd seen him, he'd appeared freshly showered, his hair still damp. For a moment, he'd disappeared again, and the sound of a key being inserted into the lock on the door had had Kennedy screaming behind the tape covering her mouth.

The man leered at her as he stepped over the dead girl's body and walked toward her. With her wide eyes glued on the leg irons dangling from his hand, Kennedy scrambled to cram herself farther into the corner. The wall against her back reminded her she had nowhere to go.

Tears streamed from her pleading eyes, but her abductor paid no attention to them. Instead, he crouched down and sliced the plastic zip ties from her ankles and replaced them with the leg irons, pressing the metal until it dug into her skin. Then, still not speaking, he latched onto her ponytail and wrenched her head backwards as he used her own hair to drag her from the corner.

Her bound hands reflexively went to her head, but he snapped her neck back and growled, his voice a low menacing snarl. 'Don't make a sound.' And then he ripped the tape off her mouth, tearing the sensitive skin around her lips when he did.

Despite the warning, Kennedy's throat automatically released the scream it had been forced to hold inside until the man's arm circled her throat and squeezed. Her eyes bulged as her lungs cried out for oxygen.

He squeezed tighter. 'What did I say? Scream again, and I'll slit your throat.'

Kennedy's legs slid out in front of her as she felt herself dropping back into unconsciousness. Just before the darkness claimed her, her abductor removed his arm and gripped her jaw, forcing her mouth open.

'Drink,' he ordered.

Liquid poured down her throat as she still gasped for air, but she knew she either had to swallow or drown. When he released her, it was only long enough to replace the tape, slapping his palm against her mouth to ensure it stuck.

Painful spasms ripped through Kennedy's stomach when his gaze swept from her to the metal rod from where the dead girl had been suspended as he beat her to death. She couldn't stop the whimpers that begged him not to kill her too.

He watched her with his soulless eyes. But instead of dragging her up, he leaned in and whispered, 'Have you been thinking about what it's going to be like? Hanging up there, helpless, while

I do whatever I want to you? Knowing that even if you could scream, no one would ever hear you?'

He traced his fingers from her face down to her stomach before he stood abruptly and walked out, slamming the door behind him and locking her in.

The next random appearance had been more of the same. By the third time, Kennedy realized that, with each visit, her abductor's wardrobe had changed. Partly in an effort to keep a grip on her sliding sanity, she used the information to calculate how long she'd been held prisoner. If each change of clothes equaled one day, then she'd been in this hell for three nights already.

The fourth night – this one – changed everything.

By then, the stringent odor of the girl's decomposing body burned Kennedy's eyes and assaulted her nose, causing her to gag.

Focused on swallowing back the bile threatening to choke her to death, she hadn't noticed her abductor had returned until the door swung open and he stepped inside wearing a pair of surgical gloves and what appeared to be waders similar to the kind her father wore whenever he went fishing. Without so much as a glimpse in Kennedy's direction, he moved over to the dead girl with a single-minded purpose. His face remained an impassive mask as he removed a rope draped over his wide shoulders and wound it tightly around the girl's feet before moving to her head, prying open her mouth, and shoving something inside.

Then he rose up, rope in hand, and dragged the girl behind him, leaving bits of rotting skin behind. Stopping just outside the enclosure, he ran one hand along the seam of the wall until a hidden panel slid open. Only then did he turn to face Kennedy.

He winked and uttered one chilling word, 'Soon,' before he stepped through the hidden doorway to a darkness that swallowed both him and the girl he hauled behind him. With visions of her own murder hammering away at her, Kennedy rocked back and forth, hitting the cement at her back with increasing force.

Chapter Six

Mingling with the pungent odor of decaying animal carcasses rotting in the hot Albuquerque sun was the even stronger, more distinct scent of a decomposing corpse. All around Alyssa, dozens of officers, evidence technicians, and crime scene analysts milled about recording the scene and snapping pictures, all while trying to preserve whatever forensic evidence they could. Shoved into a hollow space carved out just beneath a grouping of massive boulders and partially shielded by a dying juniper bush, the victim sprawled faceup, disposed of with less thought than one might use in throwing out the garbage.

Anger swirled in Alyssa's gut.

While the damage to the victim's battered and bloated face made her unrecognizable, the intricate design of the tattoo on her arm, as well as the one behind her right ear, told Alyssa the dreaded truth.

Rheagan Pembroke.

Among the hundreds of questions crowding Alyssa's mind, one demanded her immediate attention. If Rheagan's family had taken her disappearance seriously right away, would the outcome have been different?

After speaking to Bridgette and Laila, Alyssa and Cord had been remarkably unsuccessful in tracking down a single other person who might've been able to tell them anything about where Rheagan might've gone or what might've happened to her. In a nutshell, yesterday had been filled with an overwhelming display of hitting one dead end after another. And now, here she stood, faced with hunting down a killer instead of locating a missing girl.

Off in the distance, just beyond the yellow crime scene tape cordoning off the area from the gathering masses of looky-loos crowding on top of the hill, several voices shouted for Alyssa's attention. Blocking them out, she concentrated on the scene as she tried to piece together Rheagan's final hours.

Cord came up to stand beside her. 'That sure as hell didn't take long. I mean, I'm not surprised because it never does, but good God in heaven, do they really have to line up like they're waiting to board a carnival ride?'

The 'they' he referred to was the long queue of news reporters Alyssa had been actively and openly ignoring. A quick peek revealed even more of the vulturous pack had arrived and were currently in the midst of setting up their cameras for the best and most shocking shot that they no doubt hoped they could get in time for their noon newscast. Had any of them witnessed Alyssa's withering scowl, they might have had enough sagacity to back off.

Trying to remind herself that they were only doing their jobs, the same as she and everyone else on scene, she did her best to swallow back the bitter pill of annoyance she suffered from their presence. Still, she couldn't help but respond to Cord's rhetorical comment. 'Well, death and sex are what sells.' Her lips curved around the words like she'd just chugged a bitter cup of two-day-old coffee.

'Throw murder and a mutilated body on top of that, and they're worse than frenzied sharks at feeding time.'

'You're right about that.'

'I'm usually right about most things. I'd think you'd know that by now.'

Cord's sigh, born of his frustration and familiarity, had nothing to do with Alyssa's comment and everything to do with his own mounting ire at the situation at hand. 'It's her, isn't it? Rheagan?'

Tension dug its claws deeper into Alyssa's muscles. 'Yes, I'm positive of it. But we're going to need the Pembrokes to give us a formal identification to make it official.' Shrugging off her shudder at the drove of maggots and other insects crawling around the shredded remains of a shirt and the stab wounds crisscrossing the exposed upper part of Rheagan's body, making it appear as if the girl still breathed, Alyssa crouched down for a better look.

Along with the stab wounds and the battered face, a deep well of black and purple contusions blossomed with color over Rheagan's chest and stomach area.

Never an easy task, Alyssa focused on the details that would help her track down the person responsible for ending Rheagan's life so heinously. In addition to the maggots, dried blood, and contusions, she also noted the dirt, gravel, bark, and pine needles embedded in the victim's skin, almost as if she'd been dragged facedown along an unpaved road. Her eyes drifted from the familiar grooves cutting into the skin of Rheagan's wrists down to similar ones found around her ankles. Alyssa craned her neck up and pointed it out to Cord. 'Looks like whoever killed her used metal cuffs to confine her.'

Cord's mouth tightened into a thin line as he took in the damage. 'Would seem that way.'

She rose back to all of her five-foot-three-inch height just as one of Albuquerque's medical examiners, Dr. Lynn Sharp, squeezed her way through to stand next to Alyssa and Cord.

'Whoever killed your victim made it damn clear they were displeased.' Lynn huffed out a sigh. 'More and more frequently, I'm beginning to believe I'm in the wrong line of work. Whoever told me all those years ago that eventually I'd grow numb to it lied. That's all I can say.' She waved her hand over the body. 'I mean, how does anyone ever become immune to seeing something as atrocious as this?'

Cord's voice dropped to a low timbre. 'When you figure it out, please let me know, would you?'

Like Cord, Alyssa understood exactly where Dr. Sharp was coming from. Despite having borne witness to the aftermath of some of the state's most heinous crimes over the course of her more than two and a half decades fighting crime, she'd never been able to make herself immune to the inhumanity and unfairness of it all. Whereas many violent crime investigators had mastered the skill of divorcing themselves from the emotional impact and separating themselves from the job, both she and Cord tended to hold onto it because it gave them the drive to keep going. It was one of the many things that made their partnership work.

As Alyssa had done earlier, Lynn crouched so she could better examine the damage done to the victim. 'Have you had a chance to speak to the witnesses who stumbled across the body?'

Alyssa looked over her shoulder and took in three teenagers huddled together as they finished giving their statements about how they'd happened across a dead body. 'Not yet, but we'll be doing that in a few minutes.'

Lynn nodded and turned her attention back to Rheagan. Tipping her head to the side, she spoke quietly but still loud enough for Alyssa to hear. 'I know your suffering has ended and your family's has just begun, but I promise you this: I will do my utmost to make sure your autopsy releases some of the secrets your body is still clinging to, still hiding.'

As if Rheagan or the gods had heard Lynn, a huge gust of wind picked up, blowing sand in every direction, and then disappearing two seconds later as if it had never occurred.

Alyssa couldn't shake the feeling that Rheagan was trying to tell them something, begging them to listen.

Regret that they hadn't been able to save the girl her friends had described as so vivacious and full of energy seared the back of Alyssa's throat, and it took her several seconds before she trusted herself to speak. 'Let's give the techs space to finish gathering evidence and go see what our witnesses can tell us.'

Chapter Seven

Wednesday, June 1

The girls, gripping the ends of three blue blankets one of the first responders had provided, huddled close together. Despite the heat from the blankets and the rapidly rising temperature of an early June day, their bodies visibly quaked with uncontrollable shivers.

Whether they heard Alyssa and Cord's approach or spotted their shadows blocking out the sun, each of the girls jerked their heads up, their eyes revealing the impact of having their innocence ripped out from under them at the discovery of a dead – *murdered* – person. The two girls flanking the one in the middle scooted in closer until a whisper of air would have a tough time slipping through. And then, almost subconsciously, their hands all moved together as they clutched onto each other with a white-knuckled grip.

Though it was far from comfortable, Alyssa lowered herself into a squat so she wouldn't be towering above the frightened girls. Of course, at her lack of height, 'towering' might've been a stretch.

'Hello. My name is Detective Wyatt with the Albuquerque Police Department, and this is my partner, Detective Roberts. I understand you're the ones who discovered the victim. Is that correct?'

'Yes, ma'am.' The whispered words of the chestnut-haired girl in the middle were louder than her friends' but still barely audible over the rumblings of all the police activity going on around them.

'I know you've already talked to a couple of the officers here, and I know this will be difficult, but we're going to need you to go over it again. I'm sorry. But first, let me start by getting your names, all right?' Alyssa didn't bother checking to see if Cord jotted down the information; she knew he would.

The girl in the middle removed her hands from her friends' grip and picked at her already bleeding cuticles. 'Um, I don't understand *why* we have to go over it all again.' She leaned forward, searching, then pointed. 'We told those two everything we know.'

Alyssa shifted so she could see who the young girl pointed at, relieved to spot one of the officers well known for her delicate way of extracting the most information from emotionally charged victims, especially the younger ones. Even so, Alyssa still preferred hearing witness accounts firsthand and then comparing notes with the initial reports later, and that was what she explained to the three girls now.

'I understand this has been quite a traumatic experience for you, and I can completely get why you don't wish to go over it again. But it helps Detective Roberts and me to hear things firsthand while it's still fresh in your mind. And while you may not realize it, retelling us what happened might help you recall something, even a minor little detail, that you might have overlooked or simply forgotten the first time through. Something that might hold the key to helping us track down the person responsible.'

What the girls couldn't possibly know was that Alyssa's words of understanding weren't merely lip service to put them at ease; she could truly empathize with what she was asking them to do. Three short years ago, her son, Isaac, had gone through his own traumatic experience, and as his mother, standing by while he'd been asked again and again to relive his nightmare, had been one of the most difficult things she'd ever had to do.

Tears formed in the young girl's eyes before spilling over and adding to the streaks in her once carefully applied makeup. 'I'm Julia Blackwell,' the girl in the middle whispered. She first pointed to the girl on her left, then the one on her right. 'This is my younger sister, Tara. And this is our best friend, Raven Portman.'

With her raven-colored hair and round, dark eyes full of intelligence, even if they were currently marred with trepidation and mistrust, Raven had the perfect name, Alyssa thought.

While they introduced themselves, Cord took the opportunity to lower himself beside Alyssa, probably so he wouldn't appear to be hovering. Alyssa smiled gently to help put the girls at ease. 'Thank you. Now, I'd like you to take your time and just walk us through exactly what happened. Try not to leave anything out, no matter how minor or unimportant the detail might seem. In other words, just give us as much information as you can recall.'

Julia wiped her free hand across her cheek, sniffled, and closed her eyes as her head swiveled back and forth as if watching a replay of what had happened on her sealed eyelids. The seconds ticked away until a violent shudder worked its way through her entire frame, and her eyes flew open. 'We were coming back from our hike when a huge, thick dust devil kicked up, and so we just kind of raced for cover so we wouldn't get blasted by it.'

When Julia paused, Raven, intuitively understanding that her friend needed a moment to compose herself, picked up the timeline of events. Almost as if she couldn't help herself, her eyes drifted in the direction of Rheagan's body, now blocked by the thick throng of technicians collecting evidence. 'We tried to take shelter by those boulders over there. But that's when… when Tara tripped—' Raven gagged, her hand flying to cover her mouth as she fought against losing the contents of her stomach in front of strangers.

Cord signaled to one of the officers nearby, and Alyssa heard him request three bottles of water. Less than a minute later, the officer returned, and Cord handed one to each of the girls, saying, 'Here, drink this. Slowly.' He waited for them to do so before he asked, 'Better?'

All three nodded.

The first thing Raven did when she spoke again was apologize. 'I'm sorry.'

'No need to be,' Cord assured her. 'You're doing fine. Go ahead and give yourself a minute. Finding a dead body isn't something that's easy to cope with.'

The smallest lift to one corner of her mouth showed Raven's gratitude for Alyssa and Cord's patience and understanding. Only after her breathing finally returned to somewhat normal did they continue with Cord asking, 'Julia said the three of you were coming back from a hike. Do you often come out here for that?'

While she doubted the girls had noticed the underlying tension in Cord's voice, Alyssa did. Partly, she imagined, it stemmed from the fact that he didn't necessarily think the Tramway Arroyo, the main channel between the Sandia

41

and Manzano Mountains, was the safest place for three teenage girls to hike on their own. Not only was it a little off the beaten path, but it was also well known as a place for airsoft groups to play war games that sometimes looked so realistic that Dispatch often received alarmed calls regarding individuals dressed in camouflage and wielding a vast array of weapons.

In response to Cord's question, Raven shrugged. 'Not like often, I guess. But definitely sometimes, for sure. We're all really into different kinds of art, so we like to examine the new graffiti and stuff from time to time. And besides, there aren't usually a whole lot of people around. At least not when we come.'

For the first time, Tara chimed in, her husky voice not quite fitting her diminutive frame, especially with each word sounding as if it strained to leave her throat. 'It might not look like much with all the trash and stuff, and of course, the canyon is right up the hill, but believe it or not, it can be really quiet and peaceful in here. I mean, like depending on when you come and all that.'

Alyssa's eyes swept the area around her, thinking that she probably wouldn't mark this steep-sided gully of dirt, debris, and downed trees as either peaceful or quiet, but her idea of those two things clearly differed from the girls'. 'And what time did the three of you get here today?' she asked.

Both Julia and Raven looked to Tara for the answer.

'Tenish, I think.'

Alyssa nodded. 'Okay, around ten. And which way did you come in?'

Raven pointed past a thick crop of shrubbery and up the hill about five hundred yards away to what had become, over time, a makeshift parking lot for those wanting to explore the arroyo and the surrounding areas. 'We parked up there just off the side of the road like we usually do.'

Alyssa recognized the spot as the same one most hikers in this area used. 'And when you arrived today, were there any other vehicles up there?'

The three girls shook their heads. 'No,' they said in unison before Raven added, 'We usually go somewhere else if there are other cars around.'

'I see. And before today, when was the last time you came out here to hike?'

Julia, Tara, and Raven looked at one another before Julia answered. 'I think it was like a week before Memorial Day weekend.'

Alyssa started to ask a question, but before she could, Tara clapped one hand down on the bare space below Julia's shorts, leaving behind a bright red mark. 'Yes, it was Sunday, the twenty-second, remember? Because it was right after Marshall's birthday.'

In the way of many teenage girls around the world, they shared a giggly smile, and for just the space of a heartbeat, their shoulders relaxed.

All too quickly, their current reality came crashing back around them as Cord drew the girls' attention over to him. 'I know you said you don't usually stop if there are others around, but what about the twenty-second? Do you remember seeing any people on the trail that day?'

It took a moment for Alyssa to catch on to the reasoning behind Cord's question. He wanted to know if their perpetrator might've been spotted in the area, scouting things out. A long shot, maybe, but a good question, nevertheless.

'Well, when we said we don't usually stop if there are other cars here already,' Julia clarified, 'what we meant is if there's only like one or two cars, we don't stick around.'

Cord's eyebrows shot up. 'Why's that?'

'I guess we just don't feel as safe. But if there are lots of vehicles up there, like there usually are on the weekends, it's like safety in numbers, you know? I mean, we may or may not stay and hike then. It just depends. I don't know if any of that makes sense, even.'

'That definitely makes sense,' Alyssa reassured her. 'Do you recall seeing anything or anyone here that day that might've stuck out for you in your mind?'

In the first show of what Alyssa could only classify as a typical teenage response to what they deemed to be a strange – or stupid – question, Raven sniffed, lifted her chin, and shot Alyssa a look that clearly indicated that her intelligence might be in question. 'You mean like did we notice someone casing the place to see where he could stuff a body? No. Pretty sure we would've remembered that.'

Beside her, Cord covered his mouth and coughed in a poor attempt to hide his startled laugh. Alyssa couldn't really blame him since she'd been struck with the same impulse.

Before she could ask her next question, a female officer Alyssa recognized but whose name she didn't know approached, and both she and Cord rose to their feet.

'The girls' parents have arrived and are demanding to see their children.'

Alyssa turned to see two men and one woman staring down at them from atop the hill, the frantic expressions on their faces outlining their worry. She waved for the officers to let them through.

Immediately, Julia and Tara threw off their blankets and leaped to their feet so they could run into their father's arms. As they sobbed against his shoulders, he crushed them against his chest and murmured something Alyssa couldn't hear.

A little more slowly and a lot less enthusiastically, Raven also stood, opting to keep her blanket securely wrapped around herself instead of shedding it the way her friends had. Unlike Mr. Blackwell, Mr. and Mrs. Portman seemed lost as to how they should greet their daughter. Finally, Mr. Portman settled on bestowing an impersonal pat to Raven's shoulder as he asked, 'You doing okay?'

Raven kept her gaze averted as she muttered, 'Yes, sir. The detectives are just asking us some questions.'

Mr. Portman aimed a stony expression toward Alyssa and Cord. 'I see. Are the girls in trouble here?'

More put off by the man's lack of emotional support for his daughter than his question, Alyssa barely managed to refrain from growling at him. 'Not that I'm aware of. As you know, your daughter and her friends are the ones who discovered the victim, and so we're trying to gather as much information as we can.'

'And did you bother to ask any of them if they'd like an attorney present before you began questioning them?'

Before she could lose her temper with Raven's father, Alyssa heard someone shouting her name. Ignoring Mr. Portman's question, she turned to see Officer Tony White, with his recently shaved head now sporting a glowing circle of sunburn, jabbing a finger in the air as he used his other arm to wave for Alyssa to hurry.

'We'll be right back,' she said, excusing herself and Cord.

When they were close enough, Alyssa craned her neck upwards, immediately spotting what had Tony so worked up. The reflection off of a wilderness camera mounted high up in one of the trees winked down at them, and though she warned herself not to get too hopeful, she let Tony's excitement spill over her for just a moment.

'Sincerely hope that camera was activated,' Cord said as he summoned a technician over.

'And gives a clear shot of our perpetrator,' Tony added.

'Or perpetrators, plural,' Alyssa felt compelled to throw in. 'Carrying Rheagan's body down that hill couldn't have been easy, so it's possible we might be looking for more than one individual.'

Neither Tony nor Cord had time to respond as Lynn Sharp suddenly appeared, the color washed from her face as she zeroed in on Alyssa and Cord. 'You two better come with me. I found something you both need to see right now.'

Lynn's demeanor had Alyssa's nerves flaring as if stung by invisible bees. When Lynn stopped a short distance away, she held up an unfolded piece of paper.

Confused, Alyssa narrowed her eyes to focus. And then suddenly, it became clear. In her latex-covered hands, Lynn held a photocopied image of a teenage boy Alyssa immediately recognized. A bloody hammer rested near his feet. That, along with the sinister nursery-like rhyme typed at the bottom of the paper, had her head reeling with the chilling implications of this discovery.

You're going to need to run
If you want to expose the things I've done.
Better never stop to rest
Because you just might miss who I took next.

46

Chapter Eight

With a pair of binoculars in hand, his perch well hidden from prying eyes, the man watched from afar as the police descended en masse on the dead girl's location. Excitement sizzled through his veins as he paid close attention to the cop with her auburn hair pulled back into a ponytail that brushed just below her shirt collar.

Laughter bubbled up inside him, almost escaping before he caught himself. How fitting that the same detective who'd been tracking him fourteen years earlier would be the one to land this case. He couldn't have asked for a better scenario. Intuitively, he understood she'd be far more dedicated to hunting him down, not wanting the public to know he'd already escaped her clutches, but he wasn't worried. He knew she'd have no better luck this go-round. She might have years more experience under her belt, but wisdom and practice had honed his skills to perfection.

He closed his eyes, allowing the thrill of his past kills to fill him with that tingling sense of euphoria that came from each person's final moments of terrifying acceptance. The memories made it difficult not to give in to his yearning and return immediately to his latest victim so he could watch her plead with her eyes as he drained her of life. He curled his hands into fists and forced himself to remain still. He'd already acted in haste once. He had all the time in the world to play, he reminded himself. More now that he'd finally been able to get rid of the body currently surrounded by dozens of cops.

Careful not to let the sun reflect off the lens of his binoculars, he shifted his attention to the dead girl. A slow anger simmered, working its way up until it fully replaced his blissful exhilaration of moments earlier. He'd thought she was so special... different... from all the others. But he'd been wrong. She hadn't been different; she'd only misrepresented herself, and so he'd had no other choice but to kill her just like the rest of them.

Remembered fury heated his skin. She'd deserved every bit of what he'd done to her. More, even. Disgusted that he'd allowed her deceit to steal his delight, he turned his focus back to the activity of the cops and the flurry of activity on the hill above the arroyo.

For another hour, he watched, wishing he could hear what the officers below were saying. And as much as he wished he could stay, he knew his absence would be noted if he remained gone for much longer. With a disappointed sigh, he rose from his spot, brushed the dirt and twigs from his pants, and tossed one feverish final look over his shoulder before making his way back to his vehicle. After climbing inside and buckling himself in, he tuned the radio to some brain-numbing chatter and allowed his mind to drift as he drove.

From an early age – some might even argue too young – he'd known he was different, that something inside him had slipped off kilter. He remembered once hearing his grandmother – his mom's mom – hissing at his parents that something was wrong with him, that he wasn't 'quite right in the head.' He could almost hear his mother roll her eyes in that dramatic fashion of hers when she asked one simple question: 'Why in the world would you say something like that?'

'He stiffens whenever I go to hug him, he stares at people in a very odd way, and he laughs at things that aren't funny. A child shouldn't make adults nervous like that. I mean, I don't think I've ever even seen that boy cry.'

His father had snorted. 'He's a boy. Boys aren't supposed to cry over every little thing, and they're not supposed to be all touchy-feely. Too much hugging turns boys into little sissies.'

His grandmother had muttered, 'Well, some hugging and affection might prove beneficial.'

Ignoring her mother's snarky comment, his mom had hmphed and dismissed his grandmother's concerns, much like his father had.

He had no idea what it all meant, but he knew he didn't like them talking about him behind his back. In fact, it made him angry. Careful not to let his father know he'd been listening to the grown-ups, he'd slipped off to his room and sat in the corner, startling a spider out of wherever it had been hiding. He snatched it off the wall, and with his grandma's hissed words swirling like a tornado in his head, he pulled its legs off one by one, enthralled in its efforts to get away before he finally killed it.

Some days after that, he'd gone to a friend's house to play. When his friend told him about how his new puppy had been mauled to death by a neighbor's dog, he'd laughed like he'd been told the world's funniest joke. He hadn't noticed how his friend's tearful eyes had grown big as a frisbee until he'd slowly started backing away before suddenly claiming he didn't want to play anymore.

Fuming at his friend for being such a sissy baby, he'd returned home and told his mother about it. She'd stopped stirring the sauce on the stove and tossed a strange look over her shoulder at him. 'Why did you think that was funny?' she'd asked.

He hadn't been able to give her an answer, but after her lengthy lecture about his inappropriate behavior, he'd learned a quick lesson – when it came to emotions, mimic those around him.

Later that night, when his parents had settled into their evening routine of devouring the news and dissecting the state of world events, he'd brushed his teeth, donned his favorite pair of pajamas, and then shuffled into the living room where they'd stopped mid-conversation and turned to him, only slightly surprised to see him ready for bed.

Not exactly the cuddly, cooing type – not even the time he'd accidentally cut himself so badly he needed stitches (in fact, his father had immediately demanded he stop his sissy bawling before he gave him something to bawl about) – his mother merely arched her painted brows and said, 'Going to bed so soon? Aren't you feeling well?'

He'd shaken his head and claimed to be tired, to which she replied, 'Well, all right then. Goodnight,' before returning to the discussion he'd interrupted. His father acknowledged him with a nod, the way he always did.

Back in his room, he pulled out his pet gerbil and sat in the middle of his bed. Lost in thought at his friend's reaction and his mother's warning that he shouldn't have laughed, that the dog's mauling had been sad – *tragic*, she'd said – he'd grabbed his yo-yo and wrapped it around the gerbil's neck, pulling the string tighter and tighter.

When he realized it had stopped moving, he studied it for a moment. Then he'd carefully removed the string and tossed the critter back in its cage, catching a reflection of himself in the mirror as he did.

Remembering his mother's lecture, he practiced looking sad. When he found a look he thought was good, he climbed into bed, turned off his lamp, and crawled under the covers. He didn't think about the animal again until the next morning when he woke and got a glimpse of its stiff form lying in the same spot where he'd dropped it the night before. After opening the gerbil's cage, he'd pulled it out and thrown it in the garbage pail by his door.

The next day when his mother came to gather his trash, she'd turned to him, upset, and asked him what had happened. He'd told her the truth. Mostly.

'It died, so I threw it away.'

The way she studied it and him, he was sure she was going to demand he tell her how it had died, but all she'd asked was, 'Why didn't you tell me?'

He'd shrugged before remembering he was supposed to be sad, and so he stuck his lower lip out and let it quiver. His mother had stared at the dead animal for forever before finally looking back at him. Silent, she cocked her head to the side and pursed her lips. He waited, but without saying another word about it, she removed the garbage can liner, tied it into a knot, grabbed the cage, and carried it all out of his room.

As he watched her carry the dead gerbil out, he suddenly wished he could make it come back alive. Not because he missed it, but because he wanted to kill it again so he could watch what it did when it died like he had with the spider.

Since he couldn't – and his mother refused to allow him to get another pet – he found other animals instead. Each time one died, his whole body would tingle, and his brain felt super happy. And the more the animal struggled, the more elated he felt. Pretty soon, that feeling was all he found himself craving.

The sound of a blaring horn rattled the man from his thoughts, and he realized he'd dived so deeply into his memory that he hadn't moved from the four-way stop. He glanced in his rearview mirror at the driver behind him angrily jabbing his finger in the air. The guy leaned his head out his window and yelled, 'What the hell are you waiting for, man, a written invitation? It's not gonna change colors, you know.'

People should be careful who they chastised. One never knew what someone else might be capable of. If he didn't have someplace else to be, he might've considered teaching that guy a valuable lesson.

Chapter Nine

Wednesday, June 1

Nearly six hours after first receiving the call about a body being discovered in the Tramway Arroyo, Alyssa and Cord waited outside the medical examiner's office for Ben and Barbara Pembroke to arrive and give the formal, positive identification. Still feeling slightly paralyzed from the picture and note shoved inside a sandwich bag and stuffed inside Rheagan's mouth, Alyssa's head pulled her in more than a dozen conflicting directions. The most prevalent thought crowding her mind, however, was the implication that the same person who'd eluded capture fourteen years ago could very well be the same person who'd taken Rheagan's life.

And if that were true, she now had to face Rheagan's family with that knowledge weighing heavily on her mind.

Lost in a murky kaleidoscope of her past case mixed in with Rheagan's, it took some time to register Cord's garbled voice speaking to her.

'Lys, did you hear me?' A touch of concern scratched just below the surface of his question.

She unsuccessfully shook her head to try to clear it. 'Yes, I heard you.'

'I know what you told the captain, but I need you to walk me through this so I can try to understand what – or who – we're dealing with.'

Alyssa shot him a narrow-eyed glower that could be interpreted either as irritation or indignation, and not even she could say for certain which she intended. 'If I knew *who*, do you really think I'd be standing here right this second instead of doing everything possible to hunt that bastard down? The same person who murdered Gunner Galveston fourteen years ago, the one person in my career who I failed to track down or even identify, might now also be responsible for Rheagan Pembroke's death.'

Cord threw his hands up and took a step back. 'Whoa. Ease up there, my friend. We're on the same side. And I'm just trying to understand.'

Though the tension in Alyssa's shoulders remained, her brief snip of anger fluttered away, and she offered a crooked but brief smile. 'You're right, I'm sorry.'

Cord brushed her apology aside. 'Like you told those three girls today, sometimes repeating the same story helps bring to light something that might've been overlooked. And if I'm being honest, you weren't making a whole lot of sense after Lynn showed you that photograph.'

'I know.' Alyssa rubbed two fingers on either side of her temples and inhaled deeply before exhaling slowly. But the story would have to wait because she spotted Ben and Barbara's dark blue sedan pulling into the parking lot with Ellary behind the wheel.

When the three stepped from their car, the toll of guilt and grief flickered in their tired, sad eyes as their hesitant, halting steps slowly brought them face to face with Alyssa and Cord. Twice, Barbara Pembroke looked back toward her car, the longing to return to safety and denial clear in her expression, as if by avoiding the odious task of identifying her daughter's remains, she could keep herself sheltered from the truth.

Tamping back her own brewing sea of emotions, Alyssa stepped forward to greet the family. 'Mr. and Mrs. Pembroke, Ellary.' Though Mrs. Pembroke accepted Alyssa's hand, her grip remained limp and shaky, matching her outward appearance. The second she pulled her fingers away, her shoulders returned to their weighted slump, as if she were attempting to physically vanish inside her loose-fitting pantsuit.

Ellary's red-rimmed eyes skated over her mother's head to meet Alyssa's. 'Are you sure it's really Rheagan?' Her voice crackled with disbelief and something close to anger.

'I'm as certain as I can be, but we'll need you to give that formal identification.' Alyssa paused, hating to repeat this next part, but needing to remind them anyway. 'I know I already told you this when we contacted you, but I want to warn you again that Rheagan—there was a lot of damage done to her face.'

A gasping sob escaped from Barbara's mouth before she pressed her face against her husband's chest.

Mr. Pembroke cleared his throat twice before he finally managed to get his words out. 'We understand. Thank you for reminding us. We're ready whenever you are.'

With nothing left to say, Alyssa turned while Cord held the door open for the family to follow her into the building. When the calm expression on Cord's face suddenly morphed into flared nostrils and a jaw clenched hard enough for his teeth to grind, she turned back, immediately spotting the news van parked across the street.

While Alyssa willingly admitted to disliking and holding a grudge against Monty Cannon for breaking information on one of their cases last year, Cord's strong reaction outweighed even hers because Cannon's leak had endangered – almost fatally – the lives of Carter and Abigail Fleming, at the time six and three, and who now proudly called themselves Carter and Abigail Fleming Roberts after Cord and his wife won their bid to adopt the pair.

Clearly, the man's sense of propriety for allowing the Pembrokes any amount of privacy was greedily overshadowed by his need for what Alyssa deemed sensational journalism. As usual, his interests leaned more toward obtaining the horrified, grief-stricken reactions of people than he was in reporting accurate stories. The bottom line, in her opinion, was if a person were to look up life-sucking scum, a picture of Monty Cannon would appear.

Effectively shutting the nuisance of a reporter out, albeit too briefly, Cord closed the door behind the five of them. In stark contrast to the sweltering outside heat, the coolness of the air conditioner blowing on them inside the building had the effect of quickly becoming uncomfortably cold, causing Ellary to rub her hands briskly up and down her bare arms in an effort to provide warmth and tame the obvious goosebumps peppering her skin.

Dr. Sharp stepped from her office, her face a mask of polite professionalism as she greeted Alyssa and Cord with a nod and the Pembrokes with a firm handshake. 'Thank you all for coming. Being asked to identify a loved one, I know, is never an easy task.' Lynn's gentle gaze lingered the longest on Mrs. Pembroke's quaking form before she turned and said, 'Follow me.'

Like the building itself, the autopsy room was a cold and sterile space, with every outside noise resembling the sound of a ticking time bomb that added to the already macabre atmosphere. Catching Alyssa's eye, Dr. Sharp moved to the head of the table. Cord, as he usually did, situated himself closest to the family, with Alyssa standing across from them.

Bracing themselves the best anyone could in circumstances such as this, the family crowded closer together, blindly groping for and then gripping each other's hands. While Mr. and Mrs. Pembroke's eyes remained on the wall behind Lynn's head, Ellary reluctantly tipped her head forward in one jerky, nearly imperceptible motion, granting Lynn the go-ahead.

Careful to keep Rheagan's face covered to prevent the family from seeing the extent of the damage done to it and the rest of her body, Lynn lowered the sheet, exposing only the telling tattoos on Rheagan's arm and behind her right ear.

Instantly, Mrs. Pembroke's wail shattered the tense silence of the room, the tormented sound of her grief digging its sharp claw into Alyssa. Cord instinctively moved in Barbara's direction, but instead of collapsing, she clutched at her husband's arms as she burrowed herself tightly against his chest.

An image of her own mother's similar reaction decades earlier flashed briefly in Alyssa's mind before she closed the memory out and turned to Ellary, whose muffled words came through clearly, despite her hands covering her mouth.

'It's her. It's Rheagan.' Almost of their own accord, Ellary's trembling hands reached out to trace the rose tattoo. For the space of several heartbeats, her fingers

57

hovered over her sister's body before clenching into fists and dropping back to her sides. Her shadowed, grief-stricken eyes held a hint of disbelief as they drifted up to lock with Alyssa's and then Lynn's. 'Can—am I allowed to see her face?'

Lynn's startled gaze flew to Alyssa's before turning back to the Pembrokes. 'I'm sorry, but I really don't think that's a good idea right now. Perhaps you should take some time to really consider if that's what you want, but I strongly recommend against it.'

What Lynn didn't say, but Alyssa understood, was that, once done, it couldn't be undone, and the impact of seeing that kind of damage on their loved one would never leave their memories.

Thankfully, Mr. Pembroke spoke up before Ellary could push it. 'That's okay. We—we don't need to see it.' He flung an unreadable expression in his surviving child's direction before continuing. 'We can say with one hundred percent certainty that this is our—this is Rheagan.'

With compassion and understanding, Lynn carefully raised the sheet to cover the parts she'd exposed. 'While I recognize it's little consolation, I'd still like to extend my sincerest apologies.' She folded her hands together and draped them in front of her. 'At this moment, I'm afraid I don't have any real answers for you, but that's what we're hoping the autopsy will reveal.'

Ellary's eyes remained glued on her sister's covered form. Her fingers clasped tightly together, turning her knuckles white, she whispered, 'Will you be able to tell how long—'

Though Ellary's question remained frozen behind her lips, Lynn understood what she wanted to know.

'We should be able to create a window of time, but in my medical *opinion*, my initial assessment is that your sister's state of decomposition indicates she hadn't been out in the elements long before she was discovered. Of course, I'd like to reiterate that I can't officially determine that until I've finished with my exam.'

Ellary nodded once before casting one final heart-broken glance at her sister's covered body before turning on her heel and, with shoulders held stiff and high, striding out of the room.

It was difficult not to see the simmering rage bubbling just below her exit.

Chapter Ten

After giving the Pembrokes time to grapple with the realization that Rheagan had been murdered, Alyssa and Cord ushered them into Lynn's office. A long stretch of silence broken only by the sobs coming from Barbara filled the room until Ellary cast an inscrutable glimpse in her parents' direction before squaring her shoulders and facing Alyssa.

Her voice husky with the tears she visibly fought to hold at bay, she said, 'Even when my head told me otherwise, when I could sense it deep in my bones, my heart insisted Rheagan really would come waltzing through the front door any second without a care in the world for the worry she'd caused, ready to share her latest adventure with all of us.'

Her tears spilled over onto her cheeks, streaking her makeup, before she angrily brushed them away and shifted her gaze to the multitude of framed medical certificates adorning Lynn's walls before returning her focus to Alyssa and Cord.

'Despite the million times I wanted to throttle Rheagan for giving us a scare, I secretly admired her, too, you know? She just always seemed, I don't know, invincible somehow.' In her first real raw show of emotion,

Ellary wrapped her arms around her middle and began to rock back and forth. 'It was like Rheagan could always take on the worst of the world and come out the victor.' When her voice crackled and broke, she stopped talking, and her father finally seemed to remember he still had another daughter and reached out a hand to awkwardly rub her shoulder.

Whether she didn't welcome his touch, or it just happened to coincide with her movement, Ellary scooted to the edge of her seat and leaned forward for a tissue, dislodging her father's hand. After wiping her eyes and blowing her nose, she shoved the used tissue into the small purse she wore crosswise around her body.

Ben Pembroke danced his eyes in his daughter's direction before he returned to patting the back of his wife's head as she buried her face in his neck, her sorrow muffled by the collar of his shirt. An edge of angry bitterness laced through the grief when he directed a question to Alyssa. 'What happens now?'

What happened now was that Alyssa needed to determine if Rheagan had really been murdered at the hands of a killer who'd escaped justice fourteen years earlier, and what kind of cosmic coincidence would've ensured she landed *both* cases. Of course, she kept those thoughts to herself. 'I know you already told us, but I'd like to go over – again – Rheagan's last few days before she went missing. There might be a crucial detail that was overlooked or seemed unimportant at the time, that in a different light, could make all the difference to finding out what happened to her.'

Mr. Pembroke sputtered. 'Are you insinuating that this is *our* fault, that we *hid* something from you or... or... didn't tell you everything we knew?'

Alyssa raised her palm to stave off the anger radiating from Rheagan's father. 'No, that's not at all what I'm saying. I'm just saying we have the best chance at finding out what happened to Rheagan if we can retrace her steps.'

The tension in the room thickened as the urge to argue flitted across Mr. Pembroke's features. Alyssa sensed the moment the fight left him because his entire body seemed to deflate in front of them.

'When we spoke to you on Monday, you told us that you were unaware of any plans that Rheagan may have had Saturday, which was the last time you spoke with her, correct?'

Ben hesitated before he answered. 'Yes, that's right.'

Using an investigative tactic she'd learned long ago, Alyssa didn't directly ask a question with her next comment, wanting to see how the family would react. 'Bridgette and Laila claimed the three of them had plans to meet up Saturday night, but that Rheagan sent a text just after nine thirty to cancel.'

Barbara lifted her head, revealing wavy black lines of mascara that streaked through the rouge on her cheekbones. 'I truly wasn't aware of those plans.' Her voice trembled. 'But as I told you on Monday, Rheagan didn't always tell us those things.'

Ellary stiffened in her seat at her mother's words.

Knowing the potential for the kind of explosive reaction that grief sometimes wrought in others, especially when family members were desperate to place the blame of loss at someone's feet – anyone's – Alyssa changed the direction of her questioning.

'You told us that you sent Rheagan to speak to a therapist. Do you recall the name of the person she saw?' She wondered if the therapist would be willing to shed some light on Rheagan's behavior. More specifically, Alyssa wanted to know if Rheagan's seemingly reckless drive toward danger could've been at the root of what had gotten her killed.

Ben and Barbara looked at each other and then at Ellary before they each shook their heads. 'But I have his name in my files somewhere,' Ben said. 'Can I call you with it later?'

'Of course. Thank you.'

A few minutes later, Alyssa and Cord escorted the Pembrokes out, and two troubling questions wormed their way into Alyssa's mind. If Rheagan's and Gunner's killer was one and the same, as the picture of Gunner shoved in Rheagan's mouth suggested, where had he been hiding for the past fourteen years? And what else had he been doing?

Chapter Eleven

Wednesday, June 1

Assaulted by vicious waves of nausea, Kennedy lurched and swayed as she divided her attention between staring at the bloodstained concrete and the doorway where her abductor had disappeared hours ago, dragging the dead girl's body behind him like a heavy bag of garbage. Long after she could no longer see or hear him, his final word, 'Soon,' lingered in the air, a perpetual echo that held her hostage.

Choking on her sobs, Kennedy lifted her bound hands to the tape covering her mouth, but let them drop again, too terrified of what would happen if she screamed… and *he* returned instead of help.

A fresh round of tears slid down her face as she thought of her family, and she wondered if, at this very moment, her twin sister felt something off. They had that kind of bond. One time, out on a solo hike, Kennedy had lost her footing and tumbled down a steep but short hill. Her head had bounced off a boulder, and she'd been knocked unconscious. Somehow, Aubrey had sensed danger and had insisted on their parents helping her search. When they'd found Kennedy, she'd been dazed and disoriented from a concussion.

But Aubrey wasn't in the state right now, and her parents weren't even in this country, so they probably didn't realize she was missing – and that her life was about to be brought to a brutal end. Her eyes moved from the stain on the concrete floor to the metal bar stretched across the walls of the glass chamber to the sinister tools lining the shelves outside the room. Her kidnapper had told her that even if she'd been able to scream, no one would ever hear her. Meaning she must be in a remote or soundproofed area. Meaning the other girl probably hadn't been his first victim. Kennedy's heart stopped.

How many others had he killed? How long had he been getting away with murder? Would he also get away with hers?

Kennedy moaned until a voice whispered in her head. *You need to get out!* Slowly, awareness seeped back in, and it took her a moment to realize the door to her prison stood wide open. The man hadn't closed it after dragging the girl out.

A trick?

The man's evil promise, 'Soon,' ricocheted inside her brain.

Of their own accord, her eyes drifted back to the floor, reliving the memory of the sickening thud as the girl's body hit the concrete. A shudder that started at the roots of her hair rippled all the way through as terror and tears clouded her vision.

She didn't want to die.

She stared at the open door, a crushing force crowding her lungs as an idea began to take shape.

Her stomach seized with painful cramps, and her heart jackhammered with a rising panic that wrenched the remaining moisture from her mouth.

Could she be brave enough?

Chapter Twelve

By the time Alyssa and Cord left the medical examiner's office, twilight had already moved well past the point of casting its pink glow over the Sandia Mountains. Inside the oppressive, oven-like cab of the Tahoe, Alyssa cracked the windows and then cranked the air conditioner to the Antarctic setting before lowering it back to a more reasonable position. Pulling out of the parking lot, she ignored the reporters shouting out intrusive questions in the hopes of obtaining the perfect soundbite for their late-night broadcast.

In the silence as they headed to the precinct to meet up with the rest of the team, her mind couldn't stop probing around the same questions: assuming the same person had murdered both Rheagan and Gunner, where and what was the connection between the two of them? Were they his only two victims, or had there been others in between? As much as she really loathed even thinking it, she couldn't stop herself from wondering if Albuquerque had another serial killer on its streets.

The note Rheagan's murderer had left behind scratched at her. *Because you might miss who I took next.* Took. Past tense.

Cord broke into her concentration. 'Why don't you go ahead and run me through this possible link to your past case.'

A heavy weight settled on Alyssa's shoulders at the crushing disappointment that still haunted her all these years later. Being unable to deliver justice and closure to Gunner's family had left her with a prickling friction of failure that, to this day, still raked across her nerves. 'Like you heard me telling the captain when I called him, the boy in the picture is Gunner Galveston. I recognized him immediately. Back in May of 2008, he left his house to meet up with some friends to go camping. He never made it.'

In her mind, Alyssa could see the months that had followed as clearly as if they'd just happened. 'His vehicle was found abandoned on the side of the road about a mile from his house, but no usable prints were ever uncovered. No blood around the vehicle, no signs of a struggle.' She glanced at Cord. 'It was like he got beamed up. Ellie and I worked the case. Clearly not well enough since we found neither his body nor his killer.'

'Ellie, your former partner, right?'

'Right. Two witnesses, acquaintances Gunner and his friends knew from school, claimed that they thought they'd seen him helping someone change a tire, but couldn't be positive it was him. Nor were they able to describe the car, aside from dark and four doors. We turned over every rock and tracked down every lead until it dead-ended. No matter how promising something sounded, nothing ever panned out. If Gunner had been playing Good Samaritan to the person who kidnapped and then killed him, we could never find any evidence of it. Eventually, the leads slowed to a trickle and then dried up altogether.' A bitter edge of frustration leaked through her next words. 'The case went cold.'

'You said a minute ago that Gunner's body was never found. But it was. Right?'

'No, his *bones* were discovered eighteen months later. And it gave us nothing new to work with aside from the knowledge that the back of his skull had been nearly crushed. Over time, his case continued to grow colder until our captain ordered us to concentrate harder on the new missing person cases piling up in front of us. He knew Ellie and I were too bullheaded and dogged to let it go, so he stripped the case out from under us and handed it off to another team.' The fresh tightness pressing against her chest had nothing to do with her inability to solve the case. 'It still leaves a bad taste in my mouth the way our captain handled it.'

More than once, Alyssa and several others within the department had butted heads with the man. When he retired some years after Gunner's case, they'd all attended his retirement party not because they'd wanted to send him off with well-wishes, but because they were thrilled to see him go. His replacement, their current captain, Guthrie Hammond, immediately proved to be a stronger, if slightly more hotheaded, leader.

'In the end, finding what remained of their son came too late for Gunner's parents anyway because they died in a car accident three months after he disappeared.' Alyssa pressed the heel of her hand against her stomach where a knot had begun to form.

'According to Gunner's half-brother, his parents received a call from the killer saying he knew where they could find their son. I will go to my grave believing they were so distraught from that call that they didn't realize they'd crossed the center line into oncoming traffic until it was too late. Paramedics on scene said they died on impact, that they never had a chance. Nor did the driver of the car they hit.'

In her mind, Alyssa vividly replayed every encounter she'd had with Gunner's heartbroken parents, the way their crippling grief and disbelief that something had happened to their son rubbed her own emotions raw. And then she thought of Barbara Pembroke, at the way she'd crumbled into her husband at the realization that Rheagan had been slain and forever ripped from their lives.

As they arrived back at the precinct, where the rest of their team was already waiting for them, she made a vow that she'd get the Pembrokes the resolution she'd never been able to give Gunner's family.

–

Officers Tony White and Joe Roe, along with Hal Callum, all convened in the incident room Alyssa's team had long ago claimed as their own, since they occupied it far more frequently than they did their own closet space of an office, or in Joe and Tony's case, their cubicles.

With hours of work, brainstorming, and debriefing ahead of them, Alyssa nodded her greeting and headed straight for the coffee pot tucked into the corner, wanting to hug Hal for thinking to brew a fresh batch just for her. After taking a careful sip, she allowed herself a second to enjoy the burst of flavor, and then she turned to the others, ready to dig in so they could bring Rheagan's killer to justice.

Hal, who already had projected images of the crime scene onto the walls, spoke first. 'Lots of places we can start, but I think, first, you need to tell us about this possible link to your past case, Lys.'

Every bit of the monster headache that had been hinting at making its appearance came storming back to Alyssa. If she'd been thinking clearly, she would've waited to tell Cord until they were back here so that she wouldn't have to tell it twice. Or three times, as it stood, because she'd placed a call to Captain Hammond as soon as Lynn had shown them the picture.

Alyssa sighed, danced her fingertips around her temples, and told the story one more time.

'Well, if Gunner isn't deceased in that picture, he's close to it. And the way in which the killer left the image for us to find certainly points to the two cases being linked,' Hal said when she finished. He turned away from the projected crime scene photos and looked back at Alyssa. 'If it's the same person, he won't get away again. We'll catch him this time.'

Alyssa winced. Even though Hal hadn't meant anything nefarious, it still dug at her conscience. If she'd caught the bastard fourteen years ago, Rheagan might still be alive today.

Hal broke into her thoughts. 'I can hear the wheels in your head spinning like a hamster wheel. And if I know you as well as I think I do, I should make it clear that my comment was in no way intended to make you feel blame for Rheagan's death.'

Hal's sentiment didn't ease the sting, but Alyssa appreciated it nonetheless. 'I know. I can feel that guilt all on my own without anything you say. Any one of you would feel the same way, too, so spare me any lectures.' Her tired but grateful smile took any bite out of her words.

Tony shifted in his seat, drawing everyone's attention. 'If it *is* the same person, finding that connection is going to be crucial to identifying the killer. We weren't on your team back then, but I think I recall that no suspects were ever named, and any persons of interest were cleared. Did I remember that right?'

'You did. And the photograph of Gunner shoved into Rheagan's mouth takes out the "if" in this scenario. The same person who murdered Gunner also killed Rheagan. So, let's start with her. We need to interview the Pembrokes' neighbors, the Hoyts, but they're still not back, and we've been unable to reach them by phone.'

Joe lifted a finger. 'About that. Tony and I swung by there today after we left Tramway Arroyo. It wasn't out of the way since it was just a quarter, half mile down the road from where Rheagan was found. Anyway, we thought maybe they might have returned by now. Long story short, we ran into the cleaning lady who said the Hoyts were supposed to get in sometime late tonight. If you want, we can swing by there again first thing tomorrow morning.'

Alyssa thought about it a second. 'No, I'd like to speak to them myself, especially the son, Raider. Right now, I want to touch on something else you just said.' She moved over to the large map of Bernalillo County tacked to the wall. 'Rheagan was found less than a half mile from her home which, to me, indicates she was killed not far from there. But where? We already knew from her friends that she cancelled her plans with them at the last minute. So, did she leave her house to meet up with someone, maybe hook up with Raider as her friends admitted she sometimes did? Did Rheagan plan to meet up with the same person who ended up killing her, or did they come across each other by chance?' She turned to face her team. 'Most importantly, who is he?'

She moved from the map over to the projected images of both victims and tapped on the picture of Gunner; specifically, the chilling nursery-type rhyme typed at the bottom. She didn't like it, but she needed to inform her team of her fear that another serial killer could be hunting in the Albuquerque area.

But before she could, Captain Hammond appeared in the doorway, his whiskey barrel of a chest casting the illusion that he stood taller than he truly was. The hard glint in his eyes matched the grim expression on his face, sending Alyssa's heart spiraling into her stomach as she waited for the gavel to fall.

True to form, the captain didn't bother with greetings or other niceties, preferring to drop the bomb and get things moving. 'Don't get comfortable. I think we might have the answer to if or who your guy took next.' The undeniable note of... not defeat, but perhaps dismay... that snuck into his voice concerned Alyssa.

'Who? And from where?' Setting her coffee down on the table, she dug her keys back out of her pocket, steeling herself for the captain's answer.

'Kennedy Farmer, aged twenty-six.' Hammond rubbed his calloused palm over the top of his balding head. 'The sister, Aubrey Farmer, called it in.' His eyes swept the room before landing back on Alyssa. 'She says Kennedy most likely went missing from Coyote Canyon Saturday evening.'

Every muscle in Alyssa's body froze as her gaze darted back over to the map. 'Coyote Canyon is less than a quarter mile away from where Rheagan's body was discovered.'

73

Hammond nodded. 'I know. Hence, I'm standing here telling you that there's a good chance that your instincts were right, and your guy already has his next victim.'

The walls of the room closed around Alyssa, increasing the pressure in her chest at the words, "your guy." She pushed her personal feelings aside. 'What makes Farmer believe her sister went missing from Coyote Canyon? And why the delay in reporting it, for that matter?' While a tiny voice tried to reason that it could be a coincidence, the note, the proximity, as well as the similarity in the terrains, made that possibility bleak at best.

'I'll let her explain all that to you, but the short answer is Aubrey Farmer just returned home from a business trip this evening. She and her sister share a home, and when she realized Kennedy's car was missing, she checked their home security system footage and noticed the last time Kennedy had been seen coming or going was Saturday evening in her, quote, "usual running attire." And she usually runs in Coyote Canyon.'

Hal wheeled his chair over to the same map Alyssa had been staring at. 'That's not the most easily accessible trail.' He craned his neck around so he could see the others. 'I mean, it's not difficult if you know where it is, but it's definitely off the beaten path for most runners.' With his lips curled and his nostrils flared, he practically snarled his next words. 'Unfortunately, I can tell you for a fact that there are no city cameras in either the area of Tramway Arroyo or Coyote Canyon.'

Alyssa had already thought of that. Despite the chief of police's efforts to acquire funding for more closed-circuit cameras in the city, they were still sorely lacking in that department. 'That still doesn't explain why Aubrey thinks her sister disappeared from the canyon. Isn't it possible

74

something happened somewhere between their house and the trail?'

Hammond raised his hand to mimic a gun and pointed it at her. 'And that's what you and Cord are going to go find out right now.'

Alyssa turned back to Hal and the others. 'While we're gone, see if you can find any links between Gunner and Rheagan.' She paused. 'And just to be proactive, go ahead and see if you run across the name Kennedy Farmer while you're looking for connections.'

Alyssa really hoped they were wrong, and that Kennedy Farmer's disappearance wasn't connected. But if it turned out that this was the work of the same perpetrator, even if it meant she didn't sleep between now and then, he – or she – wouldn't get away with it again.

Hammond stopped at the door. 'For the foreseeable future, none of you need bother making plans for any time off. Hell, I wouldn't bother contemplating calling it a day – or night – anytime soon. Consider overtime as already approved.'

Hammond's less than encouraging words made Alyssa feel as if her thoughts had run like a neon sign across her forehead. As she jogged to her Tahoe with Cord right behind her, she reminded herself she had nearly a decade and a half more experience on her side than she had fourteen years ago. Whether the cases were related or not, the perpetrator or perpetrators shouldn't have picked Albuquerque for his hunting grounds. Because her experience, skill, and sheer determination meant she'd stop at nothing to bring him, her, or them down.

Chapter Thirteen

Her eyes glued on the open doorway, Kennedy raised her bound hands above her head, took as deep a breath as she could, and mustering her courage, brought her arms down against her stomach for the fourth time, using as much force as possible. The sting of the plastic ties cutting into her skin as they busted off brought a scream to her mouth. When the pain subsided, she reached up and ripped the duct tape from her lips, tears springing to her eyes as the sticky material took skin with it.

It took several seconds for the shock to wear off because she hadn't actually expected it to work. Eighteen months ago, she'd had the opportunity to interview an up-and-coming football player, a young man being scouted by not one, but four NFL teams. He and a buddy had gone out one night when they were stopped by the police. His friend's belligerence had earned them both a pair of zip ties and might've led to their arrest if it hadn't been for a speeding vehicle that lost control and slammed into the cop. The football player had been able to snap the ties and race to the cop's aid, a move that had ended up saving the man's life.

Both fascinated and skeptical, Kennedy had asked how he'd manage to do it. Instead of telling her, the football player had demonstrated. Afterward, he'd explained that by first tightening the zip ties and then bringing the arms down forcefully while simultaneously flaring out the elbows 'like chicken wings' made it possible to break the ties at their weakest point. Little had she known that his tutorial would one day be the tool to helping her escape a murderer.

But now that they were off, Kennedy remained frozen in place, her gaze fixed on the dried blood and bits of skin tissue where the girl's body had lain. Unless she wanted the same thing to happen to her, she needed to move.

Her heart hammered inside her chest, and her breaths came in panting gasps until dots flashed in her vision. Her eyes strayed to the shackles around her ankles and then the metal bar above her head. The brutality of the girl's beating death burned into her mind, the way she'd seemed to stare straight into Kennedy's soul before her own life slipped away.

Kennedy had no choice. Come what may, she had to escape.

Using the wall for support, she pushed to her feet and took small, shuffling steps to the door, freezing at the scraping sound of the leg irons. Terrified to move but even more afraid to stay, she leaned against the frigid glass and pressed her hands against her chest as her eyes darted to the dark tunnel where her abductor had disappeared.

What if he was hiding in there, waiting for her?

Nearly soundless whimpers slipped out as she ordered herself not to think about that.

She couldn't. She just had to do it, like she had with the zip ties.

With agonizingly slow and excruciatingly loud steps, she made her way to the array of tools outside the enclosure where she searched in vain for the key or anything that would help her remove the leg shackles.

A sudden screeching noise that hadn't come from the chains around her ankles immobilized Kennedy. Her heart thudding a painfully rapid rhythm, she strained to hear, afraid she'd waited too long and that her abductor had returned to finish what he'd promised.

The noise came again, and she whipped her head around, sending a shooting arrow of agony through her skull. When the man still didn't materialize, she decided she had no choice but to continue. Even if he'd already returned, once he found her here like this, the end result would be the same. She told herself she could deal with the leg irons after she escaped and found help.

With the sound of her blood pulsing loudly in her ears, she forced her feet in the direction of the tunnel, wincing at the grating racket of the leg irons, wishing she could rip them from her body like she had the zip ties. Every two steps, she stopped and held her breath while she listened. Finally, after what felt like two eternities, she reached the doorway that had been hidden behind the panel.

She didn't allow herself time to think about it anymore; she pushed forward, staggering on her unsteady feet into nearly complete darkness. Claustrophobia sank its claws in as images of being trapped beneath rubble swamped her memories.

You have to keep moving. It's too late to go back now. Kennedy waited until her breathing slowed and the dizziness passed before she forced her feet forward again. She could do this. She had to.

Ten feet into the tunnel, any hint of light disappeared completely, and so she leaned against the cold wall to help support her weight and guide her, kind of like she and

Aubrey did every year when they went through the Maize Maze. A gash in her arm brushed across a rough spot, and a hoarse whimper scaled her bruised throat.

Concentrating on breathing through the pain, she tripped and fell to the ground. She clawed her way back up, only to fall again. And then again. Tears burned her eyes as she pressed her lips into her arm to muffle her scream. Instead of rising again, she decided to stay down. Crawling at a torturously slow pace, inch by inch, she stopped every few seconds to listen for any inkling of sound that would tell her that her abductor had returned to discover her gone – and now followed behind her in the tunnel.

Each time she paused, she had to force herself to begin moving again. For every jagged rock and piece of what felt like broken glass biting into her hands and knees, she promised herself the pain would end and the abuse to her body would be worth it when she reached the literal light at the end of the tunnel.

But after an infinity of endless darkness and unidentifiable sounds, she began to doubt she'd ever get out. With a sense of futile hopelessness battering away at her, she lowered her head and cried.

And then she sucked in another deep breath and wiped away the blur of tears. She was not a quitter. That was when she saw it. Up ahead winked a tiny sprinkling of faint light. This time, her tears came from joy. She brutally pushed herself to the point of breaking as she crawled faster, ignoring the fire slicing across her skin and the shrill screech of the leg irons. Each time her weakened muscles sent her sprawling to the ground, she dragged herself back up.

The refreshing scent of wet earth that only rain could bring hit her nose the closer she came to the light, and the urge to curl herself into a ball and weep because she'd made it washed over her.

Finally at the end of the tunnel, with freedom a few more feet away, Kennedy spotted a thick rope hanging from a hook in the ceiling. Averting her gaze, she refused to let herself wonder about its use. Instead, she focused on the two remaining obstacles – a metal ladder bolted to the cement wall and an old, rusted grate above her head.

With her legs shackled, it wouldn't be an easy climb. She'd have to rely on her waning upper body strength to do most of the work pulling her up. Flames licked at her raw, scraped palms as she latched onto the rough surface of the ladder and hauled herself up. Gritting her teeth, she heaved herself up one rung, then another, and then another, biting her lip to hold her whimpers inside, silently cursing the shackles that made the climb nearly impossible.

Sweat soaked every inch of her skin, and just when she thought she couldn't force her fledgling strength to haul her up even an inch more, she finally reached the top of the ladder. Her breaths sawed out in great, heaping gasps as her heart pummeled the inside of her ribcage, and thunder rumbled off in the distance.

She allowed herself only a moment before she went to work trying to remove the rusted grate. When after three tries, it refused to budge, she bottled the urge to scream out to the dark clouds rolling overhead, even if the thunder would mask her cries. She didn't know how much more she had left in her.

Come on. You're almost there.

Gulping in a deep breath, Kennedy braced her back against the ladder and, straining to put everything she had into it, she pushed, shoved, and yanked until the grate finally shifted enough for her to slip her arms through. After another torturous eternity, she managed to maneuver it enough to squeeze herself through a small opening.

Once outside, she collapsed to the ground, welcoming the hot brush of air that blew against her tears.

Knowing she needed to seek help, she pushed herself back to her knees. Just ahead of her lay a boundary of massive boulders, shrub oak, Rocky Mountain junipers, and desert willows, all beckoning her with the promise of sheltering safety. Too weak to stand, she crawled their way.

Chapter Fourteen

Less than half an hour after Hammond delivered the news to the team, Alyssa parked her Tahoe outside the home Aubrey Farmer shared with her sister, Kennedy. Violet and white flowers from the three desert willows planted near the sidewalk scattered the pathway, bringing to mind the outdoor wedding venue that her daughter and her fiancé had planned in the not-so-distant future.

'I can't believe Holly will be walking down the aisle in less than a month,' Cord said as he unbuckled himself from his seatbelt. 'Some days I still think of her as the thirteen-year-old girl I first met when I moved to Albuquerque.'

The corners of Alyssa's mouth tilted up in a smile. 'Funny. I was just thinking about her wedding myself. Personally, I'm finding it hard to believe twenty-one years have gone by so quickly… and that my firstborn is, I guess, old enough to be getting married.'

Cord chuckled. 'Now, you know better than that. Holly may be twenty-one in years, but in maturity, she's more like forty most days.'

Alyssa snorted. 'You wouldn't say that if you'd ever witnessed her having one of her bridal freakouts. In fact, you'd swallow…'

She let the rest of her sentence trail off when a young woman, probably only a few years older than Holly, opened the front door of her brick façade home and stepped onto her porch clutching a wiggling Pomeranian intent on escape. Her caramel-colored pixie haircut stuck out in short spikes as if she'd relentlessly been running her fingers through it.

With the ominous note left with Rheagan's body beating out a steady rhythm inside Alyssa's head, *Who I took next*, she took a deep breath and opened her car door. 'All right then. Let's see if we can get to the bottom of this.' She tried not to let her fear get out in front of her, but the picture of Gunner and the image of Rheagan's brutal murder refused to release their hold.

When they were within a few feet, Alyssa noticed the woman's red-tipped nose and the marble splotches dotting her face, indicators she'd been crying.

'Ms. Farmer?' Alyssa asked.

The woman's voice wobbled. 'Yes, ma'am. Are you here about my sister? I'm the one who reported her missing.'

'We are.' Alyssa introduced herself and then Cord before asking, 'Do you mind if we step inside to talk?'

Still grappling with an armful of squirming dog and what looked like a cell phone with a cracked screen, Aubrey Farmer shuffled back inside her house and invited them in. Once she'd closed the door, she set the Pom on the floor. Excited to be let loose, the little dog immediately began to race around and between Alyssa's and Cord's legs, pausing every few seconds to sniff at Alyssa's pants before offering up a short yippy bark to indicate she could smell other dogs on her.

'Lucy, stop already!' Pointing to a doggy bed in front of the fireplace, Aubrey snapped the order. 'Pillow!' With her head hung low, the dog obeyed, even if she continued sneaking peeks to see if her owner truly meant it. Once Lucy settled on her oversized pillow, Aubrey apologized. 'I'm so sorry about that. She's usually not so obnoxious around strangers, but I think she's probably feeding off my nervous energy.' The hand with the phone clutched in it fluttered back and forth.

Having two dogs of her own, Alyssa wasn't bothered. 'I understand, and it's quite all right.'

Aubrey's shoulders drooped. 'She's also never been left alone by herself for so long.' She pointed toward her kitchen. 'Thankfully, she has an automatic feeder and water, as well as a doggy door, so aside from being lonely and probably scared half to death, she was fine.'

Cord used Aubrey's comment to redirect the questioning to her sister's alleged disappearance. 'Let's talk about that. When you reported your sister missing, you mentioned she might not have been home since Saturday evening. Is that correct?'

Aubrey stopped chewing at the edge of her fingernail and nodded. 'Yes, that's right.'

Concerned when Aubrey began to sway on her feet, Alyssa asked, 'Would you like to sit while you tell us what you know?'

Aubrey nodded and led the way toward a room containing a plush, cream-colored sofa with muted, barely visible azure-colored flowers, and its matching counterparts. 'Is here okay?'

'Anywhere you'd like is fine.'

Both Alyssa and Cord waited until Aubrey claimed the armchair before they settled onto the sofa. On the wall across from them, several framed, blown-up family snapshots, along with a few containing only the woman in front of them and someone who appeared to be her mirror image, added to the warm and welcoming feel of the house.

Aubrey's eyes followed Alyssa's gaze. 'We're identical twins,' she said, her voice still teetering on the edge of crying. 'Until I chopped all my hair off, it used to be much more difficult to tell us apart. My dad always teases us that no one, not even he or Mom, truly know if I'm me and Kennedy's Kennedy. It's a joke, of course. We both have a crescent-shaped birthmark' – she pointed to the right side of her forehead – 'but mine is here, and Kennedy's is on the left.'

Wary of the pressure to get answers quickly, Alyssa steered the conversation back to Kennedy's disappearance. 'Why don't you tell us what makes you think your sister's missing?'

Alyssa had seen pictures of ghosts with more color than Aubrey's face when Aubrey raised the phone that remained in her white-knuckled grip. 'I found Kennedy's phone.'

Alarm bells clanged in Alyssa's head. 'What do you mean by you "found Kennedy's phone"?'

A pale pink worked its way back into Aubrey's cheeks, enough to tell Alyssa the woman knew she shouldn't have done whatever it was that she'd done.

'I went to Coyote Canyon where Kennedy usually goes running to look for her. When I got there, I found this.'

Cord jumped in so he could clarify. 'You did this before you called the police?'

Aubrey's head dropped forward. 'Yes, sir. Because I hadn't yet considered that she might be missing. When

I got to the canyon, Kennedy's car was still in the parking lot. My mind was immediately filled with images of her lying hurt somewhere, unable to call for help, and so I headed for the trail.' She pressed the heels of her hands into her stomach and leaned forward. 'Just a few dozen yards in, I found her phone. When I went to grab it, I spotted one of Kennedy's shoes.' Aubrey's shallow breaths came faster. 'There were broken branches, and... deep gouges in the dirt, like she'd been digging her heels in.' She lifted her eyes to meet Alyssa's and then Cord's. 'Something has happened to my sister. I know it. And I know I shouldn't have taken her phone, but I wasn't thinking.'

The chasm growing inside Alyssa's gut grew wider, and she exchanged a look with Cord, guessing her face resembled the same tension marring his. She forced a calm she suddenly wasn't feeling into her voice as she turned back to Aubrey. 'Maybe you'd better back up and start from the beginning. But first I need to make a phone call.'

She excused herself and stepped out onto the front porch where she dialed Hammond. As soon as he answered, she gave him an update, ending the call with, 'I think we'd better send Joe, Tony, and a crime scene team to secure the area before we lose any more potential evidence, especially if Kennedy did go missing five days ago. Cord and I will meet up with everyone after we finish interviewing the sister.'

When she rejoined Cord a few minutes later, Aubrey was explaining why she hadn't noticed her sister missing before today.

'I've been out of town since Friday morning. I was in Durango for the annual art gallery showing I generally attend.'

Alyssa retook her seat as Cord asked, 'And when was the last time you actually spoke to your sister?'

Aubrey's hands, now empty as Kennedy's phone had been placed inside a sandwich bag, likely at Cord's request, fluttered in the air. 'We talked Saturday morning for just a few minutes. She was putting the finishing touches on an article she'd written – she's a sportswriter for several print and online magazines.'

'Did she seem upset or off in any way?' Alyssa asked.

Aubrey's head whipped side to side. 'Not at all. We talked about my showing, but we didn't really chat for long. She told me her plans for the day were to submit the article, go on her run after dinner – it's cooler then – and then she planned on coming home, showering, and binge-watching some show.'

'So, you didn't try to contact Kennedy the rest of the time you were gone?'

Aubrey reached into her back pocket and pulled out her own phone. Unlocking it and opening it to her text messages, she handed it over for Alyssa and Cord to see. 'You can scroll through. I sent a text close to midnight Saturday telling her I'd sold two paintings, was exhausted, and headed to bed. You can see she didn't respond, but I didn't think much of it because she knew Sunday would be super busy with the end of the showing, so she wouldn't want to bother me.'

More tears spilled onto Aubrey's cheeks. 'Monday, a few of us took the train up to Silverton, and again, I didn't get back to my room until after midnight, so I didn't bother texting. And yesterday, I sent a message that I was going white water rafting and wouldn't have my phone with me. The last message I sent was late this afternoon to tell her I was on my way home and would see her soon.'

'And you didn't think it was at all strange Kennedy hadn't responded?' Alyssa's question wasn't intended to sound accusatory, but she understood that, being consumed by guilt, Aubrey might take it that way.

'No. We live together, and we don't talk every day when one of us goes out of town. And I guess I was just so preoccupied that, when I gave it any thought at all, I assumed she wasn't responding because she knew I wouldn't be getting the messages anyway, or that I was driving.' Her voice broke over a sob. 'Maybe if I had thought about it, I could've asked a neighbor to check on her or something.'

Money might be the root of all evil, but hindsight was the genesis of most guilt, so Alyssa knew nothing she or Cord could say would ease that, or if it did, it would only be temporary. Instead, she redirected Aubrey's focus into an action.

'When you made the report, you told Dispatch that you'd also checked your security cameras when you arrived home. Would you mind showing that footage to Detective Roberts and me?'

Like someone had lit a fire beneath her, Aubrey leaped up. 'This way,' she said, leading the way down a small hallway and into a bedroom-turned-office. Mounted in the corner was a twenty-four-inch screen dissected into four small frames that showed the front, back, and sides of the house. 'This is where Kennedy does most of her work, but we only use this computer for the cameras.' As she spoke, her fingers flew over the keyboard. She opened a file, pointed to a list of dates, and then clicked on 'Saturday, May 28' before stepping back so Cord could scan through the videos.

'How often do these images delete?' he asked.

'I don't know. A week maybe? Or wait. Maybe it's every eight days. I can't remember. Kennedy set it up.'

Over Cord's shoulder, Alyssa studied the footage. 'What made you think to check the cameras at all? Wouldn't you just think your sister had gone to the store or out with some friends?'

'When I got home, Lucy was straight up freaking out when I walked through the door. After I calmed her down, I yelled for Kennedy, but she didn't answer. And I don't know; I just kind of got the sense that the house was empty. That's when I noticed her car was gone, so I tried texting, but again she didn't answer.' Her scared gaze drilled into Alyssa's eyes. 'I don't know if you'll believe this or if I really know how to explain it, but I got this really eerie feeling and just decided to check the cameras.'

As the words slipped past Aubrey's lips, Cord hit pause, freezing the frame on Kennedy Farmer exiting the house in jogging attire, arm raised and pointing toward her car, key in hand, to unlock the doors. Aside from the longer, slightly darker hair, the two women definitely looked identical. The time stamp in the corner showed five fifty-eight.

Using his phone, Cord snapped a picture of Kennedy so he could forward the description to Hal. He peered up at Alyssa. 'We can check with Tony and Joe first, but with this, we can at least get an APB out right away. What do you think?'

'APB. Let's get people out there looking for her as soon as possible.'

Cord hit send and then continued forwarding through the following days up until the footage of the two of them walking up the sidewalk.

Alyssa kept her gaze focused on the screen as a knife-like pain twisted inside her stomach. She could still be wrong. Just because another person had gone missing, even if she'd disappeared from a location close to where Rheagan's body was discovered, it didn't necessarily mean the cases were connected, despite the chilling note.

She turned away from the screen as Cord rewound and started over, searching, she knew, to see if anyone lurked in the background or for anything else that might give them an idea what had happened. 'Does Kennedy have any friends or a boyfriend she might've been in contact with while you were away?'

Aubrey's chuckle perched somewhere between amusement and fear. 'Of the two of us, I'm the more social one. Kennedy will do things – she's not entirely a homebody – but generally speaking, if things are too "peopley," as she calls it, she bows out. She's much more reserved and prefers to keep company with herself, our family, or the athletes she's interviewing. And up until recently, her volunteer work. Not that she doesn't have friends, mind you. But truth be told, my sister's one of those people you kind of have to drag out of the house to parties or whatnot. And no, she doesn't currently have a boyfriend. As for friends, the only two people she might've gone to visit, I've already called. One is vacationing in Maryland, and the other hadn't heard from her, but I can get you both their numbers, if you want.'

'We'd appreciate that,' Alyssa said. 'What about co-workers?'

'Well, since she's a sportswriter for a variety of publications, she's always worked remotely from home. Most of her co-workers' – she used her fingers to place air quotes around the word – 'are scattered around the country.'

Not taking his eyes off the security footage, Cord asked, 'Has Kennedy been under any increased pressure or stress lately?'

'No. She absolutely loves her job. In fact, she's been looking almost obnoxiously forward to an upcoming trip about two weeks from now. She just landed a coveted interview with the former quarterback for the New York Giants.' She half-snorted out a laugh. 'Her head's been in the clouds since she got the news.'

'What else can you tell us about your sister that might help us narrow our search on who to speak to or where to look?'

Aubrey brushed the wetness from her cheeks. 'I don't know. She used to coach volleyball, but she hasn't done that since she stopped volunteering at the Outreach Center. She hated to give it up, but she just couldn't make it fit in her schedule anymore.'

Alyssa could understand that. 'Have you notified your parents that you think your sister might be missing?'

'Yes. I called them just after I called the police. They've been in Greece celebrating their thirty-fifth anniversary, but they have their travel agent working on arrangements to get them home right away. They should be back by tomorrow if none of their flights are delayed or cancelled.'

While Cord continued looking through the security feed, Alyssa, with Aubrey watching from the doorway, went through Kennedy's room, not really expecting to find anything that would provide some answers, but hoping anyway.

Twenty minutes later, Aubrey walked them to the door. 'Please find my sister.'

'We'll do everything we can,' Alyssa promised. As she climbed back into her Tahoe, she pushed the image of Rheagan's battered body out of her mind. Whether the cases turned out to be connected or not, one thing remained clear: *something* had happened to Kennedy Farmer, and it was up to her team to find her.

Chapter Fifteen

Wednesday, June 1

Focused solely on escape, on the safety of the shelter of trees, Kennedy failed to notice the dark pair of boots off to her side.

The first kick glanced off the side of her face; the second sent her body rolling, scraping along piles of dirt, twigs, and gravel. A cascade of rocks tumbled down on top of her as she spun to her back and spotted her abductor descending on her like death come to reap her soul. She barely avoided the next kick by rolling over, a move that sent her careening down a small incline. Gravity and momentum carried her until her body slammed into a gnarled tree trunk crawling with ants the size of her hand. With the breath knocked out of her, she could do little more than squeeze a pathetic attempt at a scream past her lips.

She'd waited too long, and now there would be no saving herself.

Her abductor moved into her line of sight, blotting out everything but his furious face as he dropped to his knees. Once again, that startling sense of familiarity whispered inside. Spittle flew from his mouth and peppered her face as he clapped a hand over her mouth and squeezed his fingers across her jaw. She gripped his wrist and jerked her head to the side. If she could yell for help, someone might hear and come to her rescue.

The stinging slap across her face brought tears to her eyes. *Fight, Kennedy. You didn't get this far only to fail.*

Twisting her body back and forth, Kennedy pushed against the man's chest as she tried to dislodge him. When his weight shifted, she scrambled to get out from under him, but before she could, he grabbed her around the ears and slammed her head into the ground. Dizziness washed over her in a nauseating wave.

The sound of her weakened cries cut off abruptly when the man produced a small roll of tape from somewhere, ripped off a piece, and clapped it over her mouth. Rage bleeding from his eyes, he wrestled her wrists together, squeezing against the broken skin as he tore another piece of tape off with his teeth.

The second her hands were bound once more, all the fight melted from her body... until he leaned forward and wrapped her hair around his fist. Ignoring the ripping pain coming from her scalp, she thrashed back and forth, her heels digging into the earth for purchase, desperate not to return to his dungeon.

If her struggles had any effect on him, they didn't show as he dragged her back the way she'd come, not bothering to slow as he scraped her body over sticks and sharp rocks. When he reached the grate, he released her to kneel on the ground, his breaths heaving in and out in panting bursts, hatred and something else she didn't recognize burning from his eyes.

As he lowered himself onto the ladder, he pulled the chain on the shackles and hauled her forward.

And Kennedy finally accepted the suffocating, fatal truth of her reality.

In addition to every white-hot nerve sensor flaring to life with every breath she took, the top of Kennedy's head burned like it'd been plunged into the Earth's core. Her gaze slid to the floor where handfuls of her dark hair littered the cement floor, some stuck in the swirl of dried blood where the dead girl's body had lain in a gruesome reminder of what her abductor had planned for her. As if she could forget.

A spasm rippled through her stomach when the man reappeared carrying a small stepladder which he placed beneath the metal bar spanning the width of the room. Dangling from one of his belt loops were two pairs of handcuffs. Understanding his intent, Kennedy shook her head in wild denial, screaming out behind her taped mouth, 'Why are you doing this to me?'

He stomped down on the center of the chains shackling her legs together as she tried scooting away, though she had nowhere to go. An arrow of indescribable pain coursed through her. Smiling, he ripped a wickedly sharp knife from its sheath and waved it back and forth in front of her before swiftly slicing through the duct tape binding her wrists.

Before her blood had time to circulate back to the area, the handcuffs snapped in place with a terrifying click. Without a word, he hauled her up as if she weighed nothing and, using the second pair of cuffs, secured her to the restraint bar. Within seconds, her shoulders wept from the straining position they'd been forced into.

When he stepped even closer to her, she could feel the heat radiating off his body.

'Did you really think it would be that simple to escape *me*?' His cold laughter filled the air. 'Do you really believe you're the first one to try? Trust me. You're not. Not even close.' He dropped a pointed look at the stain on the floor before glaring back at her. 'So, whatever fruitless prayer you had of getting out with your life, let it go. Because no one but me ever walks out of here.'

Without warning, his fist slammed hard into her stomach like she was a live punching bag. Once. Twice. Three times.

Wheezing gasps tried to push their way past her sealed lips.

His crushing grip bruised her jaw. 'Do you know how many blows it takes before the organs in a human start shutting down? I do.' He squeezed harder. 'If you ever think about trying to escape me again, I'll show you how fast a two-pound hammer can pulverize your bones.'

Through blurry eyes, Kennedy watched him grab the stepladder and disappear through the door, this time locking it behind him. Unlike before, a black curtain fell across the glass, completely blocking off her view and, worse, leaving her in total darkness.

Kennedy dropped her head forward and sobbed.

Chapter Sixteen

Close to quarter to ten Wednesday night, Alyssa, weary and worn out, crossed the parking lot full of flashing red and blue strobe lights from the multitude of police cruisers and watched the tow truck loading Kennedy Farmer's vehicle onto its flatbed. Only after it had pulled away with Search and Rescue right behind it did she finally head to her Tahoe. While she waited for Cord, she observed the crime scene technicians still milling about, painstakingly gathering whatever evidence they could.

Despite clear signs of a struggle, few hard clues had been left behind. On top of that, they had to contend with the knowledge that several days had passed since Kennedy had allegedly been abducted from this spot. Not to mention the very brief, short-lived rains so well known to the area that might have wreaked even more havoc with their already compromised crime scene.

Her gut, along with decades of experience and learning to listen to her instincts, screamed that Kennedy's disappearance on the same day Rheagan had last been seen had to be more than coincidence. But based on what exactly? A threatening note? Location? Proximity of victims might be a starting foundation for building a case, but she knew they needed more than that. Her mind raced to fit the pieces together. A quarter mile down the canyon, Rheagan's body had been found – which was less than a mile from her home. Gunner Galveston's remains had been found near the Embudito Trail. Similar terrain, but ten miles from Coyote Canyon.

The sound of vehicles slowing as they drove by, passersby curious about what dreadful tragedy had occurred to merit so large a police presence, drew Alyssa's attention back to the current crime scene.

Just beyond a small grouping of boulders lay the main trailhead. Within a few hundred yards, abandoned among the juniper bushes, she'd spotted a runner's armband and a black key fob that proved to belong to Kennedy's vehicle. Several feet away, Aubrey had discovered her sister's phone.

Absorbed in her vision of how Kennedy's attacker might have overpowered her, Alyssa didn't see Cord approaching the Tahoe until he opened the passenger door and startled an embarrassing gasp out of her. She pressed the heel of her hand against her racing heart. 'Jesus! How about a little warning instead of trying to shave ten years off my life?'

'Like what? Do jumping jacks in front of the vehicle? I thought you saw me coming.' Cord snapped his seatbelt into place.

'Well, I didn't.' Alyssa's shortened temper had more to do with fatigue and the pressure of unanswered questions and a ticking clock that seemed to be spinning out of control than from being caught unaware. She cranked the ignition. 'Joe called a few minutes ago to let me know he and Tony are back at the precinct. And apparently, not that I'm surprised, Hal never left because he figured we'd need a team debrief.' She shook her head. Hal Callum might be unable to join the team in the field anymore, but never once had he allowed the circumstances of being shot in the line of duty to hold him back from the job he loved, from implanting himself forever as an integral part of the team, and someone they'd be lost without.

'I would've expected nothing less from the man,' Cord said, echoing Alyssa's own thoughts.

'Good thing, too,' Alyssa said. 'Because we're going to need everyone's collective brain power to figure out what's going on.'

Lost in their own thoughts, they made the rest of the short drive in silence.

Shortly after ten, she parked her Tahoe outside the precinct and headed up the steps. Fatigue and adrenaline-fueled energy battled against each other, confusing her muscles, so she didn't know whether she felt more like dozing for fifteen minutes or zipping around the room.

Just outside the door of the incident room, she spotted Joe talking on the phone. When he saw her and Cord, he moved out of the doorway. As they walked past him, she heard his voice pitch higher as he said, 'Daddy loves you too, baby. But you need to listen to Mommy and go back to sleep. Yes, I promise I'll read you two stories next time.'

A grin spread across Tony's face as he announced the obvious. 'He's toddler-haggling again. He's such a pushover.'

Having just ended his call with his daughter, Hailee, Joe rejoined them, rubbing a hand over his weary face while making sure his best friend spotted the one-finger salute he offered at the same time. 'I gotta say it's a sad state of affairs when my three-year-old is not only used to the disappointment of me not coming home in time

99

to tuck her into bed, but she's already learned to read my guilt and use it against me to get what she wants. Damn, if she's this good now, what will she be like as a teenager?'

Hal and Alyssa exchanged sympathetic smiles because they were both well-versed in the capability of teenage guilt trips, even though Hal's children were now adults with lives of their own while Alyssa had one about to get married and another just over seven months shy of his eighteenth birthday.

'Well, the only way we're going to get to spend any amount of quality time with our families is by solving these cases,' Alyssa said. 'We've got a murdered girl somehow connected to a fourteen-year-old case, and now a kidnapping that my gut is telling me is linked to both of those.' She pulled out a chair but didn't sit. 'Hal, you pulled the Gunner Galveston file?'

Hal flipped open a folder and slid a stack of stapled pages over to Cord, who sat nearest him. 'I did. And I made copies for everyone.'

Cord stretched his neck, trying to work the kinks out. 'So, the question becomes who or what is the common denominator in these cases? Or is there not one? I know we're basing the link theory on the note left with Rheagan's body, as well as the proximity to where Kennedy disappeared, but we need to make sure we don't get tunnel vision on this by forcing evidence we find into something that isn't really there. No matter what our guts tell us, we need definitive proof.'

'You're right,' Alyssa said.

While Cord had been talking, Hal rolled his chair over to the map and studied it. Reaching down into the pocket of his wheelchair, he pulled out a plastic container full of pushpins. He stuck a red one in the Coyote Canyon trailhead where Kennedy had disappeared, another where Rheagan had been found, and yet one more where Gunner's remains had been discovered. Then he grabbed four yellow pins and placed them all in the areas where each individual lived and, in Gunner's case, where his car had been abandoned before rolling back.

Tony, an avid outdoorsman, tracker, and hunter balanced his chair on two legs as he surveyed the pins. One finger tapped against his lips while he put his thoughts in order. 'Terrain is similar where Kennedy was taken and where Rheagan and Gunner were found. So, we're most likely looking for someone comfortable in those types of surroundings.'

Before anyone had a chance to respond to Tony's observation, the conference room door swung open, making them all whirl around, hands hovering over their weapons at the unexpected interruption. Alyssa expected to see Captain Hammond, and from the confused expressions on everyone else's faces, they did, too. Everyone except Hal, who smiled like he'd been waiting for Ruby, the perpetually grouchy precinct secretary. Like most people, Alyssa tried steering clear of approaching anything even close to the proximity of Ruby's bad side – even while she quietly admired the hell out of her.

Glancing at the time – inching close to eleven – she couldn't even manage to be surprised to see the woman whose age was as mysterious as the rest of her. If Alyssa didn't know better, she'd swear Ruby had a hidden room somewhere in the building where she lived because Alyssa couldn't recall a single time that Ruby was ever *not* present.

As usual, Ruby wore her famous scowl with the brunt of her displeasure, much to the team's relief, aimed directly at Hal. 'I guess I can add pizza delivery to my resume.'

Not in the least bit intimidated – or at least exceptionally good at hiding it – Hal rolled over with a wide grin on his face as he stretched his arms up for the pizzas.

The way the three boxes tilted precariously, Alyssa wasn't convinced Ruby didn't intend to drop the pies into his lap just to add the exclamation point to her irritation. Thankfully, Cord and Tony's quick reflexes caught the boxes before disaster could ensue. As Ruby backed out of the doorway, she narrowed her withering glare on Hal. 'You do know that I'm completely aware that you could've rolled yourself out there all on your own and met the delivery guy yourself? You are not helpless.'

Not in the least bit repentant, Hal grinned. 'Well, as compensation for your troubles, may I offer you a slice or three?' His eyes twinkled in his ever-present quest to get Ruby to smile at him. It had become such a popular pastime that someone – the who remained a mystery, though Alyssa had her suspicions – had started two different pools years ago. The pot Alyssa figured would go first and which she had tossed money into happened to be the one that claimed Ruby would clobber Hal before she graced him with a smile. That, however, didn't stop the man from trying, much to everyone's amusement – or concern in case Ruby was watching.

Slamming the door closed on his words, Ruby's response surprised no one, least of all Hal.

At the scent of roasted green chiles and melted cheese, Alyssa's stomach erupted in a chorus of hallelujahs. She searched her memory, but for the life of her, she couldn't remember when she and Cord had gotten a chance to eat beyond earlier that morning. In fact, after a quick mental replay of her day, she realized that they'd missed both lunch and dinner.

'Hal,' she said, squeezing his shoulder, 'sometimes I just want to kiss you.'

'Get in line,' Tony said as he lifted the lid off all three boxes, releasing the heavenly scent of yumminess into the air. 'Damn, I'm hungry. I haven't eaten since…'

Guilt's sticky tentacles crawled inside their heads until Cord started handing out the paper plates the team kept stashed in the room for late nights such as this. 'We need fuel to function properly, so we still have to eat.'

Hal rubbed his hands together. 'That we do, my friends. Besides, we can keep debriefing and eat at the same time.'

After everyone had taken the first few bites of food, they resettled around the table while Hal pulled up a screenshot of Kennedy's social media and flashed it onto the whiteboard. The background showed Aubrey and Kennedy posed on a bale of hay in front of an older couple whose resemblance to the two could only mean they were the twins' parents.

'Whew, identical twins is right,' Tony breathed out. 'A couple of my high school friends were identical, and man, did they pull some crazy shit back in the day.' He grinned at Cord. 'Be very glad you have fraternal twins, my friend.'

Aware of the ticking clock, Alyssa brought their attention back around before they could veer off topic. 'Our techs have Kennedy's car, but unless we get lucky and our assailant put his hands on the vehicle, leaving behind prints, or better yet, DNA, I'm not sure that it's going to yield much in the way of answers.'

'We've also got her phone,' Cord said, 'and while Aubrey gave us verbal permission to access the texts and voicemails, we need that ping warrant so we can see if Kennedy stopped anywhere along the way. Of course, we'll also be checking it for prints.' He turned to Hal. 'Can you access the city cameras along the route from Kennedy's house to the canyon?'

'Well, not up to the canyon because, as I've already mentioned, the city never saw the need to install them where there's practically nothing but trails, arroyos, and ditches.' The pinched expression on Hal's face displayed what he viewed as dangerous thinking. 'Guess no one ever thought along the lines of needing cameras in case someone decided to dump a body or kidnap someone.'

A familiar tug of frustration worked its way into Alyssa's head, not because of Hal's comment, but because she couldn't help but wonder for the hundredth time if they could've saved Rheagan if only her family had taken her disappearance more seriously. And if it turned out that Kennedy's abduction was tied to the same person, could that have been prevented as well?

'We need answers, and right now, all we've got is more questions that are leading us nowhere, not even in circles,' she said. 'Tomorrow, Cord and I will visit Jackson and Raider Hoyt, the Pembrokes' neighbors.' While she spoke, Hal projected the crime scene photos from the Tramway Arroyo onto the wall. Placed next to Aubrey and Kennedy Farmer's smiling profiles, the stark contrast of Rheagan's beaten and stabbed body put a chill in the room. 'Raider and Rheagan had some type of relationship, so maybe he can tell us something that points us to some answers.'

Tony's mouth turned down. 'Hal mentioned cameras a minute ago, and I thought I should let you know I checked out that wilderness camera we found up in the trees near Rheagan's body. Not only was the lens facing the wrong direction, as in completely away from Rheagan, but even if it had been pointing directly at our guy, it wouldn't have mattered because the batteries were corroded. Not to mention they were in backwards.'

Alyssa's sigh came from a deep well of building frustration. 'So, what you're saying is either the owner of that equipment had no idea what the hell they were doing, or someone tampered with it.'

Tony nodded. 'Yep. But based on the level of corrosion, my money's on the former.'

Alyssa's eyes drifted back and forth between Rheagan and Kennedy's images, trying to imagine what they might have in common. With each other or Gunner Galveston.

As if he'd read her thoughts, Hal said, 'I've already started looking into things, but I've got to tell you, Lys, with an eight-year gap in our victims' ages, different walks of life, et cetera, unless they hit up the same gym, shopped at the same grocery store, attended the same church or whatnot, it's going to be a battle to find the common thread that connects them.'

'Hal, if there's anyone who can find a miniscule, hidden link, it'll be you.' Hal's epic research skills were so renowned that other investigators, both within and outside the department, were known to seek his help. Because if someone needed something unearthed, Hal was the man who could get it done.

Distracted by Tony jerking to his feet, Alyssa turned to stare at him, imploring him to fill the rest of them in on whatever thoughts had sprung to his mind. 'Tony?'

Tension burrowed deep lines into his forehead as he turned to face Alyssa. 'Up at Coyote Canyon, you said that Aubrey mentioned her sister used to volunteer at the Outreach Center, right?'

'That's right.'

'And you said that Mr. and Mrs. Pembroke mentioned that, at one point, they'd had Rheagan talking to someone to see if her recklessness stemmed from something deeper than just a need for adrenaline. Right?'

Whether due to fatigue or confusion, Alyssa felt her chest tighten in impatience. 'Yes. What are you getting at Tony?'

'Did the Pembrokes ever get you the name of the therapist Rheagan had gone to?'

'No, not yet. Again, I ask why?'

'It's not in the reports you have there, at least not that I've seen, but I remember reading something years back that Dr. Frank Neely volunteered his time, free of charge, to meet with the kids at Outreach.' He shrugged. 'Could be nothing, but I'm pointing it out. Just in case.'

Cord and Joe exchanged puzzled looks. 'Should that name mean something to us?'

Alyssa's head buzzed with Tony's words. When she finally answered, her voice sounded far away, even to her own ears. 'Dr. Frank Neely is Gunner Galveston's half-brother and the only surviving member of Gunner's immediate family. The same man who blames me for his brother's unsolved case.' Her eyes swept around the room before landing on Rheagan's and Kennedy's names. That sick feeling in her stomach spread as she began to wonder if Neely's hatred toward her had manifested into murder.

Chapter Seventeen

Never had Kennedy felt such flaming agony before – not even when glass shrapnel had exploded in her face eight years ago, marking her with a lightly puckered scar that ran from the center of her cheek to her ear. Everything from the tip of her scalp to the arches of her feet felt like it had been submersed in fire as her fatigued body strained to accommodate the unnatural stretch of her muscles. Blood trickled down her arm where the cuffs cut deeper into the torn skin of her wrists.

But what threatened her sanity the most was the absolutely impermeable darkness, blacker than even the tunnel had been. Her moans and hoarse cries echoed off the glass walls, battering at her, allowing the small part of her brain not completely steeped in terror to be consumed in anger at herself.

If only she'd been paying attention to her surroundings instead of daydreaming. If only she'd fought harder. Tried to escape sooner. Moved faster. If only she hadn't chosen to run the same trail every day, making her routine memorable and easy for someone to follow.

If only…

But she hadn't done any of those things. So, now all she could do was wait. Wait for the man she knew she'd seen before to return and end her life the same way he'd ended the other girl's.

Or would he follow through on his threat and use a hammer instead of his fists, sending agonizing blow after blow to her bones until they were all shattered?

Or would he use a knife, plunging the blade into her skin over and over as she hung from the bar, helpless to shield herself from the piercing sting of steel entering her flesh?

Or would he do something else, something someone like her would never even think of?

Something he'd done to one of the 'others' who'd tried to escape him? How many others had there been? Had their deaths been quick, or had he tortured them slowly until their bodies finally gave out?

In the pitch black of her world, her mind spun with one color. Red. Pooling on the floor.

As her life bled out, would there be another girl in the corner, watching in desperate horror, as she'd done, as Kennedy pleaded with her eyes, knowing her pleas were futile but holding onto hope until her very last breath abandoned her?

A shudder rippled through her, tearing at her strained muscles.

She'd scream if only she could.

The light she'd thought she'd been craving suddenly flooded the darkness with blinding force, and the door to the chamber opened. Seeing the expression on her abductor's face, Kennedy prayed for a return to the inky blackness.

Chapter Eighteen

Thursday, June 2

Just before six in the morning, the sun peeked over the Sandias, and a little over an hour later, Alyssa and Cord found themselves making the familiar winding drive through the residential neighborhood where Rheagan Pembroke had last been seen alive. Unlike much of the city, these homes boasted huge, multiacre lots that promised privacy, despite the sprawling community-village feel. Being so close to the mountain, many families had opted to stick to the natural landscape while others, such as the mayor, preferred the perfectly green, pristine look of a manicured lawn surrounded by a small forest of trees. Few had fences surrounding their properties.

When they reached the Hoyts' massive two-story red brick home, which sat just back and below the small rise that led to the Pembrokes' house, Alyssa shut off the ignition and turned to Cord. 'How is it possible that we were able to ping Rheagan's location to within a quarter mile of her house, yet not one single person we've interviewed remembers seeing her?'

The lines around Cord's mouth tightened into a thin line as he looked around him at the tall pines, cotton-woods, junipers, oak shrubbery, and massive boulders that made up so much of New Mexico's landscape. 'With all these trees and outcroppings in the area, I can actually see how it might be easy for someone to snatch someone and slip away without being noticed, especially at nighttime. And I'm guessing whoever took Rheagan shut down her cell so it couldn't be tracked.' He swept his arm in a wide semicircle as he stared outside the SUV's windows. 'He could've tossed it anywhere. Not quite like a needle in a haystack, but pretty damn close.'

Alyssa had stopped listening because something tickled the back of her mind, drawing her out of the Tahoe. She was vaguely aware of Cord climbing out after her.

'Lys?'

She held up a finger for him to wait and then turned in a circle, her gaze sweeping up and down the street, over the Pembrokes' roof and back. It was right there on the edges of her memory. If she could just... 'That's it.' She swung around, her eyes bright with excitement. 'Gunner Galveston's parents had just moved from this area six months prior to his disappearance.'

Cord's head snapped in her direction. 'Did Frank Neely live with them at the time?'

'Not at the time. He was attending graduate school at Arizona State when Gunner went missing. But the Galvestons lived in this area for close to fifteen years, so he would've lived with them at some point during that time.' She pulled her phone from her pocket so she could text Hal.

> Re: Frank Neely – get a list of prior addresses.

As soon as she pressed *send*, she noted the time. Ten after seven. 'All right. Let's see if we can finally get some of those answers we need.' Distracted by what felt like another connection between Rheagan and Gunner, and possibly Kennedy, Alyssa barely noticed the missing front gate or the intricate design of the flagstone pathway leading to the front door.

She didn't have time to consider what that possible connection might be or the implications of it because Cord had already rung the doorbell, the sounds of the long, melodic chime reaching their ears, followed by muffled footsteps drawing closer.

A fit, middle-aged man with well-defined muscles and dark hair graying at the temples opened the door wearing a look of puzzled harassment. Both perfectly groomed eyebrows shot upward when he spotted their badges, and his head snapped around as if checking on something – or someone – behind him. When he turned back to them, the lines in his forehead had smoothed out.

'I assume you're the detectives my housecleaner told me might stop by.' His shoulders dropped, and his eyes swept up toward his neighbor's house. 'Rheagan's murder has been all over the news.'

Alyssa introduced herself and Cord. 'Detectives Wyatt and Roberts with APD. We've been trying to reach you to ask you and your son some questions.'

Dr. Hoyt stepped back, silently inviting them in. 'I don't know how I can be of much help since we weren't here, but I can certainly try to answer whatever questions you've got.'

Alyssa noticed how he'd excluded his son in that state-ment, but she let it go because she had every intention of speaking to Raider Hoyt before she left. If he was home.

'I wish I'd known Rheagan was missing before my son and I took off for Colorado. We would've stuck around to help search. But I guess they didn't notice until around noon on Sunday, and by then we were already gone.'

As a matter of habit, Alyssa's eyes automatically went to Dr. Hoyt's hands, instinctively checking for any cuts or bruising consistent with the type of damage done to Rheagan's body. She found none. At the same time, she noted he wore no wedding ring, which didn't necessarily mean anything, she knew.

Dr. Hoyt noticed where Alyssa's eyes had drifted and answered her unspoken question. 'My wife died five years ago.' He checked the time on his watch. 'Do you know about how long this'll take? My first patient comes in at eight thirty. If you had called to let me know you were coming, I could've asked my nurse practitioner to take my appointment.'

Alyssa ignored the passive dig about not scheduling the interview as she'd made that decision intentionally, primarily because they'd been waiting for days to speak to Dr. Hoyt, and she didn't want to risk being put off any longer. 'We really can't say. A lot depends on what you can tell us, but we'll try to keep things brief so you can get on with your day.'

'Appreciate it. We can talk more comfortably in the back.' As he led the way, he smiled over his shoulder. 'It's still early enough, so we might even spot a deer or two out in the yard. They tend to graze here fairly often since I don't have a fence surrounding the property. Makes slipping out for a hike a little easier, too, not having a physical boundary.'

Tony's suggestion that the person they were looking for would be comfortable in that type of environment rang in Alyssa's head, and she peered up at Cord. The way he returned her look, she knew the same thing had crossed his mind.

Dr. Hoyt stopped outside a breakfast nook and waved them to a round glass table holding a colorful centerpiece of oranges, grapefruit, apples, bananas, kiwi, and even a pineapple. 'Can I get either of you a cup of coffee, an espresso, or something else altogether?'

Dr. Hoyt's question drew Alyssa's gaze away from the beautiful display that she'd only viewed in magazines and HGTV television shows. 'No, thank you.' Apparently having a mind of its own, her stomach decided to take that exact moment to offer a highly audible protest of her refusal.

A light chuckle slipped past Dr. Hoyt's lips. 'Are you sure about that? It won't take me but a minute to brew something up.'

Quietly coveting the gleaming silver machine, Alyssa declined once more, as did Cord, though his refusal no doubt came with less regret than hers due to a bizarre lack of interest in coffee or, really, most caffeine-laden products.

Accepting their answers, Dr. Hoyt settled himself into a chair across from them.

Alyssa eased into the interview. 'Do you mind if I ask what type of doctor you are?'

'Pediatrician. I considered architecture at one time. But my mother was a family doctor, and my father worked in hospital administration, so a medical degree seemed to be the most logical, organic path for me to follow. I opened my own practice about twelve years ago, about four years after my family moved here from Colorado. My wife didn't like my unpredictable schedule and wanted me home for family dinners. Being a doctor isn't always as glamorous as television likes to portray. I imagine as detectives you understand that better than anyone. Of course, now that my son is nineteen, dinners together are rather rare.'

Since he'd brought his son up, Alyssa decided now was as good a time as any to ask about Raider's and Rheagan's relationship. 'I understand your son and Rheagan dated off and on. Is that correct?'

The corners of Dr. Hoyt's mouth tightened into razor-thin lines. 'Did Ben tell you that?' He waved off his own question. 'Never mind. It doesn't matter who told you. And yes, I suppose they did date, of a sort, anyway.'

'Of a sort?' Cord asked.

Dr. Hoyt threaded his hands together and placed them on the table in front of him. 'I mean that my son described it more as a "hooking up" from time to time, so not a whole lot of, quote, unquote, "dating" going on.'

Bridgette and Laila had used the same terminology, and while Alyssa understood, she asked for clarification anyway. 'And by "hooking up," you mean…?'

Dr. Hoyt's unflinching gaze returned to Alyssa's. 'They had sex. Whenever the itch came, if they weren't with someone else, they scratched it together. Look, I'm really sorry for what happened to Rheagan. No one deserves that. No one. But the truth is, she was just a bit too daring and perhaps a lot less discerning when it came to her sexual relationships.'

Alyssa watched carefully for the doctor's reaction to her next question. 'How were you aware of her other sexual relationships?'

If Dr. Hoyt was bothered by her question, he didn't show it. 'She didn't exactly hide the fact that she wasn't a virgin. Just ask my son.'

'We'll be sure to do that.'

Cord set his notebook on the table, placed his pen on top, and then folded his hands together. 'I take it you didn't approve of their relationship.'

'Are you asking me a question?'

Cord arched his brow. 'I suppose I am.'

A mirthless laugh fell from Hoyt's mouth. 'Do you have children, Detective?'

Cord didn't respond.

Dr. Hoyt shoveled his fingers through his hair, leaving a wake of gray down the middle. 'Fine. No, I didn't. Especially when it involved her sneaking out of her house and into ours. Rheagan, I'm sure you've been told, had quite the reckless reputation, and frankly, I didn't want my son to fall prey to her games.'

Interesting choice of words, Alyssa thought.

'Look. the truth is, I lost my wife just as Raider hit his teenage years, and trust you me, that was not an easy path to navigate. His hormones were already out of whack and all over the place, and then you toss grief onto that pile, and my son became an impressionable dry tinderbox just waiting for a lit match.'

'Implying that Rheagan was that match?' Alyssa clarified.

'Yes.' Dr. Hoyt's swift and blunt response left no room for doubt.

Alyssa still wanted to speak to Raider, but she had a few more questions first. 'When was the last time you saw Rheagan?'

'I couldn't really say. I usually didn't pay attention because I mostly just saw her coming or going.'

'And what about Raider?'

The tightness around Dr. Hoyt's mouth returned. 'You'd have to ask him. It's not something I would've asked him, nor would he have offered the information because he's well aware of my feelings – and Ben's for that matter – on his and Rheagan's... relationship.'

'What time did you say you and Raider left for Colorado?'

'Early Sunday morning. Around seven thirty. And we didn't get back in until close to eleven last night. I'm having a new outreach center built in La Plata County, and my meeting with the contractors ran a little later than I'd expected. So, Raider and I stopped in Durango for dinner and didn't start heading back until almost seven.'

Something about the doctor leaving on a Sunday and returning on a Wednesday struck Alyssa as strange. 'What about your patients?'

Dr. Hoyt stiffened his back and leveled a heavy stare in Alyssa's direction. 'I'd had this meeting set up for two weeks, so my patients were seen by my staff.'

Both his posture and snapped response made it clear to Alyssa that she'd offended the doctor. She didn't care. A young girl had been murdered, so she and Cord weren't there to make a new friend. They were there to get answers. 'Is there any chance your son and Rheagan would have met up Saturday night, maybe after you slipped off to bed?'

'I have to say I'm not liking the implications of your questions, Detective. So, let me ask you this: do I need to have my attorney present?'

'Having an attorney present is your choice, of course. And I'm not implying anything with my questions, Dr. Hoyt. We're simply trying to gather as many facts as possible in order to find out what happened to and who killed Rheagan Pembroke.'

His frown suggested he didn't believe her, but he answered anyway. 'No, Raider didn't go out. And I know that because I have an app that tracks my son's phone any time I want. It's my rule since I pay for it. The phone was here. And since I'm not entirely positive anymore that his phone isn't surgically attached to his body, I can say with a fair amount of certainty that he was, too.'

Cord looked up from the note he'd been jotting. 'And you checked the app Saturday night?'

Dr. Hoyt crossed his arms over his chest, his hands pushing against his biceps in a way that emphasized the muscles. 'No. I checked after I heard about Rheagan's murder on the news. And before you ask why, it's because I wanted to be prepared in case the police needed to question him. Which you apparently do.'

'We do. Is he home now?' Alyssa asked.

'Yes. But he's still in bed.' He inhaled slowly through his nose, checked the time, and then released his breath in a way that clearly showed his aggravation. 'I'll go get him.'

Chapter Nineteen

Thursday, June 2

While Dr. Hoyt went upstairs to get his son, Alyssa inspected the expensive artwork on the walls and the intricate vases nestled in niches or sitting on shelves. Outside the large window that framed the backyard, a beautiful doe, along with a spotted fawn, nibbled on the grass. When she leaned forward for a better look, Alyssa noticed several more deer in the back corner of the open yard near a small grouping of juniper bushes and low-hanging desert willows.

'I bet Tony would love this view,' Cord said.

'I bet he would.'

Through the vent above their heads, they heard a loud tapping and then a muffled conversation. Alyssa laughed quietly when both she and Cord cocked their heads to the side in an obvious effort to eavesdrop.

A smile tipped the corner of Cord's lips, a sure sign his mind had shifted to his children. 'Would you like to know the latest from your eldest godson's wheelhouse of wisdom?'

No matter how many times Alyssa heard that word applied to her, it still burst like champagne bubbles in her heart. Aside from being called Mom, never had she enjoyed a title bestowed upon her as much as she did godmother. 'Of course. Tell me what wisdom Carter has departed since I last saw him.'

'This morning, when I walked by Shane and Carter's room, I overheard him explaining that there is a right and wrong way to cross one's eyes. And to be clear, by "overhear," I mean I blatantly eavesdropped.'

Hit with baffled amusement, Alyssa grinned. 'First, what in the world were the boys doing up so early, and second, do pray tell, what is the right way to roll one's eyes?'

Footsteps above their head cut their conversation short, so Cord rushed an answer. 'They're always up that early, and I think I'll let him demonstrate the next time you see him. After all, seeing is believing. By the time I left for the precinct this morning, he had Shane and the girls in there practicing.'

Just as Cord finished up, Dr. Hoyt returned. 'Raider will be along in a minute.' He made a show of glancing down at his expensive watch. 'I'm afraid I'm going to need to leave soon. How much longer do you think this will take?'

Something about the way he asked rubbed Alyssa the wrong way. Probably because they were trying to solve his neighbor's murder, a young woman who'd had, at the very least, a sexual relationship with his son. 'Your son's nineteen, right?'

'Why is that relevant?' A pinched look of annoyance seized his face.

'Just reminding you that Raider is an adult; as such, the law doesn't require your presence when we speak to him, so if you need to leave to tend to your patients, we understand.'

More in line with what she'd expect from a surly teen instead of a grown man, Dr. Hoyt snorted. 'Raider's age may make him an adult in the eyes of the law, perhaps, but certainly not by responsibility.' His focus drifted to a point behind them. 'Speak of the devil.'

Alyssa and Cord met the tired, droopy eyes of Raider Hoyt, a younger, smaller replica of his father. Except that, as neat as his father's appearance was, his was equally as messy. The cowlick in the back of his head stuck out at odd angles, and a line of ridges stretched across his face where it had been pressed against a pillow. The five o'clock shadow that darkened his jaw cast him as a young man in his mid to late twenties rather than nineteen. He wore a discolored yellowish-brown shirt that bore all the signs of years of wear, and the better days of his old, tattered jogging shorts had long since passed. As Dr. Hoyt had described earlier, Raider clutched a phone in his hand.

He lifted his chin and shot his father a petulant glare, dropped his head into some semblance of what might pass as a greeting to Alyssa and Cord, and then moved past all of them over to the stainless-steel refrigerator.

'Use a cup,' his father snapped as Raider reached for a pitcher of freshly squeezed orange juice.

His shoulders stiffening in a show of sullen teenage displeasure, Raider hesitated with his hand still gripping the handle of the pitcher. Just when Alyssa thought he would ignore his father's demand, he opened the cupboard, yanked down a cup, slammed it on the counter, slammed the cupboard door closed, and poured himself half a glass of juice before returning it to the fridge. Then he downed his drink before slamming the door on the refrigerator hard enough to rattle the dishes in a nearby cabinet.

Either he and his father had a very tumultuous relationship, or Raider Hoyt did *not* take kindly to being roused from sleep. Or both.

Wiping his arm across his mouth, Raider eyed the table with discernment before latching onto the only chair available, that closest to his father, and scraping it along the floor until he was seated as far away as he could possibly be without actually leaving the breakfast nook. Stretching his shirt tight when he crossed his arms across his gym-made muscular chest, his irritated gaze bounced from his father and then onto Alyssa and Cord, his disgruntled teenage attitude on full display.

'My dad said you have questions about Rheagan. I don't know what I can tell you because I sure as shit don't know who killed her. Matter of fact, I didn't even know she'd gone missing until a couple days ago because I was in Colorado with him.' He jabbed his thumb in his father's direction. 'Because apparently, I'm a little kid who can't be allowed to stay home alone.'

'Raider.' Dr. Hoyt's voice rang out a clear warning. His son pointedly looked away and rolled his eyes.

Despite his gruff attitude, Alyssa detected the slightest wobble in Raider's voice, and understanding that neither Rheagan's father nor his own approved of the relationship, she had to wonder if his belligerence was a show he put on for his father's sake.

Both Bridgette and Laila had theorized that Rheagan's draw to Raider stemmed more from a way of going against her father's demands, but Alyssa was well aware that the age-old canon of a young girl being drawn to the bad-boy persona Raider exuded could've been just as valid a draw for her.

'Could you tell us when you last saw or spoke to Rheagan?' Cord asked.

Raider's eyes shifted to the left as he gave a one-sided shrug. 'Around noon on Saturday, I think.'

From the corner of her eyes, Alyssa noticed Dr. Hoyt's head snap in his son's direction. Clearly, he'd been unaware. 'Where was that?' she asked.

'We passed each other on Central.'

'Did the two of you talk?'

The way Raider stiffened, Alyssa didn't believe his gruff, 'No.'

She pressed him. 'Are you sure?'

As if unable to maintain eye contact, Raider took great interest in his phone's dark screen before he finally met Alyssa's gaze. 'I'm sure.'

Alyssa let the silence stretch for a moment as she studied him, and then she lowered her voice so that he'd hear the underlying warning ringing through her words. 'Raider, if there's something you know, you need to tell us now.' She paused before adding, 'It could help us find out who killed her.'

Raider lifted his eyes and leveled a steady stare at Cord and then at Alyssa. 'If I knew something, I'd tell you. But I don't. And I already told you I don't know who would've...' For the first time since he'd come downstairs, his voice cracked with emotion.

Alyssa couldn't help but notice how Raider subtly shifted his body away from his father's knowing and, from what she could determine, disappointed, eyes. Curious to hear his insight into Rheagan's personality, she changed the topic. 'You went to school with Rheagan, right?'

'Yeah. I mean, I was a grade older than her, but yeah. Why?'

'Can you tell us what she was like?'

Raider studied Alyssa as if he suspected a trap. 'Like, what do you want to know?'

'Anything you want to share. It helps us to know as much as possible about her.'

Unfiltered sorrow filled his eyes, and he snapped, 'All you need to know is she got killed.'

'Raider!' Dr. Hoyt's palm hit the table, jarring everyone.

Alyssa kept her focus glued on Raider but held up her hand to stop Dr. Hoyt from chastising his son. 'You're right. And not only was she your neighbor, but also someone you had a sexual relationship with, so I'd imagine you'd want us to do everything we can so we can find out what led up to that event. Am I wrong about that?'

Raider's chin dropped toward his chest. 'No. Look, I don't know what I can tell you that will help. I mean, girls are confusing all on their own, but Rheagan made it a sport. She ran hot and cold, depending on the day and her mood.'

'What can you tell us about her relationship with her family?'

'Not a lot. Her parents pretty much gave her freedom to do as she pleased.' Anger and something else shone in his eyes as he glared at his father before turning back to Alyssa. 'Except when it came to hanging out with me. That was a big no-no. Because apparently, I'm a bad influence. Anyway, she didn't really complain about her mom and dad like most people. The only thing she ever said about her family was that she always felt like she was living in Ellary's perfect shadow.'

That was the second time they'd heard that, and it made Alyssa wonder if Laila was right, that the insecurity of being unable to live up to the same perfect standard as her sister drove Rheagan toward a reckless need for attention, particularly from her parents, in other ways. As odd as it sounded, Alyssa, over the years, had encountered many kids who seemed to get anything they wanted from their parents – except boundaries that showed they cared – and so they acted out.

'We've been told Rheagan had an edgy personality. Did you ever witness that?'

Raider snorted. 'Yeah. If someone dared her to do something, it was like a red flag being waved in front of a bull.'

'Can you give us an example?'

'Someone once dared her to break into the mayor's house while he was away on vacation and take pictures to prove she did it.'

Alyssa couldn't hide her shocked reaction. 'And did she?'

Once again, Raider rolled his eyes. 'Yes and no. Everyone thinks she did, but she actually had permission to be in the house because the mayor's wife had asked her to water the houseplants while they were away.'

As if he'd had enough, Raider scowled. 'Look, I don't know what else I can tell you. Everyone knows Rheagan did dumb shit, but did she do something that got her killed? That's where you're going with this, right? Because I don't know. She did lots of stuff. So, yeah, I suppose she could've done something to piss off the wrong person.'

'Did she ever piss you off?' Cord asked.

Raider jerked his head up. 'What does that mean?'

'You and Rheagan had an off and on thing. Did she ever piss you off?'

A dark shadow passed across Raider's face as he shot an arrow full of resentment in Cord's direction. 'We didn't have a "thing," off and on or otherwise. We hooked up a few times, mostly about a year ago, and then our parents freaked out, and we stopped hanging out as much. And look, man, I wasn't the only one she hooked up with. Not even close. I wasn't even the first person she had sex with. That horse left the barn a long time before me. And before you ask, no, it didn't bother me because, like I said, it only happened a few times. And no, she never did anything that pissed me off. And even if she had, I sure as hell wouldn't have killed her for it.'

Alyssa's instincts told her that Raider was telling the truth. What was more, she had the distinct impression that much of his anger stemmed from feeling like he had to hide his emotions over Rheagan's death, regardless of the tragic circumstances.

She shot Cord a look, knowing he'd understand, and then she stood, indicating their interview had ended. 'If either of you thinks of anything else at all, please give one of us a call, day or night, no matter what time it is.' She pulled a business card from her pocket and placed it on the table.

Dr. Hoyt, making another show of peering at his watch, gave the card a passing glance as he pushed to his feet.

But Alyssa had one more question. 'Do either of you know or recognize the name Kennedy Farmer?'

Father and son stared at each other with arched brows and matching lines furrowing their foreheads before they both answered at the same time. 'No.'

'Why?' Dr. Hoyt asked. 'Should we?'

Alyssa didn't answer. 'Thanks again for your time.'

As she and Cord headed back to her Tahoe, they heard the smooth rumbling of the garage door opening, and they turned to see Dr. Hoyt, now sporting a dark pair of aviator glasses that shielded his eyes, slide into the driver's seat of a sleek, cobalt blue sports car that looked luxuriously expensive. While she didn't have the same appreciation for these things as her husband and son, or even Hal or Cord, Alyssa couldn't help but stop and ogle it for a moment – even if she couldn't have identified the make or model if her life depended on it. Beside her, Cord came to a complete standstill, mouth agape, gawking – and damn near drooling.

She rolled her eyes and bumped his arm. 'Are you going to stand there all day, or are you coming with me?'

Cord brushed her hand away. 'Hush. I'm having a cargasm.'

Alyssa snorted out a laugh before she could stop herself. 'Well, when you're finished, I'll be in the car. We do, after all, have a few cases we're trying to solve.' As soon as she said it, she regretted it. Not because it wasn't true, but because, as all police officers knew, they had to take enjoyment when and where they could, or they risked succumbing to the depression their jobs sometimes brought on.

Chapter Twenty

Alone, the man locked his door and opened an oversized drawer in his filing cabinet where he kept his treasured box of secrets. He lifted the lid and set it aside as he admired the stacks of photos that marked his history.

On the top, a picture of a dark-haired girl, younger than the one he had hidden away now, stared back at him with pleading eyes. He studied the blue veins popping out in stark contrast to her pale skin, remembered the way he'd ripped the tape from her mouth and listened to her screams, relived that heady sense of power he wielded over her as she'd begged for her life.

He'd taken his time with her, wanting that thrill to last forever.

He set her picture aside and grabbed another, allowing the memory to wash over him. For a moment, he relived his victim's terror as she accepted the truth, that she'd die at his hands, at his mercy, of which he had none.

And then, there at his fingertips, the one that began it all.

He remembered it like it was yesterday. He ran his finger over the picture of the boy's face, tracing the red mark around his neck, felt the strain in his arms as he pulled the rope tighter.

His pulse shot up and he dropped back in time.

For weeks, the voice inside his head had taunted him for being a sissy, too afraid to do what he knew he wanted to do. He decided to prove it wrong.

When Friday came along, he concealed himself in the trees and waited for the boy to walk by. Austin Rolling had some kind of learning disability which made it difficult for him to make friends, so luring him in would be almost as easy as stealing candy from a blind person. Like he did every day, Austin sang along to whatever music he heard in his head.

As he watched Austin's approach, his own father's voice sliced into his thoughts like a razor blade. 'Remember, boy, survival of the fittest is how you make it to the top. You always gotta be smarter and stronger than the next guy.'

When Austin came within feet of where he hid in the trees, he called out to get his attention. 'Hey. I like that song. Who sings it?' He beckoned Austin closer.

Startled, Austin stopped and stared, then looked over both shoulders before understanding that the quiet boy he passed every day in the halls was really talking to him. Austin grinned as he met him at the tree line.

God, this would be even easier than he'd imagined. His palms turned wet, not from nerves, but excitement. He needed the boy to come in a little closer. Austin named a band whose name meant nothing to him.

He patted his backpack and took a few steps farther into the dense cover of trees. 'No way. I didn't know they sang that song. I love their stuff.' Three more steps, off the trail now.

Austin's eyes widened. 'Really? You love their music? Most people laugh at me, say only babies like it.'

Five more steps, and the road completely disappeared from view. The rushing sound of anticipation buzzed in his ears. He stopped and turned to Austin. 'Some people are so stupid.' He started moving again.

Austin followed blindly, never bothering to ask where they were going. Just blissfully jabbering away, never suspecting the deeper into the trees they went, the closer they got to his death.

Just ahead, no more than a hundred feet away now, and they'd be at the spot he'd picked out ahead of time. It was far enough into the woods that no matter how loud Austin screamed, no one would hear. And if they did, they'd probably think it was nothing more than a wild animal. Fifty feet now. Twenty. Sweat flooded his pores, soaking his underarms.

He'd stopped listening and offered only noncommittal grunts as Austin rambled on.

He stepped over the broken branch he'd used to mark his perfect spot and came to an abrupt halt. Austin stopped, too.

He dropped his bag on the ground and unzipped the top, setting aside the Polaroid camera he'd gotten for his birthday the year before. Austin's yammering never slowed, not even when he saw the knife, spotted the ropes.

He pointed to something in the trees, and Austin tipped his head back to look.

He lunged, taking Austin by surprise. He wrestled him to the ground and wrapped the rope tightly around his neck, pulling tighter, mesmerized by the way the boy's eyes widened and bulged, the white orbs slowly bursting to red as the blood vessels popped. Austin grabbed the rope with his hands, trying to get his fingers beneath the thick twine to give himself room to breathe. Confusion, shock, and disbelief stretched across his face.

Smack!

The loud cracking noise startled the man back just before he'd gotten to the best part. His eyes shot toward the window where the imprint of a bird shone through. Stupid animal. He hoped its neck was broken. His gaze drifted back to the picture still gripped in his fingers. Austin Rolling. His first human kill.

He'd known even as Austin's life faded away that he'd be doing it again. He wouldn't be able to stop himself from chasing that thrill. Like the infamous Herman Mudgett had once claimed, he knew he'd 'been born with the devil inside him' and that he 'could no more help the fact that he was a murderer than the poet could help the inspiration to sing.'

'I told you I'm no sissy,' he whispered to the empty room. 'Now, it's time to prove it to the rest of the world.' He lifted his eyes to the muted television where he'd paused the screen on the cheery face of Kennedy Farmer. A banner beneath her name read: *Frantic Search*. *If you have any information about her whereabouts, please contact the Albuquerque Police.*

Oh, he was going to contact the police all right. But he had no intention of telling them where she was. No, he had a much better idea, one that promised no one would ever dare call him sissy like his father used to do.

He grabbed the things he'd need, replaced the lid on the box, and stowed it away.

This would be fun.

Chapter Twenty-One

Thursday, June 2

The illuminated clock on Alyssa's dashboard flashed eight seventeen when she finally made her way back to the main road after leaving Dr. Jackson Hoyt's home. If she turned right, it would take her but a minute to reach Tramway Arroyo where Rheagan's body had been discovered. Another minute more would lead her back to Coyote Canyon where Kennedy had been taken. Twelve minutes farther would lead her to the place a hiker had come across Gunner's remains.

'Well, what was your take on the Hoyts?' Cord's question interrupted the flow of her thoughts.

'To be honest, I'm not sure. What I can say is that unless he's hiding the fact that he murdered or knows who murdered Rheagan, I don't see Raider Hoyt as being involved.' She stopped at a red light and looked over. 'Plus, if Kennedy's disappearance and Rheagan's murder are connected with Gunner's case, then I feel the need to point out that Raider would have only been five at the time. Pretty sure that rules him out as a suspect in that instance. That being said, something tells me he wasn't one hundred percent forthcoming in his answers. And that Rheagan's death has hit harder than he wants to admit.'

'I think you're right. As for not being forthcoming, do you suppose it's something he doesn't want us to know? Or his dad?'

'Both?' The light turned green, and Alyssa turned her attention back to the traffic in front of her.

'Well, Raider's age may exclude him from our list where Gunner's concerned, but it doesn't exclude his father.'

Alyssa snorted as she muttered under her breath, 'What list?'

When her phone rang, rescuing Cord from a response, she hit the green icon on her Bluetooth. 'Detective Wyatt speaking.'

The caller's voice boomed into the cab, forcing Alyssa to turn down the volume or risk bursting an eardrum. 'Detective Wyatt, this is Ben Pembroke.'

The raspiness in his voice made him difficult to understand, so Alyssa readjusted the volume.

'I was just going through some things for...' Ben cleared his throat and started again. 'I was going through some papers for... so we can... we're trying to plan Rheagan's services, and I realized I never gave you the name of her therapist. I'm sorry. Do you still need that information?'

Alyssa did her best to keep the edge out of her voice. 'Yes, that would be great.'

'His name was Dr. Frank Neely. I can give you his number, if you'd like, but I believe he moved offices from the time Rheagan saw him.'

Alyssa felt like the wind had been knocked right out of her. 'Thank you. I appreciate you calling.'

'Before you go, Barbara wanted me to ask when we should plan for Rheagan's funeral.'

What he really wanted to know, Alyssa understood, was when would the autopsy be complete. 'I'm sorry, but I don't have an answer to that question, but I promise as soon as I know, we'll be in touch.'

'Can you tell me where you are in the investigation, at least?' The change in his tone indicated his grief had hardened into anger and frustration.

Alyssa ventured a guess that his emotions were aimed in equal parts at his own family for stalling to report Rheagan missing right away and the authorities for not yet providing them with the answers they sought. 'We're still tracking down every lead. As soon as we know anything, we'll be in touch.'

A lengthy silence followed before Ben reluctantly thanked Alyssa and hung up.

Tension that stemmed more from the call than from maneuvering through a construction zone had Alyssa's hands tightening on the steering wheel. 'If Kennedy's time at the Outreach Center coincided with Neely's tenure, we have a common link to three otherwise seemingly unrelated cases.'

Before she finished her statement, Cord had located Aubrey's number in his notebook and punched it in on Alyssa's Bluetooth.

Aubrey answered at the first ring. 'Detective Wyatt? Oh my God, did you find her? Did you find Kennedy? Is she okay?'

Because she'd experienced Aubrey's fear and desperation in her own past, Alyssa felt each question like a physical blow. 'Not yet, but we're still following leads and looking for her, which is why we're calling. You told us yesterday that Kennedy used to coach volleyball at the

Outreach Center. Do you remember how long ago she started?'

Aubrey's disappointment weighed heavily in her answer. 'She quit in January. And when she started, it had only been open a few years, I think. I don't remember how she heard about it, but she found out the center needed volunteers to help mentor the girls who came in. She knew they had a basketball court, so she suggested volleyball, and the center agreed. I mean, it's not like they competed or anything. She just knew it would help give them a sense of belonging or a place to go when they didn't really have one.'

Though Aubrey hadn't yet answered Alyssa's question, she let her talk in case there was something that might help. 'That was pretty insightful of your sister. That's precisely why the center was built.'

Aubrey sniffled. 'Some of Kennedy's best days were when she came home and talked about a positive shift in someone's behavior or whatever, like it just gave her hope that some of them would be okay. She really hated letting it go because she'd been there for four years. But her schedule got so hectic, she was afraid she'd do more damage by staying because the kids might start to think they weren't important enough for her to show up for them.' Aubrey paused. 'Do you think someone from there—'

Alyssa didn't let her finish the question. 'Like I said, we're trying to follow through with some leads. Before I let you go, do you recognize the name Frank Neely?'

'No, it doesn't ring a bell. Should I know it?'

Alyssa knew in today's technological world, all it would take was for Aubrey to run a search on the name to discover who he was. There wasn't much she could do to stop it, and so she gave the best answer she could. 'Not necessarily.'

Cord interrupted whatever Aubrey was about to say next. 'Aubrey, this is Detective Roberts. Have your parents made it back yet?'

'No. My dad sent a text early this morning to tell me their flight had been delayed. He said he'd let me know as soon as they were on the plane and it was about to take off. The last I heard was a little over an hour ago, and the situation hasn't changed.'

Alyssa thanked Aubrey, and after promising to be in touch, ended the call and immediately reached out to Hal, whose greeting could only be described as upbeat.

'Just the people I wanted to talk to. What can I do for you fine friends this morning?'

Alyssa couldn't help but smile. Hal wore optimism and cheer like witches and warlocks wore talismans. Just one more reason so many rookies and veterans alike flocked to the man for advice.

'First, we haven't heard from Joe or Tony to see how their search is going. Have you?'

'Actually, yes. They're still running down all the businesses in the area to see if any of their cameras picked up Kennedy before she disappeared. And I'm about to pull up the street cameras to see what I can find. Speaking of which, I got some information back on the Hoyts this morning. Do you want me to tell you about it now or wait to tell everyone at the same time?'

'Tell us now.'

'Well, Raider Hoyt has a reckless driving charge on his record from two years ago. But if you want my honest opinion, from the way the report reads, sounds to me like the cop was being an ass because of Raider's age. Kid skidded into a parking lot when he hit a patch of black ice. According to the report, he didn't think, just reacted because he didn't want to cause an accident, which makes sense with something else I found, which I'll get to in a minute. Anyway, cop watched it happen, decided Raider was going too fast for the conditions, et cetera, et cetera. Report states Hoyt got belligerent with the cop. In the end, ticket issued, ticket paid. Nothing since then.

'As for Dr. Jackson Hoyt, it shows he's had a few parking tickets, but none newer than four years old, at least here in New Mexico. And his wife, Evelyn Ryzen Hoyt, died five years ago of a prescription drug overdose.'

'What kind of prescription?' Cord asked.

'Toxicology report from the autopsy showed elevated levels of the muscle relaxant baclofen and fentanyl, as well as traces of what appeared to be amphetamines and dextroamphetamines, the two main drugs in prescriptions such as Adderall.'

Cord whistled through his teeth. 'Whoa. That is some combination.'

'It is indeed. But according to the records, Evelyn Hoyt suffered from a painful spinal cord injury caused when someone broadsided her in Colorado a few years before her death, which to me, explains why Raider might've been especially cautious about hitting another vehicle.'

'I agree with you,' Alyssa said. 'Regarding Raider's mother, though, what you're saying is that all the drugs found in her system had been prescribed?'

'Yes, ma'am, albeit from different doctors, which makes sense if she was abusing them. The other doctors might not have even been aware of what she was doing. But that's not the interesting part. Guess what name popped up as one of the prescribing physicians?' Hal waited a beat. 'Dr. Frank Neely.'

Alyssa's foot jerked against the gas pedal, almost careening them into a truck that had slowed for another vehicle to merge.

Hal wasn't done yet. 'Because Tony mentioned his name last night, I'd already checked out Neely's website. The man's got a whole biographical section on there. Anyway, looks like he volunteered his services to the Outreach Center from its conception until about a year ago.'

Alyssa spared a quick glance over to Cord, whose expression mirrored her own reaction. 'We just spoke with Aubrey Farmer, and that coincides with the time Kennedy volunteered there.'

'Well, if you're excited about that link, then let me toss one more onto the pile. The current director of the Outreach Center is none other than… drumroll, please… Dr. Jackson Hoyt.'

Alyssa's breath rushed out. 'How long ago was he named director?'

'Center website shows he's been active there since 2017.'

'Which means he could've come into contact with Kennedy, as well.' Alyssa's head raced with all the information. When they'd asked Jackson and Raider if either of them had recognized Kennedy's name, they'd both replied in the negative. An honest oversight or an outright lie?

'Hal, can you pull Neely's website back up and give us the address and his office hours?'

'Thought you might want it, so I've already got it.' He rattled off the address. 'Hours go from Monday through Thursday, nine to five thirty, open for emergency appointments only Friday through Sunday with a rotating on-call doctor.'

Alyssa peeked at the time, shocked to see it was already close to nine. 'Thanks. We're not far from Neely's office, so Cord and I will go ahead and swing by there to see if we can squeeze in a chance to speak to him. I can already tell you, though, that he's going to be less than thrilled to see me.'

'Well, he doesn't have to like you or even want to see you,' Hal said. 'All he has to do is answer some questions or risk impeding an investigation. I'd offer to request a ping warrant for his phone to see where it put him Saturday night or Sunday morning, but I'm afraid we'll need to establish more of a reason before a judge will agree to one.'

'Appreciate the info, Hal.'

'No problem. Next stop, leading the universe to world peace.'

Even with the knot in her stomach tightening, Alyssa chuckled as she ended the call and signaled to change lanes. 'You know, if anyone could bring about world peace, I swear Hal would be the man for the job.'

'You know it. I'd sure as hell vote for him,' Cord said.

'Wouldn't we all?'

Chapter Twenty-Two

Thursday, June 2

Two blocks from the building where Frank Neely held his practice, Cord broke into Alyssa's thoughts. 'I don't know what you're thinking, but as suspects go, Frank Neely seems kind of obvious and in your face, doesn't he? I mean, he's the half-brother of the murdered kid whose case you were never able to solve. No offense,' he rushed to add. 'On the other hand, I've gotta admit that's one hell of a coincidence.'

'No offense taken, and that "coincidence" is starting to feel like one hell of a stretch, considering he can be linked to all three victims one way or another. Even though we cleared him in Gunner's case after we confirmed he was in Arizona at the time of his brother's disappearance doesn't mean he isn't somehow involved now.' She paused, then added, 'And as much as I hate to say it, it also doesn't mean something couldn't have been overlooked fourteen years ago.'

A car wreck up ahead brought the already slow traffic to a halt, and Alyssa hit her brakes. Just a little over a block away, she could see the roof line of where they were headed. With nowhere to go, turning on the sirens would do no good, so with the seconds ticking by, she inched along with the rest of the vehicles. Half an hour later, she made the turn into the parking lot, but by then, her temper had scooted toward the short end of the spectrum.

She'd barely turned off the ignition before she hopped down to the asphalt and headed inside where Cord immediately began scouring the immense directory situated in the middle of a large open space that boasted floor-to-ceiling windows, massive plants, and a living wall. He mumbled as he ran his finger down the list of the building's occupants until he found Neely's name.

'Looks like his office is on the third floor with the rest of the therapists.'

They rode the elevator up in silence. The large white lettering in the curtain-covered window showed Neely's office two doors down. A table in the empty waiting area held a variety of entertainment magazines while a slot shelf stocked hundreds of pamphlets regarding various illnesses. Behind the glass windows separating the would-be patients from the doctors and staff in the back, three women sat at their desks, laughing about something. The one with pure white hair stopped mid-chuckle when she saw Alyssa and Cord standing there. She glanced down, presumably to check the appointment calendar, then smiled brightly and opened the window.

'Good morning. Can I help the two of you?'

Alyssa read the woman's nametag. 'Well, I hope so, Bryn. I'm Detective Wyatt with the Albuquerque Police Department, and this is Detective Roberts. We're investigating the murder of Rheagan Pembroke. You might've heard about it on the news?'

Bryn's smile faded away as she nodded. 'Yes, we did. So sad, that. I hope you catch the person responsible soon.' Her eyes drifted from Alyssa to Cord, where they lingered.

Women's reactions to her partner's good looks were commonplace, and Alyssa had gotten used to it ages ago. And while the attention made Cord a bit uncomfortable, he used it to his advantage when necessary. This being a case in point.

'We were hoping we could squeeze in a few minutes to speak with Dr. Neely. We're hoping he might have some of the answers we're looking for.' Cord flashed his megawatt smile intended to dazzle. Like magic, Bryn lit up as she rushed to accommodate.

'Of course. The doctor's next appointment isn't for another hour, so I'll just go let him know you're here. If you'll excuse me, I'll just be a moment.'

Alyssa couldn't see Bryn's face when she walked away, but the way the other two women in the office giggled and openly ogled Cord, she had a fairly good idea what had been on it. For his part, he pretended not to notice.

Two minutes, then five passed, and Alyssa felt her earlier impatience return to nip at her heels. At eight minutes, she took a step toward the window to ask if one of the other ladies could see what was taking so long. But before she could get their attention, the door separating the waiting room opened, revealing a red-faced Bryn, and Alyssa guessed the older woman had probably been scolded for not checking with the doctor before agreeing on his behalf that he'd see them. A twinge of guilt twisted her gut, but not enough to stop her from following the woman down the hall.

Bryn tapped twice on the open door.

For the first time in more than a decade, Alyssa got a glimpse of Dr. Frank Neely as he turned around from closing the filing cabinet behind him. Aside from growing older, he appeared much the same as he had the last time she'd seen him. Tall, muscular, and handsome with his dark hair and sculpted chin, she could only imagine how many of his patients ended up crushing on him. A flash of recognition and something bordering on dislike told her that she'd hit the nail on the head regarding his feelings toward her. *Happy* was clearly not the adjective one would use to describe his reaction to seeing her.

Dr. Neely grudgingly gestured for them to enter. 'Detectives, please, come in. Bryn, close the door on your way out, if you wouldn't mind.' The door had barely latched before he skipped the pleasantries and got straight to the point. 'Detective Wyatt, it's been a few years. I admit when Bryn told me you were here to see me, my first thought was that you'd come to *finally* give me some answers about Gunner's murder.'

Outwardly, Alyssa maintained her professional appearance. Inwardly, she winced at Neely's heavy emphasis on the word *finally*.

Frank steepled his fingers beneath his chin and leaned back in his chocolate brown leather chair. His eyes swept briefly to Cord before returning to her. 'Imagine how quickly my excitement dipped into abject disappointment when I learned that not to be the case. Now, how can I help *you*?'

'Well, if you already know my presence here isn't regarding Gunner's investigation, then I imagine Bryn already informed you of another case we're currently working on. Rheagan Pembroke. Just recently, Detective Roberts and I came into some information that shows you were her therapist a few years back.'

Neely arched his brows, almost mockingly. 'That's correct, I was. But without a warrant, I'm not obligated to share my sessions with her with you.'

'If we need one, we'll get one. Can you tell us how long she was one of your patients?'

'It's been several years, so no. I'd have to look in the files.'

Alyssa's eyes darted to the cabinet behind him, wondering if that was what he'd been looking at when they'd walked in. When she returned her focus to him, she had a difficult time deciphering the look on his face, which made it unclear if he was being difficult out of habit or because he blamed her for his brother's murder landing in the cold case files. She had to admit, if the tables were turned, she might've felt the same way.

Cord ended Neely's staring contest by asking, 'How about Kennedy Farmer? Do you recall ever coming into contact with her?'

Though she hadn't been the one to pose the question, Frank Neely clenched his jaw, dropped his hands, tipped forward, and narrowed an angry glare that could've burned a hole in Alyssa's skin. 'So, it's going to be like that, right? You couldn't solve my brother's murder, so you start grasping at straws. I'm not a hermit – I saw the report on Ms. Farmer's disappearance. I'm guessing that you've somehow got it in your head that there's a link between my brother's fourteen-year-old unsolved murder, my previous patient, and now apparently Ms. Farmer.'

Bright crimson stained his cheeks and spread down his neck as a kaleidoscope of emotions ranging from disbelief to fury crossed his face. 'I could psychoanalyze this one all day long, Detective. It was just a few years ago that you yourself were making headlines about your kidnapped brother. Clearly, you're carrying around a heavy dose of post-traumatic stress for something you consider to be your own personal failure. Then you allow my own brother's murder to go unsolved, and this is your way to alleviate all that guilt, by falsely trying to pin something on me. Who cares if you've got the right guy, as long as you show Albuquerque you nabbed someone, right?'

An image of Timmy, her four-year-old brother, riding around on his bike all those years ago before he'd been kidnapped flashed in Alyssa's mind. Neely was right. For decades, she had harbored all the blame because she should've been outside watching him. However, he was wrong about her objective. What had happened to Timmy had absolutely no bearing on the cases in front of her. She matched his glare with one of her own. 'I notice you didn't ask how we assume you might know Ms. Farmer.'

'Why would I? Aside from hearing her name on the news just this morning, I've never heard of her, nor have I ever seen her that I can recall.'

'Can you tell us where you were Saturday?' Cord's hard tone had Frank slowly sliding his gaze over to him.

'Are you seriously standing here in *my* office, where I agreed to see you without a bit of forewarning, accusing me of three murders?'

Alyssa stiffened, as did Cord. 'Who said anything about Ms. Farmer being murdered?' she asked.

Neely threw his hands up. 'Look, I appreciate you're trying to absolve your own personal failures, including being unable to solve Gunner's murder, by bringing Rheagan Pembroke's murderer to justice. But you're not going to do it by grilling me. And I can't tell you if this Farmer gal has been murdered or if she just ran away with the damn circus because, to my knowledge, I've *never met her.* Now, my next appointment is due in soon, and I'd rather you not scare my patients, so I'm going to insist the two of you leave.'

He pulled out his phone, scrolled through it, grabbed a piece of paper, scribbled something on it, and then shoved it across his desk at Alyssa. 'If you have any other inclination to speak to me in the future, you can contact my attorney who will be happy to try to schedule a time that's more convenient for all of us.' He nodded toward the door. 'You can see yourselves out, I'm sure.'

Because she was trying to decide if Neely's shutdown meant they were back at square one or if they'd never left it to begin with, Alyssa barely registered a more reserved Bryn offering a small wave as she and Cord moved through the waiting area and left.

Chapter Twenty-Three

Thursday, June 2

Stopped before he could make it out to Kennedy, the man ground his teeth and stashed his items before they could be seen. Maintaining natural outward appearances meant he had to endure an endless cast of ignorant people who'd probably never once considered that a monster walked among them. That at any moment he could end any one of their condescending, pathetic lives.

He pretended to listen when he was really imagining each person's reaction to discovering the face behind his mask. Who among them would scream the loudest, cry the hardest, beg the most? That guy over there with freshly ironed creases in his pants? Or the blonde-haired beauty? He should remember her name.

She turned to see him staring at her, and in his mind, he heard her high-pitched screams as she lifted her bloodshot eyes to him, recognizing that she'd fatally placed her trust in a whirling eddy of evil.

Much like Rheagan had.

Without realizing it, he took a step closer. He could change his plan, be done with Kennedy and replace her with the blonde.

No!

He heard the voice as clearly as if the person standing beside him had shouted in his ear, and the man stopped.

The blonde could wait. For now, he had something else to do, something that would cement him in the annals of history as the most terrifying kind of urban legend.

Only he'd be real.

Survival of the fittest, indeed.

Chapter Twenty-Four

Thursday, June 2

With the clock already ticking close to one in the afternoon by the time Alyssa and Cord made it back to the precinct for a team meeting, Alyssa felt the mounting pressure to locate Kennedy before it was too late. Her instincts told her that if they could solve one case, they'd solve them all.

Neely's words about absolving her own failures by bringing Rheagan's murderer to justice rang in her ears. Witnessing his simmering anger had forced her back to the last time she'd spoken to the Galvestons before their own deaths. They'd come to the station, pleading for answers she'd been unable to give them. At times, their devastated faces still haunted her dreams. Years of experience had made her a much stronger, better detective than she had been then, and she knew in her heart she'd get justice for Rheagan – and save Kennedy – in a way she'd never been able to do for Gunner. For him, for the families, for her, she wouldn't stop until she did.

She and Cord had just finished breaking down their interviews when Tony rubbed both hands over his still sunburned head, wincing at the contact as he let his body collapse back in his chair. The scowl on his face matched Alyssa's mood. 'Our work on Kennedy's case has basically gotten us nowhere. From her house to the trail, Kennedy didn't stop anywhere, or at least no place that shows up on a security feed. Hal used the city's street cameras to track her drive up to the point that they're available, and same thing, so no help there. For all intents and purposes, Kennedy Farmer climbed into her car and drove straight to Coyote Canyon where she was attacked and taken.'

'What about canvassing the neighbors who couldn't be reached last night?' Cord asked. 'Anything there?'

Joe shook his head. 'Pretty much what Aubrey already told you. From everything they've seen and heard, Kennedy is quite close to her family. According to most of them, they've chatted with Aubrey more than Kennedy as she's more outgoing, though they all rushed to add that Kennedy is also friendly, just not as willing to stop and talk. No one saw anything or anyone suspicious in the area leading up to Kennedy's abduction.'

'Text messages, call log? Anything there?' Alyssa asked.

'Nothing unusual that stood out,' Joe said. 'Not that we expected much in that way. Most messages are to or from her sister or her parents with a few thrown in regarding work. We're still trying to gain access to her emails to see if that leads us anywhere, but from what we already know, I think that's going to be a dead end, as well.'

Tony nodded his agreement. 'Her employer is headquartered out of state, but we were able to reach out to her immediate boss, and some of her – not co-workers really, but co-employees, I guess. If there's animosity there, it's hidden deep. More than anything, I got the impression that they all operate more on the level of acquaintances rather than anything else, comingling only during conferences which occur once every couple of years maybe.' Tony's eyes drifted to the whiteboard.

'And I'm going to be honest; I think one of those names up there is our man anyway.'

Alyssa agreed. She studied the names and images of their three victims: Rheagan, Kennedy, and Gunner. Several colored strings ran from each person's name down to anyone or anything they might've had in common. A yellow string connected Rheagan and Gunner's age while a blue string stretched from each individual's name down to the month of May as all three had disappeared at the end of that month with Gunner going missing in May 2008. Red string traced the connections to Dr. Frank Neely while Rheagan and Kennedy also showed ties to Dr. Hoyt. There in the center, a green string stretched from the Outreach Center to Neely, Jackson, and Kennedy.

Despite all the links, a rainbow of missing pieces left a gaping hole that needed to be filled before Kennedy suffered the same fate as the other two. If she hadn't already. Alyssa shook the thought away. She would find her in time. She had to. The perpetrator – Neely? Jackson? – had left a taunting note and the disturbing image of Gunner's body for a reason, and something told her he wasn't finished trying to get their attention.

Tony drew her back with a question: 'Is it just me, or does anyone else think it's suspect that the mayor's pet project has several players in common with Kennedy, Hoyt, Neely, and hell, the mayor himself being connected to it?'

'The Outreach Center? Yeah, you're not the only one who picked up on it,' Hal said. 'Speaking of which' – he turned to Alyssa – 'after I got off the phone with you, I left a message for Hoyt to call me. To my pleasant surprise, he did. Not that he was pleased that I was calling from the APD with further follow-up questions, mind you.

He had no problem expressing his displeasure over that. Anyway, I acted like I didn't know you'd already asked if he knew Kennedy, but whew, did I pull a pin on his anger when he let me have it. He told me you'd already asked that question and reiterated that he's never met Kennedy, and that he was beginning to feel harassed simply because his son and "the victim" had had sex. Figured since he hadn't hung up on me yet, I'd ask how often he dealt with the volunteers at the Outreach Center. He's a smart man, so he picked up on why I might be asking, and he suddenly changed his song a little. Instead of insisting he didn't know her at all, he said he couldn't say for sure whether or not she "sounded familiar" since he rarely met any of the volunteers personally. Then, he offered this tidbit: as standard operating procedure, the center keeps a documented list of all volunteers on file, so he admitted there was a chance he'd come across her name at some point or another. Even admitted he could've seen her a time or two, but wouldn't know her, in his words, "from Eve."'

Alyssa once again found herself wanting to hug Hal.

'Hmm.' Everyone shifted their attention to Tony, whose face color suddenly matched his sunburned head. 'Lys, have you considered the possibility that you being on these cases isn't a coincidence? I mean, what are the odds that the one case you're never able to close out is connected to a missing person's case – now murder – that you're currently working?'

Alyssa felt as if Tony had stuck a knife in her stomach and twisted it. 'Yes, I have considered it. But I don't see how the person doing these killings could have known I would land these cases. What I'd really like to know is why, after fourteen years, would Gunner's murderer want to bring himself back into focus when he's gotten away with it for so long?'

It was Cord who provided an answer. 'To taunt you, to show you he's smarter, a better chess player, whatever. Prove he can still outmaneuver you even with more than a decade more experience under your feet.'

'Or, like Lys said, it could just be coincidence and nothing personal at all,' Hal threw out.

'Sure as hell feels personal to me,' Alyssa muttered, even though she'd just claimed otherwise.

Tony wagged his finger between Alyssa and Cord. 'I think you two might be onto something. Intentional or coincidental aside, there's no way our perp hasn't figured out by now that Lys is the same investigator on these current cases. And with that nursery rhyme taunt he left at the scene, I think he's definitely going to want to prove his superiority in outsmarting the cops, specifically Lys. In fact, I think our lack of leads will drive him to make contact again because he's not getting the proper attention that he's clearly craving. And that's going to be the weakness we exploit.'

Where some people wore their hearts on their sleeves, Tony broadcast his emotions through the pallor of his skin and in his eyes, which now flashed cold determination.

'I happen to think you're right. He's not done taunting the police – or me,' Alyssa said. 'Which makes me afraid of what that might mean for Kennedy. Gunner Galveston was murdered fourteen years ago. If his murderer didn't strike again until Saturday, then that means he's quickly escalating into dangerous territory because he took two women within hours of each other. And that means we need to work harder at finding Kennedy because we still have a chance at saving her. If we find her, we get the answers to our other questions.'

Hal tapped his fingers on the arms of his wheelchair. 'Not to be the negative nellie of the group, but we don't know if Gunner's murderer has actually remained dormant for fourteen years. I'll start searching the national database for similar crimes. In the meantime, we can't just push Rheagan's case to the side.'

'I'm not suggesting we do. But we can look at that night and compare what we know and see how we can tie it into Kennedy's disappearance. Maybe Rheagan saw something or someone, and he caught her, forcing him to shut her up before she could tell.' As she said it, Alyssa's eyes drifted back to Dr. Hoyt's name.

Joe stood and moved over to the rough timeline he'd scribbled out on the whiteboard earlier. 'But if he kills Rheagan immediately, why hold her for three more days before dumping her body?' He tapped his finger below Kennedy's name. 'And why not kill and dump Kennedy at the same time?'

'Those are some of the missing pieces we need to find,' Alyssa said. 'Which is one of the reasons we need access to Rheagan's phone records. We know her last known location pinged in the foothills, but none of our crime scene techs were able to locate it, which tells me whoever grabbed her turned it off before disposing of it. With the terrain what it is in that area, I don't need to tell you how difficult it might be to find.'

Tony leaned his elbows on the table. 'Okay, so Kennedy left around six in the evening on Saturday. From what we can determine, she'd already finished her run when she was attacked. Now, I'm not much of a runner, but you are,

Lys, so how long would a five-mile trek through Coyote Canyon take?'

'It depends. A steady jog through that terrain would likely take an experienced runner a little over half an hour.'

Tony replaced Joe at the whiteboard and grabbed a blue marker. 'Okay, so the drive from Kennedy's place to Coyote Canyon takes just under fifteen minutes, which puts her there at quarter after six. Give her a few minutes to grab her water, lock her car, and get to the trail. By those calculations, Kennedy is attacked somewhere between six forty-fiveish to what? Seven fifteen, maybe?'

The team all nodded as they latched onto the direction Tony was trying to lead them.

He moved back to Rheagan's name. 'Okay, so Kennedy is likely snatched no later than seven fifteen, and Rheagan cancels her plans with her friends around nine thirty that night. We know her mother claims to have seen her just before she went off to bed. According to the initial missing person's report you and Cord took, she noted that nothing seemed off about Rheagan that she could tell. And yet, Rheagan blows off her friends within minutes of telling her mom goodnight. We know she still had her phone with her until at least eleven, so was she planning to meet up with someone else? She leaves her house, sees our killer with Kennedy, and gets murdered for it?'

'If that's the scenario, we'd need to figure out who she might've been meeting. Did that person see something before the killer noticed him or her?' Joe looked to Hal. 'Have you turned anything up on social media, anyone or anything that connects the two of them?'

Hal shook his head. 'Nothing and no one that stands out. And as far as Rheagan goes, if she had some kind of romantic relationship with someone we're not aware of, she kept it out of all her social accounts.'

'Well, since we're talking social media, why don't we search Raider and Jackson Hoyt, as well as Frank Neely,' Alyssa suggested.

'I've already started. If there are any golden nuggets on any of our players, hopefully, I'll be able to find them,' Hal said.

Alyssa laughed. 'You're being modest, and you know it. No one in this room thinks that if there's even a hint of a nugget, you won't magically find it.'

Hal didn't get a chance to respond because Alyssa's phone rang. A quick peek down revealed the caller as the medical examiner.

'Dr. Sharp, you've caught me with the team, so you're on speaker.'

Lynn's laugh sounded forced. 'I usually am. You might just start informing me when I'm *not.*' She cleared her throat, her way of getting back to business. 'I'm not sure how much of what I've got so far will be helpful *right now*, but at least you'll have it. But before I begin, let me ask you a question first.'

'Okay, shoot.'

'I spoke to Captain Hammond. He said your team was assigned the Coyote Canyon kidnapping case. Can you describe what your victim was wearing?'

Chapter Twenty-Five

Thursday, June 2

If Lynn was asking, then that must mean she'd found physical evidence that linked Rheagan and Kennedy either to an individual or even a specific location. Alyssa mentally crossed her fingers that the medical examiner would provide some of their missing answers. 'The security footage from the Farmer residence shows Kennedy wearing a tie-dyed tank top, a pair of black running shorts, Converse sneakers, and pink ankle socks. Why?'

Through the speakers, the team could hear Lynn tapping papers on her desk. 'If I'm being honest, curiosity made me ask simply because I know the crime scene locations are within close proximity of each other. That being said, I detected a few cotton fibers embedded in the cuts on Rheagan's body. I placed them under a microscope, and they showed up as fabric from a tie-dyed material. It could be a coincidence, of course, but if not, the transfer of fibers from your kidnap victim to your murder victim puts the two of them either in the same location or, at some point along the way, with the same individual.'

Alyssa's gaze swept over her teammates' faces, each wearing varying expressions of relief that they might have physical evidence linking their cases, anger that the person they hunted was already responsible for two murders, and fear that, if he hadn't killed Kennedy yet, that they couldn't have much longer.

'I've got more information for you,' Lynn said, snapping Alyssa back from the vivid image she had of Kennedy suffering at the hands of a sadistic killer. 'In addition to the fabric bits, I discovered long brown hairs that don't belong to Rheagan. And based solely on the photo the media showed the public, I'd say the possibility is strong that they could belong to Kennedy Farmer. Of course, that's my supposition, but I've already sent them off for testing. Of course, we might need the sister's DNA to get a match if your victim isn't in the database.'

'I'm sure Aubrey Farmer will be happy to provide whatever's necessary,' Alyssa said.

'Good. I also pulled carpet fibers consistent with car mats from the victim's wounds, but without a vehicle to match them to, I'm afraid that's not going to be of much help until you catch your perpetrator.' Lynn inhaled loudly, vibrating her lips when she exhaled. 'Now for the bad stuff.'

Across the room, Tony muttered under his breath, 'How much worse can it be with a whacked-out killer going around kidnapping and slaughtering people?'

Alyssa cringed. Silly superstition or not, she always felt as if the universe took that question as a personal challenge.

Lynn, with her bat-like supersonic hearing, heard Tony's comment and chose to respond as if it weren't rhetorical. 'Not much, I'll admit. But when I tell you what I've got, I imagine you'll want to catch this guy all the faster.'

Lynn didn't give anyone else a chance to speak before moving forward. 'Several of Rheagan's teeth had been knocked out, likely when her killer beat her. I found three in her stomach cavity, along with some undigested food, which indicates she'd eaten shortly before her death.'

More than once, Alyssa had been able to track a victim's movements by their last meal. 'Please tell me you were able to determine what it was that she'd eaten.'

'I was. Rheagan's last meal consisted of breaded chicken and homestyle fries consistent with the type served at Blake's Lotaburger. Off the top of my head, I can't think of another place that sells the same type, but you'll want to check me on that, I'm sure.' She chuckled. 'And I'll tell you the truth: I'd just finished eating some fries from there when I did the autopsy; otherwise, I might not have made the connection.'

Tony's face turned a pale, yellowish green, as if the thought of eating anything before performing an autopsy turned his stomach. Alyssa had to admit she didn't blame him. She didn't think she'd be able to eat just before – or after – cutting into another human's body either.

Hal wheeled himself closer to his laptop and pulled up a map of the city, tapping the closest Blake's fast-food chain to Rheagan's house. 'There's one on Central, about an eight-minute drive from the Pembroke residence.'

Raider said he'd passed Rheagan on Central, but he'd said it had been around noon. Had he been mistaken about the time? Or lying? And if he'd been lying, had it been to protect himself or her? Had he spotted her with someone? But why wouldn't he want to tell them that? Alyssa's nerve endings buzzed. This could be the break they'd been hoping for. 'Call the restaurant and see if we can get access to their cameras. Maybe Rheagan met up with someone there.'

Lynn's sigh signaled her fatigue and weariness all wrapped up in one disillusioned bundle. 'I hope you catch her killer soon. My examination so far shows she suffered, and if the same person has Kennedy Farmer…' With no one needing the sentence finished to understand, Lynn let her words trail off before she continued with what she'd found. 'The grooves in her wrists and the way her skin is pulled away and up toward the fingers indicates her killer secured her hands over her head using handcuffs. In addition to that, the markings around her ankles are consistent with shackles. Other debris embedded in her skin included rocks, cacti needles, desert willow flowers, juniper, and pine needles.'

Tony didn't put much stock in that bit of information. 'Most of those things are natural to the landscape and terrain where Rheagan was dumped, but it's also pretty much anywhere else in the city, so I'm not sure how much that helps. But then again, at this point, it can't hurt.'

'That's kind of what I thought,' Lynn said.

Unable to sit any longer, Alyssa rose to her feet and paced the width of the room as she tried to connect more dots. 'What about the state of Rheagan's body?'

'I was getting to that next. The severe bruising on the body shows a pattern of randomness, like the killer was enraged. Yet there are thirteen stab wounds that are primarily concentrated around her heart, as if these wounds were thought out. They were carefully placed – almost with uncanny precision. And they appeared to have been performed post-mortem. I can't quite figure out what to make of that. Maybe you all can.'

The picture of Gunner Galveston's lifeless body that the killer had left for the police to find beckoned Alyssa, and she stepped closer, angling her head to cut the glare from the overhead light. Her eyes zeroed in on the multiple stab wounds below the collarbone and above Gunner's left breast, very similar to where Rheagan had been stabbed. Unlike Rheagan, however, Gunner's wrists were bound by zip ties, not handcuffs. Nor were his feet shackled. However, that could simply be an indication of how the killer had made changes in how he kept his victims subdued.

She continued studying the picture, noticing the way blood dripped down Gunner's chest, which, to Alyssa's limited medical knowledge, implied he'd still been alive when the wounds were inflicted. Her gaze drifted to Gunner's closed eyes and the way his head lolled to the side. Had the picture been taken before he died, or as he died? Had they ever even been close to finding him? Nothing in the photo gave any hint as to where it had been taken.

Alyssa turned her attention from the image of Gunner over to Frank Neely's name. Had he killed his half-brother? Rheagan? Had he kidnapped Kennedy? Lynn had mentioned sending off the hair to try to obtain DNA to see if it matched one of their victims, but what if the hair belonged to their killer and not Kennedy? She pictured both Frank Neely and Jackson Hoyt. Both had dark hair.

Something else Lynn said suddenly clicked. 'You said Rheagan's stab wounds had been administered with uncanny precision. What did you mean?'

'Only that there doesn't appear to be ripping and shredding of the tissue around the stab wounds, as if each one was precisely placed.'

Alyssa stared at the names of their primary persons of interest for the moment and tried to picture either as a cold-blooded killer. There had to be more to the story that Rheagan's body could tell. 'What about skin cells, other types of hair, blood that doesn't match the victim's?'

'Nothing except what I've told you so far, but I'm not finished with my exam. I can tell you, however, that there was nothing beneath the victim's nails, so it's entirely possible she was incapacitated before she had a chance to defend herself.'

'What about a toxicology report?'

'Haven't heard back yet. There's still a hefty backlog, so it could be a minute or two before we can get our hands on it. I'll see what I can do to move it up the line considering what you're dealing with, but I wouldn't hold my breath, especially since I've pretty much cashed in all the favors I had coming. Still never hurts to try, right? Worst they can tell me is no.'

'I appreciate the effort, and thanks for calling, Lynn.' The rest of the team echoed Alyssa's gratitude.

'No problem. I want you to find the person responsible as much as the next gal. As soon as I have anything new, I'll give you a ring. In the meantime, good luck, you guys.'

Tony was the first to break the silence after Lynn ended the call. 'I'm going to be the one who says the bad words: serial killer. If our perpetrator, whether it's Neely or Hoyt, already killed Gunner and Rheagan with the intent to kill Kennedy, what do our victims have in common besides the person responsible for killing them?' He focused on the whiteboard while he spoke. 'Two of the victims were eighteen; one is twenty-six. We know both Rheagan and Gunner were stabbed in the chest. All three disappeared in the month of May. But aside from that, nothing else bears any similarities that I can find. Not hair color, not facial shape, hell, not even gender. So, what is it about his victims that makes him pick them?'

'I've been asking myself the same questions,' Alyssa admitted. 'Maybe if Hal finds others than the ones we currently know of, we can answer that. Not that I'm hoping he'll find any. Regardless, we're going to have to update Hammond. I have to admit that I'm a bit surprised that the mayor, being neighbors with the Pembrokes, hasn't already been breathing fire down our necks to catch this guy.' She looked to Hal, but before she could begin issuing orders, he spoke over her.

'I've already started running checks on missing person's cases that have gone unsolved in the past fourteen years, with a special focus on any that seem to fit the pattern we have here.' He glanced up. 'In response to what Tony was saying, we know Gunner was going camping and that Kennedy was out running. Tony already mentioned that our killer will likely be comfortable in that type of terrain. And you and Cord both mentioned that Hoyt stated something about enjoying hiking. Do we know if Neely is an outdoorsman?'

'No, but we can try to find out,' Alyssa said.

'Good. Anyway, I've made a note to pull up cases where an arrest was made in my searches, on the chance that Neely and Hoyt aren't involved. I'll also be conducting a cross-reference to see if either of their names pops up on our list.' Hal's heavy sigh spoke volumes. 'Unfortunately, there are a hell of a lot of cases to comb through, so it's going to take some time and patience.' He tried and failed to hide his smile when everyone but Alyssa chuckled.

Because she was well aware that her team's amusement stemmed from her infamous *lack* of patience, she rubbed both middle fingers along her nose. 'Thanks, Hal.'

'Don't thank me yet. Like I said, it'll take some digging. And if we have to go further back than fourteen years – and I sincerely hope we don't – well, I don't need to tell you what that means.'

No longer feeling like they were doing little more than spinning their wheels, the energy in the room now buzzed with hope. Hope that they'd get to Kennedy in time, hope that they would find justice for Rheagan, and hope that they'd finally bring closure to Gunner's case.

Chapter Twenty-Six

Kennedy's gaze followed the man as he stepped inside the room, the dangerous glint of intent in his eyes robbing any remaining moisture from her parched throat, reminding her it had been hours, possibly days, since she'd last had water. Maybe that was how he intended to kill her, let her slowly die of thirst. Would it hurt? Would she suffer from hallucinations like someone lost in the desert?

Almost as if he could hear her thoughts, her abductor produced a water bottle from somewhere and unscrewed the cap. 'Nothing is quite as refreshing as ice-cold water going down the hatch, right? I bet you're salivating behind that tape about now, desperate for just a tiny taste.' Condensation glistened under the artificial lights as he tipped the bottle back and gulped half of it down before recapping it and tossing it outside the room. His voice slithered around her like a snake. 'If you want it, you have to earn it.' He set aside the mini recorder dangling from his left wrist and lifted the scuffed and scratched Polaroid camera he wore around his neck.

The click and whirring sound of the camera shutter penetrated the cloudy haze in Kennedy's brain, drawing her attention away from her thirst and back to what the man was doing.

'You're big news right now, a real local celebrity!' Snap, whir. 'Every news station in the metro area has your picture splashed on their screen.' Snap, whir. 'The police suspect' – he lowered his voice and peeked over his shoulder, pretending to make sure no one could hear – 'you're in grave danger.' Snap, whir. 'These' – he waved one of the images beneath Kennedy's face – 'will ensure they *know* you're in grave danger. I mean, you should see yourself right now.' His palm cracked across her face, knocking her head to the side. 'But this is what you get when you're a creature of habit, always running in the same place around the same time, in an unpopulated, uncrowded place. I mean, what did you expect when you made it so damn easy for me?'

Sharp laughter stabbed at Kennedy's head. Was that why he looked familiar? Had she subconsciously spotted him in the area before?

As soon as the snap and whir of the camera ceased, the man picked one of the photos off the floor where he'd set them while they developed and showed it to her. In it, she could see her ribs pressed against the stretch in her skin where her shirt had ridden up to expose her midriff. Her face openly expressed the stampeding emotions she had lived with since she'd been taken – terror, torment, and torture.

When her eyes lifted from the photograph, she spotted the recorder in his hand.

He pressed the red button and whispered close to her ear. 'Scream for me. Make it believable.'

Then he ripped the tape from her mouth.

As the first blow hit her kidney, she did more than scream. She begged. 'Please, please, no more. Why are you doing this to me?'

His answer was to continue punching as agonized cries tore from her dry throat.

Then he stopped and stepped back, chuckling as he did. 'That should do nicely.'

As Kennedy gasped for breath, her abductor moved outside the room and retrieved the water bottle he'd tossed earlier. His eyes glittered as he made his demand. 'Ask me politely for a drink.'

Still desperately trying to suck air into her lungs, Kennedy wheezed out a whispered, 'Please.'

He tipped the bottle, spilling some of the precious water onto the floor. 'I can't hear you.'

She licked her lips and tried again. 'Please.'

More water hit the stained concrete. 'Please what?'

Tears streaked down Kennedy's cheeks, and she swallowed. 'Please, may I have some water? Please. I'm so thirsty.'

For what seemed to be an eternity, she was sure he'd refuse, that his demand had been intended as nothing more than further humiliation. But then he stepped forward, pressed her head to the side so that her cheek touched her shoulder, and dumped what little remained in the bottle into her mouth.

Before she could swallow, he slapped a fresh piece of tape on her face, then he disappeared, and Kennedy's world returned to utter darkness.

Chapter Twenty-Seven

Thursday, June 2

The smell of French fries and greasy hamburgers wafting through the vents of the manager's office at Blake's Lotaburger caused Alyssa's stomach to rumble in hungry protest that she hadn't fed it in… she didn't even know when she'd last eaten. For that matter, she had no idea what time it currently was. She checked her watch. Three o'clock. With all their interviews, the team debrief, and the desperate drive to locate Kennedy while also tracking down a probable serial killer, food had been low on her list of priorities. Clearly, her stomach didn't approve.

Once again pushing aside her stomach's demands, Alyssa continued the tedious task of combing through the restaurant's camera footage from Saturday, the gnawing need to be *doing*, not *sitting*, increasing with each tick of the clock. Every second that Kennedy remained missing meant one more second they might find her too late.

Beside her, Cord studied the screen, muttering under his breath the entire time. 'Come on. Show us something, Rheagan. If you tell us who killed you, we can save Kennedy from suffering the same fate.'

A light knock sounded on the door, and Alyssa and Cord turned as the manager, a man in his late twenties with a receding hairline, stepped inside carrying a tray of mouthwatering food and two fountain drinks. 'You've been in here an hour already, so I thought you might be hungry. Wasn't sure what you liked, so I brought a green chile cheeseburger, a grilled chicken sandwich, and fries. If you want—'

Tempted to leap up and high-five the man, Alyssa smiled gratefully as she cut him off. 'This is perfect and extremely thoughtful. Thank you. We hope we'll be done here soon so you can have your office back.'

The manager waved her words away. 'Take all the time you need. Like I said earlier when you called, you got lucky since the recordings are only saved for six days. Tomorrow, they would've been gone. Unless, of course, you're one of those wizards who knows how to dig into the guts of a computer and pull up everything that's ever been on it. But even if you are, I'll let you get back to it.'

Cord's thanks was lost behind the closing door, so he grabbed the cheeseburger off the tray and slid it over to Alyssa before snagging the chicken for himself. Wordlessly, they unwrapped their sandwiches and resumed scouring the security camera footage.

Fifteen minutes later, their food demolished, Alyssa's hope that they'd find something spiraled like water down a drain. 'This isn't helping us find Kennedy or Rheagan's killer. We're wasting...' She stopped talking when, on the screen, Raider Hoyt walked through the restaurant's door and headed straight for the counter. It took him less than thirty seconds to study the menu before he placed his order. Then he took his ticket and strolled to one of the far corner booths where he waited for his food, played on his phone, and glanced back toward the kitchen every minute or two.

Beside her, Cord scooted to the edge of his seat and leaned forward as they waited and watched.

Less than five minutes after Raider arrived, and shortly after he grabbed his order from the counter and returned to his seat, Rheagan walked in, and both Alyssa and Cord blew out a loud breath. The time stamp in the corner read six twenty-one, a solid six-plus hours after Raider claimed to have driven by her. By the way Rheagan did a double take when she scanned the dining area and spotted Raider, it became immediately clear that their meeting hadn't been planned. In fact, if either teen felt anything but surprise to see the other, neither of their expressions showed it.

Rheagan's smile was instant but brief as she lifted her fingers in a wave, and then she approached the counter to place her own order. Raider, wearing a grin that altered his entire demeanor, set his phone down, keeping his eyes glued to Rheagan's back. Just as she started to turn around, his expression returned to one of nonchalance, like he couldn't allow Rheagan to realize how happy he was she'd walked in.

Rheagan headed straight to her neighbor's table. With no sound, Alyssa couldn't hear what Raider said, but she could read his lips as he greeted her with, 'Hey,' then grabbed a fry off his tray, rolled it in ketchup, and popped it in his mouth.

For the next thirty minutes, the two teens kept up a steady conversation, laughing or shaking their heads at something the other said while they ate. At one point, Rheagan threw her head back, her face bright red from laughing so hard. Raider's smile spread from his lips to his eyes. In it, Alyssa saw the true depth of his feelings. Despite his gruff demeanor, Raider Hoyt, at the very least, had a major crush on his neighbor.

A feeling of immense sorrow swept through Alyssa at their exchange. Nothing in their mannerisms suggested anything outside a normal, healthy interaction between two teenagers who had a relationship, be it sexual or merely friendship. And four days later, one of them would be found tossed away, battered and dead.

'I don't know what I was expecting to see exactly,' Alyssa said, 'but I suppose, in some way or another, I expected something *more* in Rheagan's personality. I mean, everyone we've talked to, Raider, her friends, hell, her own family – they all painted this picture of a wild child, but there's nothing in her mannerisms or behavior that show it. At least not in this video.' Alyssa couldn't stop the weight of sadness from leaking into her voice.

Cord cleared his throat and spoke quietly. 'I agree. All I see are two kids hanging out. Unfortunately, one of them walks out of there and has her life cut short by some sadistic bastard. But I can definitely see how Rheagan's friends knew Raider was far more into Rheagan than she was into him.'

In the video, Rheagan checked her phone before saying something to Raider and then sliding out of the booth. With her tray of trash in hand, she hesitated. Her bottom lip slipped between her teeth before she said something else. Raider's eyes popped open in surprise, but much like he'd done when she'd come in, he masked it, shrugged one shoulder, and said, 'Sure.'

Alyssa and Cord followed the split images on the screen as Raider watched Rheagan head out to the parking lot and climb into a powder blue Volvo. He stayed for several more minutes, doing something on his phone before he, too, emptied his trash, waved absently to the person standing near the cash register, and headed straight for a blazing red Chevy Silverado.

'I don't know how this helps locate Kennedy, but we do need to find out why Raider Hoyt lied about the time he saw Rheagan, and more importantly, why did he lie about talking to her on the day she disappeared.'

After thanking the manager, they headed back out, and Alyssa dialed Hammond.

He answered the way he often did – with a question. 'What did you find out?'

Alyssa and Cord filled the captain in. When they finished, Hammond asked, 'What's your next step?'

'I'm going to request that Raider Hoyt come down to the station for an official interview.'

'And if he refuses?'

'Then we'll go back to him. Either way, we're getting some answers.'

–

Just over ninety minutes later, a reluctant and nervous Raider sat in an interrogation room, fidgeting as he alternated between drumming his fingers on the table and spinning his phone.

'Thanks for agreeing to come in and speak with us,' Cord said. 'Before we get started, can I get you something to drink?'

Raider's answer was barely audible, so he cleared his throat and tried again. 'No. Thank you. I'd rather just get this over with if you don't mind. I didn't kill Rheagan, and I've got nothing to hide from the police, so...'

'We told you on the phone why we asked you to come in. And I just want to make sure you understand your right to have an attorney present if you'd like one. But right now, all we're after is some answers.' Cord's calming voice notably relaxed the nineteen-year-old, and he stopped spinning his phone.

In a move that resembled his father, Raider raked his fingers through his hair, leaving a wake of brown and sun-kissed blond down the middle. 'If I call my dad's lawyer, then I'd have to tell him why, and for real, I have no desire to do that. I'd like to keep my old man out of this for as long as I can. Forever works for me.' He shot an apprehensive grimace over at the red blinking light that reminded him the interview was being recorded.

Alyssa scooted her chair closer and dived right in with the two most important questions. 'Why did you lie about what time you saw Rheagan Saturday, and more importantly, why did you lie about not speaking to her?'

Raider squeezed his eyes closed for just a second before releasing his breath in a loud exhale. 'One, because I didn't need my dad breathing down my neck about why I was hanging out with Rheagan, and two, because I was afraid if I told you two the truth, that you'd ask more questions, and if you knew we were supposed to hook up later that night, you'd think I offed her or something.' He winced at hearing his own callous words. 'Sorry. I didn't mean it like that.'

'Did you off her?' Cord posed the question using the same vernacular.

'No! I swear. I'll put my hand on a stack of Bibles or swear on my mom's grave.' He choked back an embarrassed sob. 'Man to man, I liked Rheagan. A lot. More than she liked me, I know, but I swear, I would never ever hurt her.'

His reaction in addition to what they'd seen on the security footage convinced Alyssa the young man was telling the truth, and she told him that. 'We believe you.'

Raider's eyes became round orbs that caused the lines in his forehead to deepen. 'You do?'

'Yes. But we still need you to provide some answers.'

Relief might've relaxed the muscles in Raider's face, but his suspicion lingered. 'Okay. Here's the truth. I'd been hanging out with some friends, playing video games, but I knew my dad wanted me home early. When I left, I realized I was starving, and I didn't feel like eating with my old man, so I decided to stop at Blake's on the way home. When Rheagan walked in, it took me by surprise.' Red circles stained both his cheeks. 'I guess I'd kind of hoped she'd seen my truck in the parking lot and decided to hang, but when she spotted me, it was pretty clear she had no idea I'd be there. Anyway, she ordered her food and came sat with me. She asked what I'd been up to. I told her. Then I asked her what she'd been up to.'

The way Raider recited the events of their meeting reminded Alyssa of someone reading the minutes from a meeting – not quite monotone, but not really adding any feeling to it either.

'Rheagan told me she had plans to meet up with some friends later that night. I told her that my dad told me I had to be home early so I could head to Colorado with him. I thought she looked a little disappointed by that but figured that was wishful thinking on my part. Anyway, she asked when we were leaving, and I told her. Rheagan knows...' Catching his mistake, Raider angrily swiped at the tears that threatened to spill over. 'Rheagan *knew* how much I hated going anywhere with my old man, but Colorado is a special kind of torture because without my mom there to act as a buffer... it's just not my jam is all. I don't know why my dad ever moved us to Albuquerque anyway, for as much as he insists we go back. Half the time, he's meeting with contractors or something else, and I'm stuck at the cabin without a ride.' He rolled his eyes. 'He refuses to let me use the car because he's afraid I'll go for a joyride and leave him hanging. Besides, he thinks if I don't have wheels, I'll suddenly start wanting to go hiking all the time, like him. Anyway, Rheagan knows – knew – I'd rather do anything else than be forced to hang out with my dad. So, she asked me if I wanted to hook up later.' He shrugged. 'I said yes.'

Alyssa thought of the text sent to Bridgette Palmer. 'What about the friends she was supposed to meet that evening?'

'I figured she'd meet up with them later or whatever. I didn't ask. Didn't matter anyway because she never showed.'

'Did you try texting her?' Cord asked.

Raider shook his head like he hadn't heard correctly and then aimed a look that all but shouted that he didn't think Cord was the sharpest tool in the shed. 'Hell no. Look, I think I've been pretty clear how *my* dad felt about Rheagan and me hanging out, but her dad wasn't fond of it either. One time last year, he caught us kissing outside, and he freaked out like I've never seen before. I don't think Rheagan had either, to be honest. I don't know if her old man talked to mine or what, but my dad didn't keep it a secret about how he could and did track my location after that. Plus, my dad reads my texts pretty regularly because apparently privacy doesn't mean shit to him. And even if I deleted them, he'd spot Rheagan's number on the bill and want to know what we were talking about. Anyway, whenever Rheagan and I would decide to meet up, we'd both sneak out after our folks went to bed and meet in the park, then go somewhere else.'

'So, the last place you saw or spoke to Rheagan was Blake's on Saturday?'

'Yes, I swear it.' He raised one hand in the Scout's honor tradition, as if that sealed his comment in truth. 'I waited in the park for over an hour, but she never showed. I finally gave up around eleven or so and went back home. I walked by her house and saw her car parked out front and figured she changed her mind for whatever reason. It's happened before.' Raider chewed at the dried skin on his bottom lip. 'Actually, when she didn't show up, the first thing I thought was that she got there first and then left because I was late.'

'Why's that?' Alyssa asked.

'My dad was outside when I thought he was in bed. I had to wait until he went back inside before I could slip out without him knowing. And because I know he tracks my phone, I left it in my room.'

Alyssa looked over to Cord only to find him staring back at her. 'Was your dad in bed when you got back home?' she asked when she turned back to Raider.

Raider shrugged. 'His light was out, but I could hear his television on, so it's hard to say.'

Chapter Twenty-Eight

Around eleven that night, Alyssa admitted to herself that if she didn't rest for at least a few hours, she'd do no one, least of all Kennedy, any good, and so she finally headed home for some much-needed sleep. As soon as she turned onto her street, she spotted Holly's car parked in front of the house. As much as she loved seeing her daughter every chance she got, Alyssa was bone tired, running on fumes, and terrified she wouldn't get to Kennedy Farmer in time to save her from the same fate as Rheagan and Gunner. If Holly was here to discuss wedding things, Alyssa didn't know how many brain cells she had left to commit to the conversation. But she knew she'd do it anyway. Because she also knew Holly, understanding that her mother lived and breathed her cases until they were solved, wouldn't come to her so late about something unless she was skating on the edge of a mental cliff, something that happened with increasing frequency the closer her wedding date came.

Inside the house, she secured her service weapon and moved into the kitchen where she noticed Holly sitting at the table, her face a hodgepodge of dismay, discouragement, and relief. Which might explain why Alyssa's husband, Brock, was notably missing. Anything wedding-related, especially when it came to his overwhelmed, nervous daughter, kept him assuredly out of striking range.

Probably because he'd learned the hard and loud way when he'd once mistakenly offered his fatherly advice of, 'Don't sweat it, baby. Everything will work out just fine.'

Ghost, Isaac's Black German Shepherd, thwapped his tail against the back of Holly's chair when he spotted Alyssa, and dutifully moved over for his head rub, pressing up against her legs to get closer, a rumbling sound coming from his chest. She chuckled. Sometimes she swore he'd been a cat in a past life.

Beside Holly, Schutz, the hybrid wolfdog the Wyatt family had adopted from the same case in which Cord had adopted Carter and Abigail, raised his head almost as if he wanted to acknowledge he'd seen Alyssa come in. But almost immediately, he dropped his nose back into Holly's palm, reassuring her he would stay true to his 'protector' moniker and wouldn't abandon her like Ghost had, not even for the head rubs he so loved.

'Mom! Thank God you're finally home.' Holly gulped down the rest of her orange juice before scooting the empty glass to the center of the table. Then she pushed – or more accurately, shoved – her wedding planning book over to Alyssa. 'Look at all that. Centerpieces, flowers, runners…' Her head plopped forward into her hands, muffling her familiar complaint. When she sat back up, she pushed both hands through her hair, pulling at the ends. 'Everything is *outside*, Mom. Why does Grandma think I need all this stuff?' Sounding like a petulant teen-ager and not a twenty-one-year-old woman about to become a bride, she crossed her arms and said, '*Do* I really need all this stuff?'

Alyssa covered her laugh when she caught the gleam of hope shining from her daughter's tired eyes. 'No, sweetie, you don't necessarily need it, especially if you don't want it. So, bottom line, if you don't want it, don't get it.'

'But Grandma—'

'Will live through the disappointment because she'll understand it's her granddaughter who's getting married, not her. And yes, she might pout a little, but in the end, you and I both know she'll still be the same grandma who swears you and Isaac hung the moon and scattered the stars and are the reason the sun shines every day. So, as long as you and Nick are happy, then the rest doesn't matter.'

Not quite convinced, Holly slid down in her chair and stared up at the ceiling the way she used to when she was ten and had been told that taking out the garbage had been added to her list of chores. At the time, she'd behaved as if her parents had informed her that her job would be to go around and kick all the animals in the neighborhood.

'God, we said we wanted simple, Mom. Why isn't any of this simple?'

'Because you're talking about marriage, and that's not simple.'

'You and Dad make it look simple.'

'That's because we communicate. But that doesn't mean it's always simple.' Alyssa eyed the open bottle of wine sitting on the counter near the sink before opting for the more sensible glass of ice water. 'Honey, if you want simple, make it simple and stop trying to please everyone else. You've already got all the important elements in place. You've got the place of your dreams secured, you've got your dress, the girls have theirs, your brother and father have their tuxes, and the invitations have gone out.' She cupped her hand around her daughter's cheek and tilted her face up until Holly looked at her. 'I understand it's easy for me to say all this, but I promise, none of this needs to be a monumental deal. And one day, you'll look back – probably if you ever have a daughter who's getting married – and see that I'm not simply spouting nonsense in order to placate you.'

To her pleasant surprise, Holly giggled. 'I've got to tell you, Mom... you should've warned me that planning a wedding would make me see sides of myself I don't necessarily want to stick around. I'm pretty sure I almost scared Nick off completely the other day when I had a meltdown over the flavor of cake.'

Isaac, Holly's seventeen-year-old brother, chose that moment to invade the kitchen and raid the refrigerator and cupboards for snacks to fill his bottomless pit of an appetite. He clucked his tongue as he rummaged inside the fridge. 'I tried to warn you and Dad years ago that Sis had a darker side.' Poking his head back up, and with his arms filled with pepper-jack cheese, salami, and mustard, he closed the door and cackled like a madman when Holly stuck her tongue out at him.

'Go away, moron.'

Isaac lifted his eyebrows in the comical way he had. 'Wow, that's a bit frosty, isn't it? What's wrong with the reigning freak-out queen now anyway?'

'Shut up, Isaac. I'm not a freak-out queen, and everything's fine – or will be when you go away.'

'Yeah. That's exactly what I was thinking when I heard your high-pitched squeak trying to break glass a few minutes ago. *Wow, Holly sounds fine.*' He pointed to the book his sister had pushed to the center of the table. 'What's that?'

'What does it look like? It's a wedding planning book.'

'Not that. Whatever's on the cover.'

Holly used her finger to drag the book over. 'Oh. That's some kind of fancy flower arrangement, I guess.'

Doubt filled Isaac's face. 'If you say so. Looks more like something the dogs yakked up.'

Instead of getting mad again, Holly laughed until she started crying. 'Oh God, Mom, he's right. It does look like dog vomit. This is all – it's just a lot.'

Isaac, in the way of younger brothers worldwide, cut straight to the chase. 'That's only because you're making it that way. Stop kissing everyone else's ass and just do what you want. Easy as that.' He took a bite of sandwich and spoke around a mouthful of food, stopping only when Alyssa reprimanded him.

'Don't talk with your mouth full. You know better than that.'

He swallowed, washed it all down with his drink, and then winked at his sister. 'Besides, if you piss Grandma off, then we'll never have to argue again about who she loves best.'

Holly glared at her brother. 'You know you're only in the wedding because we felt sorry for you, dummy. We can still kick you out.'

Isaac's eyes lit up like a fireworks finale. 'Cool. No penguin suit for me. Trust me when I assure you that I've been harboring no FOMO on being a monkey in your crazy circus. But good luck telling G-ma about that decision, especially cuz, you know, I'm her favorite.'

Alyssa sighed, used to her son's penchant for speaking in acronyms but not quite up to date on all the translations. 'Do I even want to know what FOMO means?'

Predictably, Isaac rolled his eyes. Only this time, Holly joined in, and Alyssa immediately wondered if they'd done it correctly, according to Carter. 'Fear of missing out,' they said in unison.

Then, tossing a wadded napkin at her brother's head, Holly said, 'Shoo, brat. You're not helping. And for the record, as the first grandchild, I'll always be the most special.'

Isaac threw his head back and roared with laughter. Eyes watering, he barely gasped out, 'You're special all right.' Still chuckling, he bounced back out of the kitchen with all his seventeen-year-old energy, garbling, 'Hey, D,' to his father who, like Alyssa had moments earlier, chided him for speaking with his mouth full.

Alyssa hid a smile when her husband peeked around the corner, tentatively testing the waters before risking his limbs. 'Hi, baby.' He nodded to the planner. 'Should I ask or just let you and Mom hash it out?'

'It's fine. I was just having a little angst over some stuff. I'm fine now. Promise.'

Every muscle in her husband's face relaxed as if someone had pulled a plug that let out the air.

'So, what did Nick say about all this anyway?' Alyssa asked Holly.

A deep crimson crept into Holly's cheeks. 'The same thing as you.'

'Wait,' Brock sputtered. 'How come he gets away with it while I, your beloved father, get beheaded?'

Holly rose and kissed her father's whiskered cheek before laying her head on his chest and giving him a tight hug. 'Because Dad, I've had twenty-one years of experience that promises you'll still love me even when I'm melting down to my core. I've only had three of those kinds of years with Nick.'

Full of puffed-up pride, tears sprang to Brock's eyes. 'Good answer. I'll accept it, even if it's a bunch of crap.' Then he stepped back, dropped a kiss on Alyssa's cheek, and checked the clock on the microwave. 'You'd better get some rest soon, or you're not going to do anyone any good.'

When he left the kitchen and returned upstairs, Holly propped her elbows on the table and sighed, a dreamy, faraway look in her eyes. 'I can only hope that after a quarter century of marriage that Nick and I will still look at each other with as much love and respect as you and Dad.'

It was Alyssa's turn for tears. 'I hope so, too.' She tapped the case files she'd set on the table when she'd come home. 'But your father's right. I do need to get some rest because I'm going to be back at it before dawn even begins to consider making an appearance.'

That quickly, Holly turned serious, her eyes following Alyssa's hand as it rested on the files. 'That missing woman, Kennedy Farmer, and Rheagan Pembroke's murder have been all over the news lately. Anything you want to bounce off me?'

Because she dreamed of following in her mother's criminal justice footsteps, Holly's question stretched past mere curiosity. And even though she knew Alyssa couldn't discuss her cases with her, Holly couldn't stop the gleam of hope that this might be the day that changed.

'As always, I appreciate the offer, honey, but no.' Even as she said it, Alyssa thought about how much she looked forward to the day when she could say yes.

'By the way, Sophie's pretty sure she met both of them a few years back.'

Alyssa's head snapped up. Sophie and Holly, now roommates with Rachel, Nick's twin, and Jersey, Sophie's cousin, had been best friends since sixth grade. 'What? Where? When?'

'When Sophie volunteered at the Outreach Center our senior year as part of that community service project. Remember that lady she really liked that she kind of co-coached volleyball with? I guess that was Kennedy. Sophie said she liked how Kennedy always stopped to listen to the teens there and to encourage them whenever they felt beat down.'

Alyssa's blood pressure spiked. 'What about Rheagan?'

'I guess I should've clarified before I said that because now that you're all excited, Sophie wasn't one hundred percent positive the girl she was thinking of was Rheagan. Kennedy, she clearly remembers, but Rheagan, not as much. I'm sorry if I got you all worked up for nothing.'

'Trust me. It's not "nothing." I need to make a phone call.' Alyssa snatched her phone off the table and called Cord, wincing when she realized how late it was. But crime and leads waited for no one.

Chapter Twenty-Nine

Friday, June 3

With his heart on the brink of pounding out of his chest, the man slithered through the darkness, careful to keep himself obscured in the shadows of the trees and houses as he slipped around the corner. He bit his cheek to keep his laughter from bubbling out.

Fifty feet away from the house, he stopped, and shutting out the chirping crickets providing a background symphony, he studied his destination. Its darkened porch rendered the security cameras aimed there practically useless. He had half a mind to break in and slaughter everyone inside just to prove a point. But he wouldn't. Because, in the end, he knew nothing would change his mind now, not even if there'd been a bright spotlight illuminating the entire yard. Nothing would stop what he had planned.

He set his package in the cradle of some branches while he secured his hoodie so that it covered his baseball cap. And then he tugged his gator mask up until only his eyes remained uncovered. If anyone saw him now, they would be unable to make out any individual features. All they'd see was a stealthy person dressed like a ninja. With excitement hammering away at him, he had to keep himself from sprinting the rest of the way. And then he was there. Keeping his face averted from the cameras, he placed the package where it couldn't be missed, wishing he could stick around to watch the events unfold, see the expressions on everyone's faces when they saw what he'd left for them.

But he knew better than to risk exposure, risk getting caught, especially when he'd just found a way to make things more interesting.

Only after he reached a safe distance away did he allow himself to pull out one of his many burner phones.

His entire body tingled as he punched in the number and hit *call*.

Chapter Thirty

Friday, June 3

By the time Alyssa ended her calls with Cord and then Hal and forced herself to close the files before stumbling into bed, the time on her nightstand clock read three twenty-two. But from the second her eyes closed, her subconscious began its mental assault with visions of Rheagan Pembroke's battered body, interchanging with Kennedy Farmer's face as her mind conjured up the missing woman being confronted with similar torment. Just out of sight in the background, Gunner Galveston reached out mangled arms as his twisted mouth screamed for help.

Which could've been the reason she didn't hear her phone until Brock shook her shoulder.

'Lys, babe, your phone. You need to answer it. This is the second time it's rung.' Another jostle to her body, this time with slightly more aggression.

Still in that in-between state of waking and trying to clutch onto the remnants of her dream, she mumbled, 'What?' *Tired* didn't even hit the bottom of the level of fatigue waging war with her mind and body.

'Your phone!'

Brock's sharp tone finally managed to pierce her thick armor of slumber, and she flopped her hand over to her nightstand, fumbling for her phone, knocking her alarm clock to the floor before jabbing blindly at the screen, hoping at least one of the places she hit would be the *answer* button.

Jerking the phone to her ear when it stopped ringing, Alyssa fought to keep her eyes open, to stay awake, to keep her words from slurring like she'd had one too many drinks. 'Detective—'

'Detective Alyssa Wyatt,' the caller interrupted. 'Yes, I know who you are. Just like I knew who you were fourteen years ago. Right about now, you're probably wishing you knew who I am.'

Better than a jolt of espresso injected directly into her veins, the robotic voice on the other end of the line reeled Alyssa's head back into the world of wakefulness. Afraid to miss anything the caller said, she hit the speaker button, yanked the phone away from her ear long enough to check the caller ID – *Unknown Number* – and opened the app that would record the call.

'If you're calling me at' – she squinted so she could read the time – 'four thirty-eight in the morning, then clearly *you* want me to know. So, why don't we skip the games, and you just tell me?'

Her suggestion was met with nothing less than the cold, humorless laugh she would've expected. 'Please, Detective, you're going to have to do much better than that to convince me you're worthy of my time. However, to give you just a tiny hint of who you're dealing with, let me tell you a story. And trust me when I say that you're really going to want to pay close attention.'

Fully alert, Alyssa threw the covers off her legs and slid out of bed with the intention of slipping out of the bedroom... but the caller's next words froze her in place.

'Once upon a time, there was a little girl named Miss Alyssa Archer who grew up in the Crossroads of America. While there in college, she met a man, Brock Wyatt, who she'd later call husband. Pretty soon, she gave birth to a bouncing baby girl she named Holly who grew into a beautiful young woman who attends the good ol' University of New Mexico. A woman set to marry this summer. Oh, and we mustn't leave out the essential part of our story. Little Miss Alyssa Archer Wyatt also gave birth to a boy, Isaac, who just over three years ago – and here's the important part – somehow managed to escape the now infamous Two-Faced Killer. How'm I doing so far? Do I have your full attention, Detective?'

Ice replaced the blood flowing through Alyssa's veins. The caller may think he knew her, but if he did, he would've known not to drag her family's name into his demented game.

As she moved down the hall, she peeked in at a peacefully sleeping Isaac, Ghost dozing on one side. Schutz watched her move past the room before rising and following her to the kitchen. Much like her husband had.

'Have I hit a nerve there, Detective? Am I getting a little too close to home? Is your mind, right this second, reeling in shock as you contemplate how you might possibly perform your job and still protect your family from the likes of me?'

A cold calm stole over Alyssa as she moved to where she kept her service weapon locked away and pulled it out. When she turned back around, she tried not to see the fear shooting from her husband's eyes. She realized then that he'd heard everything because she hadn't taken the phone back off speaker after activating *record the call*. Beside him, his bright, watchful eyes observing her, Schutz nudged Brock's hand while pressing himself tighter into his legs.

With a huge effort, Alyssa forced herself to turn away, loosening the grip on her phone only when her fingers began to tingle from the pressure. A warning that going after her family would be the biggest mistake of his life rested on the tip of her tongue, but she also knew the caller would take her words as a challenge.

She forced any fear she felt out of her tone. 'So far, all you've really shown me is that you're adept or at least adequate at doing research. A few internet articles, a little social media scrolling, and all that information is easily discoverable.'

Part of her comment stemmed from a conscious drive to agitate the caller, but not only because he'd indirectly threatened her family. She also knew it would keep him on the phone, talking, which would give her time to focus on any background noises he couldn't filter away. Any sound whatsoever that might give her a hint as to where he was could be the one key her team needed to unlock Kennedy's whereabouts.

The man chuckled. 'Oh, you're a tough one, I see. Or so you'd like me to believe. Okay, I'll play along for a minute, and we'll see who can last longer, hmm?' He paused. 'I've been doing a lot of thinking in the past few days, and do you want to know what I've been wondering about most, Detective? I wonder – how do you think your boy would fare with me, huh? Do you think he could beat the odds twice in his life and escape me if I chose to take him? Because I've got to tell you: I'm good. In fact, I'm better than good. I'm the best. Name one infamous killer, and I can list all the reasons I'm superior. It's why you and your sort have never been able to catch me. Hell, aside from Gunner Galveston, you haven't even been able to link anyone to the trail of bodies I've already left behind. And frankly, the only reason you've linked anything at all is because I handed it to you on a silver platter.' He chuckled. 'Or on a printed piece of computer paper stuffed in a plastic baggie. But you know what I mean.'

His eerie cackle scraped against Alyssa's nerves.

'In case you aren't quite sure what I'm telling you, let me spell it out. Gunner Galveston isn't the only failure staining your past, Detective. Don't get me wrong. I'm not judging you. After all, it's not your fault you're not as intelligent as I am. Few people are.'

With each word out of his mouth, Alyssa's muscles coiled tighter than a springboard. '*Few* people are?'

The caller clucked his tongue. 'Detective, detective, detective. Hasn't anyone ever taught you that vanity is just a fancy avenue one takes toward failure? And I have no intention of failing. Every murder I've gotten away with so far has proven that to be true. It's survival of the fittest, baby. In the end, only the smartest and strongest will last.'

The rest of the blood drained from Alyssa's face. Holding onto her control by her fingertips, she let her instincts guide her, and right now, they screamed that the caller needed to boast and brag, so the longer she listened to him, the better her chances that he would slip up.

'But discussing my past and your failures isn't the real purpose for this lovely little chat. No, Detective, I've called to inform you that I've left you a little something. Well, that's not entirely true. The truth is, I left a gift at the home of one Kennedy Farmer, right where her sister can find it. In the meantime, as you scramble your team to get over there, let me leave you with one more little token – a little motivation, so to speak.'

A loud, pain-filled scream nearly burst Alyssa's eardrum, and she had to wrench the phone away from her ear. Brock's face paled before he spun around, his wide-eyed gaze bouncing between the stairs and her, as if trying to determine if he should stay in the kitchen with her or run and check on their son.

Even knowing that Isaac slept peacefully in his own bed, the need to see it again for himself won out, and Brock sprinted up the steps two at a time. Schutz took the opportunity to move to Alyssa's side, and like he had with Brock, pressed himself into her legs.

Just as Brock returned, this time with Ghost so close on his heels that he almost tripped, the screams on the other end of the line quieted into muffled whimpers, and the caller lowered his voice, his words dark, chilling, and ominous. 'I know, Detective, that you and your team are currently looking for the person attached to that scream. That's me letting you know she's still alive – not kicking but breathing at least. But I've gotta tell you: she's not looking so good, and I'm getting kind of bored with her, so you're running out of time.'

Alyssa swallowed against the nausea burning her throat and unclenched her teeth, but the caller wasn't quite finished with his threats.

'Here are the new stakes, Detective Wyatt. You and your super squad have forty-eight hours to locate Ms. Farmer, or I will kill her, ensuring her death is torturously slow, and then I will deliver her peeled skin directly to your doorstep as a reminder of yet another of your failures. And after that, I'll make sure my next victim hits a *lot* closer to your home.'

With that final warning, the caller hung up, and Alyssa wasted no time darting into action. She stumbled over words of reassurance to Brock as she raced back upstairs, threw on the first clothes she touched, and then flew out the door.

Chapter Thirty-One

Backing out of the garage and into the street, Alyssa yanked the steering wheel so hard that the tires squealed on the asphalt as she punched the accelerator. Still on the line with Cord, who'd lost the croaked sound of a frog almost immediately after answering the phone, she barked out her orders: 'Call Hal and ask if he knows of any way to isolate the background noises of a recorded call. If he can, maybe we can pinpoint this sonofabitch's location. I'm going to call Tony. Of us all, he's the closest to the Farmer residence. Hopefully he can arrive before Aubrey wakes and discovers whatever this bastard left behind.'

The faint sounds of a zipper being yanked up whispered through the cab of Alyssa's SUV as Cord breathed out, 'What if she already has?'

'She hasn't. Whatever this guy left behind, I have a feeling she'd have already contacted us. That she hasn't tells me we've still got time.'

'I'm assuming since you didn't lead with it that you didn't recognize the guy's voice?'

'He used a voice modulator, so no. And Cord, all three cases are definitely connected.'

'Then I'm hanging up so you can make your calls. I'm already on my way – I'll meet you there.' With that, Cord disconnected, and Alyssa dialed Tony.

When he answered, he was surprisingly alert. 'Lys, what's going on? What happened?'

'I need you to get over to Aubrey Farmer's residence like twenty minutes ago. Whoever took her just contacted me.' She checked the time on her dash, stunned to see only thirteen minutes had passed, not the half hour it felt like. 'He claims he left a package for her.'

The string of curses that left Tony's mouth would've made a sailor proud. The thump of his fist hitting something preceded him stringing his next three expletives into one long word. 'Shitdamnhell. Did he say what he left? When he left it? That son of a rat's bitch.'

If the situation hadn't been so dire, Alyssa might've enjoyed Tony's creative and colorful language. 'No, but there's more. He's given us forty-eight hours to locate her before he kills her.' In her head, Alyssa could still hear the chilling vow the caller had made, and goosebumps erupted all over her skin. Through clenched teeth, she told Tony the rest, temporarily omitting the part about leaving Kennedy's skin on her doorstep. 'He threatened to go after my family next, specifically Isaac.'

'That mother—Dude must have a death wish. What a twisted—' The sound of Tony's slamming truck door caused Alyssa to miss the rest of his muffled comment, but she thought she had a fair idea of what he'd said.

'And there's that,' Alyssa agreed, the black hole in the pit of her stomach expanding. 'Whatever it is that he's left behind, his intent is to maximize the shock value and capitalize on the horror while taunting us with his supposed genius.'

'It's not just us he's taunting,' Tony warned. 'We're the cops. We might not like it, but we can handle it. The victim's family, however, might not be as prepared.

I mean, who the actual hell would be, outside of law enforcement? Shit, not even all of us could find a way to compartmentalize long enough to bring this asshole down.'

'Whatever it is he left, I'm sure it'll be something that will fuel our worst nightmares about what he's doing to Kennedy. He wants us to see what she's enduring while we scramble to locate her. And I know this sounds awful, but I'm trying to look at the bright side here, which is as long as he's not lying about giving us forty-eight hours, then that means Kennedy's still alive, and we can save her.'

'I sure as hell hope you're right about that.'

'Believe me, so do I. But right now, I'm hoping whatever he's delivered will give us a clue first to where he's keeping her and second to his identity.'

'All right. I'm about six, seven minutes away now. I'll call you as soon as I get there.'

With Hammond next on her list, Alyssa jumped when her phone rang. She peeked at her caller ID, surprised to see Tony's name again. 'Yeah?'

'What about Joe? Anyone give him a holler yet to fill him in on what's up?'

'Not yet. I called Cord, then you. Cord was reaching out to Hal—'

Tony cut her off. 'I've got Joe then. I assume you're about to contact Hammond?'

'Yep.'

'All right then. I'll let you get back to it. And Lys?'

'Yeah?'

'Let's beat this bastard at his own game!'

'That's the plan.'

After filling Hammond in, Alyssa hit her sirens and punched the accelerator, rocketing well past the speed limit, all while praying the traffic would remain light a little longer. As she drove, the three cases hammered at her in a dizzying array of information. Rheagan's body had been dumped just days after her reported disappearance. Tomorrow marked one week from the day Kennedy had been abducted. And now Alyssa had been given forty-eight hours to find her before she met the same fate as the other two. Apprehension that she'd fall short once again and fail Kennedy the same way she'd failed Gunner and even Rheagan caused her to increase her speed even more. She shook her head, wiping away the negativity. She had to believe this time would be different, that she'd get to Kennedy in time.

Without considering the early hour, she rang Ellie, her partner before Cord and the one who'd assisted on Gunner's case.

It took three rings before Ellie's groggy voice picked up. 'Lys, long time. What's going on?'

'It's a long story, and I'm sorry for waking you, but I've been meaning to call you, and now's the first chance I've had. Do you remember the Gunner Galveston case?'

'Of course.' Ellie yawned. 'I'm still pissed about the way Captain SOB ripped that case from us. It didn't have to go to the cold case files!'

Alyssa smiled at Ellie's secret nickname for the captain she'd had no respect for. 'Yeah, well, you're about to get more pissed. On Monday, Cord and I took a missing person's report for an eighteen-year-old girl who went missing in the same general area where Gunner's parents used to live before he disappeared. On Wednesday, her body was discovered with a folded copy of Gunner's tortured body placed inside a sandwich bag that was stuffed inside the victim's mouth.'

Ellie sucked in an audible gasp. 'What the…! That sick sonofabitch.'

'And then some,' Alyssa agreed. 'What do you remember about that case?'

Ellie snorted. 'I remember how every lead turned into one dead end after another, as if the killer was purposely laying down false clues for us to follow, to make us look like fools. I remember how every time we cleared a suspect, I wanted to bang my head into a wall.'

What was so sad about Ellie's statement was that more than once, Alyssa had found her ex-partner tapping her head against the table in frustration. 'What about Frank Neely? What do you recall about him?'

'Not much. I remember him flying in to be with his parents, consoling them, kind of taking charge in a way. I remember when his alibi checked out, and we cleared him from our persons of interest. And I remember after his parents died how he came in, practically foaming at the mouth, blaming us that we had gotten nowhere on his brother's case. Why? Do you think we made a mistake in clearing him?'

'I don't know. But I can tell you he's connected to two of my current cases.'

'Wait. You just mentioned one. There's another?'

'Like I said, long story, but short answer, yes. More than that, Hal's been able to cross-reference our past suspect list with our victims, and no one links to either case. Except Frank Neely.'

Ellie whistled. 'But his alibi checked out. He was in Arizona at university at the time of his brother's disappearance. What could we have missed?'

'I don't know. Maybe nothing. We have another person of interest, so I'm not saying Frank's guilty in this, but he's not looking innocent either.'

They talked about Gunner's case another three minutes before Alyssa finally ended the call with a promise to keep Ellie posted.

Then, not wanting to wake Aubrey or the neighbors, she killed the lights and sirens two blocks from the house.

–

By the time she turned into the neighborhood, Alyssa's stomach had tied itself into an enormous knot. The tangled wreck of nerves wreaking havoc with her insides loosened the slightest bit when she spotted Tony's truck already parked in front of Aubrey's driveway. Just as she hopped down from her Tahoe, Cord pulled up and parked behind her.

'At least most of the lights are still off,' he said, tipping his head toward the house. Save a soft glow from some type of night light, the house remained dark.

'Yeah, at least we got that going for us.' Using the streetlight to help illuminate the path of his finger, Tony directed their attention to a small, nondescript brown box barely visible at this distance. 'Can't say for sure, but I'm assuming that's the package in question. I just finished snapping some pics and was about to move the thing when it occurred to me that we might need to call in the bomb unit. Just in case.'

A sense of unease gripped the back of Alyssa's neck. 'I sincerely doubt an explosive is this psychopath's end game because that would take all the fun out of his taunting. Regardless, I'd already thought of that, too, and since we can't take that kind of risk based on a hunch, Hammond's already agreed to send someone out to meet us here. They'll use one of their robots to test it for – whatever the hell they test for. Once they give the green light, we can take custody of the package.'

'What about Farmer?' Tony asked.

Alyssa sighed. 'Well, unless one of you can come up with a better idea, I think we're going to have to knock on her door, wake her up, and fill her in on what's happening on her front porch. The last thing we want is for all the commotion of the bomb-sniffing robot to startle her into opening her front door and tripping over that box. Especially if my gut is wrong, and some kind of explosive is waiting to be triggered. Either way, I think it's best if we get her out of the house and away from the property.'

'And the neighbors?' Tony asked.

This time, Cord shook his head. 'Any explosive that box might contain isn't intended to blow up the entire area. If Alyssa's right, and I tend to think she is, then whatever's in there is meant to intimidate, scare, and rattle both law enforcement and the family.'

After checking the time on her phone, Alyssa said, 'We have a few more minutes before the bomb squad arrives, so let's go alert Ms. Farmer.'

Chapter Thirty-Two

Two hours later, with the sun now shining inside Aubrey's windows, Alyssa sat beside Cord at Aubrey's computer. Footage of the home security played across the screen. While Alyssa and Cord watched the video, Aubrey fluctuated from hovering over their shoulders to flitting to her door, as if half expecting the person who'd kidnapped her sister to appear.

If only he would.

Alyssa thought of the contents of the box which she'd been careful to keep Aubrey from seeing. After the bomb squad's robot images depicted no explosives inside, Tony had opened the package to discover what amounted to handfuls of dark brown hair inside a plastic baggie, as well as a small torn piece of fabric that matched the tie-dye shirt Kennedy had been wearing. Worse than that, however, had been the pile of Polaroid pictures that flaunted the young woman's torture. Her arms stretched awkwardly as her skinny frame pulled on the metal cuffs attached to a bar above her head. The shackles around her ankles cut noticeable grooves into her skin, similar to the ones found on Rheagan's body.

Dark purple, green, and yellow bruises dotted Kennedy's stomach, arms, and legs, and one side of her face appeared to have a boot print on it. In each photograph, her terrified eyes shifted toward her assailant. In them, Alyssa could see her silent screams for help, see the confusion in her mind as she wondered why this was happening to her. In all the images but one, her mouth was sealed with duct tape. A typed note accompanied the contents of the package, the words chilling in their threatening simplicity. *I wonder how much louder she can scream*. In red ink, he'd drawn a hammer below the words.

Reading those words and seeing the picture proof of Kennedy's suffering boiled inside Alyssa's gut.

Was this what he'd done to Rheagan? Gunner? Even if the caller meant what he'd said about giving them forty-eight hours, Alyssa wasn't sure Kennedy would survive that long, which meant they had to find her faster.

Already Tony and Joe had rushed to get the package and its contents off to the lab for DNA and other forensic testing that might put a name to their suspect. At Alyssa's request, Hammond dispatched a dozen officers to assist in canvassing the neighborhood and checking out any home security cameras in the area in the hopes that one of them would've picked up their assailant.

While the officers assisted with that, Alyssa and Cord stayed behind to scour Aubrey's security video.

When Alyssa's phone rang, she and Cord both stiffened until they saw Hal's name flash on the screen. Earlier, she'd asked Hal to reach out to the Pembrokes to find out if Rheagan had somehow been involved at the Outreach Center. With fingers crossed that he had some of the answers the team desperately needed, she answered the phone. 'What'd you find out?'

'I'll cut straight to the chase: we now have verification that Rheagan did volunteer at the center about four years ago. Well, actually, she was supposed to volunteer, but apparently, she mostly hung out and played volleyball. Same with Raider Hoyt.'

Alyssa sucked air in through her teeth. Cord arched one brow in question, but Alyssa didn't want to risk saying too much in front of Aubrey. She tipped her head toward the porch, letting Cord know where she was going, and he nodded his understanding before returning his attention back to the security footage.

Outside, she headed to her Tahoe and leaned against it. 'Okay, did I hear that correctly? Raider Hoyt and Rheagan volunteered at the center at the same time?'

'You heard correctly.'

'Why?'

'Well, from what I could gather, Rheagan and Raider snuck out one summer night about four years back and wreaked a bit of havoc in their neighborhood. Happened around July, so I'm guessing this was after the incident with the amusement park ride.'

'What kind of havoc?'

'The kind where they took a bat and smashed in some mailboxes, egged a couple of garages, TPed a few houses, things of that nature.'

'How did they get caught?'

'One of the neighbors happened to be getting home late from a business trip and saw the two of them running from his house. He checked his security cameras and recognized them immediately. Long story short: the other neighbors involved got together and told Dr. Hoyt and the Pembrokes that if they agreed to cover the cost of repairs, they wouldn't report the vandalism to the police. They agreed.

'Dr. Hoyt decided that part of Raider's punishment would be to volunteer at the Outreach Center, and when the Pembrokes heard about it, they decided it sounded like something Rheagan might also benefit from.'

Clearly, that had been before either parent decided the two teens shouldn't hang out together. 'I don't suppose Mr. Pembroke knew whose idea it was to vandalize the neighborhood, did he?' Not that it mattered, but Alyssa was curious.

'I thought you might ask, and according to Ben, Raider claimed it was Rheagan's idea, and when confronted, she didn't deny it. Nor did she confirm. He also admitted his wife was quite "sick about the decision." She thought placing their daughter around "riffraff" – her words, not mine – was too harsh and potentially scarring for a young girl who'd just had the misguided judgment to pull some harmless pranks.'

Alyssa's eyes rolled to the back of her head that, once again, she saw evidence where the Pembrokes could've drawn a line to show their daughter they cared.

'I guess Barbara spoke to the mayor's wife about it, and it was she who convinced her – Barbara – that it might be good for Rheagan to see what kind of hardships other kids had to endure on a daily basis. She thought it might give her a different perspective, or at the very least, be an eye-opener. So, Barbara finally agreed, albeit a bit reluctantly still. As it turns out, Rheagan enjoyed hanging out and talking with the kids she met there, though I guess she didn't maintain any of the brief acquaintances after that summer, something which Ben claimed Barbara was relieved about.'

'I think we need to dig into anyone who was involved with the Outreach Center during that time,' Alyssa said.

'I can't help but feel our answers are there somewhere. We know Jackson Hoyt and Frank Neely are or were connected to the Center, and we also know Neely is connected to Gunner Galveston. We know Gunner's connection isn't through the Center because it didn't exist when he was murdered, which means the common denominator goes back to Frank.'

'That was the same path my mind followed, and so I reached out to the mayor to see if he could email us a list of all the volunteers from over the years. You know, because I figured asking one of our *suspects* for it might not be such a wise idea. As soon as it hits my inbox, I'll have Joe and Tony get to work on contacting the individuals on it. And Hammond's already pulling in a few officers to help us out. I think we're close, Lys. I can feel it.'

'We better be. We only have forty-eight hours. Less now.' With that, Alyssa ended the call and headed back inside.

She'd barely closed the door behind her when Aubrey reappeared in the area between the kitchen and living room. Twisting her pajama top in her hands, she whispered in a voice scratchy and hoarse from crying, 'If you don't mind, I think I'd like to go take a shower.' Her puffy eyes drifted from her computer, where Cord still sat, to her front door and then down her hall before finally returning to Alyssa. 'Will you, um' – she cleared her throat and ran a crumbled tissue under her red-tipped nose – 'stay here until I get out?'

Without thinking, Alyssa reached out and touched Aubrey's hand. 'Of course. We won't leave until you're finished.'

Aubrey gave a weak nod before plodding off. As she watched her go, Alyssa felt a familiar tug in her heart, knowing from her own experience how quickly one's existence became reduced to walking around helpless, numb, and paralyzed with disbelief that any of this could be happening.

As soon as she heard the bathroom door close and the shower turn on, she filled Cord in on what Hal had said. 'I know I've already mentioned this, but I still don't understand why this guy wants to bring himself to the attention of the police now, after all these years. Why risk capture? Something isn't adding up; it doesn't make sense.'

Cord rubbed both palms down the front of his face, his heavy sigh showing his high level of fatigue and frustration. 'You said it yourself earlier. He doesn't think he's getting the proper notoriety he thinks he deserves. And if he's not lying about more than the three victims we know about, then he's starting to crave attention for his kills, which to me, means he's escalating and making him even more dangerous to the public.'

Alyssa thought of both Frank Neely and Dr. Jackson Hoyt and reviewed what she knew of both men. When his half-brother disappeared, Neely was in Arizona – an alibi that had panned out at the time. If that was true, then he couldn't be their killer now.

But what about Jackson Hoyt? According to Dr. Sharp, the stab wounds to Rheagan's body had been "precise," something a doctor would have experience in. He would also have access to debilitating drugs that would incapacitate his victims. Not that they had any proof of that sort of thing. And without a toxicology report, that aspect stood as mere speculation on her part.

Regardless, both men were tied to the Outreach Center, Rheagan Pembroke, and Kennedy Farmer. Her instincts said one of them had to be their killer. But they needed more than circumstantial connections to get a judge to issue a search warrant on either of their properties, residential or business.

Cord tapped her arm. 'Here, look at this.' He rewound the video until a person dressed in dark attire, face covered completely except for his eyes, appeared on the screen, and then hit pause. Alyssa moved in closer, trying to see if she could determine the man's identity, but though his eyes weren't covered, they were lowered. Even if they hadn't been, she had to concede it would've been too dark to tell anything. Though not surprised at the way their suspect kept his features concealed, disappointment still gnawed at her.

'If he walked in from this direction, maybe he left his car parked somewhere nearby, within two, three blocks.' Cord turned to Alyssa. 'Or maybe he lives nearby.'

'Hal's already accessing any city cameras in the area, noting any vehicles, bicyclists, or even pedestrians, especially within a two to three-hour time frame of the package being delivered. We know from the time stamp that he made the call to me shortly after dropping it, but that doesn't mean he hadn't been in the area earlier. If there's something there to find, Hal will find it.'

Alyssa listened to make sure the shower was still running before she said, 'No matter what Hal or the officers canvassing the area find or don't find, I won't be stopped like I was before. I *will* catch this guy and bring him down. He may think he's gotten under my skin by threatening my family, but what he doesn't seem to realize is that with me landing this case and him making it personal, he just cemented his own downfall.'

A muscle ticced in Cord's jaw. 'You're right about that last part, cementing his own downfall,' he agreed. 'But you're wrong about something else. *You* aren't going to catch this guy and bring him down. We *all* are. And that's a promise I intend to keep.'

'I stand corrected. But speaking of my family, I need to step outside again and call Brock. I'll be just a minute.' On the porch, she pressed the picture of her husband and listened to the phone ring.

'Babe?' The vibrating timbre of fear in her husband's voice stabbed Alyssa right in the chest.

'I've got a lot going on, so I can't talk long. I know you heard… It doesn't matter. I've been thinking… Holly's wedding is right around the corner, and things are going to get pretty hectic, so maybe now's a good time for you and Isaac to slip away for a father/son camping trip up in the mountains. Just for a few days.'

Alyssa loved that Brock asked no questions, just dove right in as if her random suggestion to spontaneously drop everything and head out of town was the most natural idea in the entire world of ideas. Of course, he understood as well as anyone that while her job remained in law enforcement, her top priority would always be her family. And despite the killer's threats, he knew she'd never allow anyone to rob Isaac of the hard-fought peace he'd finally managed to attain in the last three years.

Chapter Thirty-Three

Friday, June 3

Throughout his life, the man's father had pounded two unbreakable rules into his head: first and most importantly, sissies deserved whatever happened to them; survival of the fittest, he'd called it. And when the day came, did the world want a bunch of 'whiny bitches' in charge, people too afraid to do whatever it took to get the job done? One time, and one time only, the man had asked his father what he meant by 'when the time came.'

His father had glowered at him with disgust and told him if he didn't know, he was part of the problem.

The second rule was a lot simpler and easier to understand: if you're going to be the best at something, you'd better make damn sure people appreciate your hard work; otherwise, what was the point?

After searchers found Austin Rolling's body, his parents had been watching the news coverage. When the man walked into the room, his father had narrowed a laser-like stare at the cut on his hand before turning back to his mother. 'Kid and his folks were always sniveling about something. Maybe if he hadn't gotten himself into that situation, he'd still be alive. Survival of the fittest, after all.'

His mother, avoiding both his and his father's eyes, remained silent, the tightening of her lips the only indication she had an opinion at all.

And then, for the first time in his entire life, his father had looked right at him – not through him, not over him – but dead at him – and said, 'When you're the best at what you do, the world doesn't have to know your name; they just have to appreciate your work.' Then he'd patted him on the back, repeated, 'Survival of the fittest,' and walked away.

His father couldn't suspect what he'd done. Could he? He'd never asked, and his father never said. Five years later, both his parents were dead. Murder/suicide. His mother had served his father with divorce papers two days earlier, and he hadn't taken the news well. With their deaths, they also took to the grave the secret of whether or not they'd suspected what he'd done.

But with every one of his kills, he heard his father's voice clear as day: *The world doesn't have to know your name; they just have to appreciate your work.*

And now it was time for his work to be recognized and appreciated. It was time for him to be able to walk among the public as they cast nervous glances over their shoulders and stared intently at every stranger they passed, wondering if that individual was the person responsible for striking terror into the hearts of the nation. It was time the world knew him as the super predator he was.

He hadn't stopped to think; he'd just anonymously placed a call to a random news anchor regarding the little gift he'd left earlier for the detective. He didn't worry that the journalist wouldn't air the segment because selling fear to the public was a surefire way to jack ratings and readership. And he was about to amp up the fear.

By brazenly kidnapping the son of the detective working the case.

He hadn't known he was even thinking it until he'd said it to Wyatt, but now the very idea consumed him to the point that he found himself studying Google Maps and planning. He didn't worry himself that the detective would actually find Kennedy; there was no way she could.

He typed Isaac Wyatt's name into his search engine, scrolling until he found a picture posted on Instagram of the grinning, sweat-drenched teen holding a soccer ball beneath one arm while he draped the other around his mother's shoulder. Two dogs, one white and one black, stood on either side of the pair. He printed it out and added it to the pile of articles he'd already amassed on Wyatt's team.

Then he resumed play on the morning news program and watched as the cameraman focused on the Farmer house from down the street because the police still had the area cordoned off. In the background, Detective Wyatt stood with her back to the camera as she spoke to a couple of officers. Their eyes followed where she pointed, which happened to be the direction from which he'd approached the house to drop off the package. He grabbed the remote and turned the television off. After locking his research away, he grabbed his Modafinil and popped one of the pills into his mouth. He didn't need it for its boasted benefits of enhancing his mood and improving his memory; he needed it to keep him awake.

Because, for now, he had another role to play.

Chapter Thirty-Four

Friday, June 3

After learning that Aubrey and Kennedy's parents were finally, after a number of delayed and cancelled flights, en route to the States and would be in late this afternoon, Alyssa and Cord were ready to leave the Farmer residence. As they walked to their vehicles, Alyssa spotted a media van parked outside the police barricade where the same two officers she'd been speaking to earlier stood. Both cops ignored the woman's questions while they waited for Alyssa's okay to let traffic in and out of the area again. She acknowledged them with a wave, and they moved to their cars to open the street.

The news reporter, Shelby Morningstar, one of the few Alyssa happened to like and respect, summoned her closer instead of shouting out her question like the media were prone to do. And then she surprised Alyssa again when she gestured for her cameraman to stop panning the crime scene and cut the feed.

Alyssa turned to Cord. 'I've got this. Why don't you head back to the precinct and get started on these new developments.'

Cord eyed the reporter like he did most of them these days, with disdain. 'You sure about that?'

'Yep. I've got it under control. I'll make it short and meet you there ASAP.' As soon as Cord drove away, Alyssa strolled past the neighbors' houses to see what the reporter wanted.

'I'd say good morning to you, Detective, but I'm guessing your being here predicates the very opposite.'

'I've had better,' Alyssa agreed.

'So, full disclosure, I'm going to tell you something, but it's partly because I'm hoping you'll give us an exclusive interview, at least when you solve this case.'

Alyssa arched one brow but remained silent, committing to nothing.

Shelby smiled, understanding she'd have to go first. She waved her hands around her before looking back at Alyssa. 'Okay, first, yes, the station has aired the fact that the police were called out to this location, but not why, at least not yet. However, you might've noticed there are no other reporters here, which should make you wonder why I am. But don't worry; I'm not going to make you guess. I'll just tell you.'

Already suspecting what Shelby would say, the burning abhorrence that had been building in the pit of Alyssa's stomach since finding Rheagan's body on Wednesday grew. 'What did he say?'

A fraction of a smile lifted the corners of Shelby's mouth. 'I'm not even going to ask how you knew. He left an anonymous message – using a voice modulator – on my phone at the station that said he'd left something for Aubrey Farmer to find. I don't suppose you'll tell me what that was?'

'I don't suppose I would right now.'

'Fair enough. For now. Off the record, at least for the time being, why is Kennedy's kidnapper contacting the media? Most criminals like to stay underground, so to speak. Is there something the police haven't shared that we should know?'

Alyssa couldn't help but chuckle at the slight manipulation. She avoided giving an answer by asking another question of her own. 'What did the message say besides that?'

'Nothing. Your turn now.'

Alyssa sighed. 'Look, you know I can't share any details of this ongoing investigation, but if you hear from him again, please call me directly. It goes without saying that I mean contact me right away. And since he reached out to you, I'd like to send one of our techs over to get a copy of that recording. Anything we can get our hands on to help us track him down will help.'

Disappointment flashed across Shelby's face, but she didn't push for more details, one of the reasons Alyssa found that she didn't mind working with the anchor. 'Would you mind if I request an exclusive once the case is solved?'

'I wish I could promise that, but it's not my department. I'm sorry.'

Shelby nodded her acceptance, and the two parted ways with Shelby wishing Alyssa luck. Without Cord sitting in the passenger seat for her to talk things out, Alyssa found her mind drifting back to Gunner's case as she drove. The caller this morning had mentioned a trail of bodies and that Gunner hadn't been his first kill. That detail removed any doubt of Raider Hoyt's possible involvement, not that she'd ever actually suspected him. But it still left the door open for his father as well as Gunner's much older half-brother.

Per Hal's research, aside from the time Neely lived in Arizona while he attended university to study psychiatry, his primary residence remained in New Mexico. As a psychiatrist, Neely would have access to prescription drugs. As would Jackson Hoyt, who, again, according to Hal's research, had lived in New Mexico for at least sixteen years. Before that, his residence had been outside of Durango, Colorado. She let her mind drift to the shadowed figure on Aubrey's security cameras. Both Neely and Hoyt had similar builds and were of a similar height to the individual who'd left the package.

In other words, she couldn't rule out either man. Her ringing phone blasted through the silence of the cab and disrupted her thoughts. Without checking the caller ID, she answered. 'Detective Wyatt speaking.'

The sound that burst through her speakers resembled a gibbering chipmunk and made just about as much sense. She checked the name on her screen and shook her head. 'Sorry, Hal. I didn't catch that. Start again.'

'I said you're not going to believe this, but I just got off the phone with a possible witness to our guy dumping Rheagan's body. Cord was here when the call came in, and he's already on his way, and so is Liz, so they'll meet you there.'

Alyssa signaled her lane change so she could pull off the side of the road and input the address into the navigation system. 'What was the caller's name, and did he – or she – say why he waited so long to contact the police?'

'Arman Ramsey, and he did. Apparently, he rarely listens to the news, but this morning, he had one of the talk radio stations on, half listening, until someone called in and mentioned something about crime in the city, specifically Kennedy Farmer's kidnapping right after

Rheagan's body being discovered in the Tramway Arroyo. At first, he didn't think much of it, and then he heard that Rheagan had been found on Wednesday morning, and he remembered something. He thought it might be nothing but decided to call us just in case he was wrong.'

Alyssa did her best to temper the rising hope that this possible witness would give them something more to go on than what they had, something that would lead them to the identity of this narcissistic sociopath that they needed to take off the streets. Not only was he responsible for at least two murders, but Kennedy's life still hung in the balance. And now there was the added threat the man had launched against her own family.

–

Close to eleven and armed with a rough composite sketch of the person Arman Ramsey had spotted near the Tramway Arroyo somewhere between the hours of eleven forty-five and midnight on Tuesday, Alyssa, Cord, and Liz Waterson, a team member when she could be and the best forensic artist in the state as far as Alyssa was concerned, stood outside the witness's house.

Between the three of them, the air buzzed with electricity, chasing away the near stupor that set in after the adrenaline had worn off, reminding Alyssa she'd gotten less than two hours' sleep.

Liz practically bounced on her feet as she patted her shoulder bag containing all her sketch materials. 'I can't explain it, but I think this is going to be the break you all needed.'

Years ago, shortly before Cord became her partner, Alyssa had solved the murder of Liz's sister, and from then on, the artist did everything she could to help the team out whenever she could, though it was with less frequency lately as her skills were in high demand all over the state. Like Hal, her personality lent itself more to the glass–half–full outlook on life, despite her family's personal tragedy. Still, Alyssa felt the same way. What Arman Ramsey had described essentially amounted to a blob of darkness with the shapeless form of a body garbed in dark sweats and a hoodie, the inappropriate attire for summertime being what had grabbed Ramsey's attention to begin with. And yet, she had that itchy feeling along her skin that told her they were getting closer.

If it hadn't been for a gust of wind that had blown their suspect's hood and cap off his head, temporarily high-lighting him in the edges of Arman's oncoming headlights, he might not have taken the time to notice. Ramsey had described the person's hair as 'long enough to flop up in the wind, darkish, and probably not straight.'

What excited Alyssa was that the description could apply to both of her primary suspects. What frustrated her was the same thing because they still couldn't exclude one over the other. 'I only wish Ramsey had paid attention to the type of vehicle the man had.'

'Yeah, well, guess he was more concerned about watching out for the animals that have a tendency to dart out in front of cars up near the canyon,' Cord said. 'Be that as it may, I'm convinced the person we saw on Aubrey's security cameras this morning and the guy Ramsey described are the same person. It's only a matter of time now before he slips up and we nail him.'

Alyssa pressed the button on her remote, unlocking her car doors. 'Yeah, well, the clock is ticking, so the quicker we get back to the precinct and fill everyone else in, the faster we can stop this sonofabitch.'

By eleven thirty, the entire team, including Liz now, were all congregated back in the conference room. Foregoing greetings, Alyssa nodded to Hal. 'Tell us what you found.'

Hal clicked a few keys on his keyboard and cast the contents of his research on the wall for everyone to see while he spoke. 'Like we discussed, I ran a check for any past cases that bore similarities to what we're dealing with. And then I weeded out the ones that had been solved, as well as ones that occurred prior to thirty years ago.'

Joe interrupted. 'I thought you were only going back fourteen years.'

'Yeah, well, I decided I needed to go further. Especially after this morning's claim to Lys here that Gunner Galveston wasn't his first.'

'Narcissistic sociopathic sonofabitch,' Tony muttered just loud enough for the team to hear.

Like he was aiming a gun, Hal mock-fired at Tony. 'Bingo. We already know we're dealing with someone who's been around this block more than a few times, even if Gunner was his first murder, which we don't know. Worse, I'm convinced he's going to keep escalating, especially now that he thinks he's got us by the balls.'

The way he and the others shot unguarded glances in Alyssa's direction told her the 'balls' Hal referred to were in direct connection to the threat against her family, specifically Isaac. 'Brock and Isaac are going to head out to the mountains for some guy time, so they aren't in danger right now.' It was touching how her team needed reassurance almost as much as she did.

Hal nodded. 'That's a good idea. Anyway, regardless of how many bodies this guy's left behind, experience and instinct tell me we're probably not looking for a career criminal, at least as far as misdemeanor crimes go. Branching off Tony's comment, I do think we're looking for a narcissistic sociopath. He's manipulative and has the ability to outsmart authorities, so I don't think he's going to have a history of petty, minor offenses. He's far too methodical and organized for that.'

With his lips tightening into a thin line, Hal's doggedly determined eyes swung around the room as they landed on each member of the team. 'I don't care how successful this guy's been in the past in his ability to go undetected by authorities, the moment he contacted Alyssa was the very second he handed us our first real lead. We *will* stop this bastard before he can make good on his threat to go after her family.'

Alyssa didn't have to see the staunch expressions on her teammates' faces; she knew with absolute certainty that they had her back – and her family's, too. Just as she had theirs. 'Yes, we will,' she agreed before returning the focus back to their suspect's mindset. 'Reaching out to taunt me tells us that he self-characterizes his importance as more grandiose than he's getting credit for. His arrogance, his sense of entitlement is driving his need for validation of the crimes he's committed.'

Her gaze drifted over to the names of their two primary suspects. 'And if Frank Neely is indeed our guy, then the fact that *I'm* on the case again has boosted his confidence and fed his ego. In his mind, I've already failed once where he's concerned, so he's already predetermined I'll fail again. He's wrong, but let him think it because that'll make him sloppy. And if it turns out Neely isn't the man we're after, the perpetrator still knows about my involvement in the Galveston case, and so the same theory applies.'

Hal's head bobbed up and down. 'Exactly. And since the man's kills haven't garnered him the proper adulation he feels he's due, he *needs* us to recognize his genius, but also how dangerous he is.' He waved his hand toward the images of Kennedy, Rheagan, and Gunner. 'Exhibits A, B, and C.'

Cord sat forward and leaned his arms on the table. 'Exhibit D is the fact that he's contacted the media himself. And like Hal said, that just means he's more likely to trip up and make a crucial mistake.'

The smile that stretched across Alyssa's face fell short of reaching her eyes. 'That's going to be his downfall, and frankly, I'm not a bit opposed to us helping along the way.'

'I hope he does it sooner than later,' Joe muttered. 'I need some sleep.' Hearing how that might've sounded, his face flushed scarlet. 'Sorry. That just slipped out. Didn't mean to come across like a heartless asshole. Like I said, I'm tired.' He shrugged, lifting his hands in the air, palms up. 'What else can I say?'

'That's about all you *can* say, man. Don't worry. We all get you.' Tony clapped his friend on the back, the sound sharp as a whip being cracked against flesh. When Joe winced, Alyssa figured it probably hurt more than Tony realized.

Hal shifted so his cursor hovered over an audio box in the corner of his screen. 'Speaking of helping our guy along the way, that decision to record his call was a great idea. As soon as Alyssa forwarded it to me, I went to work. After I made a copy, I sent it off to our tech guys for a deeper analysis. In the meantime, I started dissecting it which enabled me to isolate some of the background noises, including Kennedy's scream. Listen.'

Whether consciously or subconsciously, everyone scooted forward in their seats and leaned in with their heads cocked to the side.

The moment the mechanized voice mentioned Isaac, Alyssa's brain triggered the memory of the day she'd come home three years ago and realized her son had been kidnapped. Swishing, static-like scratches screeched through the speakers on Hal's computer, and while the noise made her and everyone except Hal cringe, it helped her shove that terrifying time back where it belonged.

'What the hell was that?' Cord asked.

Hal played it again. Better prepared, the sound was slightly less abrasive the second time around. When the audio clip ended, he answered Cord's question. 'I can't be one hundred percent, but I think it's the wind. Which, can we all agree, has been off the charts this spring, including last night and this morning?' He waited for the team to nod. 'Right, so listen again. But pay close attention to the point where our perp stops talking because I managed to manipulate the audio so that Kennedy's screams aren't quite so distinct.'

Despite the fact that Kennedy's scream fell to a somewhat muted level, the young woman's tortured cries still tormented Alyssa. On the third playthrough, she finally thought she understood what Hal hoped they'd hear. 'It's almost... silent... in the background.'

Tony shot up straight. 'You're right. No wind, no dogs barking, no crickets, no cars. No... nothing.'

Hal grinned. 'Like he's not outside.'

'More than that,' Tony said, his voice pitched a tad bit higher as his words tried to keep up with the tumbling thoughts in his brain. 'There's *nothing*. Like he's in a soundproofed room somewhere.' His eyes widened. 'That wasn't live audio of Kennedy Farmer; it's recorded.'

Cord's eyes bored into Alyssa's. 'Keeping her in a soundproofed room shows premeditation. He knew he'd need to make sure no one heard his victims while he tortured them.'

'That might be true, but it doesn't tell us where he's holding Kennedy.' Alyssa turned back to Hal. 'What about past cases?'

'Well, after weeding out the ones that didn't fit our search parameters, what I found was that, of those remaining, none seemed to fit our guy's pattern.' He waited a beat. 'At least not in the state of New Mexico. That being said, I discovered three in Colorado that signal enough close similarities to what we're dealing with now that I took note.'

Alyssa's heart tried to jump out of her chest. 'Where in Colorado?'

'I'll give you three guesses, but you're only going to need one.'

Everyone except Liz made the connection at the same time, giving the answer together. 'La Plata County?'

'Told you that you wouldn't need more than one,' Hal said.

Chapter Thirty-Five

When Liz aimed her baffled expression in Alyssa's direction, Alyssa explained the importance. 'One of our primary suspects is Dr. Jackson Hoyt, Rheagan Pembroke's neighbor and the current director of the Outreach Center where Kennedy Farmer volunteered up until January of this year. After Rheagan's body was discovered up at Tramway Arroyo – a very short drive from Hoyt's neighborhood – we had to wait to interview him and his son until they returned from Colorado where he's currently building a new center in the La Plata County region.'

Alyssa turned back to Hal. 'How difficult would it be to look up building permits in Colorado to find out who the contractor is?'

'I'm already on it. I've got a buddy in the area who confirmed a new center is indeed going up, and so I asked if he'd mind driving over there and reporting back what he saw. It's still in the beginning stages, but on the fence surrounding the area, there's a big sign with the construction company's name. My buddy looked up the number and sent it to me, and right now, I'm waiting to hear back from them. As soon as I do, we should know if Hoyt's alibi checks out.'

While he was talking, Hal's phone chimed with a text message, and he peered down to read it. 'I'll be damned.' He grabbed a cord and plugged his phone into his laptop, explaining as he did. 'I asked the gal in charge of the city's website if she could check the archived photos from when the Center was built.' His cat-ate-the-canary grin had everyone sitting up straighter. 'And now we have irrefutable proof that Jackson Hoyt came into contact with Kennedy Farmer at least once.' He tapped a button on his phone that projected his screen onto the wall.

'What you are looking at, ladies and gents, is what my source called one of the mayor's many campaign photo ops.'

A total of eight people could be seen in the picture. The mayor posed with Jackson Hoyt and one other individual while three others, clearly unaware they were being photographed, hit a volleyball back and forth over a net. Just off to the side, almost out of the image, Kennedy Farmer wore an intent expression as she listened to whatever a young girl was saying to her. While Alyssa couldn't be positive, from the side, the girl resembled none other than Rheagan Pembroke.

It took a great deal of restraint for Alyssa to stay seated instead of rushing to Hammond's office. She knew he'd want more than just an old photograph to approve the request she was about to make. 'Tell us what you discovered about the cases up in Colorado, Hal.'

Hal clicked on one of his open tabs. 'I'm still waiting on some return calls, but I'll tell you what I know so far. All three of the cases I flagged were within a fifty-mile radius of where Dr. Hoyt has been building his center. Still, I have to caution that this is solely circumstantial information right now.'

'You're right, unfortunately, and as much as I'd love to request a search warrant for Hoyt's property, nothing we have so far is concrete enough to convince a judge to sign off on one. At least not yet.'

'Besides finding him standing right next to Kennedy Farmer wherever he's keeping her, how much more do we need? Why does it always seem like the damn criminals have more rights than the victims?' Tony's questions may have been rhetorical, but they all understood his frustration, especially when someone's life was at stake.

'I know Tony's being sarcastic about finding evidence that puts Hoyt with Kennedy in the moment, but he's actually on the right track,' Alyssa said. 'Hal, can you search property records and see if he's got land anywhere else in New Mexico? It's got to be close because he has to be able to move effortlessly back and forth between his practice and home without bringing attention to himself or his movements.'

'What about the center itself?' Joe threw out.

Hal shook his head. 'Doubt it. It's one story, so where would he hide someone? Plus, that's taking a pretty hefty risk that no one will stumble across a young woman suspended from a bar and looking like she has a starring role in a horror film. No. Wherever he's got her – if it *is* Hoyt – then it's gotta be somewhere else.'

'What about his current property?' Liz asked.

Alyssa thought about it. 'It's possible, I suppose. But like Hal just said, if he's keeping Kennedy prisoner at his house, he risks his own son finding out his secret. Is he that stupid?'

The expression on Tony's face spoke volumes. 'He might see it differently. Instead of it being stupid, he thinks it proves how good he is. He can hide his victims right under his own kid's nose, and worse, in Rheagan's case anyway, his victim's family's.'

Tony leaned back, his head swiveling from the picture of Rheagan's body in the arroyo to an enlarged image of one of the Polaroid snapshots of Kennedy. 'I'd suggest seeing if Hoyt has a cabin in the mountains somewhere, but if he does, even an hour's drive away would be noticeable if he does it often enough. No, it's gotta be Albuquerque. Lots of places in the metropolitan area a person could hide someone if he wanted. We just have to find where that is.'

Liz slid her sketchbook out of her bag and opened it up to the composite. Her eyes shifted from the sketch to the image still projected on the wall from Hal's phone and back again. Finally, she looked up and said, 'I don't know about you all, but I think the witness's description of the person he saw matches Hoyt's build.'

'Unfortunately,' Alyssa said, 'it also closely matches that of Dr. Frank Neely, so as much as it's looking like we've got a bead on a prime suspect, we can't rule out the other just yet.'

Joe tipped back in his chair. 'Didn't Jackson Hoyt's wife die of a drug overdose five years back?'

Alyssa, along with the rest of the team, looked in Joe's direction. 'Yes, why?'

Joe shrugged. 'Don't know. Might be nothing. But Hoyt's a doctor, so he would know about deadly drug cocktails. What if his wife's death wasn't accidental after all? What if she found out about his little pastime, and he killed her for it?'

A chill rippled through Alyssa at the thought.

'You have a good point.' Cord directed his next question at Hal. 'Do any of the cases you discovered in Colorado coincide with Evelyn Hoyt's death?'

Hal nodded. 'One. Perry Singleton, age nineteen, from Juan Lago, Colorado. It's a small town of about two hundred and forty year-round residents about thirty miles outside where Hoyt is currently building his center. At the height of the tourist season, when Singleton went missing during their annual Summerville Festival, it's nearly four times that. I placed a call to Chief William Porter, but again, I'm waiting to hear back.'

While Hal spoke, Alyssa opened her email and played the home security footage from Aubrey's residence. Despite the baggy clothing, the person on the video shared a similar build to that of Hoyt. Using the trees surrounding Aubrey's house, she estimated the man's height to be close to six feet tall, give or take an inch. The same guesstimated height of the man Arman Ramsey described. The same height as Dr. Jackson Hoyt.

Chapter Thirty-Six

Friday, June 3

Dizzy, faint, and with an unbearable scratch at the back of her dry throat, Kennedy could do little more than track her abductor's feet as he moved back and forth. She struggled to concentrate on what he said, but she found even that to be too much.

His palm slapped sharply across her face as he growled, 'Are you even listening? I told you I have some good news.' He checked the expensive-looking watch on his wrist. 'In less than forty-eight hours, this will all end for you. You'll either be dead, or the cops'll find you.'

Instant fantasies of being rescued had Kennedy lifting her head before it promptly dropped forward again, straining the muscles at the back of her neck.

Sinister laughter erupted from the man. 'That got your attention, didn't it?' He tipped his head to the side until he could peer up into her face. 'Don't worry. I'll make sure the cops find you, but it won't be here, and you'll already be dead. I told you – no one but me ever leaves here alive.'

Something about the way he sang the words in a lyrical fashion scratched at Kennedy's memory, but it slipped away the second her abductor produced a bottle of water seemingly from out of thin air. Her eyes latched onto his fingers as he unscrewed the cap. The sandpaper at the back of her throat burned as he tugged at a corner of the tape covering her mouth. If she could salivate, she would.

She should've realized his cruel game, but she didn't until he tapped her cheek and whispered near her ear. 'Just kidding. This isn't for you.' And then he guzzled the water and tossed the empty bottle behind him.

Kennedy wanted to cry. Instead, she just prayed for her suffering to end one way or another. As her eyes drifted closed, she heard her father's voice demanding she hold on. The firm command tripped another memory when she and her family had been on vacation. She and her father had just stepped outside the hotel so they could meet up with her mother and Aubrey when a loud rumble shook the earth and then the building. Within seconds, the entire structure crumbled to the ground, trapping Kennedy inside the rubble for an interminable thirteen hours until rescuers could reach her. Days later, when she'd refused to look in a mirror at the scar permanently marring her face, her father had sat down beside her, wrapped one arm around her shoulder, and touched the puckered skin. 'This, Kennedy, is not a disfigurement. This is proof that you survived something hundreds did not. Never forget that.'

Her father's voice volleyed around in her head, whispering, *You survived that; you'll survive this, too. Find a way, Kennedy.*

With her hold on consciousness slipping, she tried to latch onto hope, but like a ghost, it flitted away, leaving her only with the promise of her abductor's words. The police would find her, but she'd already be dead.

Chapter Thirty-Seven

Friday, June 3

Before they left to speak to Hammond, Alyssa asked Hal to work his magical charm to get Judge Rosario to issue a ping warrant for Jackson Hoyt's phone. Joe, Tony, and Liz were working to see what kind of financial information they could gather as it pertained to coinciding with the Colorado cases. But mostly she had them digging frantically to see if or where Hoyt tied to Gunner Galveston because if they could find that link, Alyssa was positive they could haul him in for further questioning and possibly even obtain an arrest warrant.

With the avowed forty-eight hours flying by, Alyssa and Cord crowded into Hammond's office and ran down everything they had and suspected, ending with, 'Which is why we need you to approve a twenty-four-hour, round-the-clock undercover surveillance team until we can get that last piece of the puzzle worked out so we can obtain a warrant.'

Steepling his fingers together beneath his chin, Hammond leaned back in his chair, quiet as his mind turned over this new information. The seconds stretched out before them, wearing on Alyssa's patience. Just as she thought she might snap, the captain said, 'A pediatrician without a criminal history, with good standing in the community, not to mention one who is committed to his work at the Outreach Center... If you're wrong about this, and the doctor gets wind of it, I don't have to tell you that the department will face some serious backlash. Especially if Hoyt involves the mayor, who lives close enough that they've probably stopped to chat it up in the neighborhood once in a while.'

Alyssa tried not to bristle. Not that she didn't agree with the captain. It just rubbed her the wrong way when wealth and position sometimes took a front seat to whatever evidence glared them in the face.

'I understand that, sir. Which is why we're requesting *undercover* surveillance.'

'If you're sure it's him, why not request a search warrant for his property and be done with it? Why the covert operation?'

'One, we aren't one hundred percent sure, but he's certainly where the evidence seems to be leading us. Two, because if we *are* right, the fact that Dr. Hoyt has, like you mentioned a moment ago, no prior criminal history, means he's not only smart but cunning. He knows the law, and he knows how to avoid capture. I'm afraid if we show our hand now, there's a risk we'll never find Kennedy Farmer, and that's not a gamble I want to take. If, however, Hoyt remains ignorant of the fact that we're closing in on him, there's the chance that he could lead us to wherever he's keeping her.'

His gaze steady, Hammond asked, 'You think she's still alive? That your caller meant it when he claimed he'd give you forty-eight hours?'

Alyssa couldn't see how that made a difference, but before she could respond, Cord jumped in.

'Absolutely. That she's alive, not that the caller was being honest about the forty-eight hours.' The captain raised his brows in a way that suggested he needed more information, so Cord explained. 'No body. What we can pull from all these cases is that once Hoyt tires of the game, he kills the victim and dumps the body.'

'Plus,' Alyssa added, 'the early morning call to me strongly suggests Hoyt's overactive ego is going to make him want to boast about how he's bested the authorities, specifically me, once more.'

'Careful, you two,' Hammond warned. 'Right now, Hoyt might be your primary suspect, but until we have actual proof, let's avoid affirmatively naming him as the killer.'

'Noted,' Alyssa said as Cord nodded his understanding.

Hammond placed his elbows on his desk and wagged one beefy finger between them. 'Your argument's sound, so I'll give you two days. It's the start of the weekend, and if Hoyt's our guy, hopefully he'll lead us to Farmer sooner than later.'

'Thanks, Captain.'

'I'm not finished. If it starts looking like you're barking up the wrong tree – or even if it's the right one – and we're not any closer to zeroing in on Kennedy's whereabouts, we'll need to revisit this conversation.'

'Understood,' Alyssa and Cord agreed.

'Then assemble the people you want, and I'll clear it. But rest assured, Detectives, if your evidence starts looking murky, or I suspect tunnel vision where you're seeing things that aren't there… or are there, but they're getting twisted to fit a preconceived notion… well, you don't need me to spell it out for you.'

Alyssa stood with the door open. 'No, you don't. Not any more than I have to spell out the obvious: never once have I or anyone on my team given you reason for that type of concern, nor do we intend to start now, which I'm going to assume you actually know already. So, I'm going to choose not to be insulted by that speech.'

Hammond maintained a straight poker face as he aimed his heavy stare in her direction. For several heartbeats, neither blinked nor looked away. Finally, he said, 'Let me know who you pick for your surveillance team,' which was his way of announcing the matter was resolved, and she and Cord had been dismissed.

Chapter Thirty-Eight

Friday, June 3

While Alyssa and Cord secured a surveillance team and caught them up to speed, stressing the importance of speaking to absolutely no one, even to their comrades within the department, as well as ensuring that someone, at all times, had eyes on Dr. Jackson Hoyt, both at his home and his practice, Hal was running down what leads he could regarding the unsolved murder cases in Colorado.

Heath Love, Alyssa's first choice for their eight-member surveillance team, slapped his palms down on the table and hefted his hulking six-foot-four, two-hundred-pound frame to his feet. 'All right. Let's do this. It sounds like this guy is observant and careful, so he might spot a tail, especially if he starts to become paranoid about being caught. I propose we run two shifts with people in position to watch his house and work simultaneously. Because we're looking at a serial, we'll remain paired up at all times.' He peered around the room, making eye contact with each person on his team. 'At no point do we leave our partner alone. If torturing people gets this guy off, nothing'll stop him from taking out a cop if he suspects he's being watched. Now, let's work out the logistics of scheduling. I'm willing to take the night shift. Who's with me?'

Heath's take-charge attitude was one of the main reasons Alyssa trusted him as much as anyone else on her team, why she always first chose him whenever they found themselves in need of an extra pair of hands. Knowing he would take the information she provided and do what needed to be done, she excused herself. 'Looks like you've got this under control, so I'll leave the rest up to you. As soon as you hammer out the details, loop me or Cord in. If you can't reach one of us, get ahold of Hal, but remember, because of who we're dealing with, especially as he has indirect ties to the mayor, we have to keep this on the downlow. If Hoyt gets wind we're onto him, it will spell game over, not only for Kennedy Farmer, but for stopping him, because I have zero doubt he'll pull up stakes and disappear. And if that happens, our chances are shot.'

Energized with the possibility of locating Kennedy before Hoyt could kill her, Alyssa realized she sounded almost breathless with anticipation. Like Cord had explained to Captain Hammond, Kennedy had to be alive, or he would've dumped the body already. And he would've called to gloat even before they'd found her.

His drive for attention would be his downfall. Plus, his reaching out to her and the media contributed to a theory she'd been chewing on, that the need for attention consuming him indicated an emotionally unstable person. His already diminished to absent capacity for remorse coupled with a man on the brink of losing control ensured him slipping up. And Alyssa had every intention of being there to catch him at the fall.

As she left the group, Dr. Sharp called. Plugging her ear with one finger to mute the others in the room, Alyssa moved to the door with the intent of closing herself in her and Cord's shared closet of an office. 'Lynn, give me a second to get somewhere where I can hear you,' she said. Maneuvering one of the two chairs facing their desks out of the way, she finally managed to close the door. 'Sorry about that. What do you have?'

'Well, I'm not sure. I'm still waiting to hear back on the toxicology report and the DNA results we sent in, so nothing there. But that's not the reason I'm calling. I requested a copy of Gunner Galveston's forensic report so I could compare it to Rheagan's. Before you ask, they're not the same. The weapon used to stab Galveston had to be long enough to hit bone. The puncture wounds on Rheagan, however, are smooth and neat, slicing right through her muscles and connective tissues. Remember when I mentioned the stabbing appeared more deliberate?'

'Yes.'

'The smoothness of these cuts strengthens that theory.'

'What kind of knife could've made those cuts?' Alyssa asked.

Lynn hesitated before answering. 'Something used in the medical field, possibly a scalpel, though I can't say with one hundred percent certainty that that's what it was.'

Overcome with the urge to shout and pump her fist in the air, Alyssa forced herself to take a deep breath instead. Like she'd warned her team, a growing mountain of circumstantial evidence was all they had right now, and she didn't want to pigeon-hole this news by forcing it to fit. 'Lynn, you don't know it, but you just helped cement my belief that we have the right suspect in our sights. Thanks for the call.'

'Always. I want you to catch this guy at least as much as you do.'

Alyssa stopped Lynn before she could hang up. 'You mentioned something earlier about the presence of a variety of tree species.'

'That's right. All which were consistent with the terrain where Rheagan's body was discovered, as Tony, I believe, pointed out. Why?'

Those things weren't only consistent with where Rheagan's body had been dumped, they were also consistent with Dr. Hoyt's backyard. 'Still trying to piece things together and wanted to make sure I had my facts straight. Thanks again for the update.'

'Absolutely. As soon as I hear back regarding the DNA, you'll be the first person I contact.'

Bit by bit, though more slowly than Alyssa would've liked, the pieces of the puzzle were falling into place. She could only pray they'd be able to complete the picture in time to save Kennedy.

Chapter Thirty-Nine

By the time Alyssa rejoined Cord and Hal in the incident room, the two of them were already several minutes deep into a video call with Chief William Porter from Juan Lago, Colorado. She pulled up a chair and joined the conversation, offering a hello when the chief paused long enough for Hal to introduce her.

'This is Detective Wyatt, lead investigator. She's also the one who headed up the Gunner Galveston case that I mentioned. So, you can see she has that much more motivation to see if your cases are connected to each other and ours.'

'I have no doubt whatsoever that the same guy killed all three of the victims here. More, I hope the information I provide helps you nail this guy. Nothing leaves a taste as nasty as the one where you know you've let a family down because you failed to solve the murder of their loved one.'

'You're right,' Alyssa said. 'And we appreciate you getting back to us so quickly.'

'I just finished telling Detective Roberts and Mr. Callum that we have three unsolved murders that took place out here over a period of twelve years. Like your Galveston case, Bella Teller, the only one of the three who was local to Juan Lago, was eighteen years old when she disappeared on May 20, 2005. School had just let out, and she and some friends were out celebrating her acceptance into some fancy New York art college. Being a small town of less than three hundred, I can assure you lots of folks recognized her that night. None of them reported seeing Bella talking to any strangers. At the end of the evening, close to midnight, her friends dropped her off, something her mother verified because, out of habit, she'd been up waiting for her daughter to return home before she slipped off to bed. Being a single mom after her husband died in a mountain biking accident, Mrs. Teller tended to lay down some pretty strict rules for her kids,' he explained.

'Anyway, that's where things fell apart,' Porter continued. 'Mrs. Teller saw Bella come home and the girls drive off, and she went on up to bed. She never listened for Bella to come in because she wanted to avoid an argument over what her daughter called her "overprotective hovering." The next morning, she went in to ask Bella about her night and noticed her bed hadn't been slept in. I'll cut to the end here; when Mrs. Teller went outside, Bella's phone was lying near the tree line of their property, as was her purse. There were clear signs of a struggle, and Mrs. Teller called us immediately. Needless to say, we launched a search right away. But you have to understand, the area we live in is rugged and off the beaten path, so it's easy to disappear.'

'How long before you found her?' Alyssa asked.

On the screen, Chief Porter wiped one hand down his face and leaned back in his chair. 'One week. The sonofabitch left her body in the woods right near her house, a place we'd thoroughly searched. That and the lack of blood in the area told us she'd been killed elsewhere. And with that many stab wounds, there would've been a lake of blood.' The lines around the chief's mouth tightened. 'She was nude from the waist up, and the bastard used a black marker to write *She screamed* on the part of Bella's stomach that hadn't been sliced to ribbons.'

A cold heaviness settled into Alyssa's bones as she thought of the note the killer left with the Polaroid pictures of Kennedy. 'Had Bella been sexually assaulted?'

'Autopsy saw no evidence of that type.'

'You stated there were signs of a struggle. Were you able to obtain any DNA samples from where Bella fought back against her attacker?'

By the hard expression that settled over Porter's face, Alyssa knew the answer. 'No. The medical examiner in Boulder County, where the autopsy was performed, indicated the severe burn marks on Bella's hands came from sulfuric acid. According to the doctor, it appeared her hands had been soaked in it, which told us Bella must've scratched her attacker, and he needed to make sure we didn't find his DNA.'

Anger and sadness gripped Alyssa in equal measure at the image Porter painted. And while she hadn't really expected the autopsy to reveal a DNA profile, she'd still had to ask. 'What else can you tell us?'

'Sadly, not much. The toxicology report showed traces of fentanyl, and the medical examiner noted an injection mark on Bella's neck, which we determined her killer used to subdue her. We worked that case day and night for months with not a single lead. Not one. So, either the perpetrator got damn lucky... or more likely, knew how to cover his tracks. That case is still open, and I vowed I wouldn't retire until we found Bella's killer and brought him to justice.'

The way the chief clenched one fist while the other rubbed the back of his neck revealed how the anguish of the unsolved case had never left him. Alyssa understood the feeling. 'Well, I'm hoping we can help you with that,' she said softly. 'What about the other two cases? You said Bella was a local, meaning the others weren't?'

'No, ma'am. Faith Dexter, twenty-two years old, lived in Durango but liked to hike our trails. Some of the locals knew her well enough to chat with her whenever she stopped in, but not enough to really know anything about her. We didn't know she'd gone missing until her boyfriend showed up a couple of days after she was supposed to have returned home. Off the top of my head, I can't remember the fella's name, but I can promise you we checked his alibi, and it was airtight.' Porter held up his left hand and pointed. 'Two of his fingers got damn near hacked off when the piece of wood he was sawing slipped. So, he was in the emergency room. We interviewed him, all of Faith's friends, family members, co-workers, and everyone else, but nothing ever panned out.

'When we found her body up on one of the more remote trails, we knew it was the same guy because, just like with Bella, the bastard wrote something in black marker on her stomach. Only this time it said, *She begged for her life.* Aside from what he'd written, the only difference between Bella and Faith really is that we found evidence that Faith had been killed where we found her body. Oh, and she had no stab wounds. Instead, she'd been severely beaten, and I mean to the point of permanent disfigurement had she somehow managed to survive. The medical examiner stated she'd seen mangled car wreck victims with less trauma done to their bodies. Unlike Bella, however, no drugs came back in the toxicology reports. That, coupled with the autopsy report revealing a near-fatal blow to the back of Faith's head, led us to believe her killer likely took her by surprise and never gave her much chance to fight him off.'

A chill slid down Alyssa's spine. Something told her by the time this was finished, and they brought this guy – Hoyt? – down, there'd be far more bodies than the ones they knew of and the three suspected in Colorado.

Cord rummaged through the papers in front of him, searching for something. Not finding it, he asked, 'When did Faith's murder occur?'

Chief Porter turned toward an open laptop off to the side. He scanned the information until he found the answer. 'Eleven years later, on August 27, 2016.'

'What can you tell us about Perry Singleton's case?' Hal asked.

The way his creaking chair groaned under his weight, it sounded like Porter's entire body took part in the heavy sigh he released. 'You know, before all this, the last murder in Juan Lago took place fifty years ago when a couple visitors to the area got into a drunken brawl, and one of 'em shot the other before he realized what he'd done and turned the gun on himself. Now, we have three open cases rotting like spoiled milk in my gut.

'Perry Singleton, nineteen, was from the Boulder area and had come for our annual Summerville Festival that runs from Memorial Day weekend to the following Sunday, which in 2017 ran May 27 to June 4. We get close to twelve hundred people trekking through our little town during that time, but things don't generally get out of hand. Anyway, Singleton wasn't reported missing until the final day of the festival when everyone was packing up and going home.'

'Who reported him missing?' Cord asked.

'A couple buddies he'd come with. They said the last they saw him, he'd been heading to the restroom and then he planned on stopping by the barbecue food truck to talk to one of the girls working there. When we showed the gal his photo, she didn't remember him but admitted that she didn't really get a chance to look at too many of the people they served because they were so busy. Once again, we hit one dead end after another. Even the feds, who we called in to assist, with all their advanced training, got nowhere.

'Unlike Bella and Faith, we didn't recover Perry's body for close to nine weeks, when a family out camping threw a ball for their dog to fetch. Instead of that, he returned with a human bone. They went searching and found a body in a severe state of decomposition. We confirmed Singleton's identity through DNA, but we knew from the description of what he was wearing that it was him.'

A sense of hopeless frustration tried to weave its way into Alyssa's head. If the killer was so good that not even the feds could track him, what made her think he'd slip up enough for her to do so? She shoved the pessimistic thought away so she could concentrate. 'What about the forensic evidence?'

'With the crazy weather we'd been having and the state of decomposition, we were told that the potential for locating a kernel of salt in a pile of sand would be easier than recovering any forensic evidence. In other words, nothing of note.'

Glass half full as usual, the tone of Hal's voice gave no indication that he thought they were butting their heads against a wall. 'What about the official cause of death?'

'Singleton had… what was it called… hydro—hyder… wait, hyper-inflated lungs, that's it. When I asked him what the hell that meant, the ME said it indicated there had been "interference with the boy's airway" is how he put it.'

'So, strangled?' Hal clarified.

'The ligature marks detected around the neck suggest that's what happened. The ME also noted a high number of puncture wounds along the victim's stomach and spine, but according to him, they'd been inflicted to torture, not kill.'

Alyssa asked, 'Toxicology report?'

'A heavy dose of fentanyl was detected, and according to his family and friends, Singleton didn't use opioids.'

Alyssa turned the information over in her head, but she wasn't quite convinced Perry Singleton's murder was the handiwork of the killer they believed to be Jackson Hoyt. Until Porter added one last detail that sent a jolt through her entire body.

'One more thing. We kept this next bit away from the public, but the killer left a child-like note with the body.'

'Do you recall what it said?' Alyssa held her breath.

'Not only do I remember, it still makes me want to sleep with all my lights on. *One, two, three, four; I wish I'd had time for more.* The last two lines were more of a taunt than a rhyme. *If you're worried if he suffered, I assure you he did.* The killer drew a huge smiley face on the bottom of the note and colored it yellow. But that wasn't all. He also left a Polaroid picture of Singleton handcuffed to a metal bar above his head.'

Alyssa, Cord, and Hal all stared at one another, their thoughts as clear as if someone had written them on their faces. The murders were connected to their current cases, which meant that Gunner Galveston hadn't been their suspect's first victim, nor had he been dormant in between

Gunner's murder and Rheagan's. They no longer had a single doubt they were dealing with a serial killer. The only questions that remained were: was Jackson Hoyt that killer, and where was he keeping Kennedy Farmer?

'We appreciate your time, Chief,' Cord said. 'Do you happen to know if the three victims were buried or cremated?'

'Burial. I attended all three of the services myself. Are you considering the possibility of exhumation?'

'If it comes to that, we might need to,' Cord verified. 'How do you think the families will react?'

'If it means putting an end to the person who killed their loved ones, they'd all put their hand on a stack of Bibles and swear they built the moon out of cheese themselves. In other words, I don't think you'll get any pushback from that direction. Now, before I let you go, can I ask for the name of your suspect?'

Though she'd warned the surveillance team to keep the name of their suspect under wraps, Chief Porter didn't live in Albuquerque, and Alyssa felt like he deserved to know. 'Dr. Jackson Hoyt. Does the name ring a bell?'

Porter tapped his fingers on his lips, thinking. 'Not off the top of my head. But I'll keep my ears and eyes open, see if his name pops up anywhere else on the radar. If it does, I'll be sure to contact you right away. I hope you're on the right track and you nail this man to the wall using spikes. Preferably sooner than later. Please keep me apprised of the situation, and of course, if I can offer any assistance, I'll be more than happy to do what I can. Hell, I'd like to drive down and be the one to slap cuffs on him myself.'

After promising to keep in touch, Hal ended the video call. Alyssa, unable to sit still another second, jumped up and moved over to the whiteboard. She touched her finger to the names of each of the victims both here in Albuquerque as well as those from Colorado.

Bella Teller, Faith Dexter, Perry Singleton, Gunner Galveston, and Rheagan Pembroke. At Kennedy's name, Alyssa added a silent prayer that Aubrey's twin wasn't murder victim number six. Or would it be seven, if it turned out Hoyt had actually given his wife a deadly cocktail of drugs after she somehow stumbled across his activities?

Taking a step back, Alyssa studied their rudimentary timeline. 'We need to find the proof that puts Hoyt in each of these places at the time of the murders. Which means we'll need warrants to pull his financial and phone records.'

Cord joined her at the whiteboard. 'With five murders all spread out over seventeen years, it begs the question: does his list of victims go even further back than we think? And why the big lapse between the 2005 murder and Faith Dexter?'

'Well, first, remember, Gunner went missing in 2008. But that still leaves a gap of eight years before Faith's murder. Still, I wonder that, too,' Alyssa admitted. 'We know Hoyt moved to Albuquerque sixteen years ago – so that's what, 2006? – from La Plata County, which puts him right there. We also know he maintains a cabin in Colorado, so the possibility of more victims certainly exists. But how does he pick them? Aside from Kennedy, they're all relatively close in age, but looks and build… nothing matches.'

Already clicking away on his keyboard, Hal said, 'I'll run a deeper background check, see how far back I can go. Should be easy enough to find out if Hoyt's parents are still alive or if he has any siblings, where he grew up, et cetera.' He glanced up, the look on his face serious. 'Give me a little bit of time, and I'll be able to tell you what he liked to eat for breakfast when he was six years old.'

Alyssa checked her watch. Already seven o'clock. Where had the entire day gone? 'I hate to remind you, but we don't have a whole lot of time here, Hal. I'm going to touch base with the surveillance team.'

As she waited for Heath Love to answer, Alyssa's gaze fell across the smiling image of Kennedy Farmer, whose eyes seemed to follow her around the room. 'Hang on a little longer Kennedy. We're moving heaven and hell to get to you in time.'

She didn't realize she'd spoken the words aloud until she heard Hal whisper, 'Heaven and hell and everything in between.'

Chapter Forty

Filled with a sort of peaceful quiet, Kennedy concentrated on taking one breath, exhaling, and then doing it again, focusing on the wheezing sounds coming from her chest. She knew, deep down to her soul that if she allowed herself to close her eyes and slip back into unconsciousness, she'd never wake again. And maybe that would be the better, least painful way to die, but her father's voice in her head reminded her that now wasn't the time to throw in the towel because if one thing could be said about her, it was that she'd always been a fighter. And not just when she'd survived the earthquake and building collapse.

As captain of her high school volleyball team and then earning an athletic scholarship, people had always assumed her athleticism had come to her naturally, much like Aubrey had seemed to be magically born with a paint-brush in her hands. But the truth was that as much as Kennedy had loved playing sports, she'd had to put in long, tedious hours practicing until she'd finally been good enough to try out without being laughed off the court, something that had occurred more than once.

Even before then, during their birth, Aubrey had been eager to join the world, and so their mother had been able to deliver naturally. However, when it came time for

Kennedy to make her grand appearance, complications putting both her and her mother at risk resulted in that less than five percent occurrence where, unlike her twin, she'd had to be delivered by emergency caesarean. And in case that hadn't been bad enough, her parents told her she'd had to fight those first few hours just to live. The doctors had doubted she'd make it, but her mom and dad swore they never had.

Painfully and awkwardly shy until the age of ten, there'd been many times when Kennedy had wanted nothing more than to stay home and hide away from the world. However, her parents never allowed it, always reminding her that when things seemed too tough, that didn't mean it was time to quit; it meant she needed to dig in even deeper to see herself through.

And Aubrey and her parents had always been the first and loudest to cheer whenever she succeeded when she didn't think she could.

Now wasn't the time to let them down. As if her life had come full circle, a voice inside her insisted she hadn't fought so hard the day of her birth only to die a tragic, torturous death at the hands of a monster.

He'd told her that his face would be the last she ever saw, that no one but him ever left here alive, but she knew he was wrong. Because while her abductor might see her the way she looked on the outside, weakened, starved, and horribly terrified, he couldn't see inside her head where her fighting instinct had come roaring back stronger than ever.

The police would find her in time. She'd survive this. She had to because she thought she finally remembered how she knew her abductor. And so she made a vow to herself and her family to stay strong, no matter how he tortured her, so she could be the one 'who got away,' who helped tell the story that would seal his fate and lock him behind bars for the rest of his life. Then he could find out what it felt like to be someone else's prisoner.

Chapter Forty-One

Saturday, June 4

Unable to sleep with Kennedy's life hanging in the balance, Alyssa finally gave up and headed back to the precinct with dawn still a distant tease. At three thirty in the morning, she'd half expected to see Ruby present as ever, sleeping on a cot behind her desk. She didn't know what felt stronger: disappointment that Ruby wasn't there, thus ending the theory that she truly did live at the station, or cheer that Ruby apparently had a life outside these industrial walls.

In the incident room, Alyssa set her coffee to the side and grabbed a thick pile of all the interviews they'd conducted regarding both Rheagan's and Kennedy's cases. She grabbed another stack from Gunner's case, and then she added the copies of the interviews Chief Porter had sent. Absently, she latched onto the first highlighter her fingers landed on, removed the cap with her mouth, and started searching for any similarities, any names that appeared in more than one of the cases, specifically Dr. Jackson Hoyt. And though she truly believed Hoyt was their man, she searched for Neely's name, as well. Until they made their arrest, she wouldn't close the door on either.

An hour later, the urge to hurl hundreds of pages at the wall swept over her. And she might've if Cord hadn't taken that moment to walk through the door.

He grabbed a chair and sat across from her. 'Do I even want to know what time you got here?'

'Probably not.'

'From the throttling you're giving that highlighter, I'm guessing no new answers have jumped out at you.'

Tired, frustrated, and now easily irritated, Alyssa shot her partner a withering glower of unappreciation. 'No, I've discovered all the answers. I just figured I'd sit here and give Kennedy a little more time to be tortured.'

Cord's eyebrows shot up. 'Why didn't you call me in to help?' Probably because *exhausted* had also become his middle name as of late, a slight edge of annoyance lined his question.

Guilt pushed her bad-tempered testiness out. She wasn't the only one losing sleep over these cases. 'I thought about it,' she admitted. 'But considering I know how Carter and Abigail still wake with nightmares, I think it's important that you're home. Besides, if at least one of us gets in forty winks, maybe we'll be able to obtain a fresher outlook.'

Mentioning the kids evaporated any aggravation Cord felt at her for not calling. 'Considerate. And as a matter of fact, Carter did have one of his nightmares this morning around quarter after three. I think the wind woke him up, and he got disoriented for a minute.' Pride lit up his eyes. 'But he did what he promised his therapist he would do. Instead of being embarrassed and ashamed to tell us, he came and woke Sara and me up. Anyway, after we got him settled back down, I couldn't go back to sleep, so here I am.'

Cord blurred before Alyssa's eyes. After their mother's tragic murder, Carter and Abigail couldn't have had two better people to adopt them and help guide them through life.

'I'm glad I didn't call then.'

'Any updates from the surveillance team?' Cord asked.

Alyssa's shoulders slumped in frustration. 'Nope, not since last night when Heath sent that text that Hoyt had arrived home around seven thirty and unloaded what appeared to be groceries and a gym bag.' She picked up half the stack of interviews and slid them over to Cord. 'But since you're here now, you might as well help me try to figure out what we're missing.'

Just then, Hal rolled into the room and placed the keys to his specialized van in the pocket of his wheelchair before pushing himself up to the table. 'Then you might as well put me to work, too.' His eyes swept over what appeared to be an explosion from a paper mill. 'I see I'm not the only one whose wheels were spinning faster than a hamster on speed. How long have you two been here?'

Alyssa pointed to herself. 'Three thirty.' She pointed to Cord. 'Four thirty.' She peeked at her watch. 'And you since four forty-five. What wheels were your hamsters stuck on?'

Hal reached into the same pocket where he'd placed his keys and pulled out his laptop. 'Since you asked so nicely, I'll tell you.' He opened a file and spun his screen so Alyssa and Cord could read it. 'Background check on Hoyt. Born in Denver, Colorado, to Stuart and India Hoyt. Played football in high school until an injury to the knee took him out. Attended University of Colorado School of Medicine in Aurora, which is located just outside Denver. Met Evelyn Ryzen there, though she later dropped out of the program. After he graduated, he accepted a position at Mercy Hospital in Durango.' Hal met Alyssa and Cord's gaze. 'Which is in La Plata County, which is where he's building his outreach center, but more importantly, it is the same county where our Colorado victims were murdered.'

Alyssa felt like they were getting closer to convincing a judge to issue, if not an arrest warrant yet, then at least a search warrant for Hoyt's property. However, what they had right now was still too circumstantial. 'Hal, what would we do without you?'

He winked. 'Good thing I don't plan on letting you figure that out anytime soon.'

'What else did you find?' Cord asked.

'Still trying to track down information on the parents. In the meantime, I ran property searches on Hoyt, as well as Evelyn's name, but so far, all I find are his house here, the one up in Colorado, and the land where he's having the center built. I'm not done digging, but that's where we are so far.'

–

Later that morning, the tension in the room thickened with each second that slipped away and no one coming any closer to finding the answers – or Kennedy. Scattered all around Alyssa and the stacks of witness statements were photographs and printouts of social media posts for everyone except Bella Teller who, unsurprisingly, didn't have any accounts since Facebook hadn't yet become quite so commonplace when she'd been murdered. Hundreds of hours of police work from the Colorado cases made the New Mexico ones appear miniscule in comparison.

On an easel that Ruby had brought in when she arrived shortly after Hal was a tri-fold poster board that Tony, Joe, and Hal were currently using to visually tie the victims to Jackson Hoyt.

Tuning out their conversation, Alyssa turned to Cord who had just gotten off a call. His poker face gave nothing away, so she waited.

'I think we can officially remove Neely from our list. On Friday night, he left for Montana for a mental health conference that took place on Saturday and went through Sunday. Considering he was a keynote speaker, and the entire event was recorded for non-attendees, we can say for certain he wasn't in the area when Rheagan disappeared.'

Alyssa's gaze drifted over to the whiteboard, to the smiling image of Kennedy that Hal had printed from her social media page, then down to the Polaroid pictures her abductor had delivered. As she studied them, she replayed everything she'd learned about Jackson Hoyt, dissecting every word he'd ever said to them, the movements he'd made and when, all while trying to analyze any hidden meanings. Her team called it her Monday morning quarterbacking tactic. She called it being thorough.

Her eyes drifted from Kennedy's picture to each of the other victims they knew about, whispering each of their names aloud, her way of making even the ones she didn't know personal to her. Earlier, Joe, Tony, and Hal had been on calls with the families of the Colorado victims, asking questions, and getting to know Bella, Faith, and Perry a little better. It wasn't just about the investigation; it was a way to see each person as an individual and not merely a tragic statistic.

She shifted her attention back to Kennedy, the one they could still save. 'Where are you?' she whispered.

In the background, Tony's argument with Joe about a ping warrant for Hoyt's phone barely registered.

'You really think a man suspected of at least five murders would be stupid enough to use his own phone to contact Lys? Or even take it with him when he grabs his victims? I'm telling you, even if we could get one right this second, it wouldn't tell us anything new.' Tony's agitated voice grew louder.

Alyssa studied the writing on Bella and Faith's stomachs. Would a handwriting expert be able to tie those words to Jackson Hoyt's writing? Maybe. She picked up the stack of Polaroids left on Aubrey's porch and rearranged them in front of her, studying each one like a slide under a microscope before setting it back down.

She tried to block out the way Kennedy's frame was suspended from the metal bars, tried to block out the agony and fear etched onto her face, but she couldn't. Something told her she was overlooking one critical, crucial detail, and if she looked hard enough, she'd find the answers in these photographs.

When she reached the fifth one, she turned to the side, removing the shadow that had fallen over it. Just as she went to set it down, she noticed something that made her gasp. She jerked to her feet so quickly that she knocked her chair over into the wall. Her body vibrating, she brought the picture in closer, then held it out. Her head reeled in denial with every instinct warring against the truth in front of her.

Ignoring her team as they lobbed questions at her, she grabbed a magnifying glass. Her stomach plummeted at the thought that the answer had been in front of them all this time, if they'd just looked a little harder, a little closer. In fact, Tony had even made the sarcastic remark about finding the perpetrator standing right next to his victim. Alyssa stared at the picture, not noticing the sudden silence in the room or that Cord had moved in closer to her so he could peer over her shoulder.

Her mind paralyzed with disbelief, her hands shook. Finally managing to look up and catch the strained expressions on her teammates' faces, she swallowed and then handed the magnifying glass to Cord, wanting someone else to tell her she wasn't imagining things. 'Look at the reflection in the glass and tell me what you see. It's faint, but once you get a glimpse…'

The tension in the room thickened as Cord accepted the magnifying glass and aimed it where Alyssa pointed. A second later, his pale face corroborated what she'd seen hadn't been a mere trick of the light. His head snapped up to the timeline written on the whiteboard. 'Sonofabitch. That can't—how the *hell* did we miss that? How would we *ever* have suspected it to begin with?'

Alyssa's mind buzzed with the irrefutable proof in front of her. 'But where's he keeping Kennedy?'

'Are you going to tell us, or just keep us all in suspense?' Hal barked out. He raised his brow when Alyssa shook her head, confused. 'What the hell do you see?' He waved his hand toward the photograph once again clutched between her fingers.

Chapter Forty-Two

Ben watched the two men in the car parked near his neighbor's house. They weren't the same ones he'd spotted last night when he'd slipped out from beneath Ellary's watchful, eagle eyes to go check on Kennedy. Actually, he hadn't planned on checking on her so much as killing her and then finding a way to dump her corpse on Detective Alyssa Wyatt's doorstep, just like he'd promised.

When he'd first realized a surveillance team had been placed on his street, he'd feared he'd somehow screwed up in a way he'd never done before, that the cops were finally circling around the truth. Quietly, he'd retreated back to the house where he'd moved into his office and locked the door so he wouldn't be unpleasantly surprised by someone popping in unexpectedly. Namely, his one remaining daughter. He knew Barbara wouldn't wake until morning. He'd made sure of it the same way he'd been doing for years now.

For two hours straight, he'd watched the duo in the unmarked car. He watched as one of the men climbed out and headed over to two bushes, stepping between them before reemerging a minute later, zipping up his pants and climbing back inside the vehicle.

Not once in the time he'd observed them had the men turned to watch his house, meaning he could rest assured that the police weren't onto him. He'd shaken his head at the thought that he might've made a mistake. He hadn't gotten away with murder for all these years by being stupid. But if those individuals were Detective Wyatt's best efforts at a covert surveillance team, he'd sorely misjudged his opponent as worthy of his cat and mouse game.

He peeked out the one window where he could just make out his neighbor's property. Apparently, the super squad suspected Jackson Hoyt. He couldn't help it; he'd laughed. His neighbor was what his father would've called a Class A Sissy. The way he'd carried on at his wife's funeral had been embarrassing.

Still, even though Ben knew he was in the clear, that everyone around him believed him to be steeped in grief at his youngest daughter's murder, he couldn't take the risk of something going wrong, so he forced himself to wait before he finally did what he'd intended to do a week ago – kill Kennedy. Hell, she might already be dead. He'd never tried starving one of his victims to death, preferring the personal touch, and he hadn't intended to start with her. But with people in and out of his house all hours of the day, with his daughter hovering nearby all the damn time, and being forced to play the never-ending role of concerned, strong husband to his wife, he'd simply been unable to get away as much as he would've liked. And when he had and noticed the way Kennedy's skin had begun to hug her bones, the way her breathing had become raspy and ragged, he'd been curious to see how long it would take her to die. He'd given her just enough liquid to keep her alive and lucid. After all, he enjoyed the idea of her mental suffering as she wondered when he'd be back to finish her off. But mostly, he thrived on forcing her to beg.

'Dad?'

Ellary's voice raked across his nerves. Replacing his irritation with a mask of grief, he turned around, his eyes skating past the vase of flowers offering condolences sent by the civil engineering consulting firm where he worked. *We are so sorry for your family's loss,* read the card. The company's top man had delivered the carnations personally, patting him on the shoulder and bringing him in for an awkward hug, all while assuring him he didn't need to hurry back to work.

Ben loathed the guy, but he'd played his part, bravely holding himself together for his wife and remaining daughter, all while laughing on the inside. He planned on returning as soon as possible under the guise of burying himself in work. Because it was his frequent out-of-state travels that allowed him to carry out his extracurricular activities without being detected. His father, if the bastard were still alive, would never dream of calling him a sissy now.

'Dad?'

Ellary, her tone a little more abrasive this time, called his name again, reminding him that he hadn't yet acknowledged her, though, of course, he could chalk that up to his grief. 'Yes, baby?' He watched her stop her eyeroll before it could start. She hated the endearment, though he'd never been able to figure out why. Not that he'd really cared.

'I said you probably need to eat. And I need you to help me get Mom out of bed. It's almost noon. We need to make some decisions before we meet with the funeral director tomorrow.' Her fists clenched at her sides as tears streaked her cheeks. 'I can't keep doing all this on my own,' she choked out.

Ben shuffled his way over to Ellary and tried to hug her because that's what a father would do, but her return embrace was weak, at best, so he let his arms drop. 'I know your mother and I have leaned an awful lot on you these past few days, and I'm sorry. I tell you what. The walls of this house are starting to feel like a prison I can't escape, and with all the traffic in and out… I just need an hour to myself, to clear my head and try to think. So, I'm going to slip out, and when I get back, if your mom's still in bed, I'll get her up, and we'll all sit down and figure this out, okay?' He forced a crackle into his voice. Even to his own ears, he thought it sounded pretty damn genuine.

The battle to squabble brewed across Ellary's face, and he knew she thought him leaving her here to deal with her mother while he slipped out for some alone time was selfish. But he really didn't care. Sometimes it was hard to contain the urge to see the expressions on their faces by admitting he had been the one responsible for causing their grief.

Before Ellary could argue, he kissed her cheek – because he knew it would piss her off – then grabbed his keys off the hook and headed to the garage.

He had told Detective Wyatt few were smarter than him. Maybe it was time he convinced her how cunning he really was.

Chapter Forty-Three

With her head still processing the reality that Ben Pembroke had not only brutally murdered his own daughter, but was, in fact, a serial killer, Alyssa, search and arrest warrants in hand, sped to the Cabra Hills residence with Cord. As she maneuvered in and out of traffic with Joe and Tony following close behind, pieces of the puzzle that hadn't quite fit before began to fall into place, creating a horrifyingly clear picture. One of the things still eluding her, however, was his connection to the Galveston case. He'd never been interviewed because he'd never been on their radar; hell, her team then hadn't even known of his existence. She hoped that Hal would help unlock some of those answers while digging into Ben's history.

A surge of anger heated her from the inside at how he must've laughed when she'd shown up at his house to take the missing person's report, the same detective who'd allowed him to slip through her fingers fourteen years earlier. No, not slipped – she'd let him continue to glide below the radar because she'd never even had a grasp on his identity.

And this time, she'd been so certain that Hoyt had been their guy that her mind had automatically twisted and tweaked all the incoming information to fit the circumstantial evidence they thought they had. Instead, the truth had been carefully buried under the guise of a mourning father.

She pictured Rheagan's battered body, the way she'd been unrecognizable aside from her tattoos, the way she'd been discarded like trash. Of course, none of them had suspected Ben. Who would? Because what kind of sick person could do what he'd done to his own daughter? Her stomach tied itself into knots as she imagined the horror Rheagan must've suffered as her own father ruthlessly beat her to death.

Alyssa laid on her horn when a car that ignored the warning screeches of the police sirens pulled out in front of her, forcing her to slow down until he got out of her way again. With each second that Kennedy remained captive to a monster who could wear the mask of normality and move undetected within the public, the fear that they wouldn't get to her in time increased. She pressed down on the accelerator.

By the time they reached Ben's house, Alyssa's pulse raced headlong into a full-on sprint while blood thundered in her ears. A car door slammed, and she turned in time to spot the two men tasked with surveilling Jackson Hoyt's movements join the rest of the team. With the tension in her tight enough to snap, all she could manage was a clipped nod while she gave the newcomers a two-word command. 'Back door.'

They nodded their understanding and slipped ahead to cover the back while Joe and Tony took up posts on either side of the house. Seconds later, she and Cord approached Ben Pembroke's front door. She cast one quick glance in Cord's direction before lowering one hand to hover over her service weapon and the other to pound on the front door.

'Albuquerque Police.'

Chapter Forty-Four

Saturday, June 4

Ellary Pembroke opened the door, a combination of exhaustion, sorrow, confusion, and something else Alyssa couldn't read, distorting her features. Alyssa's eyes moved from Ellary's face to span the area of the house she could see behind her. 'Is your father home?'

'No. He left about thirty minutes ago to get some fresh air.' The way her lips curled around the words made it clear she hadn't approved of her father's choice. 'Why? What's going on?' While Alyssa could hear the effort it took Ellary to put some force behind her questions, she also heard the quiver in the young woman's voice that said she knew something was wrong.

'Do you know where he went or when he'll be back?' Alyssa wished she had time to be more considerate of the truth about to hit Ellary and Barbara, but she feared they might already be out of time.

'No. Please—'

Cord interrupted. 'We have an arrest warrant for your father and a warrant to search these premises.'

Behind Ellary, Barbara Pembroke's gasp nearly drowned out Ellary's. 'For what?'

Alyssa met Ellary's eyes, breaking the news bluntly, like ripping off a band-aid, because she didn't have the luxury of time to ease into it. 'For multiple murders, including your sister Rheagan's.'

A commotion behind Ellary drew everyone's attention as Barbara Pembroke's eyes widened, her hand clutched at her chest, and she fell to the floor. Cord shoved past Ellary and rushed over to her.

Even from where Alyssa stood, she could tell Barbara's chest was barely rising and falling. Damn it! She thumbed her mic to get Joe's attention. 'We need an ambulance now. Barbara Pembroke just collapsed.'

His fingers pressed against Barbara's neck, Cord swung his head in Alyssa's direction. 'Her pulse is thready and weak. I think she might be having a heart attack.'

Alyssa barely had time to think about Dr. Hoyt being the closest doctor when he was suddenly there, shoving past her, as if she'd conjured his presence without realizing it.

Hoyt gave a brief explanation as he zeroed in on his neighbor's still form. 'I saw the police cars, was outside watching the action. Heard what you said through the mic. Here I am.' His attention now fully on the woman lying on the floor in front of him, Hoyt's demeanor instantly transformed to doctor in charge. Going to his knees beside Cord, he didn't quite shove him out of the way, but neither did he try to be polite in his brusque, 'Move. I need room to work.'

Assuring herself that the doctor had the task of stabilizing Barbara under control as they waited for the ambulance to arrive, Alyssa pulled Ellary off to the side, forcing her attention away from her mother. Though she knew the young woman was worried and that everything was happening all at once, Alyssa needed answers now. Kennedy's life depended on it.

'Ellary, I need you to listen to me and think. This is urgent. Is there any place you can think of where your father might be able to hold someone prisoner, somewhere he knows no one else will go?'

Ellary swayed on her feet before stumbling backwards, saved from falling by the wall she collapsed into. Alyssa understood that the young woman's reaction meant she had indeed thought of a place, and her hope that they were close to locating Kennedy soared.

Ellary's words were barely audible. 'His workshop.' She pointed outside. 'On the edge of the property by the trees.' Then, as if in a trance, she whispered, 'You'll need a key. But no one's allowed in it, so I don't know where he keeps it.'

They didn't need the key to gain entry because they could kick it in, but Alyssa didn't tell her that. Instead, she grabbed Ellary's arm, shaking it slightly to refocus her attention. 'Thank you. Go be with your mom. We'll have more questions, but we'll come find you. If your father calls, do *not* warn him that we're here.'

Chapter Forty-Five

Saturday, June 4

Barely contained excitement had Ben racing back to his house. While he'd been out driving around, he'd figured out his next move – after he killed and dumped Kennedy. As long as he remained patient and executed each step to perfection, the almighty Detective Wyatt would never even see it coming. If she thought not solving the Galveston boy's murder kept her up at nights… he chuckled. Well, she'd never sleep again after he snatched her partner's kids. But he wouldn't kill them right away. No, he'd keep them alive for a long, long time to prolong everyone's suffering.

The shrill scream of sirens bursting through the air, as well as the way oncoming traffic slowed before pulling off to the right, zapped Ben back into reality. Off in the distance but closing the gap in a hurry, the vehicle he recognized as belonging to Detective Wyatt led the charge up the road. A car darted out in front of her, slowing her progress, but not for long.

He laughed, imagining Jackson Hoyt's shock when they came to arrest him for a murder he didn't commit. In his mind, he sifted through options for what would pass as an appropriately horrified and outraged reaction at learning his own neighbor had murdered his baby girl.

Lost in the fantasy that had already shifted to lifelike, he almost didn't notice the car in front of him had stopped for the red light, and he slammed on his brakes barely in time to avoid a rear-end collision. Resigned to wait, his fingers tapped impatiently against the steering wheel. He didn't want to miss this.

When he finally got through the intersection and made the turn into his residential community, he forced himself to drive the insanely low speed limit. As he neared the final corner before the turn onto his own street, that fluttery sensation in his stomach heightened. He pictured screeching to a halt outside Hoyt's house, the mask of sputtering confusion on his own face as he demanded to know what was going on when he saw the cops carting Hoyt out in handcuffs. Someone would tell him, and he'd attack his neighbor. But as he rounded the bend that would bring his house into view, the scene playing out in front of him in no way matched the one in his head.

The two-man surveillance team were climbing out of their vehicles, but instead of heading down the hill, they were heading up where Detective Wyatt and another cop car had blocked off his driveway. The cops weren't at Hoyt's house. They were at his.

His levity of moments ago erupted in a red rage as the truth hit him: the detective had somehow not only accepted his challenge but had figured him out.

But how? Where had he gone wrong?

You don't have time to think of that right now unless you want to get caught. He banged both fists against his steering wheel and then shook his head to clear the voice. He needed to concentrate, to get somewhere safe where he could think.

By now, Ellary would've admitted he wasn't home, and Wyatt would be calling in reinforcements to lock down the perimeter in case he showed up, not suspecting he was about to walk into a trap.

Before anyone could spot him, he whipped his car around. Now, the battle to keep to the speed limit to avoid notice rattled him in an unfamiliar way. Back out to the main road, he headed through the canyon with no destination in mind except the one that led him away.

Chapter Forty-Six

Alyssa tried to steel herself against disappointment in case Kennedy wasn't inside Pembroke's workshop, but it didn't stop her from racing across the yard to it. The sight of the reinforced steel lock on the door pushed her hope a little higher. No one needed that type of lock for a personal workshop unless they had something to hide. Or someone. While Joe and Tony, along with help from Greg Packard and Louis Menard, the two men charged with surveilling next door, sent out an urgent request for more officers to help them secure the perimeter, she called Hammond to send in a crime scene unit. His response that they were already on the way surprised neither her nor Cord.

After quickly searching for and determining no alternate entry existed, Cord delivered three powerful kicks to the door before it finally blew inward. Alyssa cautiously but hurriedly stepped inside the workshop. Because it was darker than she'd expected due to the lack of windows or skylights, she pulled her flashlight from her toolbelt and ran it along the wall. Up high, she spotted long rows of fluorescent lights mounted on the ceiling. To the left of an industrial metal shelf, she finally spotted the switch. At the same time that she saw it, Cord slapped his palm against it, illuminating the dimness with a yellowish, sinister glow.

Quiet, straining to hear... what, she didn't exactly know... Alyssa turned in a slow circle, taking in every square inch of the shop from cement floor to insulated ceiling. Power saws, drills, mallets, blades of every imaginable shape and size, sanders, hammers, and safety equipment lined the walls and shelves, all neatly labeled and organized. Cabinets held a variety of stains and paints. But nowhere inside the shop could a person be hidden away.

But she had to be. When Alyssa had asked Ellary where her father might hide someone, she had expected, if she had an answer at all, that she'd name a place a few miles from home, at the least. That her reaction and answer had been immediate told Alyssa there had to be something in here that they were missing.

'She has to be here,' Cord muttered, as if he'd dipped right into Alyssa's thoughts.

Continuing their search in silence, listening for any sounds out of the ordinary, Cord scoured up high while Alyssa investigated low. As she did, The Toybox sex trafficking case from three years back flashed in her head. In the house where they'd found the girls, there'd been a hidden room behind a bookcase. Heart pumping faster, she ran her hand along the walls in search of a moving panel as she scraped her feet along the cement floor, feeling for a loose spot. With her heart lodged in her throat, she began to move quicker and quicker. When she'd made it around the entire workshop and still no closer to locating a hidden anything, much less Kennedy, she wanted to howl out her impatience. It took every bit of inner will she could muster not to start kicking things over.

She took a deep, calming breath and started over. From the doorway, she moved slowly along the wall until she reached the far corner where a massive, oversized ceiling-to-floor storage cabinet stood with the doors flung open from when she'd first come across it. Like everything else in the shop, it was tidy and well-organized, but as she studied it, she thought something about it seemed – not right. She took a step back and tilted her head to one side then the other as she stared. Could there be a room behind the cabinet? Her eyes landed on the low workbench where an open cardboard box held a slew of miscellaneous objects that didn't seem to fit with the other items in the shop.

Somewhere in the back of her mind, she heard Cord move up beside her and ask what she'd found, but her concentration had zeroed in on that box.

Using her foot, she pushed the top corner, surprised and thrown slightly off balance when it moved far more easily than she'd expected. A surge of adrenaline hit her straight in the heart, sending it rocketing into a near-frightening rhythm. 'Cord, look.' She pointed down where the floor of the cabinet had been removed and replaced with a thick wooden door with a rusted iron handle set in the middle.

With shaking hands, Alyssa tugged on the handle. 'Get Joe and Tony in here, and the tech team if they've arrived.' The door lifted with barely a sound, revealing a sturdy set of wooden steps. Her heart thumped hard inside her chest as her mouth went dry, and her palms began to sweat. Using her flashlight to guide the way, she began the descent into what she knew would be a hidden pit of hell. Before she reached the bottom, Cord found another switch that illuminated the entire area.

The strong odor of blood and human waste burned her nose as Alyssa took in the horrifying sight before her. Hooks lined two walls, draped with blades and ropes, chains and manacles. Assorted shelves housed hammers, scalpels, and various other items the evidence techs would have to categorize. Blood stained nearly every item her eyes landed on, including the sink. Just beneath that lay a shattered phone, and she wondered if she'd found Rheagan's cell.

Beyond this utilitarian room, a long black curtain hid whatever was on the other side of it, and Alyssa, hand on her weapon, moved carefully around it. Pulling the curtain back to reveal a locked door to the glass chamber she'd seen in the Polaroid pictures, Alyssa, at long last, found Kennedy Farmer with her head drooped forward and the pallor of her sunken face a sickly, pale yellowish white. Bones pressed tightly against the exposed parts of her skin.

Acid burned Alyssa's throat as she twisted the knob on the door constructed of more reinforced steel. 'I need keys!' Afraid they were too late after all, she pounded on the glass in the hopes of getting some type of reaction from Kennedy, even if only a wiggle of her finger – anything that would tell them she was still alive.

Nothing. Not a flicker, not even the tiniest movement of her head. Alyssa's throat clogged with emotion.

Suddenly, Cord was there, pushing her out of the way. 'Give me room.'

In his latex-covered hand, he held an awl and hammer which he used to tap the pins out of the door hinges. In no time at all, the metallic pings hit the concrete floor. By then, Joe and Tony had joined them, and they braced the heavy door from falling on Cord's head before hefting it out of the way so Alyssa could dart inside and over to Kennedy.

'Joe, Tony, we need you in here.' Cord's gruff command came as he produced his handcuff keys, so he could release the manacles around Kennedy's raw wrists. Fury etched strong lines into his face, transforming him in a way few had ever seen.

'What kind of sick sonofabitch does this to another person, much less his own child?' Tony growled.

'The human kind.' Joe's voice held a mixture of sadness and rage. 'You know, some studies claim no one is born evil, but I'm beginning to believe there might be some validity to the other side of that argument.'

Cord cut the conversation off with another gravelly command. 'Be ready to catch her. Don't let her fall.' With Joe and Tony on either side, and Alyssa in front, her shoes nearly touching the leg irons around Kennedy's ankles, he released the cuffs.

Together and in a numb but frantic state, they lowered Kennedy to the floor. While Cord worked to remove the leg irons, Alyssa, choking back angry tears, placed two trembling fingers against Kennedy's neck. 'Please don't be too late. Please don't be too late.'

Chapter Forty-Seven

Saturday, June 4

While Alyssa wanted nothing more than to accompany Kennedy to the hospital until she could be assured the woman would make it, she remained behind in the dungeon of horror. Her throat still clogged with a dizzying array of emotions, she turned to her team and said, 'I'm going to step outside for a minute so I can contact the family. I'll be right back.'

Out in the fresh air, she remembered that a beautiful June day still existed. Down in that prison where Kennedy had been held, she'd forgotten that. She pulled out her phone and dialed Aubrey Farmer's number.

Kennedy's twin answered in a breathless rush before the second ring. 'Did you find her?'

Alyssa inhaled deeply through her nose and exhaled through her mouth. 'Yes.'

Before she could get another word out, a barrage of questions bombarded her, only now they came from three markedly different voices; Aubrey had placed her on speaker phone so that her parents could be part of the conversation.

During a nanosecond of silence where the Farmer family collectively took a breath, Alyssa managed to squeeze in the rest. 'Yes, we've located Kennedy, and while she's alive, I want to forewarn you that her condition is dangerously critical. She's been transported to downtown Presbyterian Hospital.'

Another half dozen questions fired through the phone until a male voice, rough with emotion, broke through. 'I'm Kennedy and Aubrey's father. What else can you tell us? Did she say anything? Have you arrested the person who did this?'

In the background, Alyssa heard the distinct sound of three car doors slamming, a sign that the Farmers were already on their way to the hospital to be with Kennedy. Alyssa crossed her fingers that the medical personnel would allow them in to see her right away. Even if the worst happened, and Kennedy didn't pull through – she swallowed against the lump in her throat – then at least she'd be surrounded by the people who loved her instead of being another broken piece in someone else's twisted game.

'Listen, I can answer some of your questions later, but right now, what's important is that you know we've found Kennedy and you can get to her. We'll be in touch as soon as we can.'

Understanding the urgency in her voice, the Farmers thanked her and ended the call. Alyssa took another minute to brace herself before returning to Ben's secret hideaway so they could sift through the evidence and find out where he'd disappeared to. By now, he had to know his cover had been blown to hell.

Back beneath the workshop, Alyssa's heart tried to take up residence in her throat as her mind conjured every imaginable horror forced upon Ben's victims, based solely on the photos he'd supplied himself. She closed her eyes for a moment, trying to pull up a mental snapshot of the image of Gunner Galveston left with Rheagan's body. When she opened them again, she looked around before staring down at the bloodstained floor littered with what appeared to be bits of skin and tissue. She knew in her gut that this was the same place the teen who'd had his entire life still ahead of him had met his death. How many other lives had ended here, as well?

–

Nearly an hour after finding Kennedy, and with securing the crime scene and collecting evidence well underway, Joe and Tony returned to the house to execute the search warrant there – and Alyssa made another staggering discovery. On the wall opposite the glass chamber, a dark spot beckoned her. Curious, she pressed the heel of her hand against it, startled to hear something move behind the wall when she did. The hint of yet another hidden door emerged.

'Cord.'

Alyssa slid the door the rest of the way open, revealing a dark tunnel. 'Good God. I will never be able to comprehend how such evil can come across as so normal. It makes no sense.'

'Evil rarely does.' Cord flicked on his flashlight and checked that his lapel camera was still on, as did she, and then together they stepped inside to see where this new order of hell led.

Almost immediately, a cloying sense of claustrophobia threatened to steal Alyssa's control, but she battled it back and continued on, using her own light to shine up and down as they carefully made their way through. Along the ground, a light trail of blood appeared, along with evidence of what looked to be something – or someone – being dragged along. She pictured Rheagan's body; the debris Lynn had discovered indicated exactly that.

Maybe because she had realistic mental visions of what Ben had used this tunnel for, or maybe because of the darkness of it all, it seemed to take an interminable amount of time to reach the end. When they finally did, they encountered a ladder that led up to a rusted metal grate overhead. A thick rope hung from the ceiling.

'I don't want to touch anything down here, just in case,' Cord said as he stared up into the filtered light of day. 'Why don't we head back out and see if we can find it from the outside?'

'I was already on that page, too.' What Alyssa didn't say was that she had no desire to remain in this tunnel any longer than she had to. In fact, she'd love nothing more than to seal it off and keep its evil contained within.

Chapter Forty-Eight

Sunday, June 5

Slowly, Kennedy became conscious of the beeping, whirring, shuffling, and whispering sounds of a busy hospital. What she couldn't determine was if it was a hallucination. Afraid to open her eyes, yet more afraid to keep them closed, she slit one open. Everything around her remained cloudy, and while no one spoke, she sensed movement. Near the door, a dark shadow of shape shifted, and she nearly yanked the IV out of her arm, causing an alarm to blast the silence with its warning beeps.

With her heart still trying to escape the confines of her chest, her mind finally latched onto the comforting touch of a familiar hand that could only belong to her mother. Panic slowly subsiding, she turned her head and concentrated on her sister's hushed words of assurance and her father's gruff promise that she was safe now, that no one would ever get to her again, that he'd make sure of it.

An image of him building a reinforced steel castle, complete with cannons and a moat surrounding it, brought a painful, partial smile to her face.

'There she is. There's our fighter, our beautiful girl.' Her father's fingers whispered over her face and down her arm to latch onto her free hand.

'Welcome back, sis.'

Kennedy's heart ballooned at the way her twin tried to mask her cries by forcing strength into her voice. As always, Aubrey proved to be her rock.

Her mother pressed a soft kiss to her cheek. 'My baby. You're going to be okay.'

Will I? Will I ever be okay again?

As if she'd heard the doubt swimming in Kennedy's head, her mother squeezed her hand gently and murmured, 'You *will*. Just rest for now.'

Pushing the words past her cracked lips, Kennedy asked, 'Did they catch him?' When she turned her head toward the sound of her twin's sniffles, she read the answer in her face. Suddenly, her ribs felt too tight, and her breathing became labored. He was still out there. He could come back and finish what he'd promised. A ragged sob slipped out as she gasped for air.

Not understanding any of the words flying at her, she yanked away from her mother's grip so she could rip her IV out. She needed to get out of here; she needed to hide. They didn't understand – they couldn't – the danger she was in, that they all were.

Kennedy fought off the foreign touch of hands she no longer recognized. Her gaze darted blindly around the room as she opened her mouth to scream. Then suddenly, a sharp stinging sensation burned through her veins where her IV was attached. As the room began to lose focus, all Kennedy could think was that she'd lost this round, that the black walls of death had come to claim her after all.

Chapter Forty-Nine

Sunday, June 5

Mid-Sunday morning, Alyssa and Cord finally made it to the hospital to visit Kennedy. They'd been unable to come by last night because she and every available member on the police force had been on the lookout for any sighting of Ben or his vehicle. After learning Pembroke wasn't home yesterday, Captain Hammond had issued an APB and then requested a breaking news report to alert the public that they needed to remain vigilant and aware and call in immediately if anyone spotted him.

Anxious to hear how Kennedy was doing, Alyssa had breathed a sigh of relief when Aubrey called close to ten p.m. last night to inform her that Kennedy, while still unconscious due to the pain medication she'd been given, had been updated to stable but serious condition. Alyssa had thanked her and then shared the news with the team.

A medley of 'Thank Gods,' 'Hallelujahs,' and deep exhalations followed her announcement. And then they'd returned to the task of sifting through evidence, which included the laptop computer they'd confiscated from Ben's locked office, as well as a brown banker's box filled with Polaroid photographs of dead animals – and his victims, six of whom they recognized.

Now, after flashing their badges at the three individuals standing at the nurses' station as they passed by, Alyssa tapped softly before she and Cord stepped into Kennedy's room, where her family surrounded her bed. Three angst-riddled faces turned from the young woman over to Alyssa, giving her enough of a view to witness the way Kennedy's legs jerked beneath the covers and her arms tried to flail beneath her parents' grips as she mumbled something indecipherable.

'She's waking up again.' Aubrey's voice was filled with anguish. 'She had to be sedated close to three hours ago, and she's been trying to come out of it for the past twenty minutes or so. She'll open her eyes for a few minutes, then close them.' She cast her penetrating gaze in Alyssa's direction. 'She's afraid he's going to come after her again.'

Alyssa felt her heart constrict. 'We're doing everything we can to make sure that doesn't happen,' she said. 'We'll do whatever it takes to keep her safe. You probably haven't noticed them, but we have police, both uniformed and plainclothes, keeping watch to make sure of it.'

Almost as if she'd heard and understood she was safe, the muscles in Kennedy's body and face relaxed. And then suddenly her eyes flew open and remained that way as they darted left and right, stopping only when they landed on Alyssa and Cord. She directed her still slightly unfocused gaze toward her sister.

'Hey, Ken. You're okay; you're safe now.' Aubrey waved her arm behind her. 'These are the detectives who found you. They have some questions. Do you think you're ready to answer them?'

Hesitant, Kennedy nodded slowly.

'We're right here with you,' Mr. Farmer promised gruffly.

Moisture turned Kennedy's eyes glossy as Mrs. Farmer moved to the head of her daughter's bed, making room for Alyssa and Cord.

Alyssa smiled gently at the young woman she'd prayed so hard to find in time. 'Hi, Kennedy. I'm Detective Wyatt, and this is Detective Roberts. I know you're exhausted and scared, but we need to ask you some questions, all right?'

In a voice raw and scratchy yet much clearer than Alyssa would've expected, Kennedy blurted out the words, 'Ben Pembroke.' The skin around Mr. Farmer's hand turned white where she squeezed tightly.

Well, that answered one of Alyssa's questions. Kennedy had recognized her abductor. 'Do you remember meeting him?'

Kennedy took what appeared to be a deep but painful breath. 'I didn't really meet him. But I saw him a couple of times out in his car when he would come to the Outreach Center to pick up his daughter, Rheagan.' A smile tilted her cracked lips up enough to crinkle her eyes. 'She'd gotten into trouble for some vandalism, so volunteering at the center was her punishment.'

Her body still in a weakened state, Kennedy had to pause to catch her breath. For nearly a minute, her chest rose and fell in slow, even movements. When she finally continued, her voice had grown quieter. 'We bonded over our presidential names, though neither of us, apparently, was named after one, despite how it appears and what people think.' Her tortured gaze lifted to meet Alyssa's. 'Ben said it was my fault for running alone.'

The way she spoke, Alyssa had the feeling Kennedy didn't yet know that Rheagan had been murdered, too. While she tried to think of a way to approach the topic,

Cord stepped up so Kennedy wouldn't have to strain to see him. 'It is *not* your fault. That was his way of getting into your head. Don't let him keep that power over you anymore.'

Kennedy blinked once, then twice, before she tilted her chin toward her chest, which may or may not have been a sign of acceptance.

'Do you remember seeing Ben on the trail that day?' Alyssa asked, putting off raising the topic of Rheagan's death.

'No. I'd just finished my run and was distracted when he came out of nowhere and grabbed me.' As she spoke, Kennedy's breathing grew more rapid.

Mrs. Farmer brushed her daughter's hair away from her face and leaned down to kiss her forehead, whispering as she did, 'Remember, you're safe here. No one's going to let him get to you again. We promise.'

Whether it was her mother's words of reassurance or something else, Kennedy's resolve seemed to return before their eyes, but even so, the next words out of her mouth shocked everyone in the room. 'I almost escaped, but he caught me and dragged me back.'

Unsure if she'd heard correctly, Alyssa said, 'You tried to escape?'

'Yes. I watched him kill another girl in front of me.' Her throat clogged with emotion, making her next statement harder to understand. 'He'd beaten her so badly.'

Alyssa peered up at Cord before turning her attention back to Kennedy. 'Did you recognize the girl?'

Kennedy shook her head. 'Her face... I don't think even her own mother would've recognized her.'

'Do you remember when that happened?'

'I think it was Saturday, the same day he abducted me. He drugged me with something, and when I came to, she was cuffed to the bar, and he was beating the life out of her. He wouldn't stop even after it was clear she was dead. Then he uncuffed her and started stabbing...' Kennedy's entire frame shook hard enough to rattle the bed. 'He left her on the floor with me until the day when he came back and dragged her away. He used a tunnel. That's when I got the idea to try to escape.'

Alyssa knew they'd have to tell her who the young girl was, but first, they had to finish getting as much information as possible.

Forty-five minutes later, when it became evident that Kennedy could no longer fight off the fatigue draining her energy, Alyssa and Cord thanked her and promised they'd return later to check in on her. As Kennedy allowed herself to drift off, her hand with her bandaged wrists going limp in her father's, Alyssa asked if she could speak to the family in the corridor.

Outside the room, she explained that Rheagan had been the girl Kennedy had seen murdered.

'I figured that out,' Aubrey said. 'I never made the connection before, but once I heard his name on the news, it all hit me. I'll make sure I tell her before she hears it from someone else.' And then, taking Alyssa by surprise, Kennedy's twin walked straight into her arms and hugged her. 'Thank you. Thank you for saving my sister before the same thing could happen to her.'

Tears slipped down Mrs. Farmer's face as she added, 'No matter how long we live, we will never be able to express enough gratitude to your team or the Albuquerque police force for getting to Kennedy in time.'

You're welcome seemed like such an asinine response to their thanks, especially considering Ben Pembroke was still at large, and so Alyssa swallowed back her own emotions and said, 'We'll be back later to see how she's doing. If she remembers anything else or wants to talk, you all have our cards, so please don't hesitate to call.'

–

After leaving Kennedy's room, Alyssa and Cord headed for the elevators that would take them to Barbara Pembroke's private room.

Alyssa knocked before cracking the door open enough to poke her head around the corner. In a chair sitting beside her mother's bed sat Ellary Pembroke, dark lines of flaky mascara mixing in with the lighter trails streaking down her reddened face. She had a death grip on a photograph in her hands. A closer look showed it to be one of Ellary and Rheagan, their legs dangling from swings suspended in the air, their eyes beaming with laughter as their father stood behind them, ready to push. Alyssa wondered when she'd grabbed it or where it had come from.

'How?' Ellary's voice cracked, and she used her knuckles to scrub away the fresh start of tears. 'How could my *father* be responsible for ki…kill—' Unable to finish, she let the picture fall to the bed and buried her face in the palm of her hands. When she looked up again, she whispered, 'My heart feels so bruised. How did we not know? And why did he kill Rheagan? I don't understand.'

Barbara Pembroke slowly opened her eyes. Dazed and still slightly sedated, no tears clouded her vision. Just a vacant stare of nothingness, as if she either couldn't or wouldn't believe she'd been living with a monster all these years, one capable of not only allegedly murdering multiple people but also their own child, the baby of their family.

Understanding the fragility of both the women in front of her, Alyssa spoke softly. 'I know this is a very difficult and confusing time for you, but we're going to need to ask you some more questions.'

Ellary swallowed. 'Can't they wait?'

'I'm afraid not. We're still unable to locate your father.'

Ellary's entire body seemed to shrink before their eyes. With the weight of what she'd been hit with, Alyssa could understand why.

'What kinds of questions? I mean, we obviously can't tell you anything about—We never even had suspicions.' Her eyes shifted from her mother and then up to Alyssa and Cord. 'How is that something we could've possibly missed?'

'Because your father made sure of it,' Cord said softly. 'People who commit these types of crimes master the art of blending in, including becoming the picture of a loving family man.'

Despite Cord's words, Alyssa knew the Pembrokes probably hadn't missed as much as they believed, that the behaviors they would eventually come to recognize as signs would most likely have been brushed away as any number of things. Unfortunately, she'd seen it countless times over the years. In fact, far more rarely were the times when family members or close friends spotted the dangerous warning signs right off the mark.

Because people tended to see what they expected while ignoring what they didn't. It was a defense mechanism their brains put in place to protect them from things they might not be able to handle at the time. Alyssa had spent enough time in therapy after her brother's death to understand the heavy truth of that.

Witness to the devastation of Ben's now broken family, she shared her thoughts, hoping that if not today, someday they might help. 'It's difficult for us to believe, much less accept, the worst of someone we love. And while your father may have committed these crimes, including' – she forced the bitter words from her mouth – 'killing your sister, the truth, as painful as it may be, is that he was still your father, and in your mind, you're trying to find a way to connect the man you loved your entire life with the evil person capable of murder. It's not an easy leap to make.'

While Alyssa spoke, Barbara's empty gaze drifted away to stare up at the corner of the ceiling, as if she could tune out the detectives and her daughter and watch a better, happier movie in her mind.

Nearly forty years ago, Alyssa's own mother had done something similar, vacant in every way possible except physically. She looked over to Ellary. 'How long has your mother been taking opiates?' Before they'd come in, she and Cord had taken a few minutes to speak to the doctor who'd been leaving Barbara's room. He had posited that the amount of fentanyl detected in the toxicology report suggested a long history of abuse.

A purplish hue of anger flushed Ellary's face. 'I don't know that she knew she was. And when the doctor came in to tell me her heart was fine, that she hadn't suffered a heart attack, but that could change due to her opiate use, I had time to really give it some thought. My mother is a rule follower. She drove the speed limit, refused to use the express check-out lane at the grocery store if she had so much as one extra item, and got us to our doctor appointments and extracurriculars exactly on time. And yes, while she may have brushed Rheagan's antics off as insignificant, it didn't change the way she did things herself.

'Every night before my mother retired to her room, my *father*' – she spat the title out like she'd bit into something spoiled – 'brought her a glass of red wine to "help her relax." Rheagan and I used to think it was the sweetest gesture, romantic even, that he'd do that for her every night for years on end.' She forced her eyes upward to meet Alyssa's. 'Now, I realize he did that so she wouldn't wake and find him missing in the middle of the night. Yesterday, around one in the morning, she woke, inconsolable, beating herself up for falling asleep at all when her baby had been murdered. We both tried, but I nor my – Ben – could console her. So, he suggested another glass of wine might help. I suspect he might've overdone it, which is why I found it so difficult to wake her yesterday. In fact, I didn't even know she'd gotten out of bed until she collapsed when Detective Roberts announced your reason for being at the house.'

'I'm sorry about that,' Cord said. 'But I'm curious about something you just said. You mentioned your father – Ben – might've been feeding your mother fentanyl so she wouldn't wake during the times he slipped out. What about you or Rheagan? Did you ever see him leave the house after your mother went to bed?'

Ellary nodded. 'Often. Late nights were his favorite time to work in his shop. He told us he couldn't sleep with so much on his mind, and the noise of the sanders and drills and hammers helped him clear things up. Since he primarily used it at night, he soundproofed it.' She snorted. 'He even built it himself. I was maybe five or six at the time, but I still remember he wouldn't let anyone near it. The contractors weren't even allowed to begin construction on the house until he had it completed. He told us once that his mother insisted that he get a job on a construction crew back in high school. He said she thought it would help keep him out of trouble, plus give him a skill he could utilize.'

As a consultant for a civil engineering firm, it made sense that Ben would understand the intricacies of building the tunnel beneath his shop. Alyssa caught sight of the frozen expression on Ellary's face, the one that said she'd just realized that she might've touched on one of the missed signs that something hadn't been quite right.

'I used to always beg to go with him, to help him build it, but of course he wouldn't let me. However, when he finished, he made it a huge production to bring us all over there. He packed a picnic, and we ate on what would become the back lawn, and then he put blindfolds on us and led us inside. Well, not Rheagan because she was still a baby.' The memory brought a smile that reached all the way to Ellary's eyes, and as if she realized how inappropriate that might be, the smile turned almost feral.

'Looking back, he must've laughed so hard at our gullibility, our mother's. Prancing around the place like a kid in the candy shop...' A moan filled with anguish and horror escaped. Wrapping both arms around her middle, she squeezed, rocking back and forth.

Even then, Barbara remained motionless, completely unaware of the trauma crashing all around her, the tragedy befalling her disintegrating family that her oldest daughter still had to shoulder entirely on her own.

In Ellary, Alyssa spotted a bit of herself, driven by strength and determination, and she could only hope the young woman would be able to, someday far off in the future, come out stronger on the other side.

'After that day, did you ever visit your father's—'

Fire shooting from her eyes, Ellary snapped, 'Let's stop calling him that. The man I knew as my father never would've been capable of what you discovered beneath his shop. Call him anything else, but don't refer to him as my father anymore.'

Cord nodded his understanding and rephrased his question. 'Did you, Rheagan, or your mother ever visit – Ben's workshop?'

'Never. That was his sanctuary – literally what he called it. We weren't allowed in it or even near it after that first and only time. I once got spanked because I used it to hide behind during a game of hide and seek.' Her lips tightened into a thin line. 'It was the first time I ever saw my father so enraged. The only other time I saw him lose it that badly was a year or two ago when he caught Rheagan and Raider near it, making out.'

Alyssa and Cord shared a look. 'Do you remember how old you were when you were using it to play hide and seek?'

'No. Though I do recall that Rheagan wasn't quite old enough to understand how to play.' Another memory brought a brief smile. 'She would stand behind a tree and giggle or – my favorite – "hide" in front of one of the boulders in our back yard.'

'You said your father spent a lot of time in his workshop, creating things. How often did you see the items he created?' Alyssa asked.

'Every Christmas. It was a tradition. Every year, he made my mother something, sometimes big like the bureau in their bedroom and sometimes small like the cutting board or the wooden animals she lined the window planters with.'

Alyssa fell silent as she tried to lasso the million questions poking at her into a more cohesive pile. One of the things she couldn't seem to figure out was how Ben had been able to bring his victims in and out without getting caught, even if he used the tunnel. 'Did your – Ben – go for a lot of night drives?'

'I couldn't say. I know there were times I'd get up in the middle of the night for a drink of water or whatever, and I'd see his headlights coming or going, but I never gave it much thought past the belief that he must be going for a drive for the same reason he opted to work in his shop at night.'

Alyssa thought of the Colorado cases. 'Did Ben ever travel for his job?'

'All the time, mostly to Colorado.' Her gaze drifted up to the ceiling for a moment. When she looked back at Alyssa and Cord, a short, humorless laugh escaped. 'You know what just occurred to me? During those times he was gone, my mother always seemed more awake and with it. Especially if he was gone for a week or more. After the first few days, she seemed more relaxed and less sluggish. And she never needed a glass of wine before she went to bed. Now I understand why.'

The more Alyssa heard about Ben, the more she wondered the same thing as Ellary. How had he been able to go unnoticed for so long? 'Is there any place you're aware of that he might've gone into hiding? A favorite vacation spot? Anything at all that you can think of?'

Ellary's thumb stroked the top of her mother's hand, so frail and tiny in her own. 'Durango, Wolf Creek, Taos, places like that. A few years back, when he was traveling to Colorado quite a bit for work, he considered building a vacation home there, but nothing ever came of it. But even if he had, I doubt he'd go there or to any of the other places because those would be the first places you'd look.'

Ellary cast her eyes down and then out the window before looking back to Alyssa. 'Is he going to come after us, me or my mom?'

Alyssa wished she could give an unequivocal no, but she wouldn't lie to her. 'We can't know what he's thinking right now. But if he *does* try to contact you in any way, please call us immediately. In the meantime, we'll make sure the police are watching the house, in case he comes back. I would suggest, however, that you find another place to stay until we do catch him.'

'I'd already planned on staying at my apartment. Whenever they release my mother, I mean.'

Alyssa glanced at Barbara's face, but if she recognized that they were even in the room, her mental acuity gave no indication. As she and Cord left Ellary so they could return to the precinct, she felt sorry for the twenty-two-year-old girl in that room, being forced to carry this heavy burden on her own.

Ellary and Barbara, like all the others, were simply two more of Ben's victims. And he needed to be stopped before he had the opportunity to destroy any other families.

Chapter Fifty

Sunday, June 5

Back at the precinct by noon, Joe and Tony were in the midst of an intense discussion over what evidence the crime scene techs had gathered from Ben Pembroke's murder den, as they'd begun calling it. Hal, with a finger plugged into one ear and a phone pressed to the other, spoke with increasing animation to the person on the other end of the line.

Thinking she'd search Ben's laptop, Alyssa looked around the room for it before she remembered the computer technicians had taken possession while they tried to gain access to it. If it hadn't been for the blatant Polaroid images he'd kept in his office, she would've had doubts that he'd be bold or dumb enough to keep anything of importance on his computer at all.

While she waited patiently, as much as she could, for Hal to finish his call, Alyssa perused the organized chaos of scribbled notes scattered around the table. In the center of it all was the brown banker's box of photographs. Her stomach turned at what Ben had done to his victims.

Wearing a tense but excited expression that made him look like a madman, Hal finally said goodbye to the person on the other end of the line and dropped his phone into his lap. Alyssa, the team, and the captain, who had just walked in, turned to him expectantly. Already on pins and needles, she barely resisted growling out her question. 'Well, what did you find out?'

'To be clear, I'm still working on verifying some of these things, but what I've learned since yesterday is that those Polaroid pictures pretty much prove he's left a trail of bodies that extend beyond New Mexico and Colorado. Speaking of Colorado, I reached out to Chief Porter again to tell him about Ben so he could scratch Hoyt off his radar and warn him that Pembroke's on the run. I emailed him a photo so he could be on the lookout in case Ben decides to head that way. Porter said he hopes he does because he'd love to be the one to take him down.

'Now, back to what I was saying. First, Ben's an only child whose parents are deceased. Murder/suicide. Father killed his mother. So, is it a case of the apple not falling far from the tree? I don't know. Regardless, in the limited time I've been looking, I would venture to guess Ben's been exhibiting signs of sociopathy probably as early as middle school, if not before.'

When Hal stopped speaking for several seconds, the team looked from him to Alyssa who said, 'You're going to explain that, right?'

Hal shook his head. 'Sorry. Was still trying to get my thoughts in some semblance of order. Anyway, starting right around the time Ben would've been in sixth grade – so, about ten or eleven – several people in or near neighborhoods where his family lived filed complaints with the local police regarding animals going missing and later being discovered strangled and/or stabbed to death. Some had even been skinned. These complaints continued for a span of about four years. One of the last ones described spotting a boy with longish, unkempt hair, acne across his nose, and carrying a black backpack on the day his cat disappeared. Two days later, the caller found his mutilated cat in a field near his house.'

Hal's lips vibrated against the breath he pushed out. 'I used that app that can pull up yearbooks from any year, and when I came across Ben's picture, he fit the description. But to be fair, so did about a dozen other boys, and even a few girls. So, there's that.'

'Torturing animals, narcissism, lack of empathy or remorse – all those are classic signs of a serial killer,' Tony said.

'Yeah, well,' Hal continued, 'believe it or not, that's not even the worst part. When Ben was a sophomore in high school, Austin Rolling, a fourteen-year-old boy, went missing. According to his family, he had what we would probably recognize today as some form of autism, and so he was awkward and shy and struggled to make friends, which at times, they said, made him too trusting.'

Alyssa's stomach twisted at the thought of what the young boy must've suffered.

'A search party was formed, and I came across a newspaper article that shows a picture of the volunteers. And guess who was lurking in the background?'

Though the question had been rhetorical, Alyssa answered anyway. 'Ben Pembroke.'

'Wow,' Hal teased. 'You're good at this. You should think about becoming a detective.'

Because she recognized Hal's attempt to break some of the tension, Alyssa tried to smile, but it fell flat, and so he went on.

'A week after Austin disappeared, a park ranger practically tripped over the boy in a small clearing in the woods. According to the police report, the boy's hands and feet had been restrained with rope, and he'd been strangled. According to the autopsy report on file, there were also strong indications he'd been tortured for, quote, "a long time." The front of the boy's chest showed evidence of deep and shallow puncture wounds that would've been agonizing but wouldn't have killed him right away.'

'Jesus,' Cord breathed out.

'And no one was arrested?' Alyssa asked the question she already knew the answer to.

'No suspects have ever even been named. But get this – and I'll be the first to admit this could mean nothing – Ben's family upped and moved less than two months later. Not far, mind you, just a few miles away, still in the same school district, but out of that particular neighborhood.'

'Did any more complaints about missing and mutilated animals come from that neighborhood after their move?' Joe asked.

'Not that I can find. But look, I have some other news that you're going to want to hear.' He paused a beat. 'In searching for possible hideouts Ben Pembroke might use, I scoured social media. He and Barbara shared one Facebook account which, from scrolling through posts and timelines, I'd say he used less than one percent of the time. And while Barbara isn't what I'd label active, she does, on occasion, like someone else's post.'

'And?' Alyssa prodded as Hal paused to gulp down half a bottle of water.

'And I came across an incident that occurred last October when a friend of hers, Pamela Paulson, reached out and told Barbara she'd be in town for the Balloon Fiesta and would love to catch up over lunch. They agreed on a date and time, but Barbara cancelled at the last minute.' Scowling as if someone had interrupted him, he impatiently waved his hand through the air. 'I'm getting ahead of myself. More about that in a minute.

'I slid into this friend's DM, explained who I was, and requested she contact me right away, which, to my surprise, she did. I mean, within minutes. According to her, she and Barbara were best friends during college, at least until Ben came onto the scene. Anyway, in the course of our conversation, she let it drop that… you're not going to believe it…' Hal practically bounced in his chair. 'Turns out Barbara Pembroke has an older sister, Camille Bowman, from whom she's been estranged for the past twenty-five years.'

The reaction in the room ranged from astonishment to excitement. 'Tell me you were able to track this sister down,' Alyssa said.

Hal smiled. 'As luck and ingenuity would have it, I did. She still lives in Vermont where she and Barbara grew up. To call her reluctant at first would be a mild understatement, but once I explained my purpose for reaching out, she turned on like a broken spigot, and I could barely get any questions in. Figuring she was answering at least half the questions I had for her anyway, I just let her exorcize all the anger and hurt she'd been holding in for the past two and a half decades. And let me tell you, lady and gents, Camille Bowman filled in a few gaps. Not sure how the info will help yet beyond understanding Pembroke – both Ben and Barbara – but it can't hurt.'

Alyssa, Cord, Joe, Tony, and even the captain settled into their chairs, leaning forward like they were at the best part of a campfire story.

'According to the sister, Ben transferred from Frostburg State University in Maryland to the University of Vermont during his and Barbara's junior year of college when they were twenty years old. One night they attended a bonfire, and Barbara, being the social butterfly and champion of all underdogs, noticed her future husband standing off in the shadows by himself and abandoned her group of friends to coerce him into joining in the fun.'

Alyssa tried and failed to picture the woman now lying in a near catatonic state in the hospital as ever having been an outgoing social butterfly. From the very first meeting, Barbara had always struck her as meek and close to submissive. Of course, with everything they'd learned since yesterday, she could now see that Ben's wife hadn't been mild-mannered so much as well-behaved. That bit of hindsight slapped her in the face, and now that she'd labeled it, she wondered how any of them had ever missed it. Much like Ellary couldn't understand how she or her family had missed the signs that her father was a cold-blooded killer.

Thinking of Ellary, Alyssa wondered if she even knew she had an aunt. 'Did Camille ever get to meet her nieces?'

Hal shook his head. 'She said she only knew they existed because she Facebook-stalked her sister back in 2014. And she also highly doubts Barbara ever told them about her because she couldn't see Ben allowing it.'

'Did she ever try to reach out?' Cord asked.

'Nope, but there's a reason. And again, I'll get to that,' Hal said. 'Camille was a senior in college when Ben erupted onto the scene. For several months, Barbara kept their relationship strictly in the buddy zone because their father could be a bit of a controlling tyrant. And anytime either of his daughters managed to slip even a little out from under his thumb, he threatened to pull all his financial support.'

'Sounds like a pleasant man,' Tony muttered, not quite under his breath. 'Also explains why she might've been comfortable being manipulated and controlled by Ben, whether she realized it or not.'

'Right?' Hal agreed. 'Anyway, Camille mentioned that when Barbara and Ben did begin dating, Barbara hedged on introducing him to her parents which seemed to agitate him quite a bit.'

'How would Camille know that?' Alyssa asked.

'Barbara confided in her.'

'Agitate him how?' Until Captain Hammond threw out his question, Alyssa had forgotten he'd perched himself on the edge of a chair in the corner of the room.

'Camille didn't really say. But even though Barbara took great pains in keeping her relationship with Ben from her parents, they found out when the two girls returned home for Christmas break and Camille let it slip. At first, they thought their father had taken the news quite well until a couple of days later when he brandished a background report on Ben and demanded Barbara stop seeing him because he had an act of vandalism on his record around the age of fifteen.'

'That's a juvenile record, so how would the father get his hands on that kind of information?' Hammond asked.

'When I asked her that same thing, Camille simply said her father had his ways, but imagined he employed a private investigator to dig it up. Regardless of how, their father had the information and made his displeasure clear. Since Barbara wasn't in love with Ben, she agreed to break things off when they returned to school. However, when she tried, Ben pried the truth out of her, and according to Camille, he didn't take the news well at all. And since he could be pretty convincing when he wanted something,

Camille said she was actually a bit surprised when her sister remained steadfast in her decision. Though, because he was so distraught, Barbara did concede to the two of them remaining friends.

'About a month later, Camille and Barbara's parents were killed in a freak accident coming back from Mount Mansfield. It had been raining quite heavily, and the brakes on their new car failed. From the tire tracks on either side of the road, the police surmised that a deer or something leaped out in front of them, but they saw it too late. Mr. Bowman likely swerved and then overcorrected, causing him to flip the vehicle when the brakes failed to engage.'

Hal sat back in his seat and let that sink in before sharing the rest. 'Camille and Barbara were understandably shaken and in shock. She surmised that was probably why it was so easy for Ben to swoop in and take care of Barbara the way he did while they were trying to settle the estate – in which they both inherited a substantial sum of money.'

'So, Barbara told him about her parents dying even after they broke up?' Tony asked.

'No. Camille got the call from the state police, and she immediately went to Barbara's room to deliver the news to her. Since Barbara and Ben had already broken up, Camille was surprised to see him there, but she was so shaken up she didn't stop to think about asking him to leave. As soon as he heard what had happened, Ben, in her words, "leaped into action," and insisted on driving her and Barbara to their family home. At the time, both women were grateful for the offer.'

'Let's back up a minute,' Cord said. 'How much is a substantial amount of money?'

'Close to six million each.'

Joe whistled between his teeth. 'Whew.'

'But you're not asking the right question yet,' Hal hinted.

'What do you mean?' Alyssa asked.

'I mean, was Ben Pembroke somehow involved in Mr. and Mrs. Bowman's deaths?'

Alyssa shot up. 'Was he a suspect?'

Hal's lips turned down into a frown. 'Not in any official capacity, no. But according to Camille, after she and Barbara finally began to emerge from their fog of grief, she started to question certain inconsistencies in things Ben had told them.'

Until her brain sent a warning signal to uncurl her fingers, Alyssa hadn't realized she'd been clenching them into fists. The blood rushing back in needled her skin, and she shook her hands as she asked, 'Inconsistencies such as?'

'Such as where he'd been around the time of their parents' deaths. In one story, he'd been off camping – alone. In another, he'd made the nine or ten-hour drive home to visit his mother in the hospital because she'd suffered a heart attack. When Camille asked what hospital, she said Ben became agitated and angry. But the part that disturbed her the most was a comment he made while driving the girls back home right after the accident. She said he mentioned something about it "being so sad their brakes failed." At the time, she didn't think much of it. It wasn't until much later that she realized he'd made that comment *before* Camille or Barbara had learned of that particular detail.'

Chapter Fifty-One

Sunday, June 5

The flutters in Alyssa's stomach exploded into full-fledged fireworks as she shot up out of her seat. 'Did she report that to the police?'

'She claimed she tried, but the police insisted that the brakes were faulty, a tragedy sure, but' – Hal rubbed the heel of his hand across his forehead, a sign of his agitation – 'the officers she spoke with, according to her, all treated her as a "conspiracy theorist" who couldn't handle her parents dying. She said one of them also claimed, and I quote her quote: "You and your sister just inherited a buttload of dough, so why are you trying to make a suspicious death claim when all it will do is delay you getting your inheritance?" End quote.'

'Wow,' Tony said. 'Some people are real assholes, aren't they?'

'Don't we all know it? Anyway, Camille said she tried to talk to Barbara, who, of course, told Ben. And you can all guess how that turned out. Twenty-five years later, they're still not speaking.'

'You said you told her why you were calling. Does that mean you informed her what Ben is suspected of?' Alyssa asked.

'Yes. And no. I implied we were looking into some things but didn't go so far as to mention the term serial killer. And before you ask, she said she's sorry her sister's in the hospital, but she doesn't think she'll be extending an olive branch anytime soon. She tried that once in 2000, but it ended badly, and she never made another attempt. She simply moved on with her life. Of course, she might reconsider once everything comes out.'

Alyssa paced, speaking out loud to no one in particular. 'That's a classic sign of an abuser. Slowly remove your victim from their friends and family until you're all that's left.' She stopped pacing and turned back to Hal. 'Aside from learning about Camille, did you get anything else from Pamela Paulson?'

'A little. A few months after the Bowmans died, Pamela called to invite Barbara to lunch, but Barbara declined because she and Ben had gotten married by a justice of the peace and had pulled up roots and moved to New Mexico. The news took Pamela by complete surprise.'

'What a soap opera,' Alyssa mumbled. She sincerely hoped, somewhere in this episode, they'd pluck that one tidbit of information that would lead them to Ben. She grabbed onto the back of an empty chair and tilted it back. 'Okay, so in review, Ben sees a form of weakness in Barbara, probably that first night when she approached him, and begins to exploit that until he's wormed his way in. There's a strong possibility that he killed her parents by tampering with their brakes, but unless we get a full confession out of him, I doubt we'll ever really know for sure.

'We know that Ben's a consultant for a civil engineering firm, but the house they live in and their property would've been a tight squeeze on his income alone, so with control of his wife's inheritance, he moves them to a state where nobody knows them and into a nice area with a large parcel of land so that his neighbors aren't right on top of him, making it possible to go about his activities with less of a chance for being caught.'

Alyssa aimed her finger at Hal. 'Have you run a check to see about any open cases in Vermont or even Maryland that match Ben's MO?'

'Not yet. I was going to tackle that next. But I do have one final bit of information that you're all going to find interesting. Just before I hung up with Pamela, she confided the one thing that always bothered her about Ben straight from the beginning – aside from the creepy way he seemed able to manipulate people – stemmed from his bizarrely intense fascination with serial killers, especially Herman Mudgett.'

Alyssa, like the others, drew a blank.

Suddenly, Tony snapped his fingers together and jabbed his finger at the projected image of the murder den and the tunnel leading off it. 'Herman Mudgett aka Dr. Henry Holmes – I remember studying him in one of my criminal justice classes. Fairly recently, some have begun to theorize that he and Jack the Ripper were one and the same. Aside from that, though, the house he built was specifically designed for him to commit his murders. He even went so far as to install trapdoors, soundproofed rooms, shit like that.' He glanced around the room. 'Sounds familiar, right? If I remember correctly, he even used gas jets to suffocate his victims and then burned their bodies in a kiln down in his basement. I guess we can be grateful Pembroke didn't go that far.'

With that, Hammond pushed to his feet and headed for the door where he turned and pointed to Hal. 'Dig deeper and go further back into Pembroke's background. We need to find this sonofabitch fast because now that he's achieved his goal to get noticed, my gut tells me he's only going to escalate because, like all serial killers, he'll be incapable of stopping.'

'Unless we stop him or he dies,' Alyssa countered.

Joe shrugged. 'I'm good with either of those scenarios.'

'Not me,' Tony disagreed. 'I want answers. And once we catch him, I think we'll get them because he won't be able to stop himself from talking himself up.'

Mayor Kelson surprised them all by appearing in the doorway, but Cord's phone rang before he could speak. The team looked at Cord expectantly, but Alyssa already knew the answer by the way her partner's eyebrows shot straight toward his hairline.

'Unknown Number. Anyone want to bet it's *not* Pembroke?'

Chapter Fifty-Two

After realizing that the police had discovered his secret, Ben had driven aimlessly until he found himself in a familiar place, though he'd only been there on two other occasions. He backed his vehicle into the carport so that anyone out for a walk wouldn't notice his license plate. Inside, he'd immediately grabbed the remote and turned on the television, flipping through the channels until he saw his face, big as day, flashed on the screen.

Though he'd been expecting it, he erupted in a blinding rage. When he finally settled down, half the art on the walls and shelves littered the floor in shards of colorful glass and broken material.

Adrenaline still pulsed inside him, but he knew he could crash anytime, so he reached into his pocket, grabbed a Modafinil, and popped it in his mouth, swallowing it dry. He needed to think.

Another surge of fury heated his skin as he thought about Rheagan. When it came right down to it, the fault of everything happening right now could be placed squarely at her feet. She had been the first domino to fall in his carefully constructed world. Years ago, when he'd noticed his youngest daughter's desire to garner attention through outrageous stunts, a kernel of an idea began to form and grow.

Rheagan, unlike Ellary, who took after her mother, had inherited that need to feed a darker part of herself, a need that he recognized. The night he'd returned home with Kennedy stowed in the trunk of his car and discovered Rheagan hadn't gone out for the night – he'd lied to the cops when he said he'd been unaware of her plans to meet up with her two best friends – that seed had burst open. He'd seen it as a sign. After all, if Rheagan hadn't run into Kennedy at the store and stopped to talk to her, he never would've made the decision to learn the woman's routine and snatch her.

Excited, imagining a world where he and his daughter paired up to rain terror on the unsuspecting world, he'd pulled his car around to the back of the property next to the hidden tunnel. He'd pried open the grate, popped the trunk, and tossed Kennedy over his shoulder so he could descend the ladder. As soon as his feet hit the bottom, he dropped her on the ground and dragged her into his den.

And then he'd driven back around to the house where he went inside, surprised to see Rheagan getting ready to leave. He asked if she had a few minutes because he wanted to show her something. He could see the 'no' forming on her lips, and so he'd added the one thing he knew would entice her.

'It's in my shop.'

A place no one, ever, was allowed. A dangling carrot she couldn't resist.

Her animated chatter as they moved across the lawn stopped only when he placed his fingers to his lips as they stepped inside his shop. He closed the door behind them before turning on the lights. Her eyes brimming with the excitement of a shared secret, she'd turned in a circle, searching. And then he'd opened the storage cabinet, moved a box, and showed her the entrance to his secret den.

Confusion mixed with a little fear crossed her face, but her curiosity and excitement won out as, pummeling him with a ceaseless array of questions, she'd descended the wooden steps after him.

There, her fanatical curiosity gave way to a bellowing scream. He turned to see the horror written on her face at the sight of the crumpled woman in the glass chamber. And then she'd fled back up the stairs where he barely managed to catch her.

'Shut up,' he hissed.

But her screams continued as he dragged her back down. At the bottom, she tried to bite him, and so he slammed her head into the wall to get her attention.

When he did, her phone slid out of her hand and fell to the ground, and his eyes were instantly drawn to the cracked screen with a nine and one on display. She'd already been calling the police. Enraged, he'd stomped on her phone and twisted her hair around his fist as he hauled her into the glass room. He hadn't planned on killing her; he only needed her to calm down so she would understand.

And so he'd placed her in cuffs and restrained her to the bar. When he backed up, she'd raised her foot and kicked him hard in the chest, knocking the air out of him. What happened next had been a blur of disconnected memories. All he knew was that when he came back to awareness, he'd, at some point, sealed her mouth with tape, placed leg irons around her ankles, and beaten her to death, making her barely recognizable even to him.

He'd expected to feel something other than anger at what she'd made him do, but he didn't.

The next day, his wife had been frantic when she realized Rheagan was missing, and it had taken him a minute to catch on and play his part. And then when Alyssa Wyatt had shown up at his house, the same detective he'd eluded fourteen years ago after kidnapping and killing a boy who'd pulled over to help him change his tire, the thrill of taunting her had seemed too good an opportunity to pass up. That was when the nursery rhyme taunt had come to him.

And placing it on a picture of Galveston's tortured body had been the perfect touch. The kid had been one of the few he hadn't planned. The opportunity had just presented itself, and before he knew what he was doing, he'd hit Galveston in the back of the head with the tire iron and tossed him into the back of his open trunk.

A tree branch scraping against the window pulled Ben away from his memory before he could begin to relive the kid's last days.

He shook his head to clear it. He couldn't turn back time and undo whatever he'd done that had turned the cops onto his scent, he understood that. But he also found he didn't want to because now that people knew, they'd talk about him for centuries to come. His name would become synonymous with the scariest urban legends and real-life monsters alike. Even long after he died, he would live on in the stories told.

But first he needed to make sure Alyssa Wyatt and her team didn't think they'd won. He needed them to remember he was in charge. He needed them to fear him.

He grabbed a burner phone that he'd stopped and bought along the way, glad he'd chosen not to take his real phone when he'd left his house yesterday. He pulled the business card out of his wallet and called.

Chapter Fifty-Three

Sunday, June 5

Cord placed his phone on speaker and set it in front of him so everyone could listen in as he answered. 'Let me guess. Pembroke?'

Ben clucked his tongue. 'Aren't you the clever one, Detective Roberts. Now, I know Detective Wyatt must be nearby, and I know you all think you've won, but I assure you, you haven't.'

At the sound of pompous condescension and exaggerated superiority oozing from Ben's voice, Alyssa's skin tightened as if it had been encased in shrink-wrap.

'Because you haven't caught me. And you won't. Just ask Detective Wyatt about that. Even knowing my name, she can't manage to bring me down. In fact, she's proven to be quite boring, don't you think? And now, because of her pathetically failed attempts to catch me, you have to live with the worry that one day I will come for your families. Come to think of it, I recall reading in the paper how you, Detective Roberts, magnanimously adopted two little kids whose mother had been tragically slaughtered in her own home.' Ben's voice dripped with feigned sadness.

Rarely did Alyssa witness the biting heat of hatred currently flowing out of her partner. In the eight years that they'd been teamed up, more often than not, he proved to be a six-foot-two-inch teddy bear who allowed very little to pierce his outer armor of calm.

'You know, I've never killed anyone that young before, though I'm certainly not opposed to trying something new. In fact, I rather look forward to the idea.' He chuckled. 'Of course, I did consider killing Ellary once when she was about two. I didn't only because it's so much simpler to fool everyone when you're a loving family man, don't you think? I mean, obviously, the answer is yes since you never suspected me even for a minute.'

Red spread from Cord's muscled neck and throughout his face as he shot Alyssa a look – one she was all too familiar with – the near impossibility of remaining grounded in reason when your family was being overtly threatened.

'I'm going to stop you right there,' Cord said through gritted teeth, 'because now it's *my* turn for *you* to pay attention. If you're really as smart as you think you are, then you already know the hell I'll rain down on your head will make the sun feel cold in comparison if you choose not to heed every single letter of my warning. Don't ever threaten my children again, or my wife, or anyone else important to me. That includes Detective Wyatt and her family, as well as every single member on this team.' The wobble in his voice stemmed not from fear but fury.

'Again, Detective, you'd first have to catch me, wouldn't you? And we all know that's never going to happen. You may know my name, but that's as far as you'll ever get. I warned Wyatt I was the best, but she refused to believe me. So, remember, whatever happens next is all on her.'

Though his words remained arrogant, Alyssa detected an undercurrent of unease and discontent at being challenged back. She had a feeling that was because the intricate web of protection he'd woven around himself over the years had finally begun to unravel, and he was helpless to stop it.

Still, Pembroke maintained his blustery machismo with one last comment. 'I'd tell you to be on the lookout for me, but the truth is, you'll never see me coming. And neither will your families.' He ended the call without warning.

Before anyone could say a word, Mayor Kelson spoke from the doorway. 'Actually, he should be on the lookout for you because I know exactly where he is.'

Chapter Fifty-Four

While Alyssa and the team raced out of the precinct, address in hand, the mayor was on the phone requesting backup from the state police. Because Ben's personality teetered on the edge of volatility, they needed stealth and experience on their side in order to avoid further casualties or the possibility of a hostage situation.

With the end in sight, Alyssa tore down the interstate, darting in and out of traffic. Out of the corner of her eye, she spotted Cord grip the handlebar above his head.

'Here's a wild and crazy thought,' he snarled, 'practice a little patience because I don't know if you're aware of this or not, but getting into an accident before we get to where we're going isn't going to save us any time. In fact, I'm damn sure it'll delay the hell out of us.'

Alyssa let him see the exaggerated roll of her eyes. 'In the past eight years, tell me one time I've ever gotten us into an accident. Go ahead. I'll wait.'

'First time for everything, as the saying goes.' He waved her rebuttal away with an irritated wave of his hand. 'Look, you do you, but just remember you're going to be the one Carter lectures when he finds out you're driving like a lunatic.'

Despite the mission they were on, Alyssa couldn't stop the bark of laughter that erupted. 'We're on our way to take down a serial killer, and you're really going to threaten to use a six-year-old child against me? That's the best argument you can come up with?'

Cord shot her a sideways look. 'Laugh all you want, but you know I'm right.'

Though it hadn't been his intention, Cord managed to cut the tension in the vehicle as they sped down the road toward the Carson National Forest.

Long before he'd dipped his feet into politics, the mayor, passionate about hiking, had built a cabin between Santa Fe and Taos. Lately, however, he'd been unable to make use of it as often as he'd like, and so he'd hired a cleaning company to go in once a month. Spotting an unfamiliar vehicle in the carport, the crew of two had hesitated and placed a call to the mayor to see if they'd misunderstood, that they weren't needed because he'd be there.

The mayor, surprised to hear someone was at his house, asked them to describe the vehicle. As soon as they gave the make, model, and color, he'd known and run in to tell Alyssa and the others. In Ben's overinflated, confident mind, he thought no one would suspect he'd stay in New Mexico, much less use the mayor's personal property as a place to hide out, even if only temporarily.

Ninety minutes into their drive, Hal called. 'Thought you'd like the update. State police, as well as the local authorities, have all been notified. The mayor got a hold of the park rangers in the area to be on alert, so you'll have them as backup, too. And we've already tapped into the traffic cameras along the way. We can now confirm that Pembroke is in the area.'

'Did the mayor happen to mention we need to avoid using the radio as a form of communication in order to keep our arrival off police scanners?' Alyssa asked.

'He did. And Sheriff Sparks and the others all have your cell number, as well as Cord's. I'll be shooting off a text in a moment so you'll have theirs. That way, you can coordinate the takedown before you head in. In the meantime, the sheriff is mobilizing two of his deputies who will close off the area to incoming traffic. He also reached out to the owners of the cabins nearest the mayor's, and to everyone's knowledge, all are currently unoccupied. Which, as you know, doesn't necessarily translate into Pembroke being any less dangerous.'

Cord agreed. 'I'd wager to guess he could be more so considering he'll be no more than a cornered animal with nowhere to run.'

'Exactly. But at least we've lowered the risk of a potential hostage situation,' Hal said.

Alyssa found herself crossing her fingers as she clutched the steering wheel tighter. 'Let's hope that's true. And thanks for the update.'

'No problem. Just remember service is spotty out there. More importantly, stay safe. Unhinged sociopaths don't usually react the way we expect.'

'That's why we plan on going in silent and surrounding the place before we announce our presence. Trust me, Hal. Ben Pembroke won't be slipping through our fingers today. He may have eluded me before, but today there'll be nowhere for him to go except jail.'

–

Close to an hour later, Alyssa and Cord met up with Joe, Tony, the sheriff, and his team, and everyone moved into

317

place. Unless Ben managed to turn himself invisible, it would be impossible for him to slip through their nearly airtight perimeter. They had all bases covered and then a few more for the sake of insurance. Using binoculars, they'd already verified he remained inside the mayor's cabin, unaware that his days of murdering innocent people were over.

At her signal, a dozen armed officers made their cautious approach. With her nerves stretched tight enough to snap, Alyssa peeked down at her watch, waiting. When the time finally arrived, a calm settled over her. Signaling Cord and the sheriff, she held up ten fingers. They nodded, and the three of them quietly moved up the steps, trusting the others to do their part as well.

At the end of the countdown, two thunderous booms echoed off the trees around them as both Cord in the front and the team at the back kicked in the doors. Before Ben could do more than look up, startled, they had six weapons trained on him and six more at the ready outside. His head swiveled back and forth, unable to hide the stunned look of disbelief on his face.

Replacing her weapon in its holster and removing her handcuffs, Alyssa didn't give him a chance to speak as she said, 'Ben Pembroke, we have a warrant for your arrest for the unlawful flight to avoid prosecution and in the murders of Rheagan Pembroke, Gunner Galveston, Bella Teller, Faith Dexter, and Perry Singleton, as well as kidnapping and the attempted murder of Kennedy Farmer. I need you to stand up, turn around, and keep your hands where I can see them.'

Ben's eyes darted to the open front door and then to the back, weighing his chances of successfully bolting.

Though Alyssa almost wanted him to make a run for it just so she could chase him down and tackle him, she said, 'Ben, I'm warning you right now that if you make any sudden moves, force will be used.'

With his attention now focused solely on her, Ben's eyes morphed into evil black holes as he scooted his chair back and rose to his feet.

Alyssa swung him around before she latched onto one wrist and then the other, cuffing his hands behind his back while reading him his rights. When she finished, she asked, 'Do you understand the rights as I've given them to you?'

'Yes. But—'

'Good, then Mayor Kelson will be glad to know the vermin have been exterminated from his cabin.'

Instead of fear or anger or any of the other things he might've displayed, Ben gave a smug grin. 'You know the mayor isn't the only person I'm friends with. I'll be back on the streets by tomorrow, Tuesday at the latest.' He caught Cord's eyes. 'Can you surround your kids twenty-four/seven, three hundred sixty-five days, never knowing the moment I'll strike? Because I *will* definitely strike.'

Cord did the one thing he knew would infuriate Ben. He shrugged. 'I guess we'll see who's laughing in the coming days, won't we? Because none of the high-profile names you manage to drop are going to be able to ignore a murder chamber beneath the workshop on your property. Or the mountain of forensic evidence piling up. But I tell you what, if it'll make you feel better, you go ahead and compile a list of as many names as you like on the drive back into Albuquerque. In the end, it won't matter one iota because not only will you not walk out a free man tomorrow or Tuesday, but I'm betting your last moments of freedom were' – he made a show of glancing at his watch – 'seven minutes ago.'

Ben dug his feet in and lowered his voice into a menacing growl, this time directing his comment to both Alyssa and Cord. 'You know what I think? I think you brought all this backup because you're afraid of me, afraid of what I'd do if you had to face me all on your own.'

Alyssa's fingers tightened on Ben's arm as she marched him out the cabin door. 'Go ahead and keep telling yourself that, Mr. Pembroke. But the truth of the matter is: you're done. You see, since you rub elbows with so many public officials, you already know that judges and juries don't take it so lightly when someone commits multiple murders in a number of states – beginning at the age of fifteen.'

For the first time since the cuffs had been slapped on him, Ben Pembroke's arrogance vanished.

Chapter Fifty-Five

Sunday, June 5

Back at the precinct, Alyssa and Cord climbed out of her Tahoe and met Joe and Tony as they pulled Ben from the back of their car. But before they had taken ten steps toward the building, a flash of movement caught her eye. Within seconds, chaos erupted when Kennedy's father lunged across the parking lot at Ben. With his quick reflexes, Cord managed to latch onto Mr. Farmer's arms before he could make contact. Veins bulging in his temples from the exertion, Cord struggled to keep the enraged father from making the monumental mistake of letting his emotions overrule his common sense.

Amused by the attention or just enjoying Mr. Farmer's reaction, Ben grinned at the man as Cord continued to hold him back. Ben's teeth flashed as he leaned forward and whispered, 'Did Detective Wyatt here tell you how your daughter screamed for her daddy to save her, all while begging me to stop torturing her?'

Mr. Farmer shouted a string of obscenities as he fought to break Cord and Joe's hold.

In an effort to assist, Tony stepped in front of Mr. Farmer, blocking his view of Pembroke. 'Come on, man. Don't listen to him; don't let him do that to you. You've got to let the system work. Don't sink to the same level as this wasteland of pointless humanity because I'm telling you right now, sir, it might feel good – great even – in the moment, but once you've calmed down, you'll start to realize what a mistake it was. Listen to me.' He waited until Mr. Farmer's eyes met his. 'Can you tell me what good you're going to do Kennedy and the rest of your family if you're sitting behind bars?'

Only then did the fight start to dissolve, though Mr. Farmer's eyes spat fire. 'My daughter survived you, you sick bastard. Which means *she* beat *you*. Think about that while you're rotting behind bars for the rest of your miserable, pathetic life.'

Hatred burst from Ben's eyes, but Alyssa didn't give him time to respond. She hauled him up the steps and into the precinct where she locked him inside one of the small interrogation rooms and waited for Cord. As she did, she headed to the incident room where Hal had already predicted what she was after and handed her a stack of files on top of the brown banker's box they'd confiscated from Pembroke's home office.

'Here you go. You'll be wanting these,' he said. 'And just to give you a head's up, Hammond and Mayor Kelson are planning to watch the interrogation.'

'I wouldn't have expected anything less.'

Five minutes later, Cord, Joe, and Tony walked in.

'Mr. Farmer asked me to apologize to you from him,' Tony said. 'He heard on the news that we'd caught Pembroke, and he didn't stop to think beyond wanting to make the man who hurt his girl pay.'

Alyssa's heart hurt for Mr. Farmer because, even as an officer who upheld the law, she understood from the depths of her soul where he was coming from. 'I get it. I'm glad you were able to make him see reason before he did something he couldn't take back, though. I'll call him myself later.' She looked to Cord. 'But right now, let's not waste another second, and go get this done.'

In the interrogation room, Pembroke watched with a mix of anger and arrogant cunning.

Alyssa could almost see the wheels spinning in his head as she let the silence drag out while she set the box on the table. Then she pulled out one of the two remaining chairs and sat down, purposely closing the gap until less than a foot of space remained between him and her. She wanted him to feel cornered. 'I bet you recognize that box, don't you?'

Ben's smug grin returned as he shrugged. 'No, not really. Where'd you find it?'

'Do you really think playing dumb will get you out of this?'

'Not playing dumb. Just don't know what you're talking about. I'm an innocent family man that you've falsely accused.'

Cord sat across from Ben. 'That so?' He casually picked a file at random and flipped it open before moving on to the next and then the next. He glanced over to Alyssa. 'Where do you think he'd like us to start?' He turned his attention back to Ben. 'Got a favorite place, Pembroke?'

When he didn't respond, not that she expected him to, Alyssa turned the folders in his direction. 'How about New Mexico? No? Colorado? Vermont? Maryland?' With each name, she tapped the images of his alleged victims and then pushed the files in front of him. By the time she finished, the smug expression on Ben's face had disappeared.

Though she found it difficult not to, Alyssa managed to bite back her own smirk. 'I see we finally have your attention.'

Ben narrowed his eyes and turned to Cord. 'Well, have you got anything to add to this pathetic display of mind games?'

'Not really a mind game, no.' Cord leaned back and crossed his arms over his chest. 'Do you know the great thing about DNA, Ben? The technology changes all the time, making it nearly *impossible* for someone to continue getting away with murder. They've even developed a way to extract DNA from shafts of hair that don't have the root attached. Crazy, right?' He thumped his knuckles on each of the files. 'Every last one of these cold cases contains forensic evidence – blood, skin, hair – that investigators have never been able to track to any certain individual. But I'm betting all that's about to change now that we have you in custody.'

Under the harsh glare of lights, sweat began beading on Ben's upper lip, and Alyssa knew Cord had managed to strike a nerve. 'I know my rights. Which means I know you can't get my DNA without a warrant.'

With a sound far removed from humor, Alyssa laughed. 'And you don't think we have one of those coming right now? You may have been getting away with murder for more than two decades, but no more. After the state of New Mexico tries and convicts you, I imagine it'll be a toss-up over who gets you next. But you can rest assured that every state where we've contacted the cold case division is going to want their crack at you. The only thing you've got going for you right now is that the death penalty is off the table in most of the states where you committed your crimes. Which, if you ask

324

me, is good because then you'll get to live out the rest of your miserable days spinning around and around in your head trying to come to terms with the fact that you're not nearly as smart as you thought you were. That should be a fun maze for you to follow.'

Ben's eyes flashed a demonic red as the cords in his neck muscles strained to break through his skin. 'You think you've outsmarted me?' He shoved his chair back into the wall. 'The strongest and smartest will always come out ahead. It's survival of the fittest. I'm sure you've heard of it. And even if you live to be a hundred fifty, you'll never be smarter than me.'

It took effort, but Alyssa bit back her smile. He had no idea how much she counted on him thinking he couldn't be outwitted at his own games. Every narcissistic criminal she'd ever encountered imagined the same thing – no one could ever be more brilliant than him or her. With zero exceptions, they'd all been wrong. And almost always, it was their vanity that tripped them up.

Some might've been harder to crack than others, but in the end, in their quest to prove their superiority, they all gave themselves away. As much as he wanted to think differently, Ben Pembroke had been cut from the same cloth.

She leaned in close and lowered her voice. 'You didn't survive because you're "the fittest," Ben. You're not stronger, smarter, or more superior. What's more is you know it. Isn't that why you targeted' – she scooted back and rapped her knuckles against the files, ending on the one of the first murder they believed he'd committed, that of fourteen-year-old Austin Rolling – 'much younger, weaker individuals?' She leaned in closer. 'That's why you threatened to go after my son and Cord's kids, why you even considered murdering Ellary when she was a baby. Admit it. You picked out the defenseless ones because you're actually a coward inside.'

Ben reeled backwards like Alyssa had hit him with a right hook. 'I'm no coward,' he snarled.

She lifted the lid off the box and set the Polaroid images he'd taken in front of him. 'If you're not a coward, why did you detain all your victims in a way in which they couldn't fight back? Because you knew you'd lose?' Using her finger, she pushed a photograph, not a Polaroid, of Rheagan in front of Ben. 'You killed helpless animals and children, Ben.' She tapped Rheagan's picture. 'Your own child, even. How much more loathsome can a person be?'

The more she talked, the more crimson Ben's face turned until it looked ready to burst.

'I demand to speak to my attorney, Detective.'

Alyssa shot Ben a savage smile as she and Cord rose to their feet and gathered their things. At the door, she turned back to face this detestable monster one more time. 'Before we go, and while you wait for your lawyer, maybe you can think about how very much other prisoners abhor your kind. I understand it's kind of a code they live by. Maybe it'll be you sleeping with one eye open at all times and looking over your shoulder twenty-four/seven, three hundred sixty-five, wondering when someone's going to strike. To put it in terms that you'll understand, I'll tell you what you told Kennedy Farmer: no matter what, you won't be leaving there alive.'

With that, she and Cord walked out, locking the door behind them. Maybe she shouldn't have, but knowing he wouldn't talk, she'd purposely gotten under his skin by proving that he was superior only in his own mind.

After a quick pitstop to the ladies' room, Alyssa headed back to rejoin the others. They might have apprehended their suspect, but they were far from done. With the ever-growing pile of evidence against him and more to come, Alyssa's confidence in securing a conviction only increased.

On her way to the incident room, she spotted Frank Neely standing near Ruby's desk, and her heart stuttered as she headed in his direction. Not sure he'd accept it, she reached out her hand, mildly surprised when he actually shook it. 'I'm glad you stopped by. I was going to call you.'

Frank dropped her hand and took a step back. 'Is it true? You finally got him? The weak, murdering bastard who killed my brother and destroyed my family?'

Alyssa nodded. 'Yes. I'm sorry it took so long to get here. I won't offer any excuses, but I hope you know that even though he's been apprehended, we won't stop until we've made absolutely certain that the person who murdered Gunner won't ever get a chance to hurt anyone else again.'

Frank looked away and then back to Alyssa. 'I'm working hard at trying not to blame you and the rest of the police force who pushed Gunner's case to the side. In my head, I know it wasn't your fault, that you didn't make that decision. It's my heart that's still struggling with it. If I'm being honest, I know the fact that you came to question me at all, knowing how I'd react, proved you still wanted to get justice for Gunner.

'Even so, I do want to apologize for one thing. I should never have called what happened to your own brother a failure on your part. I let my emotions overrule common sense, and I knew that strike would hurt you the most, so I used it. That was wrong of me. I'm a psychiatrist, and

I know better. If it helps you to forgive me, I'm ashamed of myself for sinking that low. Besides that, what I said wasn't even true. Of course, I only know what the news reported at the time, but from everything I've heard, you were just a child yourself and can't be blamed for what happened. Again, I'm sorry, not just for what I said, but for what happened to your family.'

Blinking back tears, Alyssa swallowed past the lump in her throat. 'Thank you. I appreciate that.'

This time, Frank offered his hand and nodded toward the open door where her team waited for her. 'I should let you get back to hammering the nails into this guy's coffin.' As Alyssa watched him exit the building, a little bit of that weight she'd carried for the past fourteen years eased up. That couldn't have been easy for Neely, she knew.

Before she joined the others, she left a message for Brock that she hoped he and Isaac were having a great time, but whenever they were ready to head back home, she'd be happy to see them.

He replied with: *Glad you caught your bad guy. Having a blast. See you Tuesday. Love you.*

She sent back a heart emoji and pushed open the door to join her team.

Chapter Fifty-Six

Saturday, June 25

Beneath the canopies of fragrant flowers, close to one hundred guests – Holly's idea of a small wedding – waited to watch the young bride walk down the aisle on her father's arm. Considering the potential list from both hers and Nick's side had reached a mindboggling five hundred at one point, Alyssa conceded that a fifth of that number was small. Still, inside the dressing room, Holly tipped up on her toes before rolling back on her heels, repeating the nervous gesture over and over until Alyssa touched her arm, leaned in, and whispered, 'You're beautiful, and you're fine. Just breathe, sweetheart. Preferably before you pass out.'

'Good luck keeping her calm.' Sophie, Holly's best friend, snorted as she took a sip of bubbly champagne provided by none other than Mabel, Brock's mother.

Still fussing with her hair and makeup in an effort to provide the maximum amount of coverage over the scars she'd obtained during the time Nick and Holly met, Rachel, Nick's twin, spun around on her chair. A twinkle that had been missing for far too long but had begun slowly working its way back into her daily life lit up her eyes. Leaping out of her seat and streaking across the room, she grabbed Holly in a behind-the-back squeeze. Tears sparkled, but she swiped them away with a tissue handed to her by Jersey Andrews, Sophie's cousin and one of Holly's best friends.

'In just under an hour, Holly Renee Wyatt, you and I are going to be sisters! Can you believe it? I can't. I love my brother, but never in a million years did I ever think I'd be besties with the girl he eventually fell for.'

Of all the things that could've been said, that seemed to be the magical cure to calm Holly's nerves, and Alyssa shared a private smile with her mother-in-law. When Nick had first proposed, everyone harbored a mixed bag of emotions – not that they didn't all love the man Holly had chosen. It just seemed like the ending of a chapter in their lives, and that had brought a few minutes of sadness for Alyssa.

Until Mabel had walked into her kitchen one evening to help with dinner and provided a new outlook.

'I know it's no secret to you that I was far from thrilled when Brock asked you to marry him,' she had said, earning a snort out of Alyssa.

'That's an understatement.' She dropped the peeled potato into the boiling water on the stove and grabbed another. 'You wore black to our wedding.'

Despite the red deepening her already dark blusher, Mabel chuckled. 'I did, didn't I? I'd say I'd hoped you'd forgotten, but considering there's photo proof of my poor taste sitting on your living room mantel as a reminder… well, I guess I deserve that, don't I?'

A little unsettled at the emotion Mabel was displaying, Alyssa wasn't certain how she was supposed to act, so she smiled at this woman with whom she'd spent so many contentious years, with the only thing in common between them their unfaltering love for Brock, Holly, and Isaac. 'Well, we've come a long way from those days, wouldn't you agree?'

Mabel had set her paring knife on the cutting board, washed her hands, then dried them on her apron before leaning back against the counter and facing Alyssa. 'You're right, we have. And while I'm certainly ashamed of my past behavior, I believe it gives me insight into how you might be feeling. You think of this more as an ending to your family dynamics when really, it's just a new, bigger beginning. And while I can't promise I will *never* hound my granddaughter about when she'll give me great-grandbabies, I promise to refrain as much as possible.' Her eyes glittered with excitement. 'But can you *imagine*?' Her voice pitched high enough to nearly crack the wine glasses on the counter.

'Mom, are you listening?'

Holly's irritated voice, on the verge of another panic attack, pulled Alyssa back from her reverie just in time for Cord's wife, Sara, to bustle four hyper children into the room, along with London Brecken, who'd hidden Carter and Abigail the night their mother and another friend were brutally butchered inside their home. While she'd been kidnapped and tortured herself, London had somehow managed to survive, partly due to Schutz. The wolfdog had reappeared time and again, as if to announce himself as her guardian angel. Weeks later, after she'd finally been released from the hospital, London decided to leave Schutz with Alyssa and her family because the place where she lived didn't allow pets, he and Ghost had already become dog buddies, and she didn't want to confuse him with another move to a different home. Alyssa had agreed under the stipulation that London visit him as often as she wanted. And even while she knew London had only agreed to come to the wedding because Carter and Abigail had not stopped pleading and hounding until she agreed, Alyssa smiled, happy to see her.

Still a little uncomfortable being around so many people, London lifted a hand in greeting, offering a shy smile before turning her attention back to the children.

Carter and Shane, dressed in their little tuxedos, and Abigail and Shelley wearing miniature replicas of Holly's dress, brought a smile to everyone's faces.

And Alyssa's heart bloomed until it took up all the room in her chest. Abigail and Shelley both raced right over to Holly before Sara's reminder not to get her sticky halted them in their tracks. Snapping several wet wipes out of her bag, she handed one to Carter, one to Shane, and the other two to the girls. As soon as they'd obediently wiped their hands, they politely asked Holly if they could hug her before asking a "very serious question."

Holly settled on the bench behind her and hugged each of the girls in her arms. 'What can I help you beautiful ladies with?' she asked.

Shelley deferred to Abigail who stuck her thumb into her mouth but plopped it back out with a wet thwapping sound before Carter could admonish her. But instead of asking, she swung around to Sara, her eyes pleading for help.

Sara gave her an encouraging smile and whispered, 'You can do it.'

Abigail waved her hands at Holly so she could whisper in her ear.

Holly listened, nodding her head, as Shelley looked on intently. When she sat back up, she clapped her hands together. 'That sounds like a lovely idea.' Then she plucked two daisies from each of their flower arrangements and weaved them into their braids before turning the girls to the floor-to-ceiling mirrors so they could see.

Everyone laughed at their excited oohs and ahs as they admired each other.

And then finally, the knock came on the door, and everyone scattered into place. Before Isaac escorted her to her seat, Alyssa blew a kiss at her husband who stood with tears in his eyes as he placed his daughter's hand into the crook of his elbow, ready to walk her down the aisle and place her in the trusting care of another man who loved her at least equally as much as he did.

–

At the reception, in between the laughter and dancing, Alyssa watched Tony roar with laughter at something Lynn Sharp – his plus one – said. The way they moved around each other, danced together in perfect sync, she had to wonder how she'd never pictured the two of them together before.

Nearby, she listened to Trevor's wistful sighs as he kept his eyes glued on Holly and Nick who currently sat at a table, their foreheads touching as they smiled at each other.

'I guess there goes any chance I had of my own HEA with Holly, the girl of my dreams.'

Isaac's head snapped in his best friend's direction. 'Dude! That's my sister. What's wrong with you?'

Dumbfounded by Isaac's reaction, Trevor shook his head like he thought Isaac had lost a few brain cells, even speaking slowly as if that would help him understand. 'Uh, yeah, I know she's your sister. And what do you mean what's wrong with me? I never even came close to crossing that line into breaking the bro code territory. So, chillax, man.'

'First, just gross, dude. Second, don't tell me to chillax. And third, you're an idiot.'

Sophie, who'd been silently watching the exchange, along with Alyssa, reached up to pat Trevor on the cheek. 'What Zic here means by "idiot" is that you *never* had a chance. Like *ever*.'

Instead of being offended, Trevor trailed what he liked to think of as his sexy look up and down Sophie's figure before offering her a wink. 'Hey, it might be too late for Hol and me, but it's not too late for the two of us. Save me a dance, huh?'

Sophie wrinkled her nose and stepped back. 'That's your takeaway from what I just said? You and me hooking up? Ugh! No. Just – no.'

Alyssa bit back her chuckle as Mabel slid up beside her. 'I don't know what that was all about, but from the expression on Sophie's face, I'd sure like to have overheard it.'

Alyssa laughed and waved her arms to encompass the room. 'It turned out beautifully, didn't it?'

'Yes, it did. You and Brock have done a fine job with my grandchildren.' She turned to watch Holly and Nick. 'I can't wait until they see their wedding gift. Holly will finally get to take that European trip I got her for her eighteenth birthday.' One corner of her mouth tilted up in a crooked smile as she winked at Alyssa. 'You know the one you and Brock almost banished me for, for all of eternity?'

334

'Oh, yes, it's a little hard to forget. But be prepared for Sophie to pout, considering she was always supposed to be Holly's plus one.'

Half an hour later, Alyssa chuckled at the way Nick suddenly dipped Holly back on the dance floor and brought her back up for a kiss amidst all the foot stomping and cheering.

A tap on her arm brought her gaze around. It took her a second to recognize the person beside her as Ruby wearing an honest-to-goodness smile that traveled the expanse of her face, changing her entire appearance. Alyssa blinked, and Ruby, after peeking over at Hal who sat staring, mouth gaping open, glanced back at Holly and Nick as they continued twirling around the dance floor. 'I guess this means that you and your girl win that pot, huh? I don't think there was ever a stipulation in the wager that stated it depended on *where* I smiled, just that I did, even if it was intended to be aimed at that foolish man.' She tipped her head in Hal's direction.

Alyssa threw her head back and laughed, earning more than a few stares, including those of Holly, Nick, and Cord, who was currently spinning both his daughters out on the dance floor while Sara danced with the boys. When she could breathe again, she said, 'I always knew you had to know about that pot.'

Ruby winked once, and, as if Alyssa had dreamed the entire exchange, offered the familiar scowl that they all knew and loved. 'Sugar, of course, I knew. I know *everything* that goes on in that department and with the people I care about.' She nodded to Tony and Lynn. 'For instance, it's about damn time those two stopped merely making eyes at each other and got around to an actual date. If the sparks flying off them had gotten much bigger,

I'd have had to start carrying my fire extinguisher around everywhere I go.' She turned her head back toward Hal. 'On the other hand, that man there sometimes has far too much confidence. Why do you think I've always had to run off to the bathroom after he's been sitting at my desk for stretches of time trying to get me to smile? Can't let him gain the upper hand by thinking his charm works on me. Then where would I be? Hell, I'd probably lose all control.'

Alyssa turned her face to mock seriousness. 'Your secret's safe with me.'

'Oh, I know it is. Enjoy that pot. Take your man to an intimate dinner. You deserve it.'

With that, Ruby strolled off, and before Hal could excuse himself from his wife and come demand an explanation, Alyssa set out to drag her husband onto the dance floor with her.

Everyone she loved was all in the same room together, laughing and having a great time, and she wanted to revel in it for as long as she could before reality and another case took over.

After all, these moments were too rare.

A letter from Charly

The question of nature versus nurture is a debate for the ages, and as such, continues to hold an immense fascination for me because I'm engrossed in learning what makes someone become who they are, be it strong, weak, determined, or any of the millions of pieces shaping the many facets of a person's existence. Of course, it doesn't really matter how much I research it because there is no simple answer to that question. Which is probably why I'm compelled to write these characters.

One of the things that I've never quite been able to wrap my head around is how a serial killer can – seemingly without much effort – don a mask and live a normal, everyday existence where no one, not his closest friends or even his family, suspects what's beneath the façade. Only when it's removed for whatever reason does the darkness creep through.

And when that occurs, I can't help but wonder what becomes of the families who've had the rug ripped out from under them, when they suddenly realize they've been indelibly woven into the intricate, sticky web of someone else's lie. The ripple effect must be all-consuming as they learn how to go about rebuilding their lives when everything they ever thought they knew has been eternally shattered.

With so many variables to these questions, the intrigue holds me captive, just as I hope my stories have done for you.

Charly Cox

Acknowledgements

From the first creative spark of an idea all the way through to the finished product, writing a novel takes time and effort – and sometimes likes to steal a few tears along the way.

I'm very lucky to have such an incredibly supportive group of people around me who help nudge and encourage me along the way as they cheer me on (Kevin and Timothee). Some talk and sit with me on whatever mental roadblock ledge I've found myself on – before kindly kicking my ass right off it (Melissa Naatz). And then there's the genius–level insight that goes into helping me shape every book into what becomes the final product (Keshini Naidoo at Hera Books). And as always, I am surrounded by a steady team of friends who are always in my corner, ready to share my books with anyone and everyone who will listen (my sister Kim, Victoria, Kevin & Theresa, Susan, Karen, Drew, Hallie, Mary, Karen G., Trudy, Tam, Ang, Tracy, Annette, and Ro). Thank you. Always.

Another massive (and extremely important) thanks goes, once again, to Melissa Naatz for everything you do to keep my website looking as awesome as it does and for all you do to help guide me through all things social media. I know I've said it a million times over, but it can't possibly be said enough: Thank you. My gratitude knows no bounds. You know I'd be lost and flopping in the wind without your (step-by-step) direction.

Above all, I'd like to extend my warmest gratitude and appreciation to all the readers out there who've welcomed me into their homes. Thank you. Your kind words, emails, reviews (which are so important to all authors), and messages keep me motivated. You are all the best. Keep them coming. I truly love hearing from you.

You can contact and/or follow me at:

Charly's Chat:
www.charlycoxauthor.com

Email:
charlycox@charlycoxauthor.com

Twitter:
https://twitter.com/charlylynncox

Facebook:
https://www.facebook.com/charlycoxauthor

Instagram:
https://www.instagram.com/charlycoxauthor

Goodreads:
https://www.goodreads.com/author/show/19490745.
Charly_Cox

BookBub:
https://www.bookbub.com/profile/charly-cox